Also by Leigh Greenwood

Night Riders

Texas Homecoming

Texas Bride

Born to Love

Someone Like You

Texas Pride

Heart of a Texan

Cactus Creek Cowboys

To Have and to Hold

To Love and to Cherish

Forever and Always

Christmas in a Cowboy's Arms

No One But You

Longing for a Cowboy Christmas

When Love Comes

Leigh Greenwood

sourcebooks
casablanca

Originally published in 2010 in the United States by
Leisure Books, an imprint of Dorchester Publishing, New
York. This edition based on the ebook edition published
in 2012 in the United States by Ten Talents Press.

Published by Sourcebooks Casablanca, an imprint of Sourcebooks
P.O. Box 4410, Naperville, Illinois 60567-4410
(630) 961-3900
sourcebooks.com

Printed and bound in the United States of America.
OPM 10 9 8 7 6 5 4 3 2 1

One

BROC KINCAID STOOD BEFORE THE SPARE, SOMBER figure seated behind a plain table in what passed for the sheriff's office. He didn't want to look the judge in the eye, but his own stupidity had gotten him into this mess. He wasn't going to compound his error by adding cowardice to his list of transgressions. Getting arrested for brawling in public was humiliating enough.

"Have you been arrested for something like this before?"

"No, your honor. I've always managed to keep my temper under control."

The judge looked at a sheet of paper in front of him. "If these witnesses' statements are correct, I'm surprised you didn't do more than break Felix Yant's jaw and fracture his arm."

Broc had tried to ignore the man's vicious taunts about his face even when Felix had followed him from his hotel to the restaurant to the saloon. Broc had tried to convince himself the man wasn't worth his attention, but it was the laughter that did it. "I didn't mean to lose my temper. I apologized to his wife."

"I understand you paid the doctor's bill."

"Yes, your honor." The man had two children. They didn't deserve to suffer because of their father's cruelty.

The judge sighed. "It goes against the grain to punish you for doing what is essentially a public service."

"I understand, your honor."

The judge's features hinted at a smile. "I'm going to give you a job I expect you'll dislike even more than spending a couple of nights in the lockup. If you can accomplish it within two weeks, I'll wipe this case from the records. If not, I'll have no recourse but to send you to jail."

❧

Broc pulled his hat brim lower to shade his eyes from the intense glare. It was only mid-morning, but the Texas sun was so hot drops of perspiration had begun to trickle down his chest. It made him long for the cool days and evenings he'd spent in Rafe Jerry's home in California. Though Rafe had encouraged Broc to stay, he knew it was time to return to Texas. He wasn't sure he was cut out to be a cowboy—it was a long way from his days as an entertainer on Mississippi riverboats—but he was positive he didn't want to be a farmer like Rafe. Cabbages and artichokes held no fascination for him.

Laveau di Viere, a traitor to the crack regiment

they'd all served during the war, had escaped once again, this time after kidnapping Rafe's half brother and attempting to kill Rafe's stepmother. The only good thing to come from his latest crimes was that Broc and his friends finally had something any court in the country would accept if they managed to capture him. *When* they captured him. Every time Broc saw the reflection of his ruined face in the mirror, he renewed his vow that Laveau would not continue to escape justice.

Laveau's latest escape had left Broc in a rotten mood for most of the trip to Texas. Maybe that's why he'd gotten into the pointless fight with Felix Yant. He knew it was impossible to change the attitude of men like Yant, even by beating their faces in. The best course was to ignore them.

But he'd let his temper flare out of control, and now he was saddled with collecting a debt from a family he'd never seen before. That ought to make him about as popular as fire ants at a family picnic. It wasn't a small debt, either. Not many people in Texas had seven hundred dollars. If they did have something worth that much, it was usually difficult to turn into cash.

Virtually impossible in the thirteen days he had to complete his mission.

He couldn't go to jail. It wasn't the time he'd be forced to spend behind bars that bothered him. It was the damage it would do to his reputation. All he needed was to add *jailbird* to *scar face*, and his place in life would be fixed forever.

His unhappy ruminations were interrupted by the sight of a bull emerging from a brush-filled creek bed that paralleled the trail at a distance of about fifty yards. The beast was clearly not a range bull but a valuable blooded animal brought to Texas to improve the quality of the owner's herd. Longhorns were hardy animals, but they didn't carry much meat. Broc wondered if the owner of the bull knew it had escaped. The animal looked strong, but if it got into a fight with one of the wild-eyed range bulls, it wasn't likely to survive without injury. He supposed the best thing to do would be to lasso the bull and lead it into town. He'd seen a sign a few miles back telling him a place called Cactus Bend was eleven miles ahead. Surely someone there would know where the bull belonged.

Cactus Bend was also where he was supposed to collect the debt.

Before he had time to uncoil his rope, a young woman and a boy on horseback emerged from the streambed. The way the young woman held the rope told Broc she didn't have much experience handling it. A second rope dragged the ground from the boy's saddle. Maybe the rope that had been on the bull before it escaped. Broc uncoiled his own rope and wheeled his horse to go after the bull. The bull made an attempt to evade Broc's rope, but it was too slow and Broc's horse was too fast. The bull tried to fight the rope, but the harder it fought, the more the rope tightened around its throat. Realizing its mistake, the bull decided to charge the creature that was threatening its freedom.

"Get a rope on him!" Broc shouted to the woman. "1 don't want him to gore my horse or me."

The next few minutes were some of the most challenging of Broc's short career as a cowhand. The bull was crafty and mean, but its weight slowed it enough that Broc's horse was able to avoid its horns. Deciding to fight fire with fire, Broc spurred his horse in a different direction from the bull's charge, pulling the rope taut and throwing the bull off balance. Before the bull could regain its balance, Broc changed direction. When he changed directions so quickly the bull went to its knees, he shouted to the woman, "Throw the rope before he gets to his feet." He was relieved when, after three previous failed attempts, the woman's lasso settled over the bull's head.

"Let's hold him between us." A needless directive, for the woman's lasso was already looped around her saddle horn. The bull was smart enough to realize fighting was a waste of energy. After bellowing its rage, it snorted twice and pawed the ground before giving up the struggle.

The boy was at Broc's side almost immediately. "That's our bull. You can't steal him." The boy looked torn between his desire to stop Broc and his fear that this strange man with the terrible face might do something to hurt him.

"My brother is right." Once she was certain the bull was under control, the young woman also turned her attention to Broc. "We've been trying to get a rope on him for the last two hours."

Broc's impulse was to turn away to spare the young woman the shock of seeing the disfigured left side of his face, but rather than recoil in horror or disgust, she seemed curious, even sympathetic. Broc wanted nothing to do with either reaction. He just wanted to forget he was different from everyone else.

"I wasn't trying to steal your bull," Broc said. "I got the feeling you weren't used to handling that rope much."

The young woman flushed. "Is it that obvious?"

"My sister could have roped that old bull any time she wanted," the boy said.

"Eddie, there's no use stretching the truth further than it will go. I just said I've been trying to rope him for two hours."

"You would have roped him fine if he'd stayed in the open," Eddie said.

"If he'd stood still with his head at just the right angle," his sister said. "Sorry," she said, turning to Broc. "Eddie thinks it's his job to defend me."

"Somebody's got to," the boy said, "'cause Gary won't."

"He would if I needed it," the woman said. "Please excuse my bad manners. My name is Amanda, and this is my brother Eddie. My family owns the Lazy T ranch."

Broc had passed identifying signs of several ranches, but none of them were the Lazy T. If Amanda's bull made a habit of wandering onto other ranches, it could lead to trouble. Preventing trouble wasn't his responsibility, but he had nothing against helping a beautiful woman. She looked to be about eighteen or nineteen with her brother a few years younger. "I'm Broc Kincaid. I'll be happy to help you get your bull back home and in his pen."

"I couldn't put you to so much trouble."

"It's no trouble if your ranch is on the way to Cactus Bend."

"It's just outside of town."

"We used to own a saloon there," Eddie informed Broc. "My sister sings there."

Amanda blushed again. "It would be more accurate to say I wait tables."

"You do sing," Eddie insisted.

Broc tightened the rope on the bull and clucked to his mount. "You can tell me all about it on the way into town," he said to Eddie. "I like singing. Do you know what her favorite songs are?"

Given an invitation to talk, Eddie proved himself up to the challenge. Broc didn't have a chance to get in more than a sentence or two before they reached the lane leading to the Lazy T.

"You really don't have to come with us," Amanda said.

"I don't think your brother is ready to take on a full-grown bull."

"1 am, too," Eddied declared. "I've already done it."

"Only once," Amanda said.

Eddie stuck out his jaw. "But I done it."

"It's okay," Broc assured both of them. "I'm planning to spend the night in Cactus Bend."

"What are you doing here?" Eddie asked.

"Eddie, it's rude to ask a question like that."

"Ma's going to want to know before she lets him inside."

Broc laughed. "I'm not planning to go inside."

"You must meet my mother and allow her to thank you," Amanda said.

"If old man Carruthers had got hold of that bull, we'd never have got him back," Eddie said.

"You don't know that," Amanda said to her brother.

"That's what Ma said. I heard her."

"She was just upset. The bull is very valuable."

"She's going to be even more upset when *he* comes riding up to the house." Eddie pointed at Broc. "What happened to your face?"

Amanda gasped and flushed crimson.

"I got shot in the face," Broc explained.

"That was a mean thing to do. Who done it?"

"Eddie, you can't ask such questions."

"I already did."

"I apologize for my brother," Amanda said. "He's too young to understand that there are certain things it's not polite to mention."

"I do, too," Eddie said, indignant. "I know it's not polite to mention the black hairs on Mrs. Dunn's lip. And I know it's not polite to tell anyone that Niall Toby's thing is so small even the whores won't have anything to do with him."

Broc thought Amanda would faint from embarrassment. He knew he shouldn't laugh, but it was impossible not to be amused.

"I was shot in an ambush during the war," Broc explained.

Eddie's eyes widened with excitement. "Did you kill the man who done it?"

"No, but my friend did. He was about to shoot me again."

"That's enough, Eddie," Amanda said in a voice Eddie had obviously heard before. "My other brother and I are out of the house a lot, which leaves Eddie to look after our mother," Amanda said to Broc. "She's something of an invalid. I'm afraid she indulges him too much."

"Ma says she can't get along without me." Clearly Eddie was proud to be so valuable to his mother.

Broc was impressed by the ranch house they were approaching, a rambling, wood frame dwelling that appeared to have at least six rooms. The wide front porch reminded him of his childhood home in Tennessee. Three other buildings, all of rough-hewn timber, seemed to be a barn, a bunkhouse, and probably a henhouse.

"Nice place you have here," Broc said.

"It belongs to me, too," Eddie informed him.

"My father told us he bought it for the family," Amanda explained.

"Which part do you get?" Broc enjoyed Eddie's confusion.

"He gets the chickens," Amanda said. "That's his job."

"Chickens are for girls." Eddie's disgust with his job was plain to see.

"I gather you don't have a little sister," Broc said to Eddie.

"Just Gary and her," Eddie said, gesturing to Amanda. "Everybody bosses me around."

"Well, I won't," Broc said. "Now let's get this bull in his pen."

The pen turned out to be a large pasture. "We can't afford to let him run loose," Amanda explained, "so we bring the cows to him. We have a small herd. Without him, we'd have no hope of making the ranch pay."

"Gary doesn't want it to pay," Eddie told Broc. "He wants it to fail so he can spend all his time in the saloon."

"Mr. Kincaid doesn't want to hear about our problems," Amanda told her brother.

"I'm just passing through," Broc said. "I'll have no reason to tell anyone there's dissension in the family."

"You don't have to," Amanda said with a sigh. "Everybody knows it."

"Be careful when you drive cows into his pasture."

"That's Gary's job," Eddie informed him.

It wasn't difficult to put the bull in its pasture. Eddie jumped down to open the gate. Keeping the bull between them, they led it into the pasture. Once Eddie had closed the gate, Broc released the bull, which ambled off as though its escape were a routine part of the day. Dismounted, the three of them leaned against the gate and watched the bull try to excite the interest of a young heifer.

"Is it a lot of work to round up cows for him?" Broc asked Amanda.

"Not really. Our ranch isn't very big, and we have a creek running through the middle. Since the best grass is near the creek, our cows never wander far."

"Old man Carruthers's cows eat our grass," Eddie informed Broc.

"You know cows are allowed to range free," Amanda said to her brother.

"Amanda, who is that strange man? What's he doing here?"

The sound of rustling skirts and footsteps on gravel caused Broc to turn and face an older woman he assumed was Amanda and Eddie's mother. Her features were those of a woman still shy of her forties, but her demeanor was that of someone much older. She walked with stooped shoulders and leaned on a cane. Her face was devoid of energy or expression. Even her voice sounded thin and frail. Unlike Texas women, who wore simple dresses with only a single undergarment, her gown of rich green was worn over many petticoats. Her adornments included a necklace made of a single strand of dark green beads and a cream-colored lace cap over immaculately groomed hair. She looked like the women Broc remembered seeing before the war. Her reaction to his face was to recoil so violently, she might have lost her balance had she not held a cane. Amanda looked horrified by her mother's reaction.

"This is Mr. Kincaid, Mother," she said quickly. "He caught the bull for us and brought it back home."

Taking a moment to recover her balance, Amanda's mother paused before lifting her gaze to meet Broc's. "I'm Mrs. Aaron Liscomb. Thank you for helping my daughter."

Broc hoped he covered his surprise better than Mrs. Liscomb. Aaron Liscomb was *the man* from whom he had to collect the debt. It was all he could do to keep from turning his head to see if Mr. Liscomb might be approaching.

Mrs. Liscomb turned to look at her daughter, but did it so naturally she didn't appear to be averting her face. "Where's Gary?"

"He sneaked into town," Eddie told her.

Amanda kicked her brother's ankle. Apparently she'd intended to keep that information from her mother.

"He wouldn't do that before he'd finished his chores," Mrs. Liscomb chided. "You've got to stop being jealous of Gary. You'll be a big boy like him one day."

Amanda laid her hand on her brother's shoulder to keep him from making the sharp rejoinder Broc was certain hovered on his lips. "1 don't know where Gary is," Amanda told her mother.

"I'm sure he's with the herd. Earl Carruthers wouldn't miss a chance to run off some of our cows. He wants that bull almost as much as he wants our ranch."

Feeling he was being drawn too deeply into the private problems of people from whom he had to collect money, Broc thought it might be better to leave. "It was nice to meet you, but I need to be getting on my way. I need to find a room in town and hunt up some dinner."

"You must have dinner with us," Mrs. Liscomb said. "You won't find anything good in Cactus Bend."

"Thank you, but I don't want to put you to any trouble."

"It's the least I can do. We would be ruined without that bull."

Broc had the feeling Amanda would have preferred that he turn down her mother's offer, but he decided to accept for three reasons. For one, Eddie begged him to stay.

"I'll show you my horses," he offered. "I've got three."

Hoping to see Mr. Liscomb and finish his business quickly was his second reason for staying. The third was purely selfish. Amanda was a lovely young woman, and he hadn't had the pleasure of spending time with a woman that pretty since he'd left California. Putting up with Amanda's mother couldn't be worse than spending time in a saloon with a bunch of drunks he didn't know. "Thank you very much for the invitation. I'll accept if you're sure it won't be too much trouble."

"It's no more trouble to cook for seven instead of six."

Believing he wouldn't cause more than a mild inconvenience, Broc accepted.

"Let Eddie show you his horses," Mrs. Liscomb said. "Amanda will have dinner ready before you know it."

Too late, Broc realized it wouldn't be any trouble to the older woman because she wouldn't do any of the work. He turned to Amanda, intending to apologize, searching his mind for a reason to say he couldn't stay.

"It's not a problem," she said with a smile that made him feel better. "It'll be fun to have someone new to talk to. Cactus Bend is so small, we're all bored with each other."

"Cactus Bend isn't a suitable place for a young woman," Mrs. Liscomb told Broc. "There are too many rough men there."

"Cowhands," Amanda translated.

"You may insist that they're just as nice as Leo and Andy—they're the young men who work for us," Mrs. Liscomb explained, "—but I wouldn't want you to frequent their company if they didn't work for us."

"Don't let Eddie bore you about his horses,"

Amanda told Broc. "If you give him half a chance, he'll show you every horse on the place."

"You like horses, don't you?" Eddie asked Broc.

"I like them very much, and I'm looking forward to meeting yours."

Mrs. Liscomb offered a faint smile before turning back toward the house. "Come on, Amanda. We don't want to keep the young man waiting for his dinner."

Broc watched mother and daughter walk toward the house, confused by the mother but intrigued with Amanda. She didn't appear to mind his scarred face. That had never happened before.

"So," he said, turning to Eddie, "what makes these horses of yours so special?"

❧

"I was never so shocked in my life," Mrs. Liscomb said to Amanda. "That man's face is horrible. I don't know how I managed not to faint." Her mother had settled herself into a comfortable chair while Amanda prepared dinner.

"He told Eddie he was shot in the face during the war," Amanda said as she took a bowl of steaming potatoes to the table. "From the looks of the other side of his face, he must have been a very handsome man."

"I'm sure you're right, but how can I think of that when one side of his face looks so terrible?"

"If you feel so strongly about it, I'm surprised you asked him to stay for dinner."

Mrs. Liscomb drew herself up. "I wasn't born in Texas. I know how to treat people properly."

Amanda was sorry she'd ventured a criticism. Given any encouragement, her mother would launch into the differences between Texas and her childhood home in Mississippi. According to their father, it had been a modest dwelling on a farm her father ran without slaves. To hear her mother tell it, the place fell just short of being a plantation house.

"He seems like a nice man," Amanda said. "I expect that wound has made his life rather difficult."

"I would think so," her mother declared. "People must shrink from him."

Amanda paused in her work. "Only a cruel person would do that, but I'm sure he's suffered plenty."

"At least he wasn't killed."

Amanda suspected that sometimes a person might rather be dead than have to suffer through life with such a terrible burden. He was dressed like a cowboy, but there was something about him that said he wasn't an ordinary cowpoke. Maybe it was the quality of his horse, maybe the way he spoke and acted. Whatever it was, Amanda was curious about him. The damage to his face unsettled her because she hated to think any man as nice as Broc Kincaid would be doomed to a life of being pointed at, whispered about, and avoided because of something he couldn't help. Despite the hardships imposed by Reconstruction, Texans treated the men who'd fought in the war as heroes.

Amanda transferred the platter containing pork chops in gravy to the table. "I'll call them in. The corn bread will be ready in a few minutes."

She had prepared a more elaborate dinner than usual despite the absence of her brother and the two ranch hands. Having a guest for dinner was a rare occasion.

Her mother believed in putting one's best foot forward whenever company was around. It was a continuing disappointment to her that she'd never had the financial means to become an important force in the social fabric of Cactus Bend. She was still embarrassed that a saloon had been the main support of the family for several years after they moved to Cactus Bend. In her mind, only socially inferior people had anything to do with saloons or the men who frequented them.

Amanda was surprised to find Broc and Eddie on the front porch when she went to call them to the table. Eddie was telling Broc something, and their guest was listening with rapt attention. Amanda didn't want to think of what secrets her brother might be divulging. He was just as likely to talk about which cowhand had made a pass at her—and whether he thought she was *or should be* interested—as he was to go on about his horses.

"Dinner is ready," she told them, hoping she'd stopped the conversation before Eddie got too personal.

Eddie jumped up from the step where he'd been sitting. "Amanda is a great cook," he told Broc. "Mama says all the lazy, good-for-nothing cowhands want to marry her. Gary says her cooking isn't the reason they want to marry her, but he won't tell me what it is."

"I'm sure it's her singing," Broc said, trying to hide a smile. "Even lazy, good-for-nothing cowhands enjoy music and dancing."

"Mama won't let her dance with nobody. She says it's heathen."

"She says it puts wrong ideas in men's heads," his sister corrected him. "Now wash up."

"We already done that," Eddie informed her. "Broc made me."

Amanda cast Broc a questioning glance. No one had ever made Eddie wash up without a struggle. There was clearly more to this wandering cowboy than met the eye. "You'll have to tell me what kind of magic spell you put on him. I hope it doesn't wear off quickly."

"He didn't do nothing to me." Eddie was indignant. "He said I could ride his horse after dinner."

"Bribery." Amanda chuckled. "I've had to resort to that myself."

"I call it motivation," Broc said with an answering chuckle.

"I'm hungry," Eddie announced and marched inside.

Amanda wasn't surprised that Broc insisted she go in before him, nor was she surprised when he held her mother's chair and waited for her to be seated before he sat down. Her mother was impressed—enough to begin her usual catechism to determine whether he was worthy of her company.

"Where are you from?" her mother asked Broc as soon as they'd all been served.

"Tennessee," Broc answered. "My family had a farm there."

"I'm sure it was more than a *farm*," her mother said.

"Not much," Broc replied. "We survived mostly by entertaining on the riverboats."

"You're an actor?" She said the word as though it were an admission to some kind of crime.

"Not any longer." Broc's left hand indicated that side of his face. "I'm nothing more than a cowhand now."

Her mother looked undecided whether his current employment improved Broc's social worth or merely put him in an equally undesirable category.

"Being an actor must have been exciting." Amanda had never seen a play.

"Did your boat blow up?" Eddie asked.

"My boat never blew up." Broc's smile was reminiscent and a little sad. "My friends will tell you I'm never off the stage, that I take any opportunity to make myself the center of attention."

That admission didn't surprise Amanda. Broc had the kind of magnetism that attracted attention. He virtually bubbled with energy and good spirits. She couldn't imagine how he could be so cheerful after what had happened to his face, but he seemed to have made his peace with it and found a way to be happy. She wondered if that was a lesson he could teach her mother and brother. Their unhappiness with their lives was making them miserable.

"I don't know much about riverboats," her mother said. "When I was growing up, my father would never let us go into town when a riverboat was docked. He said the boats were overrun with gamblers."

"How did you end up in Texas?" Amanda asked. "I would have thought you'd want to go back to your home."

"My parents sold the farm. I came to Texas to help my friend Cade get his ranch back from squatters."

"Did you kill all of them?" Eddie asked, his eyes bright with anticipation.

"Only a few," Broc said. "The others ran away."

With no prospect of stories about killings or maiming, Eddie turned back to his food.

"Do you want a ranch of your own?" her mother asked.

"I don't know," Broc replied. "It's a lot easier to work for someone than to be the boss. I have another friend who owns a rancho in California. In addition to the responsibilities of his family and the farm, Rafe has to worry about the well-being of the hundreds of people who work for him and their families."

"He must be very rich," her mother said.

Amanda could tell Broc was feeling uncomfortable with the direction of the conversation. Knowing her mother was poised to ask for details, she asked, "Where is your Texas friend's ranch? It must have been difficult to return after the war and have to fight to get back his own property."

She relaxed while Broc told them about Cade's struggle to round up and brand cows that had been undisturbed for four years, having to deal with squatters, and enduring the verbal battles between Cade's grandfather and the woman who was now his grandmother-in-law. Her mother usually managed to find something to disapprove of in every story, but she laughed at some of the things those two old people had said to each other. Amanda was certain Broc had been a successful entertainer. Anyone who could cajole her mother into forgetting her dissatisfaction with life long enough to laugh had to be a genius.

She wondered if he thought he had to entertain people or they wouldn't want to be around him. He mentioned his friends with enough warmth to convince her that they weren't bothered by his scars. But she was certain most people reacted as her mother had.

Unexpectedly, she felt a kinship with him. She'd often wondered if anyone would be interested in her if she weren't pretty. She hadn't been so caught up in her own popularity that she didn't notice that many plain women were forced to marry very unsatisfactory men because they didn't have youth and beauty to recommend them. Amanda was happy she was young and attractive, but she wanted to believe she could find someone who would still love her when her youth was gone and her beauty faded. So far, she hadn't found anyone to excite her interest despite the number of men who'd shown an interest in her. She was surprised Broc Kincaid had been able to do what others couldn't.

She wasn't impressed by the handsome side of his face any more than she was repelled by the other, though she did find him physically attractive. What woman wouldn't be attracted to a man who was tall, with broad shoulders, a trim waist, powerful thighs, and such an appealing air of confidence about him? He wasn't annoyed by her brother or disapproving of her mother.

She doubted she'd ever see Broc Kincaid again, but she hoped he would find time this evening to drop by the saloon. She wasn't sure why she wanted him to hear her sing. It could be that she wanted someone with experience who could appreciate what she did. She trusted it wasn't because she wanted to add one more admirer to her list.

"I hope your friend isn't taking advantage of your kindness," her mother said to Broc. "After all you've done for him, surely he would be anxious to help you set up your own ranch."

"He's tried. I suppose I'll settle down someday, but I'm happy with my life as it is now."

Amanda sensed that her mother was about to launch into her lecture on a man and his responsibilities. The one thing her mother couldn't stand was a man who was free of obligations. She was convinced that all men were inherently bad, that only the responsibility of a family and holding a respectable place in the community enabled a man to overcome his iniquitous nature. She was kept from her lecture by the bursting open of the kitchen door and Leo's unexpected appearance.

"Andy's hurt. I think he's broken his collarbone."

Two

EDDIE WAS OUT OF HIS CHAIR AND THROUGH THE DOOR before Leo had time to turn around. Amanda rose from the table. "I'll come immediately."

"I'll be glad to help." Broc had left his chair almost as quickly as Eddie. "I saw a lot of broken bones during the war."

Amanda was relieved to have his assistance. Andy and Leo were both still in their teens, barely old enough to handle their jobs, but Carruthers and Ian Sandoval, owners of the ranches on either side of them, had hired or scared off the more experienced help. No Western man wanted to work for women, so Amanda had felt fortunate to be able to convince Andy and Leo to hire on.

"I put him in the bunkhouse," Leo said. "He's moaning some kinda awful."

"What happened?" Amanda asked.

"It was those fools who work for Carruthers," Leo said. "They started teasing Andy, saying he wasn't old enough to be a cowhand, that he couldn't do half the things they could. And you know Andy. Had to prove he was equal to any one of them. They egged him on to rope the biggest, meanest steer they could find. It pulled Andy out of his saddle. Mighty near crippled his horse, too."

Cowhands from both Carruthers and Sandoval frequently tried to intimidate Leo and Andy. She was certain her neighbors had instructed their men to cause as much trouble as they could. The sooner they drove off anyone who would work for the Lazy T, the sooner one of them could buy it.

Andy was lying on his bunk looking pitiful when they entered the bunkhouse.

"Leo said he thinks you broke your collarbone," Amanda said.

"I don't know," Andy said. "It hurts too much to tell."

"Let me get your shirt off, and I'll take a look at it," Broc said.

"He probably knows more about broken bones than any of us," Amanda said when Andy looked like he might refuse. "He fought in the war."

Andy wasn't happy when Broc removed his shirt by cutting it at the seams. "That's my best work shirt," he complained.

"It was cut it off or cause you more pain," Broc said.

"I can sew it up again," Amanda offered.

"Why does Andy's shoulder look weird?" Eddie asked.

Andy's shoulder was tilted at an odd angle. Amanda waited nervously while Broc ran his fingers around Andy's collarbone, pressing slightly every inch or so.

"His collarbone is okay," Broc said when he'd finished, "but he's separated his shoulder."

"Get the wagon," Amanda said to Leo.

"You don't have to do that," Broc said. "I can set it."

"I'd rather Doc do it," Andy said.

"It'll take you nearly an hour to get to town," Amanda pointed out. "Riding in the wagon will jar your shoulder. You'll be in constant pain."

Amanda wasn't sure why she was trying to convince Andy to let Broc doctor him. She didn't really know anything about Broc. Still, she was convinced he could set Andy's shoulder.

"Okay."

Andy's expression was in opposition to his words. He was so much like Gary, Amanda worried about him. She almost felt guilty for giving Andy a job that offered so many ways to get hurt. He was determined to be thought as much a man as someone with ten years more experience.

Broc looked around. Apparently not finding what he wanted, he picked up the sleeve of Andy's shirt, folded it several times, and handed it to him. "It's going to hurt. Bite on this."

"I'm no chicken."

"No one thinks you are," Broc assured him, "but having your shoulder put back in its socket hurts. No point in getting broken teeth in the bargain."

Andy looked as though he was going to refuse. "Take the shirt," Leo snapped. "I don't want you spitting out pieces of your teeth. You're ugly enough already."

Reluctantly, Andy took the folded sleeve and put it between his teeth.

"Try to relax," Broc said. "It'll be easier on both of us."

It quickly became apparent Andy wasn't going to relax. Each time Broc touched him or tried to get into position, Andy pulled away.

"Stop it, you fool!" Leo shouted. "He's just trying to help."

"How do I know he's not going to make it worse?" Andy asked. "It already hurts like hell."

Amanda had never realized Andy was so immature. How were they ever going to make a go of the ranch as long as the only people who'd work for them were teens?

"It's going to keep on hurting like hell if you don't get it fixed," Leo said.

"I want Doc to do it."

"Damned fool," Leo muttered. "I'm tired of baby-sitting you."

"I'm not a fool," Andy shot back. "And nobody babysits me."

"Go hitch up the wagon," Amanda intervened. "It won't take long to—"

Amanda had already turned to leave when she heard Andy utter a small grunt. When she looked back, she saw Broc standing behind Andy, Andy's treasured pearl-handled revolver in his hand. He'd just used the weapon to knock the boy unconscious. Leo stared openmouthed. Eddie muttered a word Amanda was certain he'd gleaned from Gary's vocabulary. She watched in shocked silence while Broc quickly and efficiently reset Andy's shoulder.

"He'll have a headache when he wakes up, but his shoulder won't hurt so badly. Now I'd better leave," Broc said when he stood. "He's not going to be happy with me when he wakes up."

"How long will it take?" Leo asked, awe and fear in his voice.

"Just a few minutes. I didn't hit him hard."

Eddie stared at Andy's inert form. "I think you killed him," he said to Broc.

Broc ruffled Eddie's hair. The boy pulled away. "I didn't kill him. He won't even have much of a bruise where I hit him. Let's go back to the table before all the food gets cold."

"Stay with him." Amanda spoke to Leo, but her gaze didn't leave Broc's retreating back.

"Who is that man?" Leo asked.

Amanda hardly knew what to say. She didn't want to admit she'd let a stranger take control of a situation that should have been hers to handle. "He fought in the war. He's been in California and is on his way back to a ranch here in Texas."

"He shouldn't have hit Andy."

Amanda agreed, but Broc had set Andy's shoulder in less than a minute, thereby saving him a lot of pain. "Andy was starting to panic. By the time he got to Cactus Bend, he might have been too upset to let the doctor fix his shoulder."

Leo glanced down at Andy, who appeared to be resting peacefully. "I wish he weren't such an idiot. I told him Carruthers's men were just trying to cause trouble."

"I'll speak to Carruthers about his men."

"A lot of good that will do," Leo scoffed. "He won't even listen to the sheriff."

Sheriff Tom Mercer would sympathize with her, promise to talk to the rancher, then probably go off and have a beer with him. The position of sheriff was an elected office, and Carruthers and Sandoval were the biggest landowners in the area. The sheriff wasn't likely to do anything that would cost him their support. Andy started to stir.

"Let me know if he needs anything."

"A brain would be helpful."

Amanda smiled. Leo was young, but he would make a good hand when he got more experience. Andy would probably improve if he had someone who could provide the discipline and give him the training he needed, but she didn't know of anyone who could do that. Certainly not her brother, when he couldn't even be depended on to do his own work before running off to the saloon.

She needed an experienced foreman to manage the ranch, but she didn't have the money to pay one. Until the ranch started making a profit, it would take nearly everything they earned from the saloon to support the family. Their plan to hire the bull out for stud services had come to naught when both Carruthers and Sandoval had refused and convinced—or forced— the rest of the ranchers to do the same.

Gary wanted them to sell the ranch, but her mother would never agree. She had hated depending on income that had come from drinking and gambling. She had dreamed of being a social leader in Cactus Bend, but she believed that was impossible as long as she was associated with the saloon. She'd plagued her husband until he'd bought the ranch. The Lazy T was her claim to respectability, and she would never let it go. Instead, she wanted Amanda to quit working in the saloon. So far Amanda had been unable to make her mother understand that the income from the saloon had been all that kept the ranch afloat. All too often, her mother wouldn't see what she didn't want to see.

When Amanda entered the house, Broc, Eddie, and her mother were finishing their meal as though nothing had happened to disturb it.

"How is Andy?" Broc asked when she was seated at the table.

"He's beginning to revive."

Broc studied her for a moment. "You don't think I should have hit him, do you?"

He'd given her a perfect opening. "No, I don't. Why did you?"

He shrugged. "I saw lots of boys panic during the war. We didn't have time to deal with it. Besides, it could get them killed. We had to knock that out of them as soon as possible."

"Did you knock them on the head, too?" Eddie asked.

"Sometimes."

"Isn't that dangerous?" Amanda asked.

"Not if you know how to do it."

"Will you teach me?" Eddie asked.

"No, he will not," Amanda said. "I don't want anybody knocking anybody on the head."

"I can think of several people who could benefit by a good knock on the head," her mother observed.

Amanda didn't know how things had come to such a pass. Her mother had never advocated violence. She'd always said it was unladylike. What was it about Broc Kincaid that made her mother and brother think he had the answers to everything?

"I'd like to knock Sammy Loftus on the head," Eddie said.

Amanda ignored him. Eddie's long-running feud with Sammy Loftus was well-known by everyone in Cactus Bend.

"Thank you for inviting me," Broc said to her mother, "but I need to be on my way. Can you recommend a good hotel?"

"There's only one," Amanda said.

"It's of very poor quality," Mrs. Liscomb observed. "You'll find the best food at the Open Door."

"That's the saloon we used to own," Eddie told Broc.

"It's also the name of our old diner," his mother reminded him.

"I'd like to speak to you after you saddle your horse," Amanda said to Broc. He looked surprised but left the kitchen without comment.

She wasn't sure that what she had in mind was a good idea, but it might be the perfect solution to her problems. It was clear her brother liked Broc, but it was equally clear her mother was relieved at the departure of such a severely disfigured man. She might be impressed by his confidence, but she didn't approve of unattractive injuries any more than she approved of bad manners.

For her part, Amanda had almost forgotten Broc's

scars. He had such a strong personality, it was hard to think of anything else. The scars were as much a part of him as the perfect side of his face. Somehow they represented the duality she saw in his personality, the kindness he showed to her and the rough way he'd dealt with Andy. She watched him as he emerged from the barn and led his horse toward her. She guessed he was around thirty, but it was hard to tell. The good side of his face looked very young, but he walked with the confidence of a man who had no fear of what might be asked of him. That was exactly the kind of man she needed to run the ranch, the kind of man who would stand up to Carruthers and Sandoval. Gary would be furious, her mother wouldn't like it, and it was possible Andy might quit, but she had made up her mind.

"Thanks again for dinner," Broc said when he reached her. "Now I'd better be going."

"Wait. I want to ask you something."

He paused just before mounting his horse, but now that she was on the verge of asking her question, the words seemed to stick in her throat. She would have to justify her decision to her whole family, and she had no way of doing that beyond saying that her instinct made her believe she could trust this stranger. She pushed the words out. "I'd like you to work for us. I want you to be the foreman of the Lazy T."

Now that she'd gotten the words out, the expected feeling of relief didn't come. Broc was looking at her in that inscrutable way again, making her uneasy, making her feel she'd done something stupid and he didn't know how to tell her.

"You don't have to decide right away," she said. "You can ask people in town about us. We don't have a large ranch, so I can't pay you very much, but you could sleep in the house and eat with us." She made herself stop talking. She was beginning to sound as if she was begging.

"Just because I can set a shoulder doesn't mean I know anything about ranching," Broc said.

"You said you'd worked on a ranch since the end of the war."

"I have, but I'm just a cowhand like Leo and Andy."

"I'm sure you know more than those boys. Besides, they need someone like you to organize the work for them, show them how to do it, and make sure it gets done. They're good boys, but they're young."

"What about your brother?"

"Gary is nearly as inexperienced as they are."

"I mean what would he think about me being put in charge?"

"He wouldn't like it, but he'd understand why it was necessary."

"Would your mother agree with him?"

How could he pick out the weak spots in her plan so quickly? "My mother has wanted a ranch ever since she moved to Texas. She won't care about anything if you can make the ranch pay for itself."

"I have a job that I've been away from for a long time. I have a responsibility to my friends, and I like to live up to my promises."

She wanted to argue with him, but she couldn't encourage him to ignore his obligations. She'd offered him the job because she believed he was the kind of man who *wouldn't* ignore them.

"Have your brother tie the bull up or put him in a stall when you take cows in or out of his pasture," Broc advised. "He may look docile, but any bull can be dangerous when there are cows around."

"I'll be sure to tell Gary."

Broc looked like he wanted to say something but changed his mind. "Thanks again. Watch out for your little brother. He's a good kid."

"He's too full of himself, but I know what you mean. Have a safe trip."

Broc mounted up, nodded his head, and headed down the lane. She told herself it was silly to feel that she'd lost something important. Being foreman wasn't a job that only he could do. Yet the feeling persisted that no one else would be able to do it the way he could, and that was her loss.

❧

Having had a bath and his supper, Broc stepped out of the diner and looked up and down the street. Like so many cattle towns, nearly every building of importance fronted on the main street. Scattered residences—some with well-kept yards and others with chicken coops and pens containing pigs, cows, or horses—separated the main street from the vast emptiness that was the Texas prairie. Faint trails led outward to the ranches that surrounded the town.

It was not yet dark, and the street was crowded with people shopping, visiting, or hurrying home. Now and again a child would dash between buildings or across the street, but Broc suspected most of them were at home doing their chores and getting ready for supper. That made him think of mealtime on Cade's ranch. Cade had been his captain during the war and was the friend he now worked for. Despite the efforts of Cade's grandmother-in-law to orchestrate their meals according to the aristocratic Spanish tradition, Cade's sons and his free-spirited cowhands turned every meal into a celebration of their overflowing good cheer. When Cade's grandfather showed up and the two old people started hurling insults at each other, the atmosphere became positively festive. Once, the cowhands had asked why Cade didn't try to put a stop to it, but he'd said the two old people enjoyed it too much.

Broc missed his friends, but there was a restlessness in him he didn't quite understand. He had enjoyed his time in California with Rafe, but he'd known his home was back in Texas. Not once did he consider returning to Tennessee. He was determined no one in his family would see him as he was now. They'd been told he had died in the war.

Banishing those unhappy thoughts, Broc turned in the direction of the Open Door Saloon. He wasn't in the mood to drink, but he needed time to digest what he'd learned when he booked a room at the hotel. Aaron Liscomb had died a year earlier. According to the hotel clerk—who was eager to share everything he knew or suspected—the family didn't know of the debt hanging over their heads. As far as everyone knew, Liscomb had sold his interest in the saloon and diner to Corby Wilson and used the money to buy the ranch and the bull. It was widely known that

Mrs. Liscomb had been encouraging him to do that for years.

That left Broc in a dilemma. Not only would he be the one to tell the family about an unknown debt, he'd be the one trying to collect money they probably didn't have. If he couldn't collect it, he'd go to jail, and they'd still probably lose their bull.

He was curious whether Amanda could really sing. In the years before the war, he'd gained a fair reputation as a ballad singer. But though audiences might put up with a ruined face in a villain, they wouldn't pay to see a disfigured singer of romantic ballads and nostalgic songs.

He had accepted long ago that a return to the stage was impossible. He'd learned to like his work on Cade's ranch. He especially enjoyed working with the men who'd been his comrades during the war. They shared a bond of friendship that men who'd never lived through a war together couldn't understand. He was lucky in his friends and lucky to be alive, so he threw off his ill humor and headed toward the saloon.

It wasn't a big saloon, but it was crowded. The room was long and narrow with a low stage at the far end. Lanterns suspended from the ceiling dispensed a yellow glow that struggled to make its way through the haze of cigar smoke. All the tables were occupied, as was most of the space at the bar. But he managed to find a place at the end. If he stood at just the right angle, he could turn the left side of his face away from the crowd. He'd have a hard time attracting the bartender's attention, but he had an unobstructed view of the whole room. The men ranged in age from what seemed to be teens to men in their twilight years, most still wearing their work clothes. He couldn't tell whether their high spirits were the result of some specific event or characteristic of every evening.

"What can I get for you?"

The bartender looked too young to be working in a saloon. He also bore an uncanny resemblance to Amanda. In turning, Broc exposed the left side of his face. The bartender recoiled.

"What in hell happened to you?"

"A war wound."

"From the looks of that, you ought to be dead."

"I nearly was." He hated having to talk about his wound, but it was either talk about it or appear morose and unfriendly. "I don't really want anything to drink. I just came in to hear Amanda Liscomb sing."

"Then stay in this corner. If she gets a look at that face, she won't be able to sing a note. Hell, it might even put these cowboys off their feed, and they've seen just about everything."

Encounters like this had convinced Broc to bury himself on Cade's ranch where no one but his friends would see him. It was ironic that it had been his face that had once propelled him to popularity. Now his face was condemning him to live in obscurity. Broc turned his left side back to the wall and waited. It was less than a minute before he saw Amanda.

She was carrying two plates of food. Several men spoke to her as she passed, some even reached for her, but she avoided the touches and turned aside the comments with a smile. He could see why Mrs. Liscomb said working in the saloon wasn't suitable for a young woman. The men weren't actually disrespectful, but neither were they treating her the way Broc would have wanted them to treat Amanda had she been his sister. He'd twice gotten into fights on the riverboats with men who tried to get too familiar with one of his sisters. Both men had been forced to apologize.

Amanda delivered the food and moved to a second table, where she collected some empty glasses, then disappeared through a door at the back of the saloon.

"She won't sing for a while yet." The bartender was back with a whiskey, which he set down before Broc. "You might as well have something to drink."

Broc paid for his drink and took a swallow. It wasn't in the same class with the whiskey he'd had while staying with Rafe, but it was good compared to what he'd had in other saloons. He could see why the Open Door was so popular. Too many saloon owners tried to increase their profits by watering down the beer and serving rotgut whiskey.

Over the next thirty minutes he watched Amanda serve half the tables in the room. The saloon employed two other waitresses, but every man wanted Amanda to wait on him. Broc had no difficulty understanding why. The other two women were plain, past the bloom of youth, and brusque. Amanda was young, beautiful, smiling, and willing to exchange a friendly word with any man in the room. To men who sometimes spent weeks without seeing a woman, that was like a benediction.

"You passing through, or are you looking for a job?"

Broc wasn't sure why the bartender was interested

in him, but the fellow never seemed to take his eyes off him for long. Broc wondered if the man thought he was dangerous just because he had a mangled face. "Just passing through."

The bartender didn't leave, so Broc figured he hadn't found out all he wanted to know.

"Are you interested in that waitress?" he asked, indicating Amanda, who had taken off her apron and approached the piano.

"Any man would be interested in a woman like that."

The bartender grinned. "It wouldn't do him any good. She's taken."

Broc shrugged. "The pretty ones always are." But Amanda didn't act like a woman whose affections were engaged. "Extend my congratulations to the lucky man."

The bartender's grin grew even broader. "That's him over there." The bartender pointed. "Corby Wilson. He owns the saloon."

Broc had noticed the man before. He had paraded about the saloon all evening with the self-conscious manner of a man who considered himself a person of importance. He was skinny, had a drooping mustache, and wore clothes that were so tight his lack of muscle was evident for anyone to see. "Thanks for the information." Broc offered his hand to the young bartender. "I'm Broc Kincaid."

"Gary Liscomb," the bartender replied as he took Broc's hand. "Amanda is my sister. Gotta be quiet now. She's about to sing."

Broc should have guessed. Not only did the

bartender resemble Amanda, but Eddie had also said his brother had sneaked off to the saloon.

Amanda's performance surprised Broc. Not just that she had a nice voice or that she could sing well. She seemed to enjoy it. She definitely made a connection with the audience. When she sang a funny song or something a little suggestive, they hooted and acted like young men out on the town for the night. But when she shifted to a ballad, the room got quiet. She held her audience spellbound. Afterward, he pulled out of his abstraction enough to applaud her performance.

She disappeared, and the saloon noise quickly returned to the mild roar that deadened the eardrums after a couple of hours.

Broc tried to keep from making judgments based on appearance, but he didn't understand how Amanda could be interested in a man like Corby. Forget that he wasn't attractive, that he needed to learn how to take care of his mustache, and that his complexion was sallow from spending all his time indoors. The man struck Broc as having all the integrity of a snake. Okay, it was a snap judgment, and there may have been some jealousy involved, but there was no way Corby Wilson could be a suitable husband for Amanda. She'd be better off marrying Leo. Even Andy.

Broc had swallowed the last of his drink when Amanda came back into the saloon. She walked over to where Corby was talking with a man at the bar.

"I need to leave a little early," she told Corby.

"Why? We're not ready to close yet."

It irritated Broc that Corby thought he had the right to question Amanda's reason for doing anything.

"I had a hard day on the ranch, and I have to stay late tomorrow night. I need the rest."

"Neither Gary nor I can leave yet."

"I don't need anyone to see me home."

"You know your mother will raise hell if I let you leave here alone. She acts like you're some god-damned princess or something."

Broc pushed away from the bar. He could do one of two things: he could punch Corby in the nose, or he could see Amanda home. He strode up to where the two of them were standing. "I'll be happy to escort Miss Liscomb home."

Corby took a single look at Broc and pulled his gun. "Lay one hand on her, and I'll put a bullet between your eyes."

Three

BROC'S REACTION WAS INSTINCTIVE. BEFORE HE HAD time to think, he had knocked Corby's gun hand upward, causing it to discharge a bullet into the ceiling. A quick jab from his left fist sent Corby crashing into the bar behind him. The saloon fell silent. It was into this vacuum that Broc spoke.

"Your father should have taught you it's unwise to draw a gun on a man until you're sure you have better reflexes than he does."

"I'll have you in jail for this," Corby threatened.

"You drew a gun. I only used my hands."

"You caused the gun to go off. I could have killed someone."

"I was trying to make sure it wasn't me."

The saloon seemed to come to life all at once. Men started shouting, threatening.

"Let me at him," one man shouted. "I'll teach him to insult a lady."

Amanda stepped between the men. "He didn't insult me. He just offered to see me home."

"An offer from anyone as ugly as him is an insult," another hollered.

"I can't allow a stranger to escort you home," Corby told Amanda. "Even if I would, these men wouldn't stand for it."

"He's not a stranger," Amanda said.

"I've never seen him before," Corby said.

"I knew him from before we moved here."

Broc hoped his face didn't reflect his shock at Amanda's lie.

"I never saw him," her brother said. "I'd remember a face like that."

"He hadn't been injured then," Amanda said. "He got that in the war."

As usually happened, once people learned he'd been injured in the war, they started to feel sorry for him.

"What's he doing here?" Corby asked. "Where did he come from?"

"I've been in California," Broc offered. "I dropped by to see Amanda and her mother on my way through."

"How long are you staying?" Corby asked.

"I'm thinking about heading out tomorrow."

"I hope you're satisfied," Amanda said to Corby.

Corby didn't look happy, but a wounded war veteran outranked a saloon owner. Amanda's claiming him as an old family friend settled the matter.

"I'll stop by after closing," Corby said.

"There's no reason to ride out that late. I'll be asleep." She turned to Broc. "I'm ready to go."

With that she turned and walked out of the saloon. Bemused and curious, Broc followed. "How were you planning to get home?" he asked once they were outside.

"I have a buggy."

"Give me a few minutes to saddle my horse."

"There's no need. You can drive the buggy back. Gary will bring it home when he comes."

It was one of those clear, starry nights when the moon's pale glow lent even the roughest setting a romantic feeling. "Why did you tell them I was an old friend?"

Amanda had insisted on driving, which gave her an excuse not to look up at him. "To stop Corby from making such a fuss, and to keep those men from tearing you apart."

"I can defend myself."

"Whatever you might have done would have only made things worse."

Broc wondered if she would still feel that protective of him when she learned of the debt. "Isn't your brother a little young to be working behind the bar?"

"He's seventeen."

Broc didn't think that was old enough to be a bartender in a saloon like the Open Door, but it was none of his business. Nor was Amanda's relationship with Corby, but he had to know if what Gary had said was true. "Corby seems very protective of you."

Amanda shook the reins, more as a show of irritation than dissatisfaction with her horse's performance. "I can't make him understand I'm perfectly capable of taking care of myself."

"I would have to agree that any woman who could handle that bull could handle this buggy for the few miles between town and your ranch."

"I wish you'd tell that to Corby. He stands over me worse than my father did."

"According to Gary, that's his right."

"What do you mean?"

"Gary told me you were spoken for."

This time she did look up. "Corby thinks because he was Papa's partner, he's responsible for me."

"I don't think that's what Gary had in mind." He couldn't tell in the dark, but he thought she blushed.

"I'm not *spoken for* by Corby Wilson or anyone else. And when I get through with my brother, he'll wish he'd kept his mouth shut."

Broc was surprised at the glint of fire in her eyes, the sharp edge to her voice. He suspected Gary would hear a few truths that wouldn't sit well with him.

They rode in silence for several minutes before Amanda asked, "Why would Gary say something like that to you? You're a stranger to him."

"I think he felt I was looking at you with too much admiration."

Even in the dark, it was easy to see her look of surprise.

"You're a very attractive woman. I'd think you'd be used to being stared at."

She turned away. "Being used to it doesn't mean I like it."

That was something to ponder. In Broc's experience, it was rare that an attractive woman didn't enjoy being the object of male attention.

"At least the response you get is positive. I wish people could look at me without such a strong negative reaction." He was surprised at the bitterness in his voice. "Sorry, I don't mean to complain, but I just want to forget my face and get on with my life."

What was wrong with him? He hated people who whined about the unfairness of life. He was alive. He was healthy. He had a job, friends, and an adopted family. He had more than most people.

"You probably won't believe this," she responded, "but sometimes I wish I'd been born plain. It gets old when people can't see anything but your face."

A chuckle escaped him. "It's not as comfortable when you're looking at it from the opposite viewpoint. I've been on the other side. I know."

"I guess it does sound ungrateful, but all my life my mother has told me all that matters is my looks. That's all Corby cares about because it brings in the customers."

"What about your singing?"

"He wouldn't care if I squawked like a hen. He only lets me sing because I can't wait on all the tables. He says I can pay attention to *all* the men when I sing."

"What about your father?"

"I wish I had a nickel for each time he told me he married the most beautiful woman in Mississippi. He'd have had my mother work in the saloon if she hadn't flatly refused because she said it was beneath her. I wish I could refuse, too."

Ironic that both of them should be preoccupied with their looks but for opposite reasons.

"If you don't like working in the saloon, why do you do it?"

Amanda's shoulders drooped. "I work there because the ranch doesn't make enough money for us to live on."

"Then why did your father sell his interest in the saloon and the diner?" He was asking for information that was none of his concern, but if he was to stay out of jail, he had to know everything he could about the Liscomb finances. Right now it looked like they had no way of raising seven hundred dollars in less than two weeks.

"He did it for my mother. She never liked the saloon."

Broc's parents had never concerned themselves with the gambling, drinking, or anything else that took place on Mississippi riverboats. He wondered if they were too uncaring or whether Mrs. Liscomb was too sensitive.

Broc would have liked to prolong his time with Amanda, but she drew the buggy to a stop in front of her house. A light shined from one of the front windows.

"Mother never goes to bed before I get home," Amanda told him.

"She's concerned about your safety."

"She needs more sleep. She hasn't been well recently."

Mrs. Liscomb hadn't seemed unwell to Broc, but he hadn't been around her long enough to judge. He got down from the buggy and walked around to help Amanda down. "One can't tell it by hearing you sing, but I suspect you could use more sleep as well."

Having put on the brake and looped the reins over the handle, Amanda let him help her down. "I do get tired once in a while, but I can quit as soon as the first calves from our bull go to market. Gary wants us to sell them as yearlings, but that wouldn't bring in a quarter of what we'll get when the steers are four or five."

If they still owned the ranch then.

The front door opened to reveal Mrs. Liscomb. "Amanda, come in immediately. You know the night air isn't good for you."

Amanda smiled at Broc. "She forgets it takes me twenty minutes to drive home in the night air. It gets a little wearing when I'm treated as if I'm still in pigtails."

Broc found it impossible to imagine Amanda in pigtails, but he was certain she had been adorable.

"Thanks for seeing me home. I'm sorry about telling Corby you were an old friend, but I can't stand him fussing over me, and I didn't want to stay until Gary could leave."

"Who normally sees you home?"

"Gary, but the regular bartender was sick tonight, so he had no one to take over for him."

Gary hadn't seemed concerned his sister might have to go home alone, but that was none of Broc's business. He just had to collect the debt, hand the money over to the judge, and go home. He had no intention of coming to this part of Texas again.

"I'm surprised Eddie hasn't insisted on riding with you."

"He has tried," Amanda said with a laugh, "but I won't let him."

"Amanda, come in immediately," her mother called. "Have you no concern for my health? I can't stand in this open doorway forever."

"I've got to go. Thanks for helping with the bull

and seeing me home. If you ever come through here again, you *will* be an old friend. Good night."

Broc waited until Amanda had disappeared inside before turning back to the buggy. He doubted she'd claim him as a friend after he told her about the debt. He climbed into the buggy, took the reins, and released the brake. Then he turned the buggy around and headed back down the lane toward town. He'd return tomorrow. It was probably best to time his arrival with dinner. That way he was likely to find the whole family at home.

❧

"What were you doing with that man?" Mrs. Liscomb's lips were compressed in disapproval.

Amanda unwound the scarf from around her head. "He offered to escort me home."

"Why didn't Gary come with you?"

"Gil is sick, so Gary had to work the bar alone."

"Then Corby should have brought you."

"You know he won't leave the saloon as long as it's open."

"Wasn't there anyone else?"

"Who would you choose? Bodie? Nick? Barney?"

"Stop," her mother ordered impatiently. "You know I don't permit myself to recognize men who frequent saloons. And you needn't be rude like Gary and say I married a saloon owner. I married the owner of a respectable plantation. It wasn't your father's fault that the war ruined us."

The growth in the cattle industry had turned their little town into a supply stop for cattle being trailed north, leaving her father prosperous enough to buy the Lazy T. Unfortunately, nothing had been able to turn her mother from a Mississippi belle whose ambition had been to preside over her own plantation home into a Texas rancher's wife willing to do what needed to be done to survive.

"It didn't ruin us. We're doing what we have to in order to survive. I can drive a wagon, ride a horse, and handle a rope," Amanda said. "If I have to, I will help with the branding and turning young bulls into steers."

"Amanda!" Her name wasn't spoken. It was shrieked.

"We live on a cattle ranch in Texas, Mother. This is not, and never will be, Mississippi."

"I'm painfully aware of that."

"But you haven't tried to make the best of things. Gary, Eddie, and I work on this ranch every day. Then Gary and I go into town and spend our evenings working at the saloon. I know you don't like it, but that's what we have to do to make a living."

"We wouldn't have to do it if we could sell the bull's services."

"We've tried, but between getting the bull out to service Carruthers's cows for free and Sandoval's insistence that his cows don't need to be improved, that hasn't worked."

"If only—"

"Don't start with the *if onlys*," Amanda begged. "Saying the same things over again won't change anything."

"I was only going to say that had this been Mississippi, our neighbors would have been glad to help us rather than do everything they could to make sure we fail."

"Well, we're not in Mississippi, so we have to depend on ourselves. Now I'm going to bed. Gary will check on the bull when he gets home."

Amanda hurried from the room before her mother could say anything else. She tried to have patience, but it was always the same.

Light from the small oil lamp her mother kept ready for her cast a pale yellow glow over the room. Its contents looked out of place in a ranch house in Texas. It was in essence the bedroom her mother had grown up with in Mississippi. Being an only child, her mother had inherited everything when her parents died. She had insisted upon bringing every piece of furniture, every piece of china, every item of decoration when they moved to Texas. She spent most of her day keeping the inside of the house as close as she could to what she remembered from Mississippi. Amanda had given up trying to convince her mother that the boys didn't appreciate her efforts and considered the elaborate furnishings a nuisance rather than a birthright.

Amanda did appreciate it, but she didn't want to build her life around handcrafted cherry and walnut furniture or china imported from England. Trunks in the attic were stuffed with dresses she would never wear, hatboxes that would never be opened, shoes that would be unusable after a single trip to town. She was not immune to the lure of pretty clothes, but she wanted clothes that fit the life she was leading now. She had been born in Mississippi, but in her heart she was a Texan. She liked the openness of the prairie, enjoyed working outdoors, and didn't mind the rough manners of cowmen.

Taking off her dress and petticoats, she hung them up carefully and slipped her nightgown over her head. She crawled into bed and settled the covers over her, but sleep didn't come right away. She couldn't banish a certain stranger from her thoughts.

Even though she knew virtually nothing about him, she was strongly attracted to Broc Kincaid. For some reason, his scars didn't bother her. Most of the time she was hardly aware of it. There was just something about Broc that rendered his disfigurement unimportant.

He didn't draw attention to himself, though she was certain he was the kind of person who could do just about anything he wanted. His good humor and his willingness to be so helpful would have made him a wonderful addition to any gathering. She wondered about the ranch where he worked. Did the people there treat him well despite the scars, or did he have to endure discrimination from them, too? She wondered if there was anywhere he could go where he would be treated like an ordinary person. It had to be hard to have people stare at you, especially when it was often in horror or disgust. Even when they didn't stare, Broc must know what they were thinking. It was enough to turn a normal person into a hermit.

She threw a light quilt to one side. Now that she'd taken the chill off the bed, she was too warm. Settling back, she told herself there was little point in worrying about Broc. He would leave tomorrow, and she'd never see him again. She wouldn't know how he was treated or what was happening to him.

Thinking about her own situation would be a better use of her time.

She sighed. She'd been doing that for weeks and had yet to change anything. She'd probably have to do Gary's work tomorrow. She didn't know where he disappeared to, but half of the time nobody could find him. She wished her mother would stop pretending Gary could do no wrong. The family needed a man to depend on, but Gary was never going to measure up to his father as long as his ambition in life didn't rise above serving drinks in a saloon.

She knew it wasn't the drinks that drew him. It was feeling he was part of the rugged male community that made up the ranchers and cowhands around Cactus Bend. Gary wanted to feel grown up, like a man, but he didn't understand that standing around telling coarse jokes, drinking too much, and making lewd comments to the waitresses was neither mature nor manly.

Amanda didn't want to think about Gary tonight. Instead she tried to imagine what the future would be like once she didn't have to work in the saloon any longer. Surrendering to these thoughts, she gradually fell asleep.

❧

By the time Broc got back to the saloon, the crowd had thinned, but the noise was as loud as ever. "I've returned the buggy," Broc said when he finally attracted Gary's attention.

"Stay away from my sister."

Broc had started to leave, but he turned back at Gary's words.

"What have I done to make you think I'm interested in her?"

"You offered to see her home."

"Would you have preferred one of these men do it?" The crowd was down to a hard-drinking, hard-living group Broc wouldn't have turned his back on.

"Yeah, I would," Gary responded.

"Until you get a better handle on reading character, I hope your sister stays home."

Broc turned to leave, but was stopped by Corby.

"I don't want you hanging around Amanda."

Broc wasn't used to being treated so rudely, and it was beginning to annoy him. "As long as Amanda doesn't mind, I don't see that it's any of your business." Broc had obviously hit a sensitive nerve, because Corby drew himself up to his full height, which was still several inches below Broc's.

"Amanda is going to be my wife. Everything that happens to her is my business."

"Then you ought to pay more attention to that ranch. She works there all day, cooking for the family as well as the hands, then has to work in your saloon until late at night."

"Amanda enjoys working here because the men love her."

"That's possible, but if she were my prospective wife, she wouldn't have to be in the saddle in the morning chasing down a dangerous bull, defending her cowhands from ruthless neighbors in the afternoon, and being lusted after by a bunch of drunks at night."

Corby's expression turned to anger. "If you're

thinking about trying to get Amanda to fall in love with you—"

Broc lost patience and grabbed Corby by the front of his shirt. "Look at my face. Do you think any woman as beautiful as Amanda is going to give me a second thought?" Broc released him. "That bullet ruined my face, not my brain." Hearing his words so clearly made him realize the noise of the saloon had fallen away. Broc turned to see everybody's attention focused on him and Corby. "If I'd been in your place," he added, "I'd have closed the saloon for the night rather than let Amanda go home alone. She deserves better, and you and every man in this place know it."

Disgusted, Broc walked out of the saloon, leaving a shocked silence behind him.

❧

A few hundred yards from the Liscomb ranch house Broc slowed his horse to a walk, but he was only putting off the inevitable. If he didn't do this, someone else would. "You're acting like a coward," he told himself. "You've got a job to do, so get it done."

Unlike most Texas ranch houses, this one was two stories with a wide front porch shaded by a quartet of elms that must have been planted long before the war. The exterior of weathered wood was complemented by the brown trim around the windows and doors. All the windows were curtained and closed, probably to keep out the heat and the dust. Broc saw no movement when he rode into the yard, and no one came out of the house to see who had arrived. He hoped the whole family was inside eating dinner. He hated to spoil their meal, but it would be better to talk to everyone at the same time. He dismounted, climbed the steps, crossed the porch, and knocked on the door. A moment later, the door was thrown open, and Eddie's little face grinned up at him.

"Amanda said you were gone."

"I have something I need to tell your family. May I come in?"

"The pork chops are gone. Gary ate the last one."

"I didn't come to eat dinner."

Amanda appeared in the doorway behind Eddie. "I thought you were leaving today. Is something wrong?"

"Nothing's wrong. I just need to talk to your family."

"What about?"

"It would be better if I told everybody at once."

"Has something happened to Corby?"

Maybe Corby was right. If he was the first person Amanda thought about when she believed there might be trouble, then she probably was going to marry him. It made sense on several levels, but Amanda deserved better than Corby Wilson.

"I haven't seen Corby today, but I have no reason to think anything has happened to him. I didn't realize you'd be so concerned about him."

"Corby wants to marry her," Eddie explained helpfully.

"Sorry. I had no right to say that." Now he'd done it. After the way he'd acted, Amanda couldn't help thinking he was jealous. If he'd had any doubt, her telltale blush would have confirmed her thoughts.

"Whatcha got to tell us?" Eddie asked, oblivious to the tension between Broc and his sister.

"I need to speak to your mother," Broc said.

Amanda pulled Eddie back from the doorway. "Come inside. We're just finishing up dinner."

Broc followed Amanda into the dining room. From the reactions of those around the table, it was obvious only Leo was pleased to see him. Gary looked angry. Andy acted more embarrassed than angry. Mrs. Liscomb's slight grimace indicated that she hadn't gotten past her aversion to looking at his scars. She'd be even more unhappy when she found out why he was here.

"Mr. Kincaid," she said in a cool voice. "I didn't expect to see you again. Our bull hasn't escaped again, has he?"

"I checked on the bull before I came in," Gary growled. "The lazy bastard is lying down in the shed. He doesn't give a damn about the cows he's supposed to be breeding."

Mrs. Liscomb's pained expression indicated that she regretted her son's mode of expression, but the sickly smile that followed it indicated Gary could do just about anything, and he'd still be her favorite child.

"I know nothing about the bull," Broc said. "I came here on another errand."

"Won't you sit down?" Mrs. Liscomb asked. "The pork chops are gone, but we have—"

"I don't want anything to eat."

"Then what do you want?" Her expression said that she had extended all the courtesies expected of a lady in her position. From this point on he would be treated like any other visitor who was thoughtless enough to arrive during dinnertime.

"I need to speak to you about a debt."

"We don't have any debts," Amanda said.

"Please, Amanda, Mr. Kincaid was speaking to me," Mrs. Liscomb chided. "I'm perfectly capable of answering his questions." She turned to Broc. "As my daughter said, we don't have any debts."

"According to Judge Pike in Crystal Springs, your husband still owes Mrs. Ella Sibley the sum of seven hundred dollars. I have been instructed to collect that sum. I'm further instructed to tell you that if the debt is not paid in full within twelve days, the judge will come to Cactus Bend and auction off family property until the sum of seven hundred dollars has been realized."

For a moment, no one moved. Then Mrs. Liscomb uttered a moan, her head fell forward, and she fainted.

Four

"Bastard!" Gary shouted at Broc. "What are you trying to pull?"

"I'm not trying to pull anything." Rather than look at Gary, Broc fixed his gaze on Amanda, who had gone to her mother's side. "I'm just doing what the judge told me to do."

Instead of calming down, Gary grew more agitated. "We'd be fools to give you as much as five cents."

"It doesn't matter how it gets to the judge as long as it gets there."

"What do you take me for? Any idiot would know this *judge* of yours is your partner in this attempted swindle."

Broc hadn't taken his eyes off Amanda. Her mother was beginning to show signs of reviving. "This is not a swindle. My advice is to go to Crystal Springs and verify what I've said with Judge Pike before you attempt to do anything."

"I won't waste my time. Now get out of this house."

"Gary," Amanda said to her brother, "help me get Mother to her room."

"Wait until I make sure this slimy bastard is off our property."

"No," Amanda said. "I want to talk to him."

"I'm not letting you say one word to this snake," Gary fumed.

"Gary," his mother said in a faint voice, "please help your sister. I can't stand this commotion."

Furious at being undermined by his sister and mother, Gary turned on Broc and snarled, "I'm not finished with you."

"I'm little, but I know what a debt is," Eddie said when the others had left the room. "It means you owe somebody money."

"That's right."

"Why do we owe you money?" Eddie asked.

"You don't owe it to me. You owe it to a lady named Ella Sibley."

"Who is she? Why do we have to pay her money?"

"I don't know," Broc admitted. "I'm just telling you what the judge told me to say."

"Is the judge really a crook?"

"No."

"Why did he send you?" Leo asked. "Why didn't he send some lawyer?"

"I don't know why he didn't send a lawyer," Broc said, "but he sent me as part of an exchange."

"What's an exchange?" Eddie asked.

"It's when someone does something for you, and you do something in return."

Broc looked up to see that Amanda had returned to the room alone. He wondered what had happened to Gary.

"Mother needed someone to stay with her," Amanda said, apparently anticipating his questioning look. "She's always placed her trust in Gary."

Broc thought that was a terrible mistake, but he kept his opinion to himself.

"Leo, if you and Andy are through eating, you should get back to work."

The two men wasted little time leaving the house.

"Eddie, I want you—"

"Papa's will said I had an equal part in the ranch. That means this Ella woman is going to want money from me, too. I gotta find out if what Gary said is true."

Amanda looked undecided, but reluctantly nodded agreement. "Come into the front room," she said to Broc.

"There really is nothing else to say," Broc told her. "As I advised Gary, you ought to send someone to Crystal Springs to verify what I've said."

"I intend to do that," Amanda said. "Nevertheless, I want to ask you a few questions."

"Me, too," Eddie said, following them from the dining room.

Broc had expected to confront a businessman who was in the habit of not paying debts. He certainly hadn't expected to have to deal with a fainthearted widow who was determined to live in a dreamworld, an angry teen boy, a curious and noncritical nine-year-old, and a young woman who looked too young to have to bear the burden of this dysfunctional family. He almost wished he'd told the judge to put him in jail, but it was too late to avoid being the bearer of bad news. Unfortunately, it *wasn't* too late for him to end up in jail. Whether he liked it or not, he had to stick this one out.

"Why should I believe you?" Amanda asked Broc as soon as they were seated.

"Do you believe me?"

"The scheme is too flimsy to be an attempt to steal money from us. Anyway, I don't think you're the kind of man who would do that."

Broc swallowed his surprise at Amanda's words as well as the funny feeling in the pit of his stomach. It felt a lot like indigestion, but he was certain it was the precursor of a feeling that would be much harder to swallow. Since his injury, he'd never allowed his feelings for any woman to go beyond liking, fondness at the most. Unless he was mistaken, he'd already gone past that with Amanda. Unfortunately, she'd given him no reason to do so. "Why don't you think I'm a crook? Gary does."

"I don't," Eddie said. "I like you."

Broc swallowed his smile when Amanda's expression remained unchanged.

"Intuition," Amanda said, "and what I saw of you yesterday."

"All successful thieves have a disarming charm about them. If people like you, they're more apt to let their guard down."

"I never said I *liked* you," Amanda corrected, "just that I don't think you're a thief."

That was a harsh way to learn that half a loaf wasn't better than no loaf at all.

"If none of the money you say we owe belongs to

you, how did you become involved in collecting this debt?"

As much as he disliked it, he owed her an explanation. "I was in a bad mood, and I let some guy's comments about my scars cause me to lose my temper. I ended up breaking his arm and his jaw."

"Golly!" Eddie exclaimed.

"The judge told me I could stay out of jail if I would collect this debt. If I had known then what I know now, I would have taken jail."

He saw the first change in Amanda's expression. "Why?"

Broc wasn't sure how to explain the complex lines of his reasoning. He wasn't sure he fully understood it himself. "I expected to be dealing with a man who was used to taking advantage of others, not a widow trying to take care of three children under twenty."

"Mama doesn't take care of us," Eddie informed him. "We take care of her."

Amanda's expression hardened again. "My mother suffers from poor health. The brutal way you announced this *debt* has been a terrible shock to her."

"I'm sorry. I couldn't think of any other way to do it."

"I don't understand what's behind this—I can't imagine why a real judge would make you do something like this—but we don't owe anyone any money. You've been duped, to what purpose I don't know."

"I have no personal knowledge of Mrs. Sibley, nor any substantiation I can offer to prove that your family owes her money. I am, however, certain Judge Pike is a real judge. His authority was accepted by the sheriff who arrested me. Even if you don't want to go to Crystal Springs, you'll have a chance to decide for yourself because Cactus Bend is on his circuit. He plans to be here in about two weeks."

"It seems unlikely that a sheriff and a judge would be involved in such a ridiculous scheme, but I've learned people are capable of anything. However, that's not what I wanted to say. This whole attempt to collect a debt is fraudulent. I don't know, nor do I want to know, why you're part of it, but I do know I don't want you to come to the house again. Your presence here in the house would upset my mother." After a slight pause, she added, "Please don't offer to see me home from the saloon again. If you do, I'll turn you down."

Amanda had never given him reason to think she felt anything for him beyond appreciation for a stranger who'd been able to help her, but he'd looked forward to seeing her many more times while he was in Cactus Bend. He'd found himself responding to her quiet strength of character, her steadiness when things were going wrong, and the fact that everyone seemed to depend on her. Feeling that he'd been effectively dismissed, he stood.

"I don't know that I can honor your request. I really don't want to go to jail. I would urge you to investigate the question of this debt very thoroughly. I can't help feeling there's something you don't know." There was definitely something strange about the whole situation. How could anyone be unaware of owing seven hundred dollars?

"My father told us he got the money to buy the

ranch and the bull from the sale of his share of the saloon and diner. It's as simple as that." She stood. "You'd better go before Gary comes back."

How to make the only woman he'd ever been genuinely attracted to hate him in one easy lesson. Oh well, it would save him from a good deal of unnecessary heartbreak later. *Heartbreak* seemed overly dramatic, but he had a feeling more than his freedom from jail had slipped beyond his control.

Eddie followed him outside. "Are you really a crook?"

Broc smiled reluctantly. "No, I'm not."

"Then why did you say we have to pay that lady money?"

"Because a judge ordered me to."

"Why?"

"I assume the lady showed him some evidence to support her claim."

"Is the lady a crook?"

"I don't think so."

"What does she look like?"

Why did everyone, including little boys, think looks had anything to do with character? "I don't know. I've never met her."

"Then how do you know she's not a crook?"

"I don't, but there are laws against people trying to take money that doesn't belong to them. There are also laws that force people to pay debts they owe."

"Who makes these laws? Do they get the money?"

Having younger brothers of his own, Broc knew Eddie's questioning could go on until nightfall. Amanda wouldn't be happy with that, and Gary was likely to start a fistfight. "Ask your brother or sister. I'm sure they'd do a better job at explaining."

"I don't ask Gary nothing," Eddie declared, "'cause he don't know nothing unless it's about the saloon."

Broc walked down the steps and prepared to mount his horse. "I'm sure he knows enough to explain that. Now I'd better be going."

"Will you come back?"

Standing there small, alone, and forlorn, Eddie reminded Broc so strongly of his own brothers, he wished he could give the boy a reassuring hug. "You just heard your sister tell me not to."

"She doesn't mean it. She likes you."

She might have had a liking for him at first, but not any longer. "Nevertheless, I think it'll be better if I don't come back."

"They won't let me go into town by myself."

"Why would you want to do that?"

"You promised to teach me how to rope like you."

Broc had forgotten a promise he made when Eddie was showing him the horses yesterday. Eddie had said the bull was always getting out, and Broc had said he'd teach the boy how to use a rope so he could help Amanda catch him. "Why don't you ask your brother or Leo?"

"They can't rope as good as you."

There was only one way to get around this. "If your sister will let me come out here someday, I'll be happy to teach you how to rope."

Eddie beamed. "She will. I know she will. I'm going to ask her now."

Broc decided it would be best to leave before

Amanda came out. She was bound to think he was using Eddie as an excuse to return to the ranch. He would come back. Something was wrong here, and he was determined to find out what it was.

❦

Amanda found it difficult to understand the extent of her disappointment in Broc. If he wasn't a crook, he'd allowed himself to be duped by one, and she couldn't admire any man foolish enough to fall into such a transparent trap. The difficulty lay in the fact that she couldn't really believe Broc was either a crook or foolish. The way he accepted his wound and blamed himself for losing his temper were both characteristics of a man of integrity as well as maturity. Her brain and her emotions were in conflict over him, a situation she wasn't accustomed to and one she didn't like.

When Amanda reentered her mother's bedroom, she was reclining on a silk-covered daybed next to windows hung with satin drapes. The four-poster canopy bed that dominated the room was covered by a crocheted bedspread. A huge maple armoire covered most of one wall while a marble-top table with a porcelain bowl and pitcher painted with countryside scenes stood next to her mother's bed. Three pictures depicting various scenes from the Mississippi of her mother's youth hung on walls covered with white wallpaper decorated in tiny red and blue flowers.

"Is that man gone?" her mother asked.

"I wish you'd let *me* throw him out," Gary said.

Her mother reached for Gary's hand. "I needed you

here. Amanda is very good, but she's only a woman. You know I depend on your strength."

Gary didn't appear any happier hearing that than Amanda felt, but she'd given up trying to bring her mother to a true understanding of Gary's character. Her brother wasn't a bad person, but since their father's death, he'd been too much under the influence of Corby Wilson and the men who hung out at the saloon. Amanda hated their shallow values, changeable honesty, and willingness to waste time and resources on drink and gambling when both could be better spent on their families.

"I told Mr. Kincaid not to come back," Amanda said. "I also told him we don't owe anyone any money, that he's either a crook or has allowed himself to be duped by one."

"That man made me uncomfortable from the moment I saw him."

"You mean his scarred face made you uncomfortable."

Her mother swung her gaze from Gary to Amanda. "How can you expect a man who looks like that to be honest?"

"The same way I expect a man with an amputated arm or leg to be honest."

"I'm sorry he was so hideously wounded," her mother said, "but I'm glad you told him not to return."

Gary pulled away from his mother and stood. "I need to make sure he's really gone."

"Yes, do," her mother said. "I wouldn't be able to sleep if I thought he might be lurking about somewhere."

With a brief nod to his mother, Gary left the room.

"Ask Eddie to come back in the house," her mother called after Gary. "I'll feel more comfortable once I know he's safe."

"Broc wouldn't hurt Eddie or anyone else," Amanda said. "You saw what he did for Andy."

"It doesn't matter if he was kind to Andy," her mother continued. "He tried to steal money from us. I can never forgive him for that."

"Actually, he merely told us that we owe a debt."

"Well, we don't, so that makes it stealing."

"Mother, he said we ought to check into it before we do anything. That doesn't sound like a thief to me." Why was she defending Broc? If she didn't believe he was unprincipled, why had she told him to leave?

"It doesn't matter," her mother said. "He's part of whatever terrible scheme is going on. If that doesn't make him a crook, I don't know what does."

Despite what she'd said to Broc, she couldn't push aside the feeling that something was wrong somewhere, that Broc Kincaid wasn't the kind of man to be involved in a conspiracy to steal from anyone. If he had, he could easily have tried to force her to pay for the return of the bull. Or stolen it and tried to sell it to someone else. He had no reason to set Andy's shoulder. He had even less reason to offer to see her home from the saloon.

"Well, you don't have to worry about him anymore," Amanda told her mother. "He won't be coming back."

Her mother sat up in bed. "Do you think he'll ride

to town and tell everyone we're debtors?" Her mother put a hand over her eyes. "I couldn't live with the shame."

Her mother was still haunted by the loss of her home during the war. The whole family had tried to protect their mother because they knew how devastating that loss had been, but Amanda was beginning to wonder if they hadn't coddled her too much.

"I'm sure he won't do that. Besides, you never go to town, so you wouldn't have to put up with unkind remarks or falsely sympathetic looks."

"But people would *know*."

"Everybody knows Papa was an honest businessman. That's why we always had so many customers at the saloon and the diner."

She'd heard rumors of dissatisfaction recently, but she credited that to people liking her father better than Corby. Her father was always friendly, taking an interest in people and their problems. Corby was only interested in helping himself.

"I want that man out of town," her mother said. "I want you to ask Sheriff Mercer to force him to leave."

"I intend to go into town." But she didn't plan to see the sheriff. She needed to go to the bank. She wanted proof her father had paid for everything he'd bought.

Maybe she could find something to show that Broc wasn't a part of this plot, that somehow he'd been forced into it against his will. Maybe he was married, and there had been threats against his family. Maybe *he* was in debt, and this was part of his way of working it off. There could be any number of reasons, but she hoped his being married wasn't one of them.

～

The setting sun painted the early evening sky with broad swatches of orange and red, but Broc didn't notice the sunset, the lengthening shadows, the increasing chill, or the quiet descending over the prairie as birds and small animals sought refuge for the night. Wrapped in thought, he had come to several conclusions, the first of which was that he ought to tell the sheriff what he had done. He didn't know what actions the Liscomb family might take, but they were almost certain to talk to the sheriff about him. It would be difficult to convince the sheriff of his honesty if Gary got to the man first. It was always possible to send someone to Crystal Springs to check on his story, but Texans were reluctant to approach officials. There was so much dishonesty in the Reconstruction government that ordinary people assumed you were dishonest if you had anything to do with it. Shrugging off worry about circumstances he couldn't change, he brought his horse to a stop in front of the sheriff's office. He tied his mount to the hitching post and went inside.

This office was not substantially different from the one in Crystal Springs, but it boasted two windows, two pictures on the walls, and an imposing metal cabinet behind one of two scarred, wooden desks. "What can I do for you?" the young man behind the smaller desk asked.

"I want to see the sheriff."

"I'm the sheriff. What can I do for you?" he repeated.

Broc had expected an older man instead of one

who appeared to be somewhere in his midtwenties. He knew better than to evaluate competence by age, but he also knew it was hard for a young man to get the respect of older, established businessmen. Still, the sheriff seemed relaxed and sure of himself, so maybe he'd already proved he could handle the job.

"I need to explain why I'm here," Broc said. "My presence in your town has already caused some discomfort. I expect it's going to cause more."

The sheriff's scrutiny of Broc grew more intense. "I don't like the sound of that. You're new in town, aren't you?"

"I'm really just passing through, but it's more complicated than that."

The sheriff's attention didn't falter. "Tell me."

He listened without comment as Broc told about the fight, the judge's decision, and the Liscomb family's reaction to the news he'd brought. "Either I stay here and try to collect a debt everyone in the Liscomb family says doesn't exist, or I go back to Crystal Springs and go to jail."

The sheriff didn't appear to have any sympathy for Broc's dilemma. "The Liscombs are well liked by everyone in Cactus Bend. Aaron was a respected member of the business community. I helped settle his affairs after his death. I found no mention of any debt."

Judge Pike seemed to have no doubt a debt existed. The Liscomb family and the sheriff were equally certain there was no such debt, which left Broc in a quandary. If there was no debt, he had no choice but to go back to Crystal Springs and serve his time in jail. However, if there was a debt, how was he going to prove it when everyone was convinced it didn't exist? He didn't think they were all in collusion. It was a lot of money, but it wasn't enough to get so many people to lie. He needed time to think, and he couldn't do it with the sheriff glaring at him.

"I don't know what to say," he said to the sheriff. "I can only repeat that I was ordered by Judge Pike to see that the debt was paid, or I had to go to jail. I advised Mrs. Liscomb to send someone to Crystal Springs to talk to the judge. My only interest is to do what I can to get this debt settled."

"I don't know what's going on here," the sheriff said, "but I would advise you to leave town. I don't care whether you go back to Crystal Springs, or somewhere else, as long as you don't cause trouble here."

Something was wrong, and Broc didn't intend to suffer because of it. "I haven't caused any trouble, and I don't intend to. If you don't believe what I said, *you* can send someone to Crystal Springs to talk to Judge Pike. Or," he continued when the sheriff started to speak, "you can wait until he comes here in two weeks on his circuit."

"We have no cases for him to hear, so he'll bypass us."

"You have one now."

The sheriff bridled. "Are you trying to threaten me? Because if you are, you've chosen the wrong man."

Broc smiled, though he didn't feel like it. "I'm relating facts. Whether you choose to believe them is your business. Though you might consider what you're going to say when the judge does arrive and learns you've done nothing."

The sheriff was getting angry. "I don't need advice from some drifter."

Broc didn't wear his best clothes when he traveled, but didn't think he looked like a drifter. He supposed it was his scar. He stood. "I've said what I came to say." He returned the sheriff's stare. "I won't be leaving town just yet. I expect I'll be here to welcome the judge."

"I'll be watching you," the sheriff promised.

"I hope you will. I want you to know that whatever wrongdoing is going on, I have no part in it."

Broc paused outside the door of the sheriff's office to consider what he should do next. The logical place to look for substantiation of the debt would have been Aaron Liscomb's papers, but the sheriff said he'd seen them. Broc was certain Amanda had seen them as well, so there was nothing there to tell him what had gone wrong. The bank wasn't going to give him any information, and no lawyer would speak to him except to tell him this was none of his business.

He started walking back to the hotel, his thoughts so taken up with his situation, he didn't notice Corby Wilson until the man spoke to him.

"Why the hell are you still here?"

Five

Dressed all in black, Corby appeared out of the twilight like a bird of ill omen.

"At the moment I'm headed to my hotel," Broc replied. "Is there something I can do for you?"

"You can leave town."

"Sorry. You'll have to choose something else."

"You said you were leaving."

"My plans have changed."

"Then change them back."

Broc couldn't decide whether he was angry this overdressed twig thought he had a right to tell him what to do, or amused because Corby looked so absurd. There was so much grease in his hair, the strong breeze whistling down the street couldn't blow a single strand out of place. He smelled so strongly of pomade that Broc moved to get upwind of him. And his suit had been tailored to fit his body so snugly, he looked like he ought to be uncomfortable wearing it. Despite the dusty streets, his shoes were freshly polished. What could Amanda see in this understuffed straw man?

"I'll leave Cactus Bend as soon as I complete my business."

"What kind of business can a man like you have here?"

What about that scar said he was anything but an honest, upstanding citizen with the right to be treated the way every other citizen was treated? "I'm a cowhand, and this is cow country."

"You obviously don't have any money of your own, and I don't see anyone trusting you with more than your month's wages. What can you do with that?"

"Appearances can be deceiving," he said. "After all, your clothes make you look like a popinjay."

From the blank expression on Corby's face, it was obvious he didn't know whether Broc had complimented or insulted him, but his look of irritation indicated he thought an insult was more likely.

"Sandoval and Carruthers are the biggest cattlemen around here," Corby said. "If your business isn't with them, you don't have any."

"Then I guess I'd better talk to them. Where can I find the gentlemen?"

"They come to my saloon several times a week," Corby stated with a touch of pride. "You can see them there if they'll talk to you."

"Thanks for the information. I'll let you get on your way. I don't want to keep you from any important business."

Corby was still frowning when Broc walked away. Broc thought it must be hard worrying that every comment might carry a hidden insult. Once again he found himself wondering what Amanda could see in that man.

⁂

Amanda had little appetite for the meal before her. Her mother picked at her food as usual, but Eddie and Gary ate like field hands despite their mother's efforts to instill proper table manners. Amanda had endured a difficult morning. It didn't help that she'd gotten very little sleep the night before. It helped even less that her mother couldn't stop talking about Broc's visit. The easiest part of the morning had been spent in the saddle with Leo. They weren't doing very well because they were short a cowhand, and they'd never had enough help in the first place.

"A guy can't work on a full stomach," Gary said when he pushed back from the table. "So I might as well go to the saloon and get paid for a few extra hours."

"I have a remedy for that," Amanda snapped. "Go without dinner."

"I'm surprised at you, Amanda," her mother scolded. "Gary works hard."

"So do the rest of us," Amanda pointed out, "but we're not going into town to waste the rest of the afternoon."

"Gary told you he would get paid for the extra hours. You're always telling me we need to watch our expenses because we don't have enough money."

"Things wouldn't be so tight if Gary worked more around here."

"You said we wouldn't have any noticeable increase in our income until the calves were old enough to sell."

Her mother could always find a reason for Gary to do exactly what he wanted, but she never extended the same privilege to her or Eddie. "Andy can't work with his injured shoulder. We need Gary to stay here all day so we won't get any further behind."

"I don't understand," her mother said. "Your father told me cows take care of themselves. We only have to sell them when they're big enough."

Amanda was relieved when a knock on the front door prevented her from having to explain to her mother *again* that cows really didn't take care of themselves.

Eddie was off like a flash and back a moment later ahead of their unexpected guest. "It's Corby." He didn't look any more pleased than Amanda at the interruption, but Gary welcomed Corby. Her mother's face was unreadable, but Amanda knew her mother didn't approve of Corby. Amanda wondered whether she disapproved more of the way he dressed or that he owned a saloon.

"I came as soon as I heard," he said. "I told the sheriff he ought to put that man in jail. He said he would if the fellow gave you any trouble."

"What are you talking about?" Amanda asked. "*Who* are you talking about?"

"The man who took you home the other night. He's been talking to the sheriff," Corby answered.

"He went to the sheriff about us?" Gary's face turned dark red. "I'll kill the son of a bitch."

"I don't trust the man myself," his mother said to him, "but you will not use such language at my table. What did Mr. Kincaid say to the sheriff?" she asked Corby.

"He told him you owed a lot of money and that Judge Pike was coming to auction off everything you owned if the debt wasn't paid. The sheriff said he even threatened him."

"I can't believe that," Amanda said. "Whatever mistakes Broc has made, he's not a fool."

"He is if he thinks he's going to get us to pay a debt we don't owe," Gary said.

"If he's got a judge on his side, that could be trouble," Corby said. "We all know what Reconstruction people are like. I could tell you—"

"Don't," Amanda said. "It would upset Mother. I appreciate your coming to see us, but Mr. Kincaid said we weren't to give him any money and that we should send someone to Crystal Springs to look into the matter."

"One person can lie as well as another," Corby said. "It won't make any difference that this Pike is a judge. That's why I've come to offer to marry you so I can protect the whole family."

Considering the times, Amanda supposed quite a few women had received more unflattering proposals, but she didn't personally know any. If Corby thought offering to protect her family from a flimsy threat would win her over when she'd refused all his previous offers of marriage, he understood her even less than she'd thought. But then Corby had never shown any real understanding of her—or a desire to acquire any. After her father's death, he'd assumed he would be the one she turned to in times of need, the natural choice to become her husband. Every time she turned him down, he came up with a new reason why she should marry him. This time, however, he'd miscalculated. Not even Gary liked the idea of Corby assuming the role of protector of the family.

"We can take care of ourselves," Gary said. "I can handle Kincaid by myself."

"No, you can't," Eddie said.

"I can, too," Gary insisted. "Just because I don't get into brawls don't mean I can't fight."

Amanda knew they should move into the parlor, but that would be an invitation for Corby to sit and stay longer. "This is a legal matter, not one to be settled by fists."

"It would settle his big mouth."

"I've made it plain to him that I want him out of town as soon as possible," Corby said. "He says he has business with Carruthers and Sandoval, but if he's lying, I'll see he's sorry."

Amanda had a strong suspicion Broc could take either Gary or Corby. "I appreciate your offer of help," she said to Corby, "but we can handle this by ourselves."

"There's no reason you should have to," Corby insisted. "I *want* to marry you. I *want* to take care of things for you. And your family," he added as an afterthought.

"My daughter is too young to marry," Mrs. Liscomb said.

Amanda appreciated her mother's help, but she wasn't going to hide behind anyone. "I'm not too young," she told Corby. "I just don't want to get married yet."

Okay, she was hedging, but it didn't seem necessary to hurt his feelings by telling him she would never marry him. She'd already told him she didn't love him. He said love was an invention of people who wrote poetry and silly plays to fill young girls' heads with a lot of nonsense. He believed respect and admiration were the feelings on which successful marriages were founded.

"You should think of your family," Corby said. "They need a man to guide them as well as protect them."

"I don't need nobody to protect me," Eddie insisted.

"You shouldn't confuse an offer of assistance with an offer of marriage," her mother said. "It complicates one and undervalues the other."

"I've offered to marry Amanda many times before. I hoped this situation would make her think more about her future and less about the present."

Corby couldn't get it through his head that she had refused him because she *was* thinking of her future and didn't want to spend it with him.

"I'd never marry anyone just to get out of a difficult situation," Amanda said. "Once the situation resolves itself, what reason would I have for wanting to stay married?"

"Security," Corby said.

"Your vows," her mother added.

Gary winked and made a silly face, which was his way of saying he thought the physical side of marriage was an inducement all its own.

"I don't want to be in a marriage where that's all that keeps me with my husband," Amanda told her mother and Corby. "I want to love the man I marry. I want him to depend on me as much as I depend on him."

"Why?" Gary asked.

Her mother and Corby just stared at her as though bereft of speech.

"Why not?" Amanda replied.

"Gary likes Priscilla because she's rich." Eddie hid behind his mother before his brother could grab him.

"I do not," Gary insisted. "I mean, that's not the only reason." Gary could be a slacker, but at least he was straightforward about it.

"I'm just saying that women want to be married to men they like and enjoy being with," Amanda said.

"You like me and enjoy being with me," Corby said.

"I know, but that's not enough for me. I just told you I want to be in love with the man I marry."

"You're nineteen," Gary said, "and you haven't found anybody you love yet. What if you never do?"

Amanda had thought about that on many lonely nights, but she believed not being married was better than being married to the wrong man. "Nineteen isn't old," she told Gary. "I doubt I'll wind up an old maid aunt to your children."

"How about my children?" Eddie asked.

"You won't have any children," Gary said. "No woman would marry you."

"I don't want to get married," Eddie said. "Girls are afraid of horses."

"Priscilla isn't," Gary said.

"Sammy Loftus says she only rides in a buggy," Eddie told him. "She won't even harness her own horses."

"You're a liar." Gary grabbed for Eddie, who escaped by diving under the table and hiding behind Amanda.

"I'll spare you my brothers' embarrassing behavior and refuse your kind offer. We really can handle the situation on our own."

"I haven't given up." Corby gave Amanda his most engaging smile. "I'll keep the offer open because you'll need me soon. Now I do have to get back to town. I'm never comfortable leaving the saloon for long."

Amanda wondered if he realized he was already married—to the saloon.

"I'll see you out," Gary said to Corby.

"It would have been nice to have the security he could provide," Mrs. Liscomb said to Amanda after Corby had left, "but I can't like a man who dresses so badly."

Unwilling to laugh in her mother's face, Amanda said, "I want to make sure Gary doesn't keep Corby standing on the porch forever. He's nearly as bad as Corby when it comes to that saloon."

"I don't understand this liking for low company," Mrs. Liscomb said. "There was nothing like that in *my* family."

Amanda didn't have to go outside to hear what Gary was saying. The front window was open, and he was making no attempt to keep his voice down.

"Don't give up," he was saying to Corby. "She'll marry you as soon as she gets tired of this ranch."

"She can have the ranch, too," Corby said. "I just want to marry her."

"I don't know why my mother ever wanted this place. I hate it."

"I can see why your mother likes this house," Corby said, "but it's too far from town for my taste."

"Just keep after Amanda. I know she likes you. She thinks everybody in the world is crazy about her. Once she starts to look old, she'll change her mind."

It was all Amanda could do to refrain from bursting through the doorway and setting her brother straight on quite a number of things, but she wanted to hear Corby's response. She would deal with Gary later.

"Do I look like a man who wants a wife who looks old?" Corby attempted to puff out his skinny chest, but the effort yielded barely visible results. "I deserve the best-looking wife, because I'm the best-looking man in Cactus Bend."

Broc's image sprang into Amanda's mind. Most people would think she was crazy, that his disfigurement would make it impossible for a woman to think he was attractive. She didn't like the scarring because of the pain and suffering it must have caused Broc, but she thought it gave him character, a kind of strength nearly every man she'd met lacked. She just couldn't understand his part in the attempt to gouge money from her family.

"Sure you are," Gary told Corby, "which is why Amanda will change her mind. Just give her time."

She wasn't going to change her mind as long as she couldn't get a certain cowhand out of it.

"Where is she going to find a more suitable husband?" Corby asked. "I could have any woman within a hundred miles, but I want only Amanda."

"You'll get her. I'm sure of it," Gary said. "Once she marries you, Ma won't have anybody to help her on the ranch, and she'll have to sell it. Mr. Carruthers says he'll give her any price she wants."

Only because he was determined to get the ranch instead of Sandoval.

"I'll hire extra cowhands if Amanda will marry me."

"Don't! Then Ma will never sell, and I'll be stuck here forever. Priscilla will never speak to me as long as Ma and Amanda think everything that happens is her father's fault."

Amanda felt sorry for Gary. Priscilla Carruthers was a nice girl, but even if she had been interested in Gary, Amanda was certain her father wouldn't allow his only daughter to throw herself away on a bartender.

"Earl Carruthers is one of the most outstanding men in the county," Corby said.

"I keep telling Ma he's not behind the trouble that keeps happening on the ranch. It's just his cowhands fooling around, but she won't listen."

If it had been just the incident with Andy, Amanda might have agreed, but there was much more. Carruthers was growing increasingly insistent in his efforts to buy the Lazy T.

Corby took out his pocket watch and looked at it. "I can't stay away from the saloon any longer. I'll be back, but I can't wait forever. A man like me deserves to have children."

Corby was a vain peacock who was fortunate to have had her father as a partner when he wanted to open a saloon and a diner. Both establishments were on solid footing now, but her father had taught Corby how to attract and hold customers, how to handle the business end. Corby had been a good student and had become a decent businessman, but he would never be the man she wanted to marry.

"Is he gone?" her mother asked when she returned to the dining room.

"He's leaving."

Her mother sighed. "Your father admired his business ability, but I simply can't feel comfortable with him."

"You don't have to. Now I need to clean up. I want to run into town this afternoon."

"What for?" her mother asked.

"To put an end to this question of debt. I'll be very curious to know what Mr. Kincaid will do then."

"I really should be talking to your mother rather than you," the president of the bank said to Amanda. "It's not that I don't trust you or don't think you're capable of understanding financial matters. It's just that your mother is the senior member of the family."

The bank was the most substantial building in Cactus Bend, but her mother had characterized it as a general store with an ugly grille and badly scarred woodwork.

"I understand, but my mother has always left financial matters to my father or me."

Amanda felt uncomfortable facing the bank president. Roger Evans was one of those men who appreciated women—Amanda wished he wouldn't look at her quite like she was a tasty morsel to be consumed—but felt they ought to stay at home where they belonged.

"What exactly is it that you want to know? I explained everything about the provisions of the will last year." Dressed in black, Evans regarded her with an equally dark expression.

"It's not about the will." She hesitated, hating to involve an outsider in family business. "Before he died, my father sold his interest in the saloon and the diner."

"Is there some question about that?"

"I don't know how he paid for our ranch or for the bull. He said he had no debts, but I don't have any contracts to show what his arrangements were."

"Have you looked through his papers?"

"Yes."

Apparently, Evans thought she was an idiot. "Have you talked to his lawyer?"

"My father distrusted lawyers. He insisted that two honest men could handle any business arrangement between themselves."

"Unfortunately, that's not always true. What are you concerned about?" Evans leaned back, complacent in his position of power.

"A man came to the house yesterday saying we owe seven hundred dollars to a woman in Crystal Springs. I think it's for the bull my father bought. He says if we don't pay the debt, a judge will be here in two weeks to hold an auction of our possessions so that the debt can be satisfied."

The banker lost his appearance of disapproval and boredom and sat forward in his chair. "You didn't give him any money, did you?"

"No. He advised us to go to Crystal Springs and look into the matter ourselves."

The banker settled back in his chair. "That's what a reputable lawyer would advise."

"He's not a lawyer. He's a cowhand. He said the

judge offered to commute his jail sentence if he could collect the debt."

"That doesn't sound like something a reputable judge would do."

Amanda didn't know how she was to determine who was reputable and who wasn't. Her father had said the war had changed everyone. He had been particularly critical of the Reconstruction government and its appointments to the courts. Near universal use of the "ironclad" oath had deprived virtually every Texan of elected or appointed office.

"You have the only bank in town, so you must have handled my father's business."

"He deposited very little money with me." Evans sounded resentful.

Her father had kept large amounts of cash in his safe because he preferred cash dealings in everything he did. "I didn't come to ask about his deposits. I came to ask about the arrangements for paying for the ranch and the bull."

"Your father didn't handle either of those transactions through me. I'm familiar with his purchase of the ranch only because the previous owner deposited the funds with me before he moved away."

"You know nothing about the purchase of the bull?"

"The first I heard about it came from your neighbor, Ian Sandoval."

Amanda found it hard to believe her father could have handled such a transaction without anyone knowing.

"You should talk to Corby. Being your father's partner, he might know something I don't."

She should have asked Corby when he was at the house earlier today, but she'd been too anxious to make him understand she was never going to marry him. She'd try to talk to him tonight, but he believed women were incapable of understanding anything about business.

"If this was a cash transaction, you might never find any record of the purchase," the banker told her. "If Corby can't help you, I think your best alternative is to go to Crystal Springs and talk to the person who says you owe the money. If this woman doesn't have a written agreement, the dispute could end up in court unless the two of you can come to a settlement."

Amanda's spirits sank. Instead of providing her with proof the debt had been paid, the banker had left her with the prospect of having to come up with a way to settle the debt or end up in court. She was certain her mother would rather pay money she didn't owe than go to court. It was her oft-stated opinion that only criminals and the lower classes found themselves in courts with all their private business being aired in public.

"Thank you for your time," Amanda said as she got to her feet. "If you should learn anything about this business, I'd appreciate your letting me know."

"I will," the bank president said as he stood. "These are difficult times. It's necessary for all Texans to stick together."

Amanda didn't see how sticking together would help. What she needed were answers to a lot of questions. Why hadn't the person who was owed the money contacted the Liscombs before now? How could she prove the debt had been paid? If her father had paid for the bull, someone should have received the money. Where was it?

Almost as important, why couldn't she get Broc Kincaid out of her mind?

❧

Broc approached the bunkhouse from the opposite direction of the house. He wanted to make sure neither Amanda nor her mother saw him. He was hoping Eddie was either inside or away from the house. He had to take his chance that Leo and Gary were out working on the ranch, leaving only Andy in the bunkhouse.

"Come in, fool," Andy shouted when Broc knocked. "You don't see no lock on the door, do you?"

Broc smiled to himself before he opened the door and went in.

Andy's expression went from sour annoyance to unhappy surprise when he saw Broc. "What are you doing here?"

"I found the bull loose again. I need you to help me get him back."

"Gary and Leo are out looking for him now. Where is he?"

"Tied to a tree."

"My shoulder's not well yet."

He sounded like a spoiled child. "I'll put your rope on him and loop it around your saddle horn. All you have to do is keep the rope taut so he can't attack either of us."

"Why don't you wait until Leo and Gary get back? You can tell them where the bull is, and they can get him."

"I don't want the family to know I was here. I'm not very popular with them right now."

"You're not very popular with me, either. I haven't forgotten that you knocked me on the head."

Broc knew there was no point trying to convince Andy he'd done it because it was the fastest and least painful way to set his arm. "Just help me get the bull back here."

"Amanda told me I wasn't to do anything until I was better."

Broc was saved from having to find a way to change Andy's mind when Leo entered the bunkhouse. His tall, sinewy frame contrasted with Andy's shorter, broader build.

"What are you doing here?" he asked Broc.

"He says he found the bull," Andy told him. "He wants you to help him bring him back."

"Where was that damned critter?" Leo didn't wait for an answer. "Gary and me have been looking for him for hours."

"I found him on Carruthers's land. I thought I'd better get him back onto the Lazy T before he caused some trouble."

Leo muttered a curse. "I told Gary the critter musta gone that way, but Gary insisted that Sandoval took him."

"Can you meet me where the lane runs into the road to town?"

"Give me time to saddle a fresh horse."

Broc followed Leo through the bunkhouse door and nearly bumped into Amanda. For the third time in just a few minutes, he was faced with the same question.

"What are you doing here?"

Six

AMANDA HADN'T EXPECTED TO SEE BROC AGAIN. MUCH to her shock and dismay, rather than feeling angry he'd disregarded her wishes, she was relieved. No, she was almost happy, and she couldn't accept that. He'd caused her family too much distress. She was even more dismayed to discover she had smiled at him.

"I found the bull."

She could feel a question hovering in the air between them. Did that smile mean she was glad to see him, or was it merely a polite response because Leo was watching? She knew the answer, but she wasn't going to let Broc know.

"Where? Gary said he and Leo spent hours looking for him."

"We was looking in the wrong places," Leo said with disgust. "Gary won't never listen to anything I say." He followed that statement with another curse under his breath. "We was lucky we didn't get shot at."

"Where is the bull now?" Amanda asked Broc.

"Tied to a tree. I couldn't get him back here without being gored."

"I'll saddle a horse and be back in a minute," Leo said.

"Saddle one for me," Amanda said. "I'm going with you."

"That's not necessary," Broc said. "Leo and I can handle him between us."

"I appreciate your having caught the bull, but this isn't your responsibility," Amanda told him.

"Maybe not, but I'm going, too." His answer was firm. It was clear there'd be no budging him from his decision.

Amanda had a wide experience with men, but she was coming to the conclusion she had no experience with a man like Broc. She could tell from the light in his eyes he was attracted to her, but she suspected his disfigurement made him feel he was unacceptable to any woman. She hoped he hadn't let it make him think he had nothing to lose if he decided to step outside the law.

"I saw you coming out of the bank yesterday," he said after they'd stood in silence for a long moment. "I hope it wasn't bad news."

She didn't feel comfortable sharing this kind of information with him, but he already knew more than she wanted. "Papa didn't trust banks or lawyers, so I didn't learn anything. The bank president assured me Papa wasn't a man to refuse to pay his debts. I won't be sending money to Mrs. Sibley. Does that mean you'll still go to jail?"

"That's what the judge said."

"But you can't go to jail for not collecting a debt that doesn't exist."

"The judge believes the debt is real."

She didn't understand how Broc could discuss it so calmly. Going to jail wasn't something to be taken lightly. A prison sentence would follow him for the rest of his life. "My father said all the Reconstruction judges were crooks, that you couldn't get a fair verdict unless you paid for it."

"I got a fair verdict."

"You call being forced to collect a debt that doesn't exist a fair verdict?"

"I could have served my time in jail."

"Why didn't you?"

He pointed to his face. "This is enough of a handicap. I don't want to add another."

"Do you have to go back? Couldn't you go to your friend in California? The law would never find you out there."

"The judge trusted me enough to let me go. I can't betray that trust and still respect myself."

Now she felt terrible that she'd suggested he do something she wouldn't have done herself. "Sorry. What you do is your business, but not everyone judges you by your scar. I think you were quite heroic to have endured so much and to have handled it so well."

His smile was half-hearted. "I didn't always handle it well."

"I wouldn't believe you if you said you had. I'm surprised you don't hate every Yankee you see."

"They did what they thought was right, just like we did. At least I'm alive. The man who did this isn't."

She hoped Leo would hurry up with the horses. This conversation was making her uncomfortable. She preferred to believe people were honest, that good would prevail, and everyone would find someone to love. Seeing Broc's wound, knowing how people treated him, forced her out of that comfortable state of mind, and she didn't like it.

"I don't understand how the bull keeps getting out," she said, changing the subject. "He doesn't look like he's capable of jumping the fence."

"He didn't. Someone let him out."

"How is it possible for someone to sneak onto the ranch at night and let him out without anybody knowing?"

She didn't understand why Broc was so slow to answer. He'd been quick enough to say the bull wasn't getting out on his own.

"You don't have a dog, and I doubt Leo or Andy has been sleeping with one ear to the ground. Gary gets home so late, a stampede wouldn't wake him."

What he said was reasonable, but she got the feeling he was thinking something else.

"All anyone has to do is ease the gate open, wait for the bull to leave, then close it. If the person walked in from behind the barn, you'd never see or hear him."

"Do you think Carruthers has been sending one of his men over so the bull can breed with his cows?"

"Maybe. He could also be hoping the bull would get killed in a fight with one of the range bulls."

Loss of the bull would nearly guarantee her mother would have to sell the ranch. She would have to talk to Leo and Andy. Gary, too. All of them would have to be more vigilant. Maybe it would be a good idea to set up a watch. With five of them—she didn't count her mother—it shouldn't be too hard on anybody.

Leo came up leading two saddled horses. "Ready to go?"

"Yes," she said, coming out of her abstraction. "I need to get back so I can start supper."

Burrows dug by small rodents and rocks that could get jammed in a horse's hoof made it preferable to use the road rather than head directly across the prairie despite the dust stirred up by their mounts' hooves. For the first few minutes of the ride, Leo complained about not having enough time to do all the work. "Andy's laid up, and Gary is gone half the time. I don't see how you expect me to do everything," he said.

"I don't," Amanda said. "I've never asked you to."

"Somebody's got to do it," Leo said. "If we lose any more cows, this place ain't going to make it."

"What are you talking about?"

"Didn't Gary tell you?"

"Tell me what?"

"We've been losing cows for at least a month. I don't know how many are gone. Maybe a hundred."

Amanda felt faint. "A hundred!"

"Could be less. Could be more," Leo said. "I haven't had time to make a count, but it seems we're missing mostly cows with calves by the bull."

"I can't understand why Gary didn't say something," Amanda said.

Leo shrugged. "I guess he didn't want to worry you."

"He didn't want to worry me!" Amanda pulled her voice down to a nearly normal level. "How is going broke going to worry me less?"

Leo looked uncomfortable at having divulged information Amanda didn't know. "I think I'll ride ahead, put my rope on the bull so we'll be ready to go when you get there."

"I tied him to a post oak next to the dry wash," Broc told Leo.

As Leo loped off, a couple of riders approached, nodded a greeting, and rode past. Amanda didn't recognize either man. After they'd ridden a few minutes in silence, Broc said, "I heard Gary doesn't like working on the ranch."

Amanda looked up, felt her face flush. "What do you mean by that?"

"I don't know that I mean anything," Broc said.

"Yes, you do. I've thought from the first you knew more than you were saying."

"I know almost nothing beyond what you've told me. Anything else is just conjecture."

"Tell me what you conjecture. I saw something in your face when Leo first mentioned the missing cows."

"If the cows really *are* missing, it's because someone wants you to have to sell the ranch. I've been wondering who that someone could be."

"It would have to be Carruthers or Sandoval."

"Are you sure? Your father's partner wants to marry you, but you won't agree. Maybe he thinks losing the ranch would change your mind."

"Corby would never do anything like that. He was here yesterday offering to marry me so he could help us keep the ranch," she argued. "What else have you been conjecturing?"

"I'm not sure I should tell you."

"Why?"

"Because you'll be even angrier with me than you are now."

"I'm not angry with you."

"Do you tell all the men you're *not angry with* to leave your ranch and never come back?"

"That's different. You'd upset my mother."

"I didn't upset you?"

"Yes, you did." It wasn't a hot afternoon, but she was feeling warm from irritation. Frustration. Attraction.

"I don't want to upset you again."

She didn't want to be upset, either, but he was the only experienced cowhand she could trust to tell her the truth. "I promise not to get upset."

"You'll hate what I'm going to say."

She couldn't imagine what he could say that would be that terrible. "I'm sure I won't, but even if I did, I need to know. It might help me figure out what's going on and who's behind it."

He hesitated.

"Come on. Leo already has a rope on the bull. If what you say is going to upset me so much, I'd rather it didn't happen in front of him."

"I'm not saying this is what's happening, but you've got to consider all the possibilities."

"Stop stalling. Spit it out."

"Your brother hates working on the ranch and hopes your mother will sell it. Have you considered that he might be letting the bull out? And who would be in a better position to hide some of your cows until you're forced to sell?"

Amanda was so appalled by his accusation, she was speechless. She wondered what kind of family he'd grown up in to make him think her brother would even think of doing something so horrible. Gary did hate to work on the ranch, but he was young and easily bored by hard work.

"Gary doesn't enjoy working on the ranch, but he'd never do anything to hurt his family. How could you even think something like that?"

"I'm an outsider, so I'm not influenced by knowing anything about the people involved. I just look at facts and draw possible conclusions."

"Well, that conclusion isn't possible." She was relieved to have reached the tree where Broc had tied the bull. She didn't want him to know he'd upset her a lot more than she let on. If she hadn't overheard what Gary had said to Corby yesterday, she wouldn't have given Broc's accusation a minute's thought. But she *had* overheard it, and she couldn't get it out of her mind.

She would have to talk to Gary. She didn't believe he was responsible for any of their troubles, but he needed to stop broadcasting his dislike for the ranch. He also had to start telling her when something went wrong, especially when a hundred cows were missing.

She had intended to help with the bull, but he followed so docilely between Broc and Leo, she wondered what made the bull leave his pasture so often. She followed, relieved not to have to ride next to either man.

All the way back to the ranch she tried to convince herself neither Corby nor Gary was responsible for any of the trouble. She was satisfied her arguments against

Gary's involvement were solid. She was equally sure of her reasoning against Corby's involvement. The difficulty came when it occurred to her that they might be working together. Forcing her mother to sell the ranch would accomplish what each of them was after. It upset her that she'd let someone she didn't know cause her to question the honesty of two people she'd known most of her life. She didn't know whether it was Broc or the logic of what he said, but she felt alone with only a stranger to depend on.

Her heart sank when, as they approached the ranch house, her mother came out on the porch. She took one look at Broc and gripped the porch rail for support. She wouldn't say anything while Broc was here, but she'd fill Amanda's ears with complaints as soon as he was gone. They had to ride past the house, the bunkhouse, and the shed to reach the bull's pasture.

"Has anyone checked the fence?" Broc asked Amanda.

"I've been around it twice," Leo told him. "Ain't no way he could have gotten out except through the gate. You'd think if someone was trying to make us think the bull was getting out by itself, they'd put a break in the fence, but any fool knows there ain't no bull can open that gate."

Amanda thought maybe Leo was wrong. A circle of rope was looped over the end post of the fence and the end of the gate. It was conceivable the bull could have learned to lift it with his nose and push the gate open. Amanda explained her theory to Leo.

"Maybe it happened that way before, but not last night," Leo said. "I tied a rope farther down between the braces. Show me a bull that can untie a knot, and I'll show you a bull that ought to be in the circus."

"Let's put him in his pasture," Broc said. "I need to get back to town."

"Mind if I go with him?" Leo asked Amanda. "I'm tired of doing my work and Andy's."

"Go have a good evening," she said, "but don't drink too much or stay too late."

Leo grinned. "Yes, Ma."

Amanda blushed. "Sorry."

Now it was Leo's turn to look uncomfortable. "It's okay. It's nice to have somebody to worry about me."

Before she could respond, Eddie and Gary rode up.

"What's he doing here?" Gary demanded, pointing at Broc, "and what's he doing with our bull?"

"The bull got out again," Leo told him. "He couldn't untie the knot I made in the rope, so some-one had to let him out."

"That doesn't tell me what *he's* doing here," he said, indicating Broc.

"He found the bull," Amanda told her brother. Her mother, seeing that her sons had returned, had left the house and was walking toward them.

"How is it he's always finding our bull?" Gary demanded.

"Because he's smart," Eddie said. "He likes horses."

"Maybe he's the one letting the bull out," Gary said.

"Why would I do that?" Broc asked. "I didn't even know who owned him when I found him a few days ago."

"Maybe you did," Gary accused. "Maybe you

knew all along. Maybe you're trying to make us so afraid something will happen to our bull that we'll sell him and give you the money you say we owe."

"He wouldn't do that," Eddie said.

Amanda thought the same thing but was relieved Eddie had said it for her. She had no rational explanation for her belief.

"I'm certain Earl Carruthers is responsible for this." Her mother had arrived in time to hear Gary's accusation. "He will do anything to force me to sell this ranch to him."

"Why do you always blame everything on Mr. Carruthers?" Gary demanded, his anger growing.

"Because his men are the ones always causing us trouble," Leo said.

"And he is the most insistent that I should sell the ranch now that your father has died," her mother added. "He says it's impossible for a woman to manage a ranch successfully. He says no cowhand with an ounce of self-respect would work for women."

"I'm not a woman," Gary said.

"Neither am I," Eddie added.

"Mr. Carruthers thinks my being a widow is more important than having two sons," her mother said.

"Sammy says he just wants to have a bigger ranch than Mr. Sandoval," Eddie said.

"What would you or Sammy Loftus know about something like that?" Gary demanded.

"Sammy is a lying coyote, and I hate him," Eddie declared, "but he said his friend Pete overheard Mr. Carruthers telling his pa he wasn't doing any of those things we said he was doing. He said he was just waiting for us to sell so he could buy our ranch and be bigger than Sandoval."

Amanda had reported the harassment to the sheriff, but she wasn't surprised Carruthers had been able to convince Tom Mercer he was innocent. Mercer had the makings of a good sheriff, but Carruthers was rich and powerful, and they couldn't prove anything beyond ordinary rivalry between cowhands.

"It doesn't matter what Mr. Carruthers's motives are," her mother said. "They don't change the fact that he'll do anything to drive us away."

"It's unfair to keep saying that when you can't prove it," Gary protested.

"You're only objecting because you like Priscilla, and she doesn't like you." Eddie had a way of reducing things to their essentials.

"She does like me," Gary said, "but she'd like me more if my whole family wasn't ready to point a finger at her father every time a cow got a pimple."

"What about the bull getting out all the time?" Amanda asked. "And what about the hundred cows and calves Leo tells me are missing?"

"A hundred cows!" her mother gasped. "That man will ruin us."

Gary threw Leo an angry glance. "We don't know how many are missing."

"Only because we haven't counted," Leo said.

"Why haven't you counted?" her mother asked.

"Cows wander all over looking for water and better grass when they're not fenced," Broc explained. "They scatter worse during storms, especially if there's lightning. They also tend to stay away from people."

"Why aren't our cows in pens?" Mrs. Liscomb asked. "That's what my father did."

It wasn't the first time Amanda wondered why her mother had insisted that her husband buy a ranch when she knew nothing about ranching and couldn't seem to remember anything she'd been told.

"Nobody in Texas fences their cows," Gary said, exasperated.

"Wood or timber fences are too expensive and take too much time to build and maintain," Broc explained. "A Frenchman has been experimenting with twisting sharp points around wire, but so far I haven't heard of anything like that for sale."

"I never heard of such a thing." It was obvious Gary thought Broc was lying.

"You will if he succeeds in producing a commercial product. It will end the open range. Ranchers will have to own the land they graze, not merely control it."

"Is this true?" Leo asked.

"Of course not," Gary said. "Nothing like that will ever happen."

Both Amanda and her mother turned to Broc.

"The cattle industry in Texas is exploding. A cow that used to sell for three dollars in Texas can bring twenty dollars in Abilene. One that carries more meat can bring thirty or even forty dollars. Every rancher will soon be trying to do what you're trying to do with this bull. It will be a lot easier and faster with fences."

If Amanda had had any doubt that Broc was an experienced cowhand, she didn't doubt now.

Her mother looked slightly dazed by Broc's

knowledge, but she recovered quickly. "That's all the more reason for Carruthers to want us to fail," she said.

"If Carruthers wants you to fail, it's because you keep accusing him of everything that goes wrong here." Gary turned to his sister. "Priscilla wouldn't even talk to me after you went to the sheriff."

"You should have been the one to do that," Amanda told her brother.

"What we should do is sell this ranch and this damned bull and go back into partnership with Corby or start our own saloon." Gary glowed with the enthusiasm of a zealot. "I know all we need to know. With Amanda singing and waiting tables, we'd soon have all the business we could handle."

"I'm not very good with figures," her mother said, "but if this man—" she pointed to Broc rather than using his name—"is correct in asserting that we can get as much as forty dollars for one cow, we'll make more money with the ranch."

"It depends on how many cows you have and whether you can get them to Abilene carrying a lot of weight, but a hundred cows at forty dollars each is four thousand dollars."

Now Amanda understood more clearly why the only cows missing were those with calves by the bull.

"You've got to stop working in the saloon until we find the cows," her mother said to Gary.

"We won't have money to pay Leo and Andy."

"Can we sell some of our yearlings?" She turned to Broc. "Is there a market for yearlings?"

"Not as much as for a mature steer."

"I'll stop working here before I stop working in the saloon," Gary said. "I hate this ranch. I hate cows. I argued with Pa the whole time he was considering buying the ranch and the bull."

"It's not respectable to own a saloon," their mother said.

"It is more respectable to starve?"

"There's no question of starving," Amanda said, trying to calm her brother's burgeoning anger.

"I don't mind working without wages for a time," Leo volunteered. "Since Andy has a bum shoulder, you don't have to pay him, either."

"I couldn't let you work without pay." Their mother turned to Gary. "Amanda can keep working in the evenings. You have to stop."

"No."

Their mother looked stunned by Gary's flat refusal, but Amanda wasn't surprised. Her mother drew herself up in what Amanda privately referred to as her imperial mode.

"We need you here," their mother said. "Amanda will tell Corby you've quit when she goes in this evening."

"The hell with that!" Gary shouted. "Amanda will have nothing to tell Corby because I'm leaving."

Seven

BROC WATCHED GARY STORM OFF TOWARD THE HOUSE.

"I'll have everything out of the house before supper," he shouted over his shoulder before turning and pointing to Broc. "You can let him have my place at the table."

"Come back. Don't walk away from me."

Broc wanted to tell Mrs. Liscomb her attempts to establish control over her son were futile, but he'd already caused enough trouble in this family. All he wanted was to find a way to disappear quietly.

"Let him go," Eddie told his mother. "Broc can work for us."

Mrs. Liscomb looked as though she'd been slapped. "I'm sure Mr. Kincaid is quite capable, but Gary is your brother."

"I bet Broc is better than Gary," Eddie said. "He likes horses."

"This has nothing to do with horses," his mother snapped. "I'll talk to Gary. He'll change his mind."

"I hope he doesn't," Eddie said after his mother left for the house.

"Edward Liscomb!" Amanda said, scandalized. "How can you say a thing like that?"

"Because Gary's mean." The boy looked defensive, but he wasn't backing down.

Broc had several younger brothers. He knew how they felt about being bossed around by an older brother. Gary struck him as an unhappy young man who was just looking for an excuse to rebel. Hating the ranch and believing it stood in the way of his infatuation with Priscilla Carruthers was more than enough reason.

"I hope you don't expect me to do his work as well as Andy's," Leo said to Amanda.

"Of course not," Amanda said. "Eddie and I will help as much as we can."

Leo looked at the bull, which had wandered off to a more inviting patch of grass. "I'm certainly not sitting up all night to see how he's getting out."

Amanda looked so tired, so defeated, Broc wanted to offer to do Gary's work for her, but he could help her best by leaving. Maybe he could talk to her brother later that evening in the saloon. He didn't think the boy was a bad kid; Gary was just trying to establish his independence from his mother and survive his first serious romance at the same time.

"How long before supper?" Leo asked. "I got a couple of things I need to do."

"Will an hour give you enough time?" Amanda asked.

"I guess." Leo disappeared into the lengthening shadows on the east side of the bunkhouse.

"I'll be going," Broc said.

"I would like to talk to you if you have time," Amanda said.

"I don't know anything more about the debt."

"It's not about that. I wanted to ask some questions about ranching."

"If you really want to know what's going on, let me put you in touch with the friend I work for. He's dealt with cows all his life."

"I'd rather talk to you."

Broc didn't like the way her words made him feel. He could deal with being attracted to Amanda as long as there was no possibility she might return his interest. Even the possibility that she might like him would raise hopes that would be painful to extinguish. He had thought he was beyond such struggles. It was a bitter surprise to learn he was probably no more immune than Gary.

Deciding it would be better to do anything rather than continue to stare at Amanda, Broc led the horses to the shed to be unsaddled. "You ought to hire an experienced cowman. He could teach you what you need to know."

"I've tried, but we don't have enough money to compete with Carruthers or Sandoval. Every time I've found someone, they hire him or drive him off."

He had never met either man, but he'd learned a little of their reputations in town. They were accounted to be hard but fair competitors. "How do they do that?"

"Mostly they either offer more money or make it clear it would be easier to look for a job elsewhere. I only got Leo and Andy to work for us because they were too young and inexperienced for Carruthers to bother."

"Have you talked to the sheriff?"

"He said he couldn't go up against two such powerful men without solid proof."

Broc would have expected him to do just that. During the war, the Night Riders had attacked trains, supply wagons, munitions dumps, anything that stood in the way of victory. They never asked whether the opponent was too big or too powerful because the opponent was *always* too numerous and too powerful. Yet they'd never suffered defeat or significant casualties until one of their own had betrayed them.

"Have you talked to the two men?" Broc asked.

"Yes, but they denied doing anything."

"I'd begin by putting a padlocked chain on the gate to the bull's pasture. If someone is letting him out, they'll have to take down some fence. Then you'll have something to show the sheriff."

"What about the missing cows?"

"As long as you only have one man working for you, I don't see how you can do much more than try to keep them away from Carruthers's range."

He would have done more. He'd have searched the surrounding land, even if he'd had to do it at night. He'd have put a halt to the harassment by the cowhands. He'd have had the sheriff out there looking into things if he'd had to drag him by his shirt collar.

"Andy will be back in the saddle soon."

He didn't think Andy would contribute much, but he had eyes and could look for the cows. Rustling was a serious offense that was always sure to unite cattlemen regardless of what they thought of each other individually.

But why was he worrying about Amanda's problems? She wanted nothing to do with him. No woman who wasn't desperate would. She was only talking to him because she didn't have anyone else. He really needed to get back to town. Staring at her, thinking of how nice it would be if she would smile at him again, if he could just touch her hand, brush her cheek, kiss—

He snapped that thought like a thread. It was mental and physical torture. If he didn't concentrate on something else, his body was going to make it obvious what he was thinking. After that, she wouldn't even speak to him. That would probably be the easiest way to get over his infatuation, but he didn't want it to happen. It was pathetic to admit, but even a tiny bit of attention was better than none.

"Look, bring the cows with calves by the bull closest in. When you breed a cow with the bull, mark it so you'll be able to track it until it calves. If you've got anyplace that offers natural barriers, like a canyon, even a wide streambed, keep as many of your cows there as you can. Keep them away from points of contact with Carruthers's and Danoval's ranges."

"That sounds like a lot of supervision."

She looked so overwhelmed, he wanted to take her in his arms and assure her that everything would work out. More than that, he wanted to pound some sense into Gary's head. The young man should be helping his sister, not causing more trouble. He also longed to have a few words with Mrs. Liscomb. She was using her position as their mother to keep her children dependent on her, making them feel guilty if they didn't respond to her every need. Broc didn't care where she was born, who her parents had been, or if she'd lived in a mansion. She was in Texas now. Women with more exalted backgrounds and greater privilege had plucked up their courage and decided honest work wasn't beneath their dignity. It was time Mrs. Liscomb learned the same lesson.

But he wasn't the one to teach it to her. She thought he was a hideously disfigured crook who was trying to steal money from the family.

"Amanda, come talk to your brother."

Broc turned to see Mrs. Liscomb standing on the porch, wringing her hands. He wanted to tell her to gather up Gary's stuff and throw it after him. The sooner her son realized running away was stupid, the sooner he would be back.

"I have to go," Amanda said. "Thank you for finding the bull."

"I wish she'd let Gary leave," Eddie said.

Broc had forgotten the boy was still there. "He'll come to his senses soon."

"No, he won't," Eddie said. "He hates the ranch. He told me he hopes the bull runs away and never comes back. He told me he hopes all the cows get stolen so Mama has to sell the ranch. He said then she'd move back to town, and he could work in the saloon all the time and marry Priscilla."

"It's hard to be in love with someone who doesn't love you in return."

"I don't want any girl loving me," Eddie declared.

Broc hid his smile. "You won't always feel that way. Now, I'd better go, and you need to help your sister."

Eddie squared his shoulders. "If I was bigger, I'd punch Gary in the nose."

Broc did smile then. He remembered one of his younger brothers saying the same thing. "I don't think that would make things any better."

"I'd feel better," Eddie declared. "A *lot* better."

Broc chuckled as he watched Eddie head toward the house with a walk that was more of a swagger. It was a shame he wasn't the older brother instead of Gary.

But as Broc rode back to town, he found himself thinking about Amanda, the swell of her breasts, the softness of her lips, the way her hips moved under her dress. He could empathize with every man who watched her each night, knowing he would never get any closer. The Open Door might be the only decent saloon within twenty miles, but he would have been better off drinking his beer down by the creek with only stray dogs for company. Or in the livery stable with nothing but drowsing horses to witness his misery.

Thinking about Amanda's body got his blood so warm, he became uncomfortable in the saddle. If he wasn't able to get his thoughts under control, it would be better for him to go back to Crystal Springs and let the judge put him in jail. At least that way he wouldn't be able to wander the countryside hoping the bull would escape again so he would have an excuse to see Amanda once more.

But he wasn't going back to Crystal Springs yet. If he had to go to jail, there was no sense rushing. He would hang around, keeping his eyes and ears open. Something was wrong on the Lazy T, and he intended to find out what it was.

"There's no use asking me to follow him," Amanda said to her mother after Gary had slammed through the front door. "He's not going to listen to me if he won't listen to you."

"But he can't leave. What am I going to do without him?"

Amanda wanted to tell her mother they had already been doing without Gary, but she swallowed the words. "Let him find out what it's like to live without someone to cook his meals, clean his room, and wash his clothes."

"What will we do without the money he earns?" her mother asked.

Amanda didn't have an answer for that. "I don't think he'll stay away long, but I'll speak to him about the money."

"If he won't give us any money, you'll have to work more." Her mother looked chagrined. "I don't know how I can stand the humiliation."

"I don't see why not. It isn't you the men will be gaping at."

Her mother stiffened; her eyes flashed. "How can you speak to me like that after the way Gary behaved?"

Normally Amanda would have backed down, but her blood was up. "How can you believe my working in the saloon embarrasses you and not me?"

"I never wanted you to work in that place," her mother said. "That's why I begged your father to buy this ranch."

"Didn't you stop to think that once you had this ranch, you would have to work to make it successful?"

Her mother looked at her in surprise. "Your father never wanted me to work."

"Why is it beneath you but fine for me?"

Amanda felt as horrified as her mother looked. She'd never spoken to her like that. She'd never even argued with her. She didn't know what had gotten into her, but once the words started, she couldn't stop them. And she wasn't ashamed. She was angry, so angry she was trembling. Far too angry to apologize. She couldn't stay in the house. The way she was feeling right now, she had no idea what she might say.

Without a word of explanation, she headed straight for the door and out into the yard. She didn't turn back when her mother called after her. She didn't slow down when Eddie wanted to know what was wrong. She kept walking until she found herself on the far side of the bull's pasture. The fat lazy beast was lying down under a tree, chewing his cud as though he didn't have a care in the world. At that moment, he represented everything that had gone wrong with her life: the ranch that was going to fail and leave them bankrupt, this mysterious debt Broc Kincaid said they owed, Gary's break with the family, Andy's dislocated shoulder, and the lack of a document that said her father had paid for the bull.

Yet he was the reason Broc Kincaid had come into her life.

That thought stopped her. Why would she think Broc had *come into her life*? He was just a stranger who'd found their bull and had come to collect a debt they didn't owe. He was passing through, on his way to jail or to the ranch where he worked. He was an ordinary

cowhand. He had a ruined face that either shocked
or repulsed people. He hadn't shown any signs that
he felt anything more than admiration for her beauty.
He'd given no indication he *wanted* to come into
her life. On the contrary, he'd kept his distance and
seemed anxious to leave.

His disfigurement had never upset her. Rather,
she'd felt sorry that he'd suffered such a terrible injury,
that such a handsome man now had to accustom himself to repelling people. Despite that setback, he was
cheerful and appeared to have a sense of humor. Aside
from the matter of the debt, he appeared to be honest,
unassuming, and willing to help. He had beautiful
manners and was as happy talking to Eddie as he was
to her. Even though he said he had to collect the debt
to keep from going to jail, he'd advised them to give
him no money and to go to Crystal Springs to verify
what they owed.

It was possible that these admirable characteristics
weren't the real reason she was so out of sorts. If she
was honest with herself, she'd have to acknowledge
that she'd never been as physically attracted to any
man as she was to Broc Kincaid. Just thinking about
being in his arms made her body ache with desire.

And that realization shocked her. She'd never felt
this way before and didn't understand why she should
be feeling this way now. Broc had an outstanding
body, strong legs, trim waist, well-muscled shoulders.
Lots of cowhands had similarly developed bodies, but
theirs didn't come together in a mesmerizing whole
like Broc's did. The ruined side of his face didn't
cause her to ignore the side that said he used to be an

exceedingly handsome man. The scars couldn't dim the twinkle in his eyes, or the way he had of looking at her as if she were the only person in the universe. Whatever battles he fought in his own mind didn't impair his cheerfulness or his ability to cause people to feel better just because he was there.

Most of all, she was horrified to acknowledge that her gaze had been drawn more than once to the bulge in his jeans. She'd never thought she had a carnal nature. The discovery came as a shock to her. Yet it also brought with it a low-key sense of excitement that kept her blood simmering. Was this how some of the men in the saloon felt when they looked at her? Did they have disconcerting dreams? Did they feel embarrassed to have so little control over their own minds?

"This is all your fault," she said to the bull, "and you don't care at all."

She had to back up. There was plenty of fault to go around. Her mother was to blame for urging her father to buy a ranch they couldn't manage. Her father for giving up a dependable source of income to feed his wife's vanity. Gary for not pulling his weight. She supposed she could blame herself for not being more understanding of her mother and brother. Eddie, bless his soul, was probably the only one free of blame.

She wanted to blame Corby, but it was hard to fault a man who wanted to marry her and take care of all the family problems. She wanted to blame Broc, but he was caught in circumstances not of his making. She had to stop thinking about blame. All that mattered now was figuring a way out of the mess they were in.

"I guess you're doing your part by siring as many

calves as you can," she said to the bull. "It's not your fault we keep losing them."

"Why are you talking to the bull?"

Eddie didn't look surprised, just curious. Her mother would have thought she was crazy. "I guess because he's the only living thing close by. Besides, he can't argue with me."

"I won't argue with you."

He looked so worried, she gave him a quick hug. "I'm just irritated. It helps to say things, even if it's only to a bull."

"What are you irritated about? You can tell me."

Even if she could have forced herself to divulge her attraction to Broc, she'd never do so to a nine-year-old boy. She nearly blushed at the thought of describing her dreams. She didn't want to think what her mother would say if she knew.

"It's a lot of things," she said to Eddie, "starting with Gary."

"I hate Gary," Eddie declared.

"No, you don't."

"I love you and Mama. I loved Papa, too, but I hate Gary. I like Leo," Eddie continued. "Andy not so much. I like Broc, too. Do you like him?"

This time she did blush. "I don't know him well enough to be able to answer that, but," she added before she told a lie, "I think I could like him a lot."

"Mama doesn't like him. She says he's ugly."

"It's not his fault."

"I think he was very brave."

She did, too. Strong to survive such an injury, brave to face the world without flinching, courageous to blame no one, wise enough to expect no favors. She'd never found so many wonderful qualities in one man.

"I want him to teach me how to rope a cow."

"You'd better ask Leo. I doubt we'll see Mr. Kincaid again."

"He said he'd teach me."

"When?"

"When I showed him my horses."

That was before he'd told them about the debt. "Things have changed."

"I know. Gary is acting like an ass, and Mama is mad at you."

"Where did you learn such language?"

Eddie grinned. "From Andy. He cusses a lot when you're not around."

Amanda knew it was inevitable that every boy would learn to cuss. It seemed to be as much a part of the growing-up process as starting to shave. "You'd better not talk like that around Mama."

"I'm not crazy." He acted insulted. "You're not the only one around here with a brain."

She wasn't sure about that. The way she was reacting to Broc didn't speak well for her intelligence. It was a good thing she wouldn't be seeing him again. Unfortunately, not seeing him didn't mean she would forget him. She had a sinking feeling Broc Kincaid had ruined her for any other man.

Broc looked across the saloon, his gaze narrowing until he saw only Earl Carruthers. The man looked about as he had expected: big, handsome in a rough way, and exuding a kind of confidence that came with years of getting what he wanted. He didn't look like the kind of man who would try to badger a widow into selling her ranch, but Broc had learned long ago that you couldn't judge a man's character by his looks or his background. Cain and Abel had nursed at the same breast, and Absalom had been beautiful to the eye.

He wanted to speak to Carruthers, but they didn't know each other, and he had no business to conduct with the man. Carruthers had no reason to speak to him, even less to tell him anything incriminating. Broc would have to wait for an opportunity to present itself. In the meantime, he could listen. Maybe he could learn something.

Tonight he found a place near the middle of the bar. Gary scowled at him, then proceeded to ignore him. Broc didn't say anything, just let a hint of a smile play on his lips.

"You gonna ask this man what he wants?"

Broc had been so busy watching Carruthers in the big mirror behind the bar, he hadn't paid attention to the man standing at the bar beside him. He was big, stocky, powerful-looking.

"No, I ain't," Gary said, sulking. "I don't like him."

"You don't have to like him," the man said. "Ask him what he wants."

"Don't bother," Broc told the man. "I'm not especially thirsty."

"You don't have to drink if you don't want to, but he's got to ask you what you want." His long arm snaked out and grabbed Gary by the apron tied around his waist. "Ask this man what he wants before I come around there and see how your head fits in one of them slop buckets."

"Is something wrong?" Corby had come up to see what was going on.

"Your snot-nosed bartender won't ask this man what he wants to drink. That's what you get for letting kids tend bar."

Corby didn't look any happier to see Broc than Gary did. "I told you I don't want you around here."

"Why not?" the man asked. "What's he done?"

"It's not something I care to make public," Corby said.

"I don't care if it's made public," Gary said. "He's been turning up at our ranch causing trouble."

"What'd you do?" the man asked Broc.

"I found their bull loose," Broc told the man. "I returned it."

"I don't see nothing wrong with that," the man said to Gary.

"He drove my sister home."

"I offered when neither you nor Corby would go with her."

"Now you're trying to squeeze money out of us for a debt we don't owe."

"I advised you to go to Crystal Springs and look into the problem before you paid anybody anything."

The big man had been turning from Broc to Gary and back with each accusation and each reply. Now he focused on Gary. "I don't see anything wrong with that. Sounds to me like he did you a service."

"I don't want him doing us any services. I don't

want him anywhere around. It makes me sick to look at him."

The big man regarded Broc for a few seconds. "I admit he doesn't look very pretty, but I doubt it's something he asked for. In any case, I'd rather look at him than at your sour puss."

"Serve him whatever he wants," Corby said to Gary. "I hope you'll leave once you're finished," he said to Broc.

"Not very friendly," the man remarked. "If it wasn't for that pretty waitress and her singing, I'd never step foot in this place."

Gary slapped a beer in front of Broc and turned to help someone else.

"My name's Dan Walch," the big man said. "I ain't seen you around before."

"I'm new in town. Won't be here long, but it'll be long enough to need a job. Never could hold on to money very long."

"Ain't that the truth," Dan said. "What do you do?"

"I'm a cowhand."

Dan picked up his drink. "Come with me. I want you to meet my boss."

"Who's your boss?"

"Mr. Carruthers. He's right over there."

Eight

Picking up his beer, Broc followed Dan as he wove his way across the crowded saloon to a table in the corner where Carruthers was seated with three equally prosperous-looking men. The fourth man was the young sheriff.

"What's up, Dan?" the sheriff asked. He looked at Broc with raised eyebrows.

"I wanted to introduce this man to the boss," Dan said. "He's a cowhand, and he's looking for a job."

"I didn't say—" Broc began but Carruthers cut him off.

"You've come to the right place. I run the biggest spread in the county," he added with a self-satisfied smile.

"The biggest after mine."

Broc turned to find himself facing a man he guessed was Ian Sandoval. He wasn't as tall or imposing as Carruthers, and his swarthy complexion gave him a Mediterranean look.

"We'll find out after roundup." Carruthers appeared unusually confident his boast would be confirmed.

"We'll be taking a herd up the trail to Abilene," he said to Broc.

"I work with a man who's sent a herd up the last two years."

"Would I know him?" Carruthers asked.

"Probably not. His name's Cade Wheeler. We served together in the war."

"Is that where you got those?" Sandoval pointed at Broc's scars.

"My patrol was ambushed in the middle of the night. I'm lucky to be alive."

Sandoval asked several questions about the conditions of the troops during the war, wanted a description of one of their raids, and said he appreciated the sacrifice men like Broc had made. Carruthers was obviously uninterested and continued his conversation with the other men. When Sandoval went back to his own table, Carruthers turned back to Broc.

"I'm hiring men for the roundup and the drive. Dan will tell you how to find your way to my ranch. Be there tomorrow morning."

"I'm afraid I wasn't very clear when I was talking to Dan," Broc said to Carruthers. "I didn't say I was *looking* for a job. I said I'd stayed here long enough that I *needed* one. A man likes to look around first to make sure he's got the best scenery."

Carruthers's friendly smile turned to cold scrutiny. "If you're thinking about working for Grace Liscomb, don't."

"Thanks for the offer, but—"

"You can't work for Grace. I won't let you."

Broc had expected Carruthers to argue with him,

but he hadn't expected a flat order not to work for the Liscombs. Just as surprising was the fact that neither of the two prosperous-looking men appeared to find anything wrong with the order. Only the sheriff seemed uneasy.

"Earl, you can't tell the man where he can work," he said.

"I can, but it wouldn't make any difference if I didn't. Grace doesn't have any money to pay him. I'll see you at my ranch tomorrow."

Broc had never been one to fling down a gauntlet. First, he wasn't the type to enjoy confrontations. Tempers always got out of hand, and something was said or done that made things worse. Second, he'd learned there were dozens of ways to solve a problem without using force. Also, he enjoyed figuring out what people wanted and giving it to them. He could even make them like something they thought they were going to hate.

Carruthers's cold assumption that he could order any man to do as he wished caused Broc to lose any desire to find a way around this man.

"I'm afraid you're too late," he said with a calm he didn't feel. "I've already signed on as foreman for the Lazy T."

❧

Now that Broc's anger had cooled, he kept wondering why he hadn't just agreed with Carruthers, then failed to show up the next day, but there was something about Carruthers that hit him wrong. Maybe it was the assumption that he deserved to have everything he wanted. Maybe it was Carruthers's feeling that he had the right to tell other people what they could and couldn't do. Maybe it was Broc's certainty Carruthers was the kind of person who would do anything to get what he wanted.

"You'd think learning to ignore insults about my face would have taught me to keep my mouth shut," he said to his uninterested horse. "Or at least control my temper so I don't end up in worse trouble."

His horse continued to lope along at a comfortable canter, more interested in getting the man and the saddle off his back than in listening to the ramblings of its owner.

"Now I've got to convince Amanda to give me a job."

That wasn't going to be easy. There were times he thought she trusted him a little, maybe even liked him, but most of the time he felt she would have been happier if he had just disappeared. Most likely, he'd have been happier, too. It would be a lot easier to get over his infatuation if he didn't have to see her every day. It was as if she had become a reference point for his life. That was a foolish mistake. In a short time he was going to have to go back to Crystal Springs and serve his time in jail before going back to his old job.

The trouble with that was he wasn't sure he could go back to his old job and be content. Something had changed, and that something was Amanda.

How stupid could he be! He was a grown man obsessing over a woman who didn't like or trust him. What was the advantage of getting older if a little wisdom didn't come along with it? He was acting like a youngster falling in love for the first time, ignoring common sense, the obvious, even facts. And just what did he expect to accomplish if he did get the job?

The sound of a rider coming up quickly behind him broke off his dismal train of thought. He pulled his horse to the side of the trail to let the rider pass, but the other man slowed down. Broc was surprised when Dan Walch came alongside. He wondered if Carruthers had sent him.

"Why did you tell me you wanted a job?" Dan asked. "You got me in trouble with the boss."

Dan looked more irritated than angry, which made Broc feel guilty. "I didn't say I *wanted* a job. I said I was going to be here long enough to *need* one."

"Sounds like the same thing to me."

"The situation is complicated. I apologize for involving you in it."

"What's so complicated about needing a job? You look like an okay fella. I'd welcome you to the crew."

"Are you Carruthers's foreman?"

"Not exactly, but close enough. You shoulda told me you were foreman at the Lazy T. I never would have taken you over to the boss."

That comment gave Broc pause. If Dan was close to being foreman, then he would know just about everything that happened on the ranch, but Broc's instincts told him Dan was a straight shooter. He might bend a few rules, but he wouldn't break them. Broc wasn't ready to trust the man yet, but he needed to be honest with him.

"The situation is far too complex for me to explain

right now, but I don't actually have that job. I'm headed to the Lazy T right now to see if they'll hire me."

Dan looked at him without understanding.

"Your boss made me so mad when he said he wouldn't allow me to work for Mrs. Liscomb, I lost my temper and did something I shouldn't have." He seemed to be doing that a lot these days.

A lazy chuckle escaped Dan. "Gary hates your guts. If I know Mrs. Liscomb, she'll take one look at your face and faint dead away. Amanda is practically engaged to Corby Wilson, who also hates your guts, and Andy Kilburn is a fool. Why would you want to work for them?"

Broc sighed. "It really is too complicated to explain in the short time before we reach the ranch."

"Maybe it's so complicated you don't understand it yourself."

"That's part of the reason I want the job. Something is wrong here, and I want to find out what it is."

Dan regarded him thoughtfully. It was early evening, but the moon was bright and millions of stars filled the cloudless sky. Broc figured Dan could read his expression fairly well. He just hoped his uncertainty didn't show too clearly.

"You think my boss is involved in whatever it is?" Dan asked.

"I know he'd like to get his hands on the Lazy T, but I don't know how far he'd go to do that."

"He's not a crook."

"There are lots of ways to get control of a spread without doing anything illegal."

"And you think you can figure it out?"

"It's not what I want to be doing, but I let my temper get out of hand a few days ago, and I got into some trouble."

"Anything to do with your face?"

Broc nodded.

"How'd it happen?"

"The judge gave me a job to do so I could avoid spending time in jail. It's beginning to look like I can't do that job without figuring out what's going on."

"I'm sorry about your face," Dan said. "I figure you used to be right good-looking before. Must be hard now."

Broc forced a laugh. "I don't have to look at myself, at least not very often." He sobered quickly. "It's only hard when people recoil."

"I expect you get that a lot."

Broc was relieved Dan wasn't one to waste time trying to soothe his sensibilities or reassure him with useless platitudes. They'd reached the lane leading to the Liscomb ranch, so Broc pulled up his horse. He glanced at the ranch house in the distance and back at Dan. "Wish me luck."

Dan shook his head. "If I really wanted to wish you luck, I'd hope they'd refuse to hire you, and you'd come to work with me."

"I doubt Carruthers would have me now."

"If he wouldn't, Sandoval would. They both believe Mrs. Liscomb is wasting the best grazing land in the county. They can't wait for her to fail and sell up."

Broc wondered how much longer they were willing to wait.

Dan offered his hand. Broc took it, liked the firm

grasp that didn't try to impress him by its strength, but did impress him with its genuineness.

"Let me know if I can do anything to help," Dan said. "I'd hate to see a man go to jail because of a wound he got in the war."

❧

Mrs. Lipscomb said, "I hate for you to have to ask Corby about working more nights, but I don't see any other solution if we have to do without Gary's money."

Amanda's mother had repeated herself so many times during the evening, Amanda was beginning to believe working would be easier than staying at home. Her mother had largely ignored the complicated piece of embroidery she'd been working on for months. Amanda squinted over a repair she was making to one of Eddie's shirts. They both needed more light than the single lamp provided, but her mother insisted they use expensive oil rather than the cheaper kerosene.

"Don't worry about that yet," Amanda said to her mother. "I'll talk to Gary when I see him tomorrow. I'm sure he will have cooled off by then and be ready to move back."

"I don't want him to move back," Eddie said.

"He's your brother," their mother said. "Of course you want him back."

"No, I don't," Eddie insisted. "He's mean."

Eddie had said that so frequently Amanda had started to wonder if she'd missed something important in the way Gary treated his brother. She'd assumed it was natural when brothers didn't get along, but now she was beginning to wonder if Gary had been too rough.

"Gary is never mean," their mother said. "He's just firm."

Amanda tried to ignore her mother's argument with Eddie. She was so tired at the end of the day that she didn't want to deal with anything, just go to bed and rest up for the next day. Not that she'd gotten much rest the last few nights with dreams of being in Broc's arms causing her to wake up embarrassingly warm. Her thoughts once she was awake were just as vivid as they had been in her dreams. She was relieved when Leo's entry caused her mother and brother to break off their argument.

"What brings you to the house at this hour?" her mother asked. It was her frequently stated opinion that cowhands should only enter the house to eat.

"It's Andy," Leo said. "He's threatening to quit."

While Amanda was worried about how the ranch would survive with only one cowhand, it would be a relief not to have to deal with Andy's immaturity. "Why? Does he want more money?"

"He said Sandoval offered him a job. Said he wouldn't have to do any work until his shoulder was completely healed."

Andy had complained when she'd made him saddle up and ride with them that afternoon. She'd said his shoulder didn't affect his eyesight. He could look for the lost cattle.

"I'm not sure Andy will really quit," Leo said. "He's mad at you for making him work while his shoulder is hurting, but he's more afraid of Sandoval's men treating him like Carruthers's men do."

"What ingratitude," her mother exclaimed. "We gave him a job when no one else would. Now he decides to leave us when we need him so much."

"What about you?" Amanda asked Leo. "Are you planning to leave, too?"

"No, ma'am."

Something about the way he shifted his weight and didn't meet her gaze told Amanda he wasn't as certain as his words indicated. If he quit, it would be impossible to run the ranch. She'd been racking her brains to figure out how she could get more time in the saddle until Andy was fully recovered. It would take several days before Gary cooled off enough for her to talk to him. How was she going to work more at the saloon at the same time she worked more at the ranch?

Her mother turned to her. "You will just have to hire someone else. You can go into town early tomorrow." She assumed the attitude of a martyr. "I can fix Eddie something for lunch."

The pleading glance Eddie sent her way caused Amanda to stifle a laugh.

"I can—" The sound of someone knocking at the door stopped her.

"I'll see who it is." Eddie jumped up from his seat and ran to the door. He peeked out the door, then ran back into the house before letting the visitor in. "It's Broc."

From the way he acted, Amanda would have thought his best friend had arrived. From the way Amanda's body went rigid, then flushed hot, she'd have thought her worst nightmare had arrived. In a sense, it had.

"What is he doing here?" Her mother dropped her embroidery in her lap. The bright colors of the silk threads contrasted sharply with her cream-colored silk gown, which had been made for her before the war.

"I expect he'll tell us." Amanda's voice came out as a thread, not surprising given that she felt barely able to breathe. She heard the front door close.

"He can have nothing to tell us," her mother insisted.

"He must have. Otherwise, why would he be here?"

"I don't want him—" Her mother broke off when Broc entered the room.

"Good evening."

Amanda thought he looked as uncomfortable as she felt.

"If you've come to ask for money, you're wasting your time," her mother said. "We don't owe anybody any money, and I wouldn't give it to you if we did."

"That's not why I'm here," Broc said.

"Has the bull gotten out again?" Eddie asked.

"I don't know. I didn't check."

"Why *are* you here?" Amanda asked.

"I've come to offer to work for you," he said. "To be your foreman."

Amanda could hardly have been more surprised if he'd—well, she didn't know what would have surprised her more.

"How did you know Andy was threatening to quit?" Leo asked.

"I didn't."

"I can appreciate your feeling responsible for

causing Gary to leave his home," her mother said, "but it's unnecessary for you to feel you need to take his place until he returns."

"I don't feel the least responsible for Gary," Broc said. "He's spoiled, self-centered, and impressed with glitter over substance."

"How dare you speak of my son in that manner." Her mother was so incensed, she half rose from her chair.

"It's easy to speak the truth. It's lies that take work."

"I want you to leave this house at once."

Amanda ignored her mother's outburst. "Why do you want to work for us?"

"He's probably going to try to steal our bull to pay off this ridiculous debt." Aware no one was listening, her mother settled back in her chair.

"If he wanted to do that, why did he bring it back, twice?" Eddie asked.

The answer was too obvious to deserve a response.

"I'm embarrassed to have to explain," Broc said, "but I let my temper run away with me. Carruthers offered me a job, but I turned him down. When he thought I intended to ask you for a job, he told me he wouldn't allow me to work for you."

"He's done that before," Amanda said.

"I told him I had already taken a job as your foreman. Now I'm here to ask you to help me out of this lie. I don't know what's wrong with me that I can't control my temper lately."

Amanda put a stop to her imagining—even hoping—that he'd come back because of her.

"I'm sorry you find yourself in this situation, but I

don't see how you can expect us to help you out of it," her mother said.

"You need another cowhand," Leo reminded her.

"Gary will be back soon," her mother said. "He will take care of everything."

"He never did," Leo responded, "so I don't see any reason why he would start now."

"What do you mean?" her mother asked.

"He was always sending me in one direction and himself in another. Half the time he didn't do what he said. The other half he left for the saloon early. That's all he ever thought about. Hell, Andy did more work than he did, and Andy's the laziest man I've ever been around."

"I'm sure you mean well," her mother said in a voice that contradicted her words, "but you don't have sufficient experience to judge my son." She kept glancing nervously at Leo and Broc's boots, apparently afraid they were getting dirt on her prized Aubusson carpet.

Leo didn't back down. "It don't take experience to know when someone's slacking off. Even a kid like Eddie can see it."

"Gary's work isn't the issue here," Amanda said, in an attempt to end an argument that was causing her mother to become increasingly agitated. "Mr. Kincaid has offered to ride for us, and we're in need of a cowhand. I can't pay you much," Amanda said to Broc, "probably only a little more than we were paying Andy."

"I'm not worried about the pay," Broc said. "I just want the job."

Probably he'd stay just long enough to save face, then go. Unless she could find a reason to make him stay. What was wrong with her? She was acting like a schoolgirl over a man she barely knew. She'd never known herself to behave so irresponsibly. Maybe the best thing would be for her to hire Broc and work with him as much as she could. After a few days, she was bound to realize he was just an ordinary man, not some demigod who was going to solve all her problems and make love to her until she was weak in the knees.

Just thinking about her latest dream caused heat to flame in her cheeks. She hoped no one could see her embarrassment in the dim light coming from the single lamp.

"It's not really a matter of money," her mother said. "I wouldn't feel comfortable with you working for us."

"Why?" Eddie asked. "I like him. I like him better than Gary."

"Edward, you will not speak of your brother in that manner."

"It don't matter if I say it or not," Eddie argued. "I do like him better than Gary, and you can't make me feel different."

"Why would you feel uncomfortable with him working here?" Amanda asked her mother. She was certain she knew one reason, but she wanted to see what her mother would say.

"It was kind of him to return the bull," her mother said, "but his insistence that we owe that woman money has forced me to question his honesty. I could never be certain he wouldn't do something that... might be involved in something that could cause...I don't know," her mother finished lamely as she averted her face. "I don't know what a dishonest person might do."

"I don't think you can accuse him of being dishonest," Amanda said. "He returned the bull twice and never even asked for thanks."

"I know, but—"

"If you don't hire him, I'm quitting."

Leo's declaration fell into the pool of their conversation like a large rock. The splash hit everyone in the room.

"I can't do everything by myself," Leo explained. "There'd be too much even if Gary came back. Besides," he added, appearing a little uncomfortable, "I ain't looking forward to facing Carruthers's men by myself."

"Do you think you could stand up to those men?" Amanda asked Broc.

"I'm sure I can stand up to them," Broc said with what she suspected was a trace of a smile, "but I can't guarantee the outcome."

"I bet you could shoot their whiskers off," Eddie said.

"I won't have any shooting," their mother said.

No one paid that statement any attention.

"I can't say that I can do all of Andy and Gary's work," Broc said to Amanda, "but I can give it a try."

"I'll help," Eddie offered eagerly. "I got three horses."

Amanda made a snap decision. Avoiding her mother's gaze, she turned to Broc. "From now on Mother will do the cooking. I'll be in the saddle with you all day."

Nine

WHEN THE DOOR CLOSED BEHIND BROC AND LEO, Amanda braced herself. From time to time her mother had had to do things she didn't want to do, but no one had ever made the decision for her.

"Does she have to do all the cooking?" Eddie asked. "I'll starve."

"No, you won't. Mother is a good cook."

"Thank you for that compliment," her mother said, her lips folded in an expression Amanda recognized as one which meant she was prepared to dig in her heels, "but I doubt you believe it."

"I remember when you did all the cooking," Amanda said. "Papa always said he liked your pot roast."

"I like pot roast," Eddie said. "Why don't we ever have any?"

"That's not the issue," their mother said.

"It ought to be," Eddie insisted. "If I got to eat your cooking, I ought to like it."

"I will not be cooking. It's more than my nerves can stand now to keep this house clean. My mother's house was never like this when I was a girl."

Something snapped in Amanda. She wasn't sure whether it was the *when I was a girl* phrase which always preceded a complaint, or whether it was her mother's refusal to realize that the world had changed, and she had to change, too, if she wanted the family to survive.

"Nothing is like it was when you were a girl," Amanda told her mother, "and it never will be again. If you don't change, if all of us don't change, we'll go under."

"I will not compromise my standards," her mother declared.

"I'm not asking you to compromise anything," Amanda said. "I'm just asking you to realize that what it's going to take for us to survive has changed. We live in Texas, not Mississippi."

"No one is more aware of that than I," her mother stated. "I never forgave your father for bringing us to this awful place."

"Papa made a good living for us."

"By running a saloon and a diner." Her mother held her scented handkerchief to her nose as though to eradicate a bad smell. "My mother would have turned over in her grave if she had any idea what I've been reduced to."

Amanda had a very different memory of the woman who'd been her grandmother. According to her grandfather, she had been instrumental in building the success that had allowed their daughter to grow up with privilege.

"I don't think Grandmother was made of such weak stuff," Amanda said. "I remember her as a forceful woman who knew what she wanted and didn't let anything stand in the way of her getting it."

Her mother looked uncomfortable. "My mother had to do some things that shouldn't have been required of a lady."

"When did the definition of a lady come to mean a woman who was incapable of doing anything, whose purpose was merely decoration?"

"I'm not a mere decoration," her mother declared, "and I'm capable of many things."

"I know that, and now is the time to put those capabilities to use. I'm capable of riding a horse for much of the day, of working with cows. It's not what I thought I would be doing, but it's work that needs to be done. I might even learn to like it."

"When I asked your father to buy this ranch, I never envisioned having my own daughter act as a ranch hand or sing in a saloon. I wanted more for my children."

"The only way I'm going to be able to stop working in the saloon is to make this ranch a success. That means we can't keep losing cows. It means we have to find the ones we have lost. It means we have to keep the bull from getting out. It also means I have to keep working in the saloon. The only way I can do all of that is for you to do all the cooking."

Her mother opened her mouth to object.

"It's either that, or we lose the ranch," Amanda told her. "Then you'll have to do a lot more than cook." Amanda looked around at a room decorated with furnishings her mother had brought from Mississippi at great cost and trouble. "Are you willing to see Carruthers living in this house? I'm sure his wife would enjoy the way you've decorated it. She hasn't stopped badgering her husband to refurbish her entire house since the day you invited her to lunch."

"It would kill me to sell a single thing in this house," her mother declared. "It all belonged to my mother."

"If we lose the ranch, we'll have to start selling things so we can eat."

"I don't care what you sell," Eddie said, "but I got to eat." He looked at a tray table that was one of her mother's most prized possessions. It was an heirloom that had come from England. "What good is that old table? All you need is a box to set a lamp on."

If the discussion hadn't been so serious, Amanda would have laughed at Eddie's impatience while her mother detailed the origin and history of the table. And that included the ordeal of transporting it and other valuable possessions from Mississippi to Texas. When she nearly cried over a scratch that had occurred sometime during the journey, Amanda lost patience.

"You have to decide how much you're willing to do to keep the things that are important to you. I'm willing to spend my day in the saddle and my evening working in the saloon."

"I'll be in the saddle, too," Eddie said.

"That leaves the chickens and the milking to you," Amanda said to her mother.

"I don't know how to milk a cow," her mother stated.

"It's easy," Eddie said. "I'll teach you."

"You can't say you don't know how to feed chickens or pick up eggs," Amanda said.

"Or slop the pigs," Eddie added.

With a sigh of surrender, her mother said, "I'm not stupid."

"We need your help, Mama, if we're going to pull out of this mess."

"Are you depending on me, or that man out there?" She gestured in the general direction of the bunkhouse.

"I'll take any help I can get," Amanda said. "I don't expect Broc to stay long, but he knows more about cows than I do. I hope he'll teach me as much as he can."

"If he brings up that debt again, I won't have him in the house," her mother said. "I will not feed a man who's trying to steal from me."

Amanda kept forgetting about the debt. She didn't know if it was real, but she had to find out. If it was valid, they would have to sell something. "I think he's washed his hands of the debt."

"I'd like to wash my hands of him," her mother said. "I don't like him, and I don't trust him."

"I like him," Eddie said.

Amanda liked *and* trusted him, but she thought it would be better not to say that to her mother.

"You sure you want to work here?" Leo asked as he and Broc walked toward the bunkhouse. "Carruthers is gonna set his men on you first chance he gets."

"I can take care of myself." Carruthers was arrogant and bullheaded, but he had to know harassment could only go so far before he ran afoul of the law. Broc didn't have a high opinion of the sheriff, but he didn't think Mercer would stand for that.

"I'm not sticking my head in a noose just because you got Carruthers mad at you. It's for dang sure Andy won't do it."

It quickly became apparent Andy wasn't going to do anything to help Broc.

The bunkhouse was no exception. It had been built to house six men, with the bunks evenly spaced around the room and a table and chair provided for each. A trunk at the foot of the bed and shelves above each bunk provided each cowhand with more than enough space for his personal belongings. A stove with a pipe going through the roof stood in the middle of the bunkhouse. A lantern suspended from the ceiling provided the light. When they walked in, Andy was lounging on his bed, flipping through a catalog, smoking a small Mexican cigar. When he saw Broc, he gathered up some pictures lying on the bed and slid them under his pillow.

"What's he doing here?" he demanded.

"Amanda just hired him to be foreman," Leo explained.

"I ain't working for him," Andy said.

"You'll be working for the Liscomb family," Broc said. "They pay your wages."

"You know what I mean," Andy barked. "I ain't taking orders from you."

Broc decided it would be best to calm Andy down. The boy hadn't yet decided to quit, and they needed his help. "Amanda will be riding with us. She'll be giving the orders, not me."

Andy's disbelief was obvious. "She's never ridden with us before."

"Things have changed now that Gary has moved out."

"He never did much," Andy complained. "I don't imagine she's gonna be any better."

"Maybe Eddie will make up the difference."

Andy sat bolt upright. "I ain't riding with a kid."

Broc had never had a high opinion of Andy, and it wasn't getting any higher. "For a man who's being paid to do very little, you've got a lot of requirements."

Andy turned sullen. "She makes me get in the saddle every day even though I got a bum shoulder."

"There's nothing wrong with your eyes."

Andy's feelings weren't assuaged, but Broc had enough brothers to know Andy was at a difficult age.

"You ain't getting those cows back," Andy said. "Carruthers or Sandoval got them. They're probably halfway to Kansas by now."

Broc knew no sensible rancher would attempt to trail calves more than a thousand miles. "For the family's sake, I hope not. Now does anybody care where I drop my stuff?"

"I don't," Leo said.

Andy didn't say anything.

"Good. I'll take the bunk by the door."

"You'll get a draft every time Andy or I open that door."

"I don't mind. Maybe it'll blow away some of Andy's smoke. If he sets the bunkhouse on fire, I'll be the first one out."

Andy snuffed his cigar out. "At least I don't chew tobacco or use snuff."

Broc would have preferred either to smoking, but he didn't say so. "Glad to hear it. Now I'm going to bed."

"I'm not ready to blow out the light," Andy said.

"I can sleep in broad daylight with people talking, playing cards, even singing. You won't bother me."

Broc hadn't brought the majority of his belongings, because he wasn't sure Amanda would hire him. Since he didn't know how long he would be here, it might be better to leave them at the hotel.

Broc changed his mind. "I'm going to check on the bull," he said.

"Want me to come with you?" Leo asked.

"Only if you want."

Leo grinned. "I'll stay. No point in working if I don't have to."

That attitude would keep Leo working for someone else for the rest of his life.

The sky was blotted with dark clouds that blocked the moonlight and filled the landscape with dancing shadows and eerily dark corners. It would have been easy to stumble over anything lying in his path.

The horses in the corral were like ink blots against an even darker background. Those with white splashes in their coats looked like puzzles with pieces missing. All stood quietly, their heads hanging down, sleeping standing up. A sorrel looked up when Broc passed, then dropped his head once more.

It took Broc several minutes before he found where the bull had lain down in the shadow of the shed provided to shelter him from the worst weather. The cows, being wild creatures, were as far away from the house as they could get.

Broc stood watching the bull for several minutes. It seemed odd that the future of a family should rest on the genes of an animal that would run away the first chance he got. The bull couldn't understand that he received food, protection, and an endless procession of wives in exchange. The animal didn't know he wouldn't last long in a fight with one of the range bulls. He just responded to his instincts to bolt to freedom when he got the chance.

Ironic that Broc was doing his best to ignore his instincts to stay as far away from Amanda as possible. Losing his temper had twice given him a reason to stay close to her. It would have been impossible to predict the consequences of the first outburst, but he wondered if the second loss of temper might have been a subconscious attempt to find a reason to go back to the Lazy T ranch. He didn't trust himself where Amanda was concerned. He'd lost control of his thoughts. It was going to be difficult to be around her all day and not betray his feelings.

She'd shown no sign that she liked him, but what if she was holding back? What if she was interested in him but didn't feel she could express such an interest in a man she probably thought was trying to extort money from her?

Even if she didn't think Broc was a crook, she had to have doubts about his honesty. Her giving him a job as her foreman wouldn't change that. She had probably decided to work with him because she didn't feel she could trust him. Her mother didn't like or trust him, either. Andy had already made his feelings plain. Having Eddie and Leo on his side would only help so much. If he had any sense, he'd leave the Liscombs to solve their problems by themselves and go back to Crystal Springs to get his time in jail behind him.

With a muttered curse, he pushed away from the fence. He might as well accept that he wasn't going anywhere. He didn't know what would happen in the next several days, but he had to be a part of it. If Amanda didn't like him, he would have to live with that, too. It wasn't the end of the world.

"But it will feel like it," he said to the bull, which ignored him. "It will feel exactly like that."

༄

Amanda was relieved when breakfast came to an end. She was anxious to get to work, but she was even more anxious to get out of the house. Her mother had been in a rotten mood all morning, not answering Amanda at least half the times Amanda had spoken to her. Amanda hated that kind of tense atmosphere, but she was determined to stand by her decision.

"That was a fine breakfast," Broc said to her mother. "I'm already looking forward to supper."

"It wasn't anything much," her mother replied in a voice that didn't reflect her usual rigid civility. "It's not hard to cook breakfast."

To hear the way her mother had talked while she was fixing it, you would have thought it was one of the labors of Hercules, a mythical figure her mother always mentioned when faced with anything she thought was beyond human capabilities. Amanda was glad she wasn't going to be around when her mother tackled preparations for supper. She felt sorry for poor Eddie. She was tempted to let him ride with them, but she wanted to wait until she learned enough about the work to know if it would be safe. It was clear Eddie wouldn't be satisfied going with Leo or Andy. Even her. He wanted to be with Broc.

"It may be a simple task for a woman of your talents," Broc was saying, "but it's beyond my abilities."

Amanda sensed her mother was responding to Broc's compliments. She didn't smile or relent in her disapproval—she was also angry he'd taken Gary's place at the table—but she didn't look quite as moody as before. It would be amazing if he could charm her into a better frame of mind. Only Gary and her father had ever been able to do that.

"I'd like to get started," Amanda said to the men. "That includes you, Andy." He was so sullen, she wondered if he might quit even though he was afraid of how Sandoval's men would treat him. "I want everybody to be ready to ride out in thirty minutes."

The men didn't linger. While Amanda made her final preparations, she ran through the things she hoped to accomplish during the day. By the time she slipped out the back door, she had the whole day organized. She would soon know if she was any good at running a ranch, or whether she should try to convince Broc to become her permanent foreman.

She didn't know whether it was that thought or the sight of him waiting with the horse he'd saddled for her that was responsible for the surge of warmth coursing through her body, but she hoped it wasn't as obvious to an observer as it was to her. She'd given up telling herself she shouldn't have such a strong physical response to him. Instead, she had to concentrate on keeping the few facts she knew about him from getting buried under the weight of the attraction. He was a stranger about whom she knew virtually nothing. He'd arrived with a claim against her family that everyone believed to be a crude attempt to rob them. He had been a very handsome man before he was wounded so severely.

It was the areas of supposition, of conjecture, that had the potential to lead her into great trouble.

Despite what appeared to be evidence to the contrary, she believed he was a man of principle. Though she knew he found her attractive, he had never made her feel that her appearance was all he noticed about her. If he really was a cowhand, he knew more about running a ranch than she did. But maybe the most compelling reason for her interest in him was the feeling that he was a leader who had the ability to command the loyalty and confidence of others. She was certain he wouldn't back down from a challenge. She didn't have proof of any of this, but she hoped to be in a better position to judge by the end of the day.

"What are your first orders?" Leo asked. He seemed to be as amused at the prospect of taking orders from a woman as Andy was irritated by it.

"I feel uncomfortable directing you. I know less about this job than any of you do."

"You're the owner," Broc said. "That gives you the right to give any orders you like."

"Well, the first thing I want to do is to become familiar with every part of our range. Since you know even less than I do, I'm depending on Leo and Andy to tell us everything we need to know."

"All in one day?" Andy gave the impression that it would take weeks to learn what he knew.

"I learn quickly," Broc said. "I'm sure Miss Liscomb does, too."

"Call me Amanda. Hearing myself called Miss *Liscomb* makes me feel like I ought to be back at the house doing needlepoint."

Andy muttered something under his breath. From the look on Broc's face, Amanda decided against asking him to repeat it.

"My first concern is finding the missing cows and calves," she said. "The future of the ranch, and the future of your jobs, depends on it."

"Then let's get to work," Leo said. "I need some new boots."

"Since Leo is the one who knows the ranch best, he'll ride with me," Amanda said. "Andy, you can answer any questions Broc has."

"I know as much as Leo," Andy protested.

"Then you can ride with me in the afternoon."

Broc didn't know how much of Andy's rotten attitude came from having a bum shoulder and how much came from a poorly developed personality, but he wasn't a man Broc would have hired to work on any ranch he owned. They were supposed to tally the number of cows, calves, bulls, and steers. They also were supposed to keep a record of how many calves were sired by range bulls and how many by the home bull. Broc had volunteered to keep the written count because of Andy's shoulder. He'd ended up doing the physical count as well, because Andy couldn't remember which cows he'd counted and which ones he hadn't.

"How many calves do we have by range bulls?" Amanda asked.

"One hundred eighty-two so far," Broc responded.

"How many by the home bull?"

"Forty-seven."

"It ought to be close to half the total number of calves."

"We know we've got at least a hundred missing," Leo said.

In less than two hours, Broc knew Gary Liscomb had been useless as a ranch foreman. Rustlers could have robbed the ranch blind, and he probably wouldn't have noticed.

"There's no point in arguing about that," Amanda said. "What we need to do is find out what happened to them."

"They probably wandered off," Andy said.

In open range ranching, cows were free to wander anywhere they wanted. The only way to know what you had was to round them up and count them. You had to depend on other ranchers to tell you how many of your cows were on their range. Laws passed by the Reconstruction government had made it so easy to cheat that Cade had insisted all the ranchers in his area do the roundup together. Broc was going to recommend the same thing to Amanda.

"Is there any way to know where they went?" Amanda asked.

"It's impossible to follow cows," Andy said.

"Not always," Broc intervened. "If you watch them every day, you'll soon learn their pattern. Cows are like all herd animals. They tend to stay in their own territory."

"Do you think the missing cows will come back to the ranch?" Amanda asked.

"It's hard to say. They may have found better pasture, been incorporated into another herd, or been prevented from staying on their familiar range."

"How do we start looking for them?"

"I'd begin by going over to see Carruthers and Sandoval. Tell them that a large number of your cows are missing and ask them to have their cowhands look out for them and let you know what they find."

"Neither one of them will do that," Leo said.

"Maybe not, but we won't know until we ask them."

"We're not far from Carruthers's ranch now," Amanda said. "We can ask him first."

"You'll ask him without me," Andy said. "I'm not giving any of those bastards a chance to break my other shoulder."

Broc had a low opinion of Andy's courage and common sense, but he decided the boy was probably right this time. If nothing else, the men would probably enjoy jeering at him.

"You and Leo continue counting the cows," Amanda said. "Broc and I will go see Carruthers."

"Do you think that's a good idea?" Leo asked.

Broc wondered why Leo would ask such a question, but he could tell the boy had done so reluctantly.

"Why not?" Amanda asked.

Leo studied the pommel of his saddle. "It's not a good idea to go off alone with a man you don't know much about."

"I came home with him from the saloon in the dark. Why shouldn't I trust him in the daylight?"

Leo didn't answer.

"Come on, Leo. What are you hiding?"

"Your mama made me promise I wouldn't let him get you alone."

Amanda blushed. "I appreciate your wanting to honor my mother's request, but I'm quite safe with Broc. I don't know how long this will take, but we'll be back before suppertime. In the meantime, keep counting."

The boys had different reasons for being unhappy with her decision, but they rode away bickering softly until they were out of hearing range. Then, judging from their gestures, they started shouting at each other.

"Maybe you should take Leo. I don't mind staying with Andy," Broc offered.

"They bicker all the time. It used to drive Gary crazy."

They rode in silence for a few minutes before Broc asked, "Why did you choose me?"

Amanda kept her gaze straight ahead. "I wanted to ask you to teach me as much about ranching as you can while you're here."

Broc leveled an inquiring glance at her.

"You said the judge only gave you two weeks to

collect the debt. That means you have little more than a week before you have to leave."

"There's a lot more to know about ranching than you can learn in a week. There's even more I don't know. If you really want to learn, you should spend some time at my friend's ranch."

"I can't leave the Lazy T or my job at the saloon. I'll have to be satisfied with what I can learn before you leave."

They were riding through prairie covered by bluestem and Indian grass that grew well in the deep clay soil. Single trees and small groves dotted the gently undulating prairie with some areas of marshy ground bordering the stream that flowed through the heart of the ranch. Songbirds flitted in and out of the grass looking for insects and seeds, seemingly unconcerned about a hawk that circled overhead. A large king snake slithered through the grass in search of field mice or a spot out of the sun. A group of cows and calves was resting in the shade of a post oak, the cows chewing their cuds and watching, the calves sprawled out on the grass, confident of the safety provided by their mothers.

"I can see why you love this place so much," Broc said.

"I didn't at first. The ranch was my mother's idea. She thinks a saloon isn't a place for a respectable woman to work." She laughed. "Ironically, Mother thinks working on a ranch is also something a respectable woman shouldn't do, but there's no going back."

They rode in silence a bit longer before she turned to him and asked, "Is the debt real?"

"I don't know. I can only tell you what the judge told me."

"There really is a judge?"

"Yes, and he's really coming here to settle the debt unless you can show him proof that your father paid it before he died."

"My father handled everything himself and in cash."

"There has to be some record of it, or the judge wouldn't have anything to base his decision on."

"Why would my father have left a record with someone else but not with us?"

"I can't answer that. Have you talked to Corby? He was your father's partner. He's more likely to know than anyone else."

"Not yet. I—"

She broke off when she saw a group of riders come into sight from behind a hardwood grove.

"That's Carruthers and some of his cowhands," she said.

Broc hadn't gotten a good impression of Carruthers when he'd met him in the saloon. When Carruthers recognized him, he had a feeling that impression was about to be reinforced.

Ten

"WHAT ARE YOU DOING ON MY LAND?" CARRUTHERS demanded of Amanda in a harsh, accusatory voice. He jabbed a thick, stubby finger at Broc. "And what are you doing riding with him?"

Broc got the feeling there was something more than simple arrogance in the man's attitude. He had the burning hot eyes of a fanatic, though Broc had no idea what he could be fanatical about.

"One of my cowhands says we've got about a hundred cows missing," Amanda told the other rancher. "I was coming to ask if your men have seen many of our cows on your land."

He looked pointedly at Broc. "You're a fool if you believe anything that man says."

"He's not the one who said it. He's just come to work for me. He's going to teach me what I need to know to manage this ranch successfully."

The fire in Carruthers's eyes flared hotter. "I don't want you learning anything from him. I don't want him anywhere near Cactus Bend. I particularly don't want him on my land."

Carruthers's men were impassive in the face of his denunciation, but Dan Walch's uneasy gaze swung from Carruthers to Broc to Amanda and back.

"He's a stranger, an outsider," Carruthers declared. "For all we know, he could be a murderer."

"I'm sure he's not," Amanda said.

"He *is* a thief," Carruthers declared. "Your brother said he's claiming you owe a lot of money, and he's come to collect it."

"The debt is a misunderstanding that will soon be cleared up."

"Only one way to clear up something like that." The light in Carruthers's eyes glowed even brighter. "You got to get rid of the problem. For good."

Broc didn't like the way things were going. He'd witnessed one case of vigilante justice and had no intention of becoming a victim.

"I advised Mrs. Liscomb to refer the question to her banker or lawyer," Broc said. "I took myself out of it altogether."

"It doesn't look that way to me," Carruthers said. "It looks like you put yourself right in the middle. Now you're pushing your way onto my land, no doubt looking for a way to cause more trouble."

"He's here because I asked him to be," Amanda said.

Carruthers ignored her. "In Texas we have a way of dealing with thieves."

Broc had a rifle in his scabbard, but he knew he could be cut down before he had time to get off more than one or two shots. He didn't intend to let anyone hang him, but neither did he intend to die in a shoot-out. "You have sheriffs and judges, jails and courts," he said, "just like every other state."

"We don't like to depend on judges and courts appointed by the Reconstruction. They favor carpet-baggers and thieves like you too much for the liking of real Texans."

Broc didn't like the way Carruthers's men were fanning out. It wouldn't be long before he was hemmed in on all sides.

"This is crazy," Amanda said, clearly surprised at the way the situation was developing. "You can't possibly mean you want to hang him."

"It's the only way to protect you and every other innocent woman in Cactus Bend," Carruthers assured her.

"He's been protecting me."

"That's how he gets close to you," Carruthers said, "causes you to let down your guard. You should have listened to your brother. He knew what kind of coyote this man is right from the first."

"Gary's angry because Mother won't sell the ranch," Amanda explained.

"You should listen to him. I'll give you twice what your father paid for it."

"My mother doesn't want to sell."

"How are you going to make a go of this place when your only two cowhands don't know enough to get out of their own way?"

"I'm depending on Broc to change that."

Her words caused Carruthers's eyes to blaze dangerously.

"Don't you have enough sense to see what's right in

front of your eyes, girl?" Carruthers demanded. "He's nothing but an agent of the Reconstruction sent to steal everything we decent Texans have managed to hold on to. You can tell by his accent he isn't from Texas."

"I'm from Tennessee," Broc said. "I've never been part of the Reconstruction. They wouldn't have me if I tried."

"And just why is that?" Carruthers's attitude said he was expecting another lie.

"Because I fought under Generals Lee and Jackson during the war." He pointed to his scars. "That's where I got these."

"You can't touch a wounded Johnny Reb," Dan Walch told Carruthers. "People around here would hang you next to him."

"There's not a soul in the county that would touch me," Carruthers declared.

"It would be nothing but murder," Amanda said. "It's against the law."

"I'm the law on my own land," Carruthers shouted. "I can do what I want."

"You'll do it without my help," Dan said. "Any of you boys willing to risk your neck?" he asked the assembled hands.

"I know every one of your faces." Amanda let her gaze travel around the circle of men, stopping briefly to concentrate on each face before moving to the next. "I promise I won't forget a single one."

The men slowly moved from their circle to positions behind Walch.

"You can't listen to her," Carruthers shouted. "Nobody pays attention to what a woman says."

"You do, if you're a gentleman," Broc said.

Carruthers reached for his gun, but Broc had his rifle out and pointed at the man before he could get his gun out of his holster.

"I don't feel much like dying today." He waited until Carruthers released his grip on his gun and dropped his hand to his side. "Miss Liscomb wanted to ask if you would assist her in looking for her missing cows. I take your actions to mean you won't do that, so we'll leave. People would be angry at you for shooting a wounded war veteran in the back, but they'd tear you apart if you shot a lady. It was nice to meet you fellas," he said to the assembled cowhands. "Have a good day." He turned to Amanda and said, "Let's go."

"Don't ride away from me," Carruthers shouted. "I'm not done talking to you."

"Keep riding," Broc said to Amanda. "Don't respond or turn around."

"Grace Liscomb is a fool," Carruthers shouted after Amanda. "She'll lose that ranch, and I'll get it for pennies. You're a dead man, Kincaid. I don't believe you got that wound in the war. You probably got it trying to steal chickens from some poor Confederate widow."

Carruthers continued to shout, but his words gradually grew less understandable. When they rounded a grove of post oaks and the ground dropped away toward the creek, his voice faded to a sound only slightly louder than the rustling leaves. Broc could see some of the tension go out of Amanda.

"I don't know what got into him," she said to Broc. "I've never seen him act like that."

"Some men can't stand not getting their own way. I didn't realize turning down his job to work for you would set him off like that."

"I'm sorry he was so cruel. For a minute I could almost believe he was serious about hanging you."

Broc was sure Carruthers had been serious. The question in his mind was whether the cowhands would have stood for anything more than a good roughing up. He was relieved to know Dan Walch wouldn't.

"Some men like Carruthers have had their own way so long, they don't understand they are subject to laws like the rest of us."

Amanda shook her head. "Are all men like that?"

"No, but women can be like that, too."

Amanda looked thoughtful. "My mother is, a bit."

Broc thought it wisest not to respond.

"She was brought up to expect a certain kind of life. When the war took it away, she couldn't understand. My father brought everything he could from Mississippi to make her feel less cut off from the life she knew, but she has never been able to adjust to Texas. Since Papa died, she's grown a little angrier each day."

"Maybe having more work to do will take her mind off her troubles."

"I hope so. Now that Gary has left, she's going to have to do a lot more than clean house." She uttered a mild expletive. "She has always been convinced Papa or Gary could make things the way she wanted if they would just try. Gary's leaving has been a shock to her."

"I'm sure he'll come back once he's had time to cool off."

"He'll come back tonight, or he'll hear some words from me that will take a few layers of skin off his hide."

Broc was certain that being treated like an errant little brother would only serve to put Gary's back up. "If you'll take the advice of a man who has several younger brothers, you won't say anything to him tonight. You might even sympathize with his frustration."

Amanda looked surprised, maybe even a little annoyed. "You think I should pretend what he did was right?"

"No, but he doesn't want the same things as his family. That's unfortunate, but it's not his fault that he prefers working in the saloon to working around cows."

"I think he should come back to the ranch whether he likes it or not."

"He has the right to look for the kind of work that will make him happy."

Amanda pulled up her mount and turned to fix him with a steady gaze. "I don't understand you."

Broc laughed. "What's so hard to understand?"

"Everything. Why you're here in the first place. Why you felt compelled to work for me rather than Carruthers. Why you're defending Gary when you know he practically hates you. Why Eddie likes you better than his own brother." She paused.

"Is there more?" Why had he asked that question? He couldn't expect her to tell him what he wanted to hear.

"Yes and no." She shook her head. "Sometimes

I think you must be a crook, and I ought to order you off our land. But the next minute I'm convinced you're a good man who has handled misfortune with great courage."

"Why would you think I'm a crook?" Why did he need to ask that question? Did he hope she would somehow talk herself into thinking he was a man she could be attracted to? He told himself she might sympathize with him, even learn to like him, but she could never love him. Regardless of how deep his feelings for her might become, he could never accept a relationship based on sympathy. It would eat him alive.

"The debt."

"Doesn't my refusing to accept any money make a difference?"

"Yes, but I can't forget that you made the request in the first place."

Maybe it did sound suspicious that a judge had threatened to send him to jail if he didn't collect a debt, but the judge was real, and he was coming to Cactus Bend intent upon collecting it. Whether the debt was real or imaginary, Broc would bear the blame.

"Don't worry about it. I won't be here long."

There was no need for her to think about him ever again. He wouldn't be coming back through Cactus Bend after he'd served his time in jail.

❧

He should have stayed at the ranch. There was plenty there he could be doing. Talking to Leo to learn as much as possible about the land and the cows. Trying to get on better terms with Andy. Spending time with Eddie, who wanted little more than to follow Broc wherever he went. Even spending some time with Mrs. Liscomb in hopes of convincing her he wasn't a thief, but what was the point in building bridges when he would be gone in little more than a week? The closer he got to people, the harder it would be when he left.

So why had he offered to accompany Amanda into town and stayed to escort her home after work? He wasn't fooling himself that he did it because Gary wouldn't be coming back until later. He wasn't even doing it to keep Corby from volunteering. He was doing it because he couldn't stop himself from wanting to be with Amanda as often as possible.

"What do you want?" Gil, the second bartender, leaned on the bar in front of Broc. He nodded his head in Gary's direction. "He refuses to serve you, so if you want anything to drink, I'll have to get it for you."

"Nothing yet," Broc said. "It's going to be a long evening."

Being in the saddle early the following morning would feel a lot better without a hangover. Still, he didn't know how he could get through an evening of watching men gape and grope at Amanda without getting a little drunk. He hated it when she smiled at the men. He knew she was doing it because it was part of her job, but he hated it just the same. He had no right to feel that way, but he couldn't stop himself.

The piano player was irritating him. The man was probably doing his best, but his best was rotten. From the time Broc was little, his parents had made extra money by entertaining on riverboats. All of the children had learned to sing, dance, act, and play a musical instrument. Broc had been forced to learn to play the piano. He quit playing when the war started, but he'd gotten back into practice singing and playing duets with Rafe's wife during the months he'd spent in California. Now his fingers were itching to show this man how a piano should be played.

Unable to stand the double torture, he got up and hurried outside. He could still hear the piano, but he didn't have to watch the men lusting after Amanda.

The night sky was nearly cloudless, the moon and countless stars shedding their pale light on the dusty streets and creating deep shadows between the hastily constructed wood frame buildings that made up the town. People, mostly men, moved along the boardwalks and crossed the streets with a purpose born out of the fatigue and frustrations of the day. Greetings were curt, expressions barely altered. All passed Broc as though he wasn't there.

A couple of men Broc recognized as working for Carruthers entered the saloon without speaking to him.

"You don't like what we can offer you to drink?"

Broc turned to see Corby had followed him. "It's not that. I'm just not in the mood right now."

"I thought cowhands were always in the mood to drink."

"I guess it wouldn't be good for business if most men drank as little as I do." When he did drink, he preferred wine, a fine whiskey, or an aged cognac. His time at Rafe's ranch had spoiled him.

"Amanda said she hired you to be her foreman."

"Yeah." He didn't offer any more. He waited to see what Corby would say.

"I also heard you were on Carruthers's range."

"Amanda went to ask him to help her look for some lost cows."

"Carruthers doesn't allow strangers on his land."

"How are people supposed to talk to him?"

"Meet him in town or at the saloon. Everybody knows he's liable to shoot first and ask questions later."

"Why didn't you tell Amanda?"

"I didn't think she needed to know."

"She does if she's going to work alongside her cowhands."

"I don't want her working alongside her hands. I don't want her working on that ranch at all."

Broc knew where Corby was going, but he was determined to make the man say what he wanted instead of hint at it. "Why should she pay any attention to what you want?"

"I intend to marry her."

"Maybe she *wants* to work on the ranch. Maybe she likes making the important decisions about her life."

"A lady shouldn't want to work, and she should leave all the important decisions to her husband. That's what Amanda's mother wants for her."

Apparently, when Amanda and Corby were together, he did all the talking and none of the listening. If he had, he'd know Amanda wasn't like her mother. She had enjoyed her day in the saddle. She'd been intent on learning everything she could from him and Leo, from the kind of grass under their feet to the varieties of birds in the trees. She'd even asked Broc to write out a schedule of the things that should be done each month during the year.

"If you want to marry Amanda, you should talk to her more, find out what she wants. It's not what you might think."

The magnitude of the condescension in Corby's smile made it downright insulting. "I know all there is to know about Amanda. I know her better than she knows herself."

Right then and there Broc decided that if he did nothing else before he left Cactus Bend, he was going to see that Amanda didn't marry Corby Wilson. It would be better for her to die an old maid than have to suffer living as his wife.

"No man knows all there is to know about any woman, not even after being married for fifty years. That's part of the wonder of females. No matter how much you know, or think you know, they're full of surprises. It's like a treasure hunt that never ends but just keeps getting better."

What was wrong with him? He was sounding like his happily married friends, not the self-possessed, cynical bachelor he'd become. He didn't know a damned thing about women, didn't like surprises, and had never been on a treasure hunt. Obsessing over Amanda was affecting his mind.

"That's all the advice I have for the evening. Now I think I'll have that drink."

"You're wasting your time with Amanda."

Broc had started to reenter the saloon, but he turned back to Corby. "What makes you say that?"

"I know you've fallen in love with her. She's so beautiful you couldn't stop yourself. Nobody can."

Whatever the state of his feelings for Amanda, they were none of Corby's concern. "I'm only going to be here for a little more than a week. I doubt Amanda will feel more than a twinge when I leave."

Corby laughed. "I'm not worried about Amanda. She could never be interested in anyone who looks like you. I just wanted to let you know she's already spoken for."

His face again! Was it possible for anyone to see beyond the scars to the man inside? Before the war he'd been a song-and-dance man, dazzling people with his performances and his looks. It seemed no one had ever been interested in who he was as a person.

"I'm not normally one to tell another man his business, but I'm not sure Amanda knows she's spoken for."

Corby's confidence remained unshaken. "We've had an understanding for a long time, even before her father died."

And they weren't married yet? All the more reason for Broc to think Amanda wasn't nearly as enamored of Corby as he thought. There was no more to be said, so Broc nodded to Corby, went inside to the bar, and asked Gil to bring him a whiskey. He needed something stronger than beer. Over the next two hours, Corby came over to talk to Broc at least once every fifteen minutes. That annoyed Broc so much he had a second whiskey. Corby was standing next to him when Amanda approached them.

"I need to talk to you," she said to Corby.

"We can talk after I close up."

"I have to go home before my usual time so I can get up early tomorrow. That's part of what I wanted to talk about."

Corby wasn't happy about that. Broc figured he had no right overhearing any part of this conversation, but he couldn't make himself leave. Amanda wasn't his responsibility, but he was determined Corby wasn't going to pressure her into doing something she didn't want to do.

"You know the men depend on you being here," Corby said.

"I don't have any choice," Amanda said. "Now that Gary has left home, I have to take over what he's been doing."

"I'll tell him to move back. I'll fire him if he doesn't."

She glanced at Broc. "Don't. It would just make him angrier, maybe angry enough to leave town."

"He's only a boy. He couldn't go anywhere."

"He's seventeen," Broc reminded Corby. "I'd been working away from home for nearly ten years by then."

Both looked at him in surprise. Apparently Amanda was going to ask what he'd been doing, but Corby spoke first.

"I'll marry you and take care of everything. Just set the date."

Amanda didn't meet Corby's gaze. "We've already been over this. I'm not ready to get married."

"You're nineteen years old!" Corby exclaimed. "How much older do you have to be?" He'd spoken so loudly, several heads turned in their direction.

"You know my feelings on this." Amanda spoke so softly, Broc had to strain to hear her over the noise in the saloon.

"I know all about your wanting to be in love, but I've told you that's not a sound basis for marriage."

If Broc hadn't disliked the man so much, he might have felt sorry for him. He knew what it was like to be in love with a woman who wasn't in love with him.

My God! Had he fallen in love with Amanda? She hardly knew he existed. As a potential husband, he was essentially invisible. It was incredibly stupid to have let his emotions get so far out of control. What was it about Amanda that had dismantled his common sense?

What an idiot! He deserved to be locked up in jail.

"...more money as long as Gary isn't helping us."

Broc had been so caught up in his own thoughts, he'd lost track of the conversation. He wasn't surprised Amanda would ask for more money, nor was he surprised Corby didn't want to give it to her.

"You know the only reason I can pay you more than the other girls is that you sing a couple of songs now and then. If you worked more hours, the men would slip you a few more coins."

"Corby, I just said I needed to work *fewer* hours, not more."

"I can't pay you more money for less work. That ought to make sense even to a woman."

Maybe Corby understood how to run a saloon— decent food, decent liquor, and pretty girls were a good combination—but he didn't know how to make himself attractive as husband material.

"I understand, even though I'm a woman," Amanda

Eleven

"YOU CAN PLAY THE PIANO?"

Broc didn't know why Amanda should be so shocked. She really knew nothing about him.

"Amanda doesn't need anyone who can play with just two fingers." Clearly, Corby didn't believe he could play.

"I'll show you."

They followed him over to the piano, which had been mercifully quiet for the last several minutes.

"What do you want to hear? A waltz? A march? A ballad?"

"Play whatever you want," Amanda said.

Broc played one of the dance tunes that had been popular when he played for the riverboats. When that was over, he played a waltz. It wasn't until he'd finished that he realized the noise in the saloon had fallen so low, he could barely hear the whispered voices.

"Can you play 'Turkey in the Straw'?" someone asked.

Broc broke into a rendition so spirited, several men started dancing. It was twenty minutes before he stopped taking requests. By the time he finished, the top of the piano was lined with drinks and coins from grateful patrons.

"Can you sing something?" someone shouted.

Broc obliged with a tune that was as racy as it was lively. The men wanted more, but Broc said it was time for Oscar to take over again.

"You gotta get rid of Oscar and hire this man," one of the men said. "I ain't heard nothing that good since I left New Orleans."

Broc gathered up the coins and handed them to Amanda. He wrapped her fingers around them when she tried to refuse.

"You were wonderful," Amanda said. "I couldn't believe it when you just sat down and played like it was the easiest thing in the world. I've never seen anybody do that. It's just amazing."

Broc was caught between happiness that Amanda thought he was wonderful and sadness that it was only because he could sing and play the piano. He wanted to be more than a trained bear whose only value was to entertain people. He wanted to be a person who was loved and valued for himself. So far it seemed the only people who saw his true self were the men who'd served with him during the war.

"I'll give you Oscar's job," Corby said. "He never got the men to stop talking long enough to listen to anything he played."

"I don't want his job," Broc told Corby, "but I'll play for Amanda so she can earn more money and work fewer hours."

"I'll pay you twice what I pay Oscar to work here

full time," Corby offered. "If you can entertain every-body like you did tonight, this place will be packed."

Broc could practically see dollar signs in Corby's eyes, but he had no desire to add to the man's wealth or importance in town. "I'm going to be here for only a little more than a week, so it would be unfair to push any man out of his job." He turned to Amanda. "What songs do you sing?"

Amanda knew only six songs she felt comfortable singing. He knew five of them and figured he could fake the other one after she hummed the tune.

"Let's try one and see what happens," Broc said.

"But we haven't practiced together," Amanda protested.

"Just ignore me and sing like you usually do," Broc said. "I'll follow you."

Amanda appeared skeptical, but Broc had spent several years accompanying anybody who wanted to get up and sing. That included farmers who couldn't carry a tune, spoiled children with high squeaky voices, over-the-hill opera singers, and women who were convinced their local church choir would have fallen apart without them.

"I'm used to Oscar."

"Then pretend I'm Oscar," Broc said.

Amanda shrugged, turned to face the men in the saloon, and started to sing. Broc found the key and began with a simple single-note accompaniment. Once he was sure they were feeling the same rhythm, he started to add more notes until both hands were busy. Amanda's singing gained confidence as they went along. By the time she finished the third verse, she had all the men in the saloon tapping their feet. When Broc sang a harmony line on the last verse, Amanda's eyes widened in surprise. The saloon erupted in applause as they finished. She had to sing all six songs before the men would let them stop.

Amanda looked so happy and excited, Broc felt the same way. It didn't matter that they weren't happy about the same things. He was willing to take what he could get. She went back to waiting on tables, and he went back to the bar to kill time until her evening was over, and he would escort her home. He was surprised when Gary approached him.

"I didn't know you could play like that," he said.

"Your sister is a fine singer. You should be proud of her."

Gary's expression clouded. "I would if she wanted to work here instead of on that ranch. I hate cows."

Broc laughed. "Lots of people do."

"Then why do Mama and Amanda like them so much?"

"I doubt it's the cows they like so much as the kind of life owning a ranch gives them."

"What does it give them but getting up with the chickens—I hate chickens, by the way—and working until you're so tired you don't feel like eating?"

"Some women don't like being stared at. Others think certain kinds of work aren't respectable. Others simply like different things. I think your sister likes the freedom the ranch gives her."

"The freedom to work like a slave and still not make money."

"The ranch will become very profitable in time.

Your father made a wise decision when he bought that bull. Nobody says you have to like the Lazy T, but don't let it drive you away from your family."

"It didn't. They did. I gotta go. Seems like everybody's thirsty at once."

"Think about it," Broc said. "They miss you."

Broc couldn't tell whether Gary believed him. He just hoped the boy wouldn't cut himself off from his family. Broc's scars had done that for him. Much of his family's success had been based on the handsomeness of the family. They would have no place for a disfigured monster. It was better for him to stay in Texas. Cows didn't care what he looked like.

～

"I still can't get over it."

Amanda had said that so many times, Broc cringed.

"It's not so surprising," he said. "It's what my family did. It was our work, just as waiting tables is yours, or tending bar is Gary's."

"It doesn't take any talent to do what we do," Amanda said.

"Everything takes talent, even serving beer. It's just a different kind of talent."

"I refuse to let you make light of your piano playing," Amanda said. "It was wonderful. Incredible. You had everybody in the saloon whistling, humming, tapping their feet, even singing. Corby was so happy I thought he'd burst his buttons."

"Forget about Corby. He was thinking only about how much more money he could make, which is good, because I intend to make sure you get a chunk of it."

Amanda turned to gaze at him. "Why are you doing this? You're going to jail if you don't collect this debt we don't owe. You should be trying to prove the debt is real. Instead you've forgotten about the debt and are helping me on the ranch as well as in the saloon."

The light buggy bounced uncomfortably over the wheel tracks in the road, but the sky was clear, the air soft and mild. It was the kind of evening when the drive between town and the ranch would be much too short, when the words that could never be uttered were the only words he wanted to say. It was also the kind of evening when a man who wasn't careful to keep a tight rein on his heart could imagine anything could come true. When that man was sitting next to a beautiful woman whose eyes sparkled with excitement and whose face was wreathed in smiles, keeping a tight rein on his emotions was impossible. It was too easy to invest that excitement, that happiness, with another meaning.

"I suppose there are lots of reasons why I'm doing it," he said, "but the only one that matters is that I want to."

"Why? You don't know me or my family. You're going to jail because of us."

Why? Because he was certain there was something going on here that needed to be brought to light. Because he was certain the Liscombs *did* owe the debt. Because he had to do something to fill up the days before he went back to Crystal Springs. Because they needed help and didn't have it. Because he hated to see someone like Carruthers bully people who weren't as rich or strong as he was. Because he didn't want them to lose the ranch. Because it gave him a chance to perform again, to enjoy the nectar of applause. Because it gave him a chance to spend whole days with a beautiful woman he was falling in love with.

But maybe the real reason he was doing all of this, or any of this, was because Amanda was the only woman he'd ever met who seemed unaware that his face was hideously scarred.

"What else am I going to do?" That wasn't what he wanted to say, but it was safer.

"You could go back to California."

"I have to serve my time in jail. I'll figure out what to do after that."

"You could come back here. Corby would practically get down on his knees and beg."

If she had said come back and *work with me,* he might not have been able to resist, but she didn't. "We'll see. Now we need to talk about teaching you some new songs."

They talked about which songs she thought the men would like best, when to practice, whether she should sing solo, or if he should add harmony, but he was barely able to hold up his end of the conversation. His mind was consumed by the effort it took to keep from touching her, putting his arm around her, even kissing her. The only thing he'd ever done that was harder was to accept what had happened to his face. It was almost a relief when he pulled the buggy to a stop before the ranch house.

"Thanks for seeing me home," she said as he handed her down, "and thanks for volunteering to help me at the saloon."

"I enjoyed both."

"I can hardly wait for tomorrow. I haven't been so excited about anything since we moved from Mississippi. Please come back after you get out of jail. You've only been here a few days, and already I feel like I've known you forever. I'd love for us to work together."

She said it! Us. Him and her. Not her family. Not Corby. Not anyone else. Just him and her. "I'll think about it."

She gripped both of his hands and looked full into his eyes. "Are you sure?"

For a moment, he wasn't sure of anything. He could barely form a coherent thought. Visions of impossibilities bloomed with the profusion of bluebonnets in the spring. He looked into her eyes and saw the possibility of happiness. What had seemed impossible for so long now seemed to be within his grasp. All he needed to do was reach out and take it.

So he kissed her.

It was impossible to tell whether it lasted a second or a minute. Everything around them—the horse blowing through its nostrils, the breeze that teased her hair, moths that danced in the light from the window—faded into nothingness. Nothing existed but the two of them.

Her lips were unbelievably soft and sweet. He had imagined they would be, but reality outstripped his imagination. Everything felt so different, he might as well never have kissed a woman before. Was this how it was supposed to be when everything was right, when a man found the one woman meant for him? If this was a dream, he didn't want to wake up. If it was his imagination, he didn't want to face reality. If this was his only chance, he wanted to stay here forever. Nothing else mattered. Only this. It was perfect. It was sublime. It was magic.

Until Amanda jumped back with an expression on her face that would haunt him for the rest of his life. He tried to speak, but his words came out in a strangled whisper. She opened her mouth to speak, then changed her mind. She turned and ran inside without looking back.

It took a moment for the importance of what had happened to sink in. When it did, Broc felt the strength go out of him in a rush. He stumbled as he turned and walked back to the buggy. He leaned against it and took deep, controlled breaths to slow his racing heart. Gradually, the pounding in his head began to ease. Slowly, inevitably, he returned to reality and the grim realization of what he'd done.

He might as well saddle up and leave tonight. She would probably fire him first thing in the morning. She certainly wouldn't want him to play for her in the saloon. Once she told Corby what he'd done, Corby wouldn't want him, either.

He took an exceptionally deep breath and forced himself to stand erect. There was no point in feeling sorry for himself. He'd done what he knew he shouldn't have done. Now he'd have to abide by the consequences.

"Come on," he said to the horse. "It's time for both of us to get some sleep."

The horse didn't seem particularly interested in

Broc's need for rest, but he was eager to get out of the harness, so he followed readily. Broc's steps were heavy and slow, which caused the horse to nudge him along.

"Impatient, are you? I was, too, so let that be a lesson to you."

But as he walked, his steps grew lighter, his spirits started to rise. Finally a smile played across his lips.

"At least I got one kiss."

❧

"You're home early," her mother said when Amanda walked into the house.

Amanda's mind was in such turmoil, she couldn't concentrate. She didn't want to talk to her mother, but she knew it would be worse if she went straight to her room. Her mother would know something was wrong, and Amanda couldn't explain to anyone what she couldn't explain to herself.

"I told Corby I had to leave early because I need to get up early now that Gary has left."

Her mother's expression grew animated. "Did you talk to him? When is he coming home?"

"I don't know. I didn't talk to him."

"Why not? I told you just before you left you had to talk to him. I even told you what to say."

"Broc convinced me that would only make Gary angrier, more reluctant to come home."

"You listened to that man instead of your mother?"

"He has lots of brothers. He understands how boys think."

"I'm Gary's mother. I know how *he* thinks."

Amanda's control broke. "If you knew how he thinks, if you cared *what* he thinks, he'd be here now."

"Amanda Elizabeth Liscomb," her mother intoned in that awful voice mothers have when they're about to pronounce that you're an unnatural child and they don't know what they did to deserve you, "I never thought I'd live to see the day you'd speak to me like that."

"Neither did I," Amanda said, too emotionally exhausted to mince words, "but I never thought I'd be in a position of having to support the family, trying to hold it together, when you were doing all you could to tear it apart."

"I have never, I *would* never do anything to hurt my children. Their happiness has been my only desire in life."

"No, Mother. Your primary desire in life has been *your* happiness. If it had been otherwise, you'd have more interest in this ranch you badgered Papa to buy than in all the furniture and other stuff you forced him to drag from Mississippi. He was happy running the saloon and the diner, and we had enough money to live comfortably, but that wasn't good enough for you. He had to have a respectable job so you could be a social force in Cactus Bend." She drew a shuddering breath and went on before her mother could interrupt her. "Well, you have your ranch, which none of us knows how to run, but Papa is dead, Gary has left home, and I'm forced to work in the saloon you hated, being gaped at, pawed at, and slavered over by strangers, so you can stay here and dust furniture. Yet you want me to turn away the one person who's volunteered to help me."

"His face is horrible."

"No, it's not. It has more character than any man's in Cactus Bend."

"And he's a crook. A thief."

"He's not that, either."

"Then how do you explain his trying to force us to give him money?"

"He didn't." Her head was throbbing so she could barely think. She had to go to her room before she said something truly awful. "I have a terrible headache, and I'm too tired to think. We can talk about this tomorrow."

"Don't walk away when I'm talking to you."

Amanda looked her mother square in the eye. "When you spend the whole day in the saddle, then work all evening in the saloon, I'll listen to anything you have to say. Until then, I'm tired, and I'm going to bed."

Amanda practically ran to her room, closed the door, staggered over to the bed, and collapsed on it. It didn't matter that she'd forgotten a lamp, that the only light in the room filtered through the lace curtains at the window. She welcomed the darkness because it closed out the world around her, a world that was growing increasingly beyond her ability to control or understand.

She didn't know what had caused her to speak to her mother like that. She ought to apologize now, but it would have to wait until the morning. She had more important things to think about, like why had Broc kissed her, and why had she kissed him back?

Because she wanted to.

The truth was frightening in its simplicity. Why had

she wanted it? How did she expect *or hope* Broc would respond? Worse yet, what was she going to do when they came face-to-face in the morning? What would he expect of her now?

She was overwhelmed with questions she'd never asked about Broc or any other man. She didn't have answers to them because she'd never thought of them before. But she'd allowed him to kiss her, she had kissed him back, so some part of her mind must have been thinking about it.

She rolled over and sat up. She heaved herself off the bed and walked over to the window. If she looked sharply to the right, she could see the black hulk of the bunkhouse silhouetted against the velvet sky. What was Broc doing? What was he thinking? Was he wrestling with the same questions, or did he chalk it up as just a kiss, roll over in his bunk, and sink into a sound sleep? She wondered if he had planned the kiss, or if it had been spontaneous, something he wanted to do but wouldn't have done if he'd had time to think about it.

She turned away from the window and began to undress. The simple, familiar, oft-repeated motions served to soothe her spirits and calm her tumultuous thoughts. By the time she crawled between the sheets, she was able to think more clearly.

She'd been attracted to Broc from the beginning. There was something about him that made him stand out from other men. His scars made him different. They told her he was a man who had made his peace with what could have been a life-changing tragedy and didn't intend to let it determine the course of the rest of his life. They told her he was a man who had the courage to face the world knowing a large part of it would be repelled by him.

But his disfigurement was only part of what made him a man who captured her attention. There was the other side of his face that spoke of the man who had honor, integrity, dignity, generosity, kindness, and a willingness to help whenever he could, to share his knowledge without expecting payment in return. Even before tonight, he'd been a man who had exceeded her expectations in every way.

Tonight she'd realized her admiration for Broc had turned into something much warmer and more serious. She didn't just admire him. She liked him. She liked him a great deal. She liked him so much she wondered what she would do if he never came back.

Amanda came awake slowly. With her eyes still closed, she stretched lazily, enjoying the warmth of the bed and a sense of peace and well-being. That vanished as soon as she remembered the events of the night before. Eyes open now, she could tell from the amount of light coming in her window that she had overslept. She scrambled out of bed and practically threw herself into her clothes. It took several minutes to brush her hair and pin it atop her head so it would fit under her hat. Next she put away her nightclothes and made up her bed. Looking around to make sure her mother would find nothing to complain of, she left her bedroom and hurried to the kitchen.

"Mama said to let you sleep all day if you wanted," Eddie announced the moment she entered the kitchen.

Her mother didn't look up from where she was scrambling eggs. Food warming in pots on the stove and bowls covered with towels revealed that everything was ready to serve the minute the men arrived. "Is there anything I can do to help?"

Her mother didn't turn around. "You can pour the milk instead of Eddie. He has to call the men. If they don't arrive soon, the eggs will be cold, and the biscuits will burn."

Eddie happily abandoned his task and bounded through the door before his mother could change her mind. The fact that her mother had made biscuits signaled to Amanda that her mother was still angry with her and had responded to her criticism by preparing an enormous breakfast.

"I didn't mean to lose my temper last night," Amanda said to her mother's back. "I was tired and upset."

Her mother looked at her over her shoulder. "I thought you were too mature to let being tired and upset cause you to say things you don't mean."

Amanda took a deep breath to steady her hand as she poured milk into a glass. "I apologized for losing my temper, not for what I said."

Any thawing in her mother's expression stopped immediately. "I see." She turned back to the eggs.

"I'm not sure you do."

"I'm not stupid, Amanda." She scraped the eggs onto a serving plate. "I can understand things that are said to me."

"All I was trying to say was that we need to work together to make this ranch a success and to find a way to get Gary to come home."

Her mother placed the eggs next to one of the bowls and opened the oven to check on the biscuits. "I had thought that in my declining years I wouldn't have to slave the way I did when your father and I first got married, but I see that is not going to be the case. I will never be a burden to my children."

Amanda didn't know where to start with that statement. Her mother had never had to do any real work until the war broke out. Even then, Amanda, who had just turned eleven, was drafted to help her mother. By the time they moved to Texas, Amanda was doing most of the cooking while her mother concentrated her efforts on caring for all the fine things her parents had left her.

"Things haven't worked out as planned," Amanda said. "Papa's dying was just the first upset."

"I never thought he would leave me," her mother said with a sob.

"He didn't want to." Amanda felt like an idiot stating the obvious. "He loved you very much."

Her mother smiled wistfully, and it was easy to see the beauty that must have enthralled her father twenty years ago. "He called me his gardenia. He said its fragrance made him dizzy the way holding me in his arms did."

Amanda couldn't imagine her practical father saying such a thing, but he had been deeply in love with her mother. That was the kind of love Amanda was looking for. It was one reason she continued to turn down Corby's offer of marriage. She had no desire to—

The back door opened, and Eddie bounded in, followed by Leo and Andy. "Broc says he's going into town for breakfast. Can I have his biscuits?"

Twelve

Broc stuffed his last shirt into his saddlebags. The only decision left to make was whether to stay in Cactus Bend or go back to Crystal Springs and start his jail sentence early. Either prospect was depressing, but he might as well get it over with. He wasn't doing any good here. Amanda didn't need any more trouble to deal with. He tossed his saddlebags over his shoulder and turned to leave the bunkhouse. He'd already tied his bedroll to the saddle. He stepped through the doorway and almost ran into Amanda.

He didn't know how it was possible, but each time he saw her affected him more powerfully than the last. He should have left before breakfast. Now he was going to have to do the one thing he wanted to avoid: explain his behavior last night.

The explanation was simple enough. He had fallen in love with her.

Amanda backed up a couple of steps and held out a folded piece of paper. "This says you're quitting. Why?"

"After last night, I thought it was the best thing to do."

"You think leaving me to try to figure out how to run this ranch on my own is the best thing to do?" She gestured vaguely in the direction of town. "You figure leaving me to keep struggling with Oscar's piano playing is the best thing to do?"

"You can hire someone to teach you, and Corby can hire someone to play for you."

"The men reacted to *your* playing and singing, not someone Corby might hire. There's no one else with that kind of talent in the area. And you were going to stay here long enough to teach me about running the ranch."

"Anybody can do that."

"Carruthers wanted to hang you for working for me. Do you think anybody else is going to risk that for the few dollars I can pay?"

"But I kissed you last night."

"It was just a kiss."

For a moment, he couldn't catch his breath. What did she mean it was *just a kiss*? Did she mean it was so unimportant she'd already forgotten it? Did she mean she remembered it but didn't expect it to happen again? "A cowhand can't go around kissing his boss."

Her gaze intensified. "Do you want to kiss me again?"

Was she laying a trap for him? He'd already quit. There was nothing else she could do except get the sheriff to chase him out of town.

"I think about you—about kissing you—all the time." There. Now she knew how he felt.

Her gaze fell to the ground. "So you *do* want to kiss me again?"

He was sure he couldn't be hearing her correctly. Was she trying to lead him deeper into a trap, or was it possible she hadn't disliked being kissed? "It would depend on whether you wanted me to."

"Kissing the foreman wouldn't be a proper way for a boss to act, would it?"

"I don't know that I would say it was improper, but it's not usual." He wanted her to look up so he could see what was in her eyes, but she kept her gaze averted. He dropped his saddlebags, stepped over to her, put his hand under her chin, and lifted her head slowly. "Are you saying you want me to kiss you?"

"I didn't dislike it."

"That's not what I asked. Do you want me to kiss you?"

"If you want to."

The warmth in her eyes should have been a sufficient answer, but Broc needed words, something concrete he could point to when he was shaken by doubt. "Look at me. Are you sure you want a man with this face to kiss you?"

"There's nothing wrong with your face."

He didn't know whether she was trying to be kind or simply didn't have the courage to say what was in her mind, but he couldn't let her stop there. He knew what he looked like. He saw his face every time he looked in a mirror, passed a store window, saw his reflection in still water. "Look at me. How can you say there's nothing wrong with my face? Half of it is destroyed."

"But the other half is beautiful."

"I don't come in separate halves. You can't take one side and ignore the other."

"It was just a kiss, Broc. That doesn't require a pledge of lifetime commitment."

He knew it was unreasonable, but that was what he wanted. "You've never given me a reason to think you'd welcome a kiss. And with this face…" He let the sentence trail off.

Much to his surprise, Amanda stepped closer and placed her hand on the left side of his face. He had to fight the impulse to pull away. No woman had ever touched his scars.

"To me this is a testament to your bravery. It took courage to fight in the war, but it took even more to make peace with the terrible thing that happened to you."

She gave him too much credit. For a long time he had been bitter. In the days after he was shot, he prayed he would die. It was the fierce love and unyielding support of his friends that had enabled him to come to terms with what had happened to him, but he still wasn't beyond bitterness or anger. Every time someone turned away from him or flinched at seeing him, he was angry all over again that for the rest of his life he would be judged by one side of his face rather than the rest of him.

It was the reason he'd never gone back to Tennessee.

"Last night was more than just a kiss. I was attracted to you the first time I saw you. The more I'm around you, the more I like you. I've wanted to touch you, to kiss you, to tell you I enjoy being with you."

"Why haven't you?"

"Because I look like this. Because your mother and brother think I'm a crook."

"I don't understand about the debt, but I don't think you're a crook."

"Why?"

"Crooks and thieves don't act the way you've acted."

"I could be working for you so I could steal your mother's silverware."

Amanda laughed, and some of the tension between them eased. "I can't imagine anyone wanting that horrible stuff."

"It's silver, and many people lost everything in the war."

"Did you lose everything?"

"I had no material possessions, but I lost my career on the stage. It was the only way I knew to make a living."

"Now you know all about ranches. Will you stay and teach me what you've learned?"

Broc felt tension crawl along the back of his shoulders. "If I stay, I'll want to kiss you again."

"That's okay."

"I don't mean I'll just *want* to kiss you. I mean I'll *need* to kiss you."

Amanda's gaze didn't waver. "That's okay."

Broc couldn't believe she really meant what she said, but now was a good time to find out. He moved closer, slipped his arm around her waist, and pulled her to him. She didn't resist even when her breasts came in contact with his chest. Slowly, still afraid he might be asking more of her than she was ready to give, he lowered his head until their lips met.

Her mouth was as soft and sweet as he remembered.

He had lain awake most of the night reliving their kiss, trying to imprint on his mind every moment, every sensation, every feeling. Now he didn't have to try to remember because he would never forget this kiss. He hadn't acted on impulse. His thought processes hadn't been suspended. He had approached this as a test, but once their lips met, all that mattered was holding Amanda in his arms and kissing her.

He had kissed many women during his days on the riverboats, young women and not-so-young women, eager to indulge in a moonlight tryst with a handsome actor. Some had been beautiful, several rich, others amorous—some were rich, beautiful, *and* amorous— but nothing had affected him as powerfully as this simple kiss from Amanda, because she was kissing him back with as much purpose and vigor as he was kissing her.

It was enough to make a man lose his moorings and start imagining that anything might be possible. To hold her, breathe in her scent, feel the heat of her body against him, was more intoxicating than the finest cognac. He didn't want to get his hopes up too soon, but—

"Why are you kissing Amanda?"

Eddie's voice cut though the bubble of unreality around them like a knife through soft butter.

"Mama said Amanda has to come to breakfast. She said if she had to cook it, Amanda had to eat it. I thought you were going into town," the boy said to Broc. "I asked Mama if I could have your biscuit. She said she was going to give it to the chickens. I don't like chickens. I don't want to give them your biscuit."

Amanda had busied herself straightening her clothes and schooling her expression to impassivity before she turned to face her brother. "I was just trying to convince Broc to stay here rather than go into town."

Eddie looked uneasy. "Do I have to kiss him if I want him to stay?"

Amanda put her hand over her mouth to keep from laughing, but Broc let his roll out without restraint. "No," he said when he caught his breath, "but it would be nice if you asked me to stay."

"Mama doesn't want you to stay." Eddie hadn't yet learned that some things were better left unsaid. "But Leo and I do. I don't count Andy."

"I'm going to stay, but I'll have to leave soon."

"If Amanda kisses you again, will you stay longer?"

Amanda blushed and giggled.

"We'll have to see," Broc said. "Now I'd appreciate it if you didn't tell your mother you saw me kissing Amanda."

"Hell, no!" Eddie exclaimed. "She'd have a conniption fit."

Broc was able to contain his amusement, but Amanda was overcome with a very undignified fit of giggles. "Go back and tell your mother we'll be in shortly."

"Can't. She said I was to come back with Amanda or I wouldn't get any breakfast. I gotta eat so I can grow big enough to beat up Gary."

"Okay." Common sense told Broc not to be foolish, but he couldn't extinguish the tiny flame of hope that his future might not be as bleak as he'd always imagined it would be.

"Do you think these are some of the one hundred cows you said we're missing?" Amanda asked Leo.

"I don't know," the boy replied.

"What do you think?" she asked Broc.

After two days' hard work, they'd finished the rough tally of the cows on their range. When they came across cows belonging to Carruthers or Sandoval, they'd hazed the cows back to their own range. They'd been in the process of returning a cow to Carruthers's range when they noticed a Lazy T cow and calf. When they went to chase that cow back to their range, they found another. That had led to another until they had found five, two of them with calves by the stud bull.

"It's hard to say," Broc said. "We're still fairly close to your range. They could have wandered this far on their own. If you really have lost over a hundred cows with calves by your stud bull, then my guess would be that they were stolen. It sounds like someone was choosing which cows he wanted."

That's what she thought, but she'd hoped Broc would tell her something different.

"I don't see how there could be rustlers around," Leo said. "Sandoval or Carruthers would have lost enough cows to be suspicious."

"It's hard to know when you have so much land to cover," Broc said.

The glance he sent Amanda's way told her he was thinking what she was thinking: this was no common rustling operation. Whoever had taken the cows had concentrated on the Lazy T herd, with special attention to calves by the stud bull.

"What do you think we ought to do?" she asked Broc.

He took a moment to survey the prairie that stretched before them. "There are so many trees on Carruthers's land, it's hard to tell if there might be more Lazy T stock there. Why don't you and the boys take these cows back while I look around?"

"If Carruthers finds you, he'll kill you," Andy said. "He's in town interviewing drovers to take his herd to Abilene. Sandoval, too. I heard them talking about it last night."

Amanda was feeling exhausted from working on the ranch during the day and in the saloon every night, but the men had responded well to her performing with Broc. Every time Corby saw a man who usually went to another saloon, he rushed over to tell her. She suggested that he add a dollar to her night's pay instead, but he wasn't that grateful.

"Andy and Leo can take the cows back," Amanda said. "I'll go with you."

Broc tried to talk her into going with the boys, but she refused. She didn't think it was good leadership to ask people to take risks she wouldn't take herself. That was no way to build loyalty or respect, and being a woman in a man's world, she needed a lot of both.

"Be careful," Leo said as he and Andy were getting ready to leave. "Even if Carruthers is in town, his men could cause trouble."

"We'll be okay," Amanda assured him. "I've got Broc to watch out for me."

She didn't know how much faith Leo had in Broc's

ability to protect her, but Andy's sneer implied he
didn't have any.

"You really think I'll watch out for you?" Broc
asked after the boys had left.

"You've been doing it for close to a week. I don't
know why you'd stop now."

Broc grinned in a way that had come to be very
special to her. "Then let's go. You look for cows, and
I'll watch for Carruthers's men."

It was hard to think of cows when she was with
Broc. The last two days had been wonderful and terrible at the same time. She found it hard to believe
how much she liked being with him. It didn't make
any difference whether they were in the saddle, taking
care of their horses after a long day, talking about
problems over a meal, or working together in the
saloon. Being with him was like being with a part
of herself. That is, if she could discount the growing
physical attraction.

She couldn't.

Her mother still sulked when she had to be around
Broc, but Amanda was finding it increasingly difficult
not to show her growing attraction to him. Especially
when he kissed her, which he did as often as he could
manage to be alone with her for a few minutes. It
wasn't as hard as she'd thought to find these isolated
moments. The hard part was keeping them short to
avoid suspicion. How could she have known that
being wrapped in Broc's embrace, being kissed by
him, would be something she'd want to do as often
as possible? She hadn't wanted to kiss or be held by
Corby or any of the other men she knew. She'd

been uninterested in men for so long, she'd begun to wonder if she was too coldhearted to fall in love.

All that had changed with Broc. They worked together nearly all day, but that wasn't enough. When she wasn't with him, she was thinking about him. When she was sleeping, she dreamed about him. When he talked to her about the ranch or the cows, it was all she could do to keep her mind on what he was saying. She didn't understand why any woman would notice his scars when there was so much more of him to appreciate. She felt herself grow warm remembering some of the dreams that had been inspired by his strong arms or powerful thighs. Why would any woman care what kind of clothes he wore when they clothed a body that seemed perfect in every way?

She felt guilty hiding her feelings from her mother, who still insisted Broc was a thief. She was irritated that Corby watched the two of them with the suspicious eyes of a jealous lover. Gary was irritated, Andy angry, and Leo amused. Eddie was just happy to have Broc around. She wondered, not for the first time, why everybody couldn't keep their opinions to themselves.

"There's one."

Amanda came out of her abstraction and turned her gaze in the direction Broc was pointing.

"She has twins," Broc pointed out. "That almost never happens. Let's make a big circle around her. She looks ready to bolt."

The cow eyed Amanda suspiciously, her two calves huddled against her flanks. Amanda decided to ride on the far side of a thick grove of post oak tangled with grapevines. When she did, she found herself

confronting one of Carruthers's men. She recognized
him as the one who'd told Carruthers he wouldn't
help him hang Broc.

He looked behind her, then over his own shoulder.
"What are you doing here?"

"We're after a cow that strayed off our land."

"We? Who's with you?"

"Broc."

"Shit!"

The expletive surprised her.

"Carruthers has ordered us to shoot any of your
men we find on his land. He was especially insistent
that we keep a lookout for Broc."

"We were bringing some of your cows back when
we noticed a few of ours," she explained.

"That won't make any difference to Carruthers."
They had cleared the thicket, and Amanda saw that
Broc had circled the cow and was hazing her back
toward her ranch. "Come with me," the cowboy said
and put his horse into a gallop.

Amanda saw Broc tense, then relax a little when he
saw who was with her.

"Dan," Broc called out. "What are you doing here?"

"We have to hide," Dan replied as soon as he got
close enough for Broc to hear. "There's no time to ask
questions. I'll explain later."

He looked over both shoulders. Amanda didn't see
anybody, but it was clear Dan was expecting someone
very soon. She looked at Broc, but he nodded his head
to indicate they were to follow Dan.

"This isn't the best place," Dan said, "but I don't
have time to find another."

Amanda was unprepared to see Dan gallop his horse toward a post oak thicket about a hundred yards away. It wasn't until their horses' noses were touching the branches that Amanda saw the small break in the trees.

"In there." Dan pointed to the opening. "Don't leave until I come for you. It may be a long time, so just stay put."

Without hesitation, Broc rode his horse through the opening and disappeared into the thicket. Giving Dan one last look, Amanda followed.

What had looked like an impenetrable thicket proved to be quite open once they passed the tangle of vines. The trees provided a canopy so dense that the lower branches had died and fallen off. The ground was covered with damp leaves that muffled the sound of their horses' hooves. Broc motioned her to dismount.

"Hold your hand over your horse's nose so he won't nicker if he scents other horses."

Being careful to move quietly, Broc approached the edge of the thicket.

"Why did you follow Dan without question?" she whispered. "He works for Carruthers."

"I've talked with him a couple of times. I trust him."

"Why did he want us to hide? If he was afraid of what Carruthers might do, why didn't he just tell us to go back?"

"I expect some men he doesn't trust are close enough he thought they might see us."

Amanda wanted to say more, but her horse suddenly jerked his head up. She covered his nostrils just as his belly tightened up for a nicker.

"Somebody's coming," Broc warned.

Keeping a tight hold on her horse, Amanda strained her ears for the slightest sound. She was surprised at the number of little sounds she would never have noticed at any other time. But she wasn't interested in rustling leaves, birds, small rodents, even the breathing of the horses. It wasn't long before she heard approaching horsemen coming from two directions, one from the Lazy T and one from the Carruthers ranch house.

"What are they doing?" she whispered.

He shrugged his shoulders and indicated she wasn't to talk. She suddenly realized why. The riders were approaching the thicket where they were hiding.

Thirteen

"THIS IS A WASTE OF TIME."

"It's what the boss wants, and he's the one paying our wages."

"That guy would be a fool to come back."

"The boss is certain he will. He says he's the type to get in trouble trying to help a woman." The man laughed. "Hell, *I'd* get in trouble, if I could get a piece of that woman."

Amanda felt heat flame in her face, but it was impossible to move away. The speakers were too close.

"I think it's stupid to waste time chasing cows off their land just to tempt them to come after their beeves. I don't like this kind of stuff. I'm thinking about shoving off."

"Why should you care?"

"What do you think, Dan?"

"Not my decision," Dan replied. "I just take orders."

"That's what you ought to do."

"I don't know. I'm getting tired of riding around

looking for chances to make trouble. Besides, I don't see why that lady can't send her hands over to look for stray cows."

"Don't worry about it," Dan said. "They all get sorted out at roundup."

"Then why are we chasing her cows over here?"

"Just to cause trouble," the other guy said.

"Well, I'm fed up with it. She seems like a nice woman. Even the guy ain't too bad."

"Carruthers is just angry the fellow refused to work for him and hired on with that woman instead."

"I'd work for her if she offered me a job."

"You'd be a fool."

"Time you boys get back to work," Dan said.

"Want us to take that cow along with us?"

"No. She's more likely to attract attention if she's close enough for someone to see her."

"Carruthers said chase every cow with calves by that stud bull as far away from her land as we can."

"This cow can't be bait if she's five miles from here."

"Let's go. I'm starting to feel hungry. You coming?"

"Not yet," Dan said. "I want to look around some more."

"Make sure you give a signal if you find him. I don't want to miss the fun."

"You mean like when you caused that fool kid to bust his shoulder?"

"Nobody forced him to lasso that steer."

"Get going," Dan said. "You can argue on your way home."

"Which way did the other hands go?"

"They're making a broad sweep about a mile this side of the creek on their way back to the ranch," Dan told them. "You ought to catch up with them in about ten minutes."

"I'm not riding that hard. My horse will sweat, and I'll have to wash him down."

"You shouldn't mind doing it after he's carried your sorry ass all day."

"Quit bitching and ride," Dan ordered, "or you'll be rubbing down every horse that went out today."

The two men headed off at a canter. Amanda didn't know whether Dan had gone with them until he spoke. "Wait about ten more minutes, and you can leave. Head back toward that row of hills. It's about twice as far that way, but no one will see you."

Amanda wanted to thank him for helping them, but he rode away too quickly. She had some questions she wanted to ask, too, but this wasn't the time.

"That clears up the mystery of why so many cows keep wandering in this direction," Broc said.

"Why would Carruthers chase them off if we get them back at roundup?"

"He doesn't care about the cows, just causing trouble. He's determined to have your ranch, and he'll do anything he can to make that happen. One of the best ways is to make sure you don't have anybody working for you. That's why he's so angry with me."

"Do you think those men would have tried to hang you?"

"No. It's just Carruthers who seems to want me dead."

"Why? I'm sure other men have refused to work for him."

"But they haven't worked for you instead. I think ten minutes have passed. Let me take a look."

Amanda waited until Broc signaled it was safe. She had a lot to think about, but she intended to talk to the sheriff. He had to bring Carruthers to his senses before someone got hurt.

Or killed.

❦

Amanda left the sheriff's office feeling angry and dissatisfied. She'd explained her situation to the sheriff, told him everything Carruthers had done, including running off her stock so he could cause trouble, but the sheriff had told her there was no proof.

"None of his cowhands are going to admit he has told them to run off your cows, intimidate your hands, or threaten to hang Broc Kincaid," the sheriff had said.

"Doesn't my word count for anything?" she'd asked. "Broc, Andy, and Leo will vouch for everything I've said."

"He has more hands than you do, and every one of them could say just the opposite. I will be on the lookout for trouble, but he hasn't done anything I can call him on. When something concrete happens, let me know."

And that's where the sheriff had left it. What use was a sheriff if he couldn't do anything to prevent trouble, only react when it was too late?

"Amanda Liscomb, may I speak to you?"

Amanda turned around to find Priscilla Carruthers

behind her on the boardwalk. She was surprised the girl had spoken to her, since Gary said she was angry at Amanda for accusing her father of causing trouble.

"Sure. What can I do for you?"

Priscilla was a tall girl of nineteen, the same age as Amanda. She had her mother's pretty face and reddish-brown hair combined with her father's imposing height and broad shoulders. She was expensively, though simply, dressed. Her manners were too queenly for Amanda's taste, but she laid responsibility for that at the feet of Priscilla's mother. Today, however, Priscilla looked like a nervous and unsure young woman.

"It's not you exactly," Priscilla said, looking even more uncomfortable. "It's the man who plays the piano for you."

"Broc?" Amanda was so surprised, she was certain she was standing there with her mouth hanging open.

Priscilla nodded. "I heard one of Dad's hands, Dan Walch, saying he played the piano and sang. I want to know if he would help me."

"Help you do what?" Amanda couldn't imagine what Priscilla could want Broc to do. If her father found out she'd even talked to the foreman of the Lazy T, he'd probably lock her up.

Priscilla blushed and lowered her gaze. "I like to sing. My father bought me a piano, but I don't have anyone to play for me."

"I doubt your father would allow Broc on his ranch. He's furious Broc decided to work for me."

"I don't want him to come to the house. Pastor Burns has given me permission to use the church."

"Broc and I don't get into town until evening."

"Papa will let me come in at night as long as he thinks I'm going to the church. We could meet there before he goes to the saloon."

Amanda could tell the girl was eager for some help, but she didn't think it was a good idea for Broc to get involved. Her uneasiness must have shown in her expression.

"I can pay him," Priscilla said. "Papa paid Oscar, and he was awful. I want to sing opera. Mama says I have a good voice, but Papa hates opera and wouldn't let me sing anything but silly songs."

Amanda didn't know much about opera or why Carruthers should hate it, but she did know he would be furious if he found out Broc was helping his daughter.

"I don't think—"

"Please. Just talk to him, tell him what I said."

"I'll tell him, but—"

"All I ask is that he listen to me sing. If he doesn't think I have the voice to sing on a real stage, I won't bother him again."

"Okay, but I can't guarantee he'll help you."

"Dan said Mr. Kincaid used to sing on riverboats." Priscilla's expression turned dreamy. "I'd love to sing for people like that."

Amanda doubted her parents would be happy about that ambition.

"I have my own music." Priscilla laughed. "Papa says it's a terrible waste of money, but Mama says—"

Priscilla's expression changed, and she broke off. Amanda turned to find what had disturbed her and saw Gary hurrying toward them with a face-splitting grin. Her heart sank. It was obvious from Priscilla's expression she didn't want to talk to Gary.

"I went out to your place, but your mama said you'd come into town." Gary spoke directly to Priscilla, ignoring his sister's presence.

"I was talking to your sister, but now I have to go. I still have several errands to run."

"I'll be happy to go with you, carry packages, help you across the street."

"I'm perfectly capable of doing that for myself. You may have noticed I'm a rather big girl."

Priscilla had to be taller than half the men in Cactus Bend, something no woman was likely to consider an advantage.

"A lady shouldn't have to carry her own packages."

Gary ignored the fact that Priscilla had neither returned his smile nor appeared eager to accept his assistance.

"I wouldn't like my father to see you helping me. He's not very happy with your family."

"That has nothing to do with me," Gary said, pressing his case. "I already told him I'd be happy to sell him the ranch. I hate cows."

"I doubt he'd appreciate that attitude either," Amanda pointed out, annoyed that Gary had tried to undermine the family's position.

"Not every man wants to be a rancher," Gary said angrily.

"I'm sure Priscilla's father knows that," Amanda said. "However, since ranching is his chosen profession, I doubt he would approve of your lack of appreciation."

Gary glared angrily at his sister, but Amanda was irritated Gary was practically begging Priscilla to like him. Didn't he have any pride?

Priscilla looked as uncomfortable as Amanda was annoyed. "Papa has Dan Walch accompany me when I ride into town without him or my mother. I see he's through with his business. You don't need to accompany me," she said to Gary. "It's only a short distance." Before he could object, she turned and strode off with a rapid stride more characteristic of a man than a woman.

"I know you couldn't see the foolish expression on your face," Amanda told her brother, "but you could hear the silly words falling out of your mouth."

"I just offered to help carry her shopping. I didn't know that big ox was with her."

"You were virtually begging for the attention of a woman who was looking for a way to refuse without being rude. Face it, Gary, she's not in love with you. She doesn't even like you."

"She does like me," Gary insisted. "I've talked to her hundreds of times. Well, dozens. Anyway, she won't tell me she loves me as long as you and Mama blame her father for everything that goes wrong on the Lazy T. Why can't you leave her father alone? Don't you care anything about my happiness?"

Amanda cared about Gary's happiness, but he wanted to spend his life working in Corby's saloon while Priscilla wanted to go to big cities and sing opera. They had nothing in common. "Of course, I care about your happiness," she said.

"Then why won't you help me with Priscilla?"

"Did you know she wants to sing opera?"

"What's that?"

"She wants to go to cities like Chicago, perform on a big stage, and sing foreign music in a foreign language."

"Why would she do that?" Gary's lack of comprehension would have been funny if it hadn't been so pitiful.

"She probably would have gone to New Orleans or St. Louis by now, but her father won't let her."

"I don't care," Gary declared. "I'll follow her anywhere."

"Mama said opera singers have to go to Europe. Sometimes they stay there."

"Why would she do that? Texas is better than anyplace in Europe."

Amanda sighed. "People like different things. I'm afraid Priscilla doesn't like cows, Cactus Bend, or Texas. Besides, she's two years older than you."

"It doesn't make any difference to me," Gary insisted. "I love her anyway."

Amanda decided she'd said all she could at this time. "If you want some advice from another woman, don't press her too hard. No woman wants to feel she's been pushed into a corner."

"I'm not pushing her. I'll wait for years if I have to."

Amanda hoped her brother would gain a little maturity and perspective in a couple of years. Right now, he was acting as if he were fifteen rather than seventeen.

"Then don't follow her around. Be cheerful, polite, and casual when you run into her. Let her talk about what she's been doing. Let her decide when to end the conversation. If you don't seem too anxious, she'll be more likely to decide she likes you."

Gary looked suspicious. "How do I know you're not telling me all the wrong things? I know you don't like her."

"I like her just fine," Amanda tried to assure him, "but I love you. I don't want you to get hurt."

"What do you know about things like this? You've never been in love. You don't even like Corby."

Amanda thought of the kisses she'd shared with Broc and felt heat flame in her face. Fortunately, Gary was too preoccupied with his own troubles to notice.

"Just because I don't want to marry Corby doesn't mean I know nothing about love."

"How? You've never even kissed anybody."

Amanda didn't think she blushed, but something about her reaction caught Gary's attention.

"You *have* kissed somebody. It's not Corby, because he would have told me."

"I didn't say I'd kissed anyone."

Gary ignored her. "It's got to be somebody new. The only new man in Cactus Bend is Broc, but not even his horse would kiss a face that ugly. You're not sneaking around with the sheriff, are you? I know all you women yammer about how good-looking he is, but he's married."

"I wouldn't kiss Tom Mercer if he were unmarried and the only man in Cactus Bend," Amanda stated emphatically.

"Well, you kissed somebody," Gary said. "You had

guilt written all over your face, and you were just in the sheriff's office."

"If I kissed anyone, it would be a man I cared about very deeply so I'd have no reason to feel guilty."

"Does Ma know?"

His relentless questioning was making Amanda uncomfortable. "There's nothing for anybody to know."

"There's something," Gary insisted. "And I'm going to find out what it is. When I do, I'm going to use it to force you to help me make Priscilla love me."

"You can't make a person to fall in love with you, Gary. It doesn't happen that way. Now I've got to get back to the ranch."

But Amanda didn't have many thoughts to spare for the ranch. She was too busy analyzing her feelings for Broc and coming to the disturbing conclusion she hadn't been entirely truthful to Gary. If she wasn't feeling guilty about kissing Broc, why was she anxious that no one know? Was it possible she was ashamed of kissing someone everyone else considered too ugly to like?

"She says she just wants you to play the piano for her," Amanda said to Broc when they stepped outside the saloon to get a breath of fresh air after performing their first group of songs.

Amanda hadn't seen Broc when she went back to the ranch, and he and Leo hadn't come in from work by the time she had to leave for town. He'd reached the saloon so late, they'd barely had time to choose their songs before it was time to perform.

"She said she would come into town one evening and you could work together before it was time for us to perform. She has permission to use the church. She says she wants to be an opera singer. I don't know anything about opera. Do you?"

"A bit. Can she sing?"

"I don't know. I've never even heard her in church, but she said she'll give up her ambition if you don't think she has the voice to sing on a professional stage."

Broc looked thoughtful, and Amanda found herself prey to an unexpected pang of jealousy. She told herself it was stupid, but that didn't make it go away. She'd never thought of Priscilla as competition, but what if Priscilla did have a fine voice? The other girl would be working with Broc as often as possible. They would have something in common that Amanda couldn't share.

She told herself not to be foolish. Broc was leaving Cactus Bend in a few days, and neither she nor Priscilla was likely to see him again. She ought to get her feelings under control so she wouldn't be hurt when he left.

"I wouldn't mind listening to her, but I'll have to do it soon."

As if she needed a reminder that he would be leaving. "A few of her father's cowhands are in the saloon this evening. I'll see if I can get one of them to tell her to be here tomorrow." She was relieved Broc didn't seem eager.

"What are you doing out here?" Corby had apparently come looking for them when he realized they weren't in the saloon.

"We came out for some fresh air," Broc said. "All that cigar smoke is bad for Amanda's voice."

"It hasn't bothered her before now," Corby said.

"How would you know when you've never heard her sing in better conditions?"

"Her voice sounds fine to me. It always has." Corby looked at Amanda as if he expected some sort of praise.

"It would sound better if she didn't have to wait on tables when she wasn't singing."

"The men come here because they like to see her. They don't really care if she sings or not."

"If they didn't care, you wouldn't be paying her more to sing," Broc said. "We won't stay out here long, but she needs to clear her lungs."

"That smoke can't be any worse for her than the dust at the ranch," Corby said. "I end up coughing and sneezing every time I go out there."

"Then I would suggest that you stay in town where you're safe."

Amanda tried to hide her amusement at Corby's irritation. "I'd live on that ranch all the time if Amanda would marry me. I'm so crazy about her I'd even learn to like cows."

Amanda nearly laughed. Corby would die of boredom in less than a week.

"It's time to sing again," Corby announced. "The men are getting restless."

"Are you ready?" Broc asked Amanda.

She nodded and led the way back into the saloon.

The next twenty minutes went by quickly. Amanda couldn't believe how easy it was to sing when Broc played or how much she enjoyed it when he sang duets with her. She moved among the tables trying to pay a little attention to each man so no one would feel overlooked. The only thing she refused to do was dance with the men whenever Broc played a lively number. She couldn't stand the thought of any man's arms around her except Broc's.

She noticed Dan Walch was in the saloon this evening. She didn't remember having spotted him before, but she hadn't forgotten that he'd helped her and Broc avoid being caught by Carruthers's men. She decided to ask him to take the message to Priscilla, so when she finished her last song, she worked her way over to where he was leaning against the bar. When the applause died down, she turned to him. "I wanted to thank you for what you did for me and for Broc," she said in a voice she hoped was soft enough that it wouldn't be overheard. "I realize it could have gotten you into a lot of trouble."

He nodded his head, looked uncomfortable, and glanced to where some of Carruthers's men were seated at a table together.

Amanda wondered why he wasn't sitting with the other men and why he seemed so uncomfortable. "I want you to take a message to Priscilla Carruthers for me." Dan's mood immediately went from uneasy to agitated.

"I'm sorry," Dan said, "but I can't do that."

Amanda wondered if there was some reason for his refusal. She didn't want to get anyone in trouble with Carruthers. He could be dangerous when crossed.

"That's all right. I'll ask someone else."

"It's not that," Dan said. "I need to talk to you and Broc."

"Why?"

"I know where to find your missing cows."

Fourteen

"I don't know where Dan is," Amanda told Broc. "He just said he'd meet us, then left the saloon. I didn't see him again."

They were two miles out of town, about three miles from the ranch. Amanda would much rather have been riding her horse, but her mother still insisted that she continue to use the buggy.

"I only talked to him a couple of times," Broc said. "But he seemed like an honest man."

She wanted to think he was, but she couldn't completely trust anyone who worked for Carruthers. "Why would he say he wanted to meet us, then not show up? Why would he say he knows where our cows are if he doesn't?"

"I don't know," Broc said. "Something must have happened."

If he'd asked them to meet him at a special place, she might have suspected a trap, but he hadn't. One of the other men had been eager to take the message to Priscilla, so that wasn't the problem.

"I wish he hadn't said anything," Amanda said. "I

couldn't think about anything else all evening." She noticed a horseman a good way up the trail. "Do you think that's him?" she asked Broc.

"We'll know in a few minutes."

Apparently Dan felt it was safer to meet them where it was unlikely anyone else might see them together. "I thought you weren't coming," she said when he fell in beside them.

"Are you in any danger?" Broc asked.

"I would be if Carruthers had any idea what I'm doing."

"He wasn't in the saloon tonight." She wouldn't have missed him. He always insisted that she wait on him.

"But some of his men were. Two of them even followed me out, anxious to know what I'd said to keep you talking to me so long." His laugh was mirthless. "They wanted to try the same thing."

"Where are our cows?" she asked.

"On a bit of low land on the far side of the ranch."

"How did you find out where they were?"

"I've known where they were for some time, but today Carruthers told me to round up a crew and start branding the calves...with his brand."

"That's the same as rustling," Amanda exclaimed.

"Carruthers doesn't care," Dan said. "All he can think about is getting your land and that bull."

"When does he intend to start the branding?" Broc asked.

"Tomorrow."

"Then we need to get the cows tonight."

"There's no way you can drive that many cows

back on your ranch before morning. If Carruthers caught you with them, I wouldn't put it past him to shoot you and have the men swear you were stealing his cows."

"What do you suggest?" Broc asked.

"You and Amanda need to ride into town first thing in the morning and bring the sheriff. I'll do what I can to put off the branding until you all show up."

"Amanda doesn't need my help to bring the sheriff," Broc said.

"Don't think about coming on the ranch by yourself," Dan warned. "Carruthers hates you more than ever. If I didn't know better, I'd swear he knew you were on the ranch today. The men aren't crazy enough to shoot you for trespassing, but I wouldn't put it past Carruthers."

"Are you sure you can hold things up long enough for us to get there?" Broc asked.

"I think so. Carruthers likes to give orders, but he doesn't like to do the work, especially when it's hot, nasty work like branding and castrating."

"I'll go back to town now and wake the sheriff," Amanda said.

"Don't," Dan said.

"Why?"

Amanda thought Broc sounded a bit distrustful.

"The sheriff won't take any stand against Carruthers without hearing his side first," Dan explained. "If he does that, it will give Carruthers time to move those cows. We might not find them again. I'd better be going. I'm already going to have to answer a lot of questions about where I've been for the last couple of hours."

"You got a good excuse?" Broc asked.

Dan grinned. "Yeah. I'm seeing a girl."

Amanda was surprised. Cactus Bend wasn't that large. She'd have thought she would know if Dan was seeing anyone in town. "I gather she doesn't live in town."

"I'm not telling," Dan said. "A man needs a few secrets. Don't forget to be in town early. The boss is an early riser."

"I always thought Carruthers was behind all our trouble," Amanda said as she watched Dan ride off into the night. "Now we'll be able to prove it. We'll take Leo with us. With four of us against him, Carruthers won't dare to try anything."

"There'll be just three of you," Broc said. "I'll be hidden out of sight, keeping an eye on those cows when the sun comes up."

❧

"Here, let me," Leo said to Amanda. "If the sheriff sleeps like Andy, it'll take a mule kick to wake him."

Leo pounded the door with his fist. Amanda hated to wake the sheriff's wife or his young children, but her need was too urgent to worry about that this morning. If she failed to convince the sheriff that her neighbor was trying to brand her calves, Broc would have to face Carruthers and his men alone.

A very sleepy and very angry sheriff yanked the door open.

"What in hell do you mean by banging on my door at this hour of the morning?"

"Carruthers has stolen more than a hundred of our

cows," she told the sheriff. "He's going to start brand-ing the calves this morning."

The sheriff's expression was filled with disbelief. "We've been over this before. You've got no proof of your accusations."

Amanda put out her hand to keep him from closing the door. "I'm not asking you to arrest him, just go with me to where the cows are being held."

"I can't go traipsing all over his ranch looking for a few cows. Do you have any idea how much range Carruthers controls?"

"I know where the cows are, but it will take us a couple of hours to get there."

The sheriff sighed in frustration. "You just won't listen, will you? I don't have any evidence, and I can't take your word he's got the cows because you're not an impartial witness."

"Do you consider Dan Walch an impartial witness?"

"Yes, but he's Carruthers's foreman."

"Dan told me Carruthers had ordered him to start branding the calves today. He promised to hold off as long as he could."

"When did he tell you this?"

"Last night. He came to the saloon but didn't want to talk there. He met Broc and me when we were halfway home."

The sheriff looked thoughtful. "I did see him leave town early. I spoke to him, but he wasn't in a talking mood."

"That's because he didn't want to do what Carruthers said. He's helped us once before."

"When was that?"

"I'll tell you on our way," Amanda said. "We've got to leave now."

"I'll need to dress, eat, saddle my horse, stop by the office to—"

"I've got a horse already saddled and some hot biscuits and sausage you can eat on the way. I'll write a note for your deputy while you dress. If we're not there in time, Carruthers might try to kill Broc again."

"Again? Only a crazy man would try anything like that."

"Carruthers just might be crazy."

⬥

Comfortably settled in his hiding place, Broc glanced up at the sun, trying to gauge the time, wondering who would show up first. Amanda had said she'd be in town before the sheriff had his breakfast. Even if she could convince Mercer to leave immediately, Broc doubted they would arrive before Carruthers and his men, which was why he'd been determined to be here before dawn. Come hell or high water, he was going to make sure no calves were branded before the sheriff arrived.

Broc didn't know why Carruthers was so eager to claim the water and grass on the Lazy T ranch. A nearby creek provided enough water to create a small lake and an extensive marsh area populated by at least a dozen kinds of songbirds. He had watched a pair of osprey circle and dive for fish. A snowy egret shuffled through shallow water in an effort to frighten prey out of hiding. A careless bullfrog had settled himself on a lily pad to catch insects skimming over the water. In the pale light of dawn three deer had emerged from a blackjack and post oak thicket to drink from one of the shallow inlets. The stolen cows had long since begun to graze. Their calves, having fed and frolicked, were now lazing in the morning sun. It seemed impossible that such a pastoral scene could soon be the setting for a potentially deadly showdown.

Not for the first time he wondered about the wisdom of the Liscombs trying to hold on to their ranch. With her father dead, Gary gone, and Eddie too young, most of the work and all the responsibility would devolve on Amanda. What she needed was a husband.

A husband like Broc.

He had tried to prevent that thought from crystallizing in his mind, but, aided by the kisses they'd shared, it had assumed a life of its own. He still couldn't accustom himself to the fact that she had allowed him to kiss her, or that she kissed him back. He'd spent too many years convincing himself no woman would want to be with him, much less welcome his embraces. Yet it had happened again and again. Each time made him more eager for the next opportunity. More than once he'd had to force his brain to stop searching for ways and times for them to be alone and pay attention to his work. He was starting to get questioning glances from Leo.

The more time he spent with Amanda, the less he was able to imagine his life without her. Whether they were working on the ranch or in the saloon, they had formed a connection that kept them attuned to each other. It had shown up first in their duets, when, even though they had their backs to each other most of the time, they sang as though they'd practiced together for weeks. They slowed together, swelled the tone together, even emphasized the same words. To him, it seemed proof they were meant to be together.

The sound of approaching horses broke his train of thought. It was impossible to tell until they came into sight, but it sounded like about a half dozen men were approaching. Broc had left his horse on the other side of an oak thicket so there wouldn't be any danger of the animal's giving away his hiding place. The men were here earlier than Broc had anticipated, but he believed Dan would find a way to hold up the branding operation until Amanda and the sheriff arrived.

That hope was shattered when, one by one, the riders crested a small rise about a hundred yards away. Earl Carruthers was the first rider to come into view.

Broc had to do some rapid recalculation. Dan couldn't delay the branding indefinitely with Carruthers in charge. That meant Broc might have to try to stop it, but how could he do so by himself? Even if he could count on Dan, his one gun couldn't be depended on to stop the seven men who would be against him. It certainly wouldn't stop Carruthers.

Nor could he take it for granted he would be safe if he went unarmed. Under normal circumstances, no one would shoot an unarmed man, but he couldn't be sure about Carruthers. The man seemed unswayed by law or common sense. Broc would just have to watch and make his decision at the last minute.

As the riders came closer, Broc could see that Dan was arguing with Carruthers, and Carruthers was yelling at Dan. About the only words Broc could hear clearly were profane. He tensed when he realized they were headed straight for the thicket where he was hiding; at least there were no hoofprints to give him away. It had been dark when he rode in, but he'd been careful to approach from the side away from Carruthers's ranch.

"Stop worrying," Carruthers told Dan. The riders slowed as they drew closer. "Nobody's going to know."

"What about the sheriff?"

"He knows which side his bread is buttered on."

"He's not going to protect a rustler. Every cowman in the state would be after his head if he did."

"Nobody's going to touch him without my say-so."

"Rustling is a hanging offense. They'll be after your head, too."

"Nobody's going to lift a finger against me. I'm too rich."

Broc had seen that attitude in a few men before the war. Since then it seemed to be growing more prevalent, especially in the parts of the West where the law was ineffectual or nonexistent. Powerful men like Carruthers seemed to feel that they could do anything they wanted. They would have to be controlled—or eliminated—if the West was to become a safe place for ordinary people to live and raise a family.

"What you're doing will endanger these men as well." Dan gestured to the six men who, having brought their horses into a tight group, were carefully listening to him. "You may be too rich and powerful to be arrested, but we aren't. We'll be the ones actually wrestling the calves down and slapping your branding iron on them. We'll be the ones the sheriff arrests."

Carruthers dismounted and signaled to the men to follow. "Nobody's going to be arrested." He glanced around. "This looks like a good place. There's enough blow down around this thicket for the fire, and the ground is dry. You ought to be done with the branding in a couple of days, but take more time if you need it."

"This is crazy," Dan said. "Anybody taking just one look at calves wearing different brands from their mamas will know they're stolen."

"I'm not stupid," Carruthers shouted. "We'll drive the cows back to their range once the calves are weaned." His laugh was a high-pitched, unnatural sound. "Maybe I won't take the Lazy T just yet. It might be more profitable to keep taking half her calves. In a few years, I'll have so many young bulls I won't need her stud. *Then* I'll take the ranch."

Broc couldn't believe Carruthers was so confident he was beyond the reach of the law that he would outline his criminal activity in front of seven people.

"What if somebody sees these cows before then?" Dan asked.

"Nobody will dare set foot on my range."

"But what if somebody does?"

"You'll kill him. Dead men carry no tales."

"You can't shoot people just for crossing your range."

"I'll say they were trying to steal my cows. That's a hanging offense, so nobody will care if they're already dead."

"I'm not shooting anybody."

"You'll follow orders just like the rest. Now let's get started before it's too hot. You," Carruthers said, pointing to two men, "start gathering wood. I'll need enough to last the whole day. Dan and I will heat the irons and brand the calves. The rest of you start rounding them up."

Broc backed deeper inside the thicket so there wouldn't be any chance the men gathering wood would see him. In the meantime, he listened to Dan put forth one argument after another. Carruthers ignored everything Dan said. He appeared so focused on heating the branding irons, he didn't seem to notice he was doing all the work while Dan did nothing. If this ever went to court, Dan couldn't be accused of participating.

"The irons will soon be ready," Carruthers told Dan. "Tell the men to start roping the calves."

"I've got to ask you again not to do this," Dan said. "It can only end up being bad for everybody."

Carruthers appeared to lose control of his temper. He waved his fists in the air and got so agitated, his face turned dark from the force of his anger. He made Broc think of one of his younger brothers who used to throw a tantrum when he didn't get his way.

"Nothing is going to happen to anybody!" Carruthers shouted. "Now stop talking and take one of these branding irons. Sully will have that calf on the ground any minute now."

"I'm not picking up one of those irons," Dan stated. "I'm not going to brand any calves that I know don't belong to you."

Carruthers let out a strangled shout of anger, yanked one of the red-hot branding irons from the fire, and turned on Dan, waving the rod like a weapon.

Dan evaded Carruthers's attack, then moved in to get a grip on the man's wrists and hold them immobile.

Unfortunately he didn't have eyes in the back of his head to see one of the men sneak up behind him, pick up a rock, and hit him over the head. Dan crumpled into a heap on the ground.

"Son of a bitch!" Carruthers said. "He turned on me."

The men, shocked by the unexpected turn of events, had frozen into a tableau.

"Shoot him," Carruthers shouted to the man with the rock. "Shoot him and throw his body into the marsh."

The man froze.

"Shoot him!" Carruthers screamed. "I want him dead."

"I don't have a gun," the man stammered.

Broc wondered if he would have shot Dan if he *had* had a gun.

"Any one of you got a gun?" Carruthers asked the other men.

One by one they shook their heads. Apparently thinking they were only going to brand calves, none of the men had come armed.

"You're all spineless, useless bastards. If your mothers could see you now, they'd be ashamed they gave you birth. Looks like I have to do it myself."

When he strode over to where his horse stood munching on the rich grass, and yanked his rifle from its scabbard, Broc knew the decision about what to do had been made for him. Pushing aside the foliage blocking his sight, he took careful aim with his own rifle and fired.

Carruthers's weapon exploded into three pieces

and flew from his hands. Everyone knew the shot had come from within the oak thicket, so Broc had no option but to show himself.

"You!" Carruthers exclaimed when he saw Broc. "I'll kill you for being on my land. Shoot him!" Carruthers shouted at his men, apparently forgetting they'd already told him they were unarmed. "Shoot him! He tried to kill me."

"If that's what I'd meant to do, you'd be dead instead of acting like a crazy man. I just wanted to stop you from shooting Dan."

"I have another rifle."

Carruthers turned to where his horse had been, but the rifle shot had caused the animal to run off.

"You're not going anywhere," Broc told him. "Amanda knows where we are and what you intend to do. She and Leo are bringing the sheriff."

The announcement appeared to make no impact on Carruthers, but it had an immediate effect on his men. The man who had wrestled a roped calf to the ground jumped up to let the animal scramble to its feet. A second cowhand released the pressure on his rope, which allowed the calf to shrug off the lasso and run bawling to its mama. A third cowhand released his calf. The others backed away from the animals they were holding in a tight circle. In a matter of seconds the scene had changed from one of a branding to men sitting their horses. The only evidence of what was meant to happen was the fire and the still red-hot branding irons.

Broc knew that would be enough. Carruthers recovered enough from his rage to realize that, too.

"Scatter the fire and throw the branding irons in the marsh," he ordered.

"No one is going to touch that fire until the sheriff gets here," Broc said.

"Rush him," Carruthers ordered. "Without the fire, there's no evidence against you."

The last word was hardly out of his mouth before Carruthers turned and started running after his horse. It was clear Carruthers didn't intend to be caught in case the sheriff really did show up. Broc had a decision to make: did he keep the men covered and allow Carruthers to get away, or did he go after Carruthers and let the men get away? He didn't know if he could trust them to be more concerned about their own skins than Carruthers's anger, but he couldn't allow the boss to get away. He started after Carruthers.

Running in boots was hell, but Broc ignored the pain. What he couldn't ignore was that Carruthers had gotten a good head start and was incredibly fast for a man his age. If Broc didn't do something, he might get to his horse before Broc reached him. Hoping he hadn't lost the accuracy he'd gained playing darts with rich men on riverboats, Broc threw his rifle at Carruthers's feet. His luck held. The rifle struck one leg, causing the rifle to spin and catch the other leg. Carruthers hit the ground hard.

Broc was on him before he could get to his feet.

Carruthers wasn't ready to give up. He did his best to hit or kick Broc. Neither scratching nor biting was beyond the man. Broc finally wrestled him flat on the ground, face pushed into the grass, and locked his arms behind his back.

"I'll kill you for this," Carruthers threatened in a muffled voice.

Broc ignored his threat.

Much to Broc's dismay, when he looked back Carruthers's men were busy scattering the fire. He didn't know how he could prove Carruthers had meant to brand stolen calves, but he would think of something.

Apparently Carruthers could see well enough to realize what his men were doing, because he laughed. "You might as well let me up. It's over."

Broc sighed in relief when he saw a horse's nose appear above the crest of the nearby hill. It was immediately followed by Amanda, Leo, and the sheriff. "No, it's not," Broc said to Carruthers. "The sheriff is here. Even if your men have scattered most of the evidence, there's still enough to convict you."

"It won't matter what they find. They'll never convict me of rustling."

Broc couldn't believe the man would continue to pretend innocence. If nothing else, Dan could testify to what his boss had intended to do.

"None of my men moved a single one of those cows. Gary Liscomb brought them here. Even Dan Walch will testify to that."

Fifteen

At first Broc didn't believe him. He couldn't understand why Gary would do such a thing, but then the sinking feeling in the pit of his stomach made him reconsider. Gary wished his mother would sell the ranch. He hated it so much he'd quit rather than continue to work on the Lazy T. Then there was his obsession with Priscilla Carruthers. How far would he go to win favor with Priscilla and her father?

"Let me up," Carruthers said. "I'm not going to leave now that you have nothing to hold against me."

No one could remove the scorched spot where the men had built the fire. The ground would still be warm. With some effort, the sheriff could probably recover at least one of the branding irons from the marsh, but no one could prove they'd been intended for use today. The fire could be explained as a way to heat coffee. Cowhands needed coffee to drink almost as much as they needed air to breathe.

Broc got up off Carruthers and started toward the site of the fire. He was more worried about Dan. Amanda and the sheriff rode up as he was helping Dan sit up. Amanda looked around, obviously confused by what she saw.

"Amanda told me Carruthers was going to brand her calves." The sheriff looked around. "I don't see any cows."

"They were here a few minutes ago," Broc said, "but Carruthers's men drove them off when they realized you were on your way." He pointed to the scorched place on the ground. "They scattered the fire and threw the branding irons into the marsh. The ground is still warm."

"He's lying," Carruthers called out to the sheriff as he approached. "He was hiding in those trees. I'm sure he would have run off my cows if we hadn't found him."

"I couldn't run off cows that aren't here." Broc's sweeping gesture took in the panorama of the empty prairie.

Carruthers acted as if Broc hadn't spoken. "He tried to kill me when I told my men to run him off." He pointed to the pieces of his rifle. "Any one of them will tell you he did that when he shot at me."

"I can produce a half dozen men who will testify that I can shoot the heart out of a card at a hundred feet," Broc said. "I can prove it right now if you'll hold up a card." Carruthers didn't seem anxious to volunteer. "I shot that rifle out of your hands to keep you from killing Dan while he was unconscious."

Dan stopped rubbing the back of his head and directed a startled glance at Carruthers. "You were going to kill me?" he asked in disbelief.

Carruthers pointed at Dan. "He hooked up with

Kincaid to rustle my cows. One of my men knocked him out when he attacked me."

"You attacked me with a branding iron when I refused to brand Lazy T calves." Dan turned on the assembled cowhands, who were watching warily. "It shouldn't take more than a day to find out which one of you knocked me out. If you're smart, you'll be gone before then." The guilty cowhand flinched. Dan started to laugh. "I should have known it was you, Lakey. You'd empty the pockets of a passed-out drunk."

"Lakey deserves a reward for coming to my rescue," Carruthers said, "and he'll get one. I take care of hands who ride for the brand."

The sheriff turned to Amanda. "I don't see any evidence Carruthers was going to brand your calves."

"Both Broc and Dan will testify that he was."

"My men will testify I wasn't," Carruthers countered.

"Don't waste your time," Broc said to Amanda. "They're not going to incriminate themselves." He turned to the sheriff. "I realize you don't have the proof you need to arrest Carruthers, but you will have to agree that the circumstances look suspicious. If you'll ride around a bit before you leave, you will find plenty of Lazy T cows in this area. If you don't look around," Broc added when it was clear the sheriff didn't believe a word Broc said, "you'll be neglecting your duty to investigate any allegation of rustling or illegal branding. When it comes out that this is exactly what has been happening and that you ignored it, you will be as guilty as Carruthers."

"I'm not guilty of anything. Gary brought his cows here," Carruthers told the sheriff. "My men had nothing to do with it."

"I was against keeping them here," Dan said, "but Gary said Sandoval had been stealing any cow that dropped a calf by the stud bull."

Amanda looked so horrified, so nearly destroyed, Broc ached to take her in his arms, to tell her it wasn't true, but he couldn't. He would have enjoyed pounding Gary's head against a wall until the boy came to his senses, but that wouldn't help things now.

"I don't see any proof that Mr. Carruthers or any of his men were attempting to brand calves, his or anyone else's," the sheriff said to Amanda. "Since your brother was the one who brought your cows here, there's no point in my looking around. There's nothing I can do." His expression hardened. "This is the last time I let you involve me in an attempt to incriminate Mr. Carruthers. It won't do you any good to object," he said when Amanda started to speak. "I won't listen to anything you say. Now I think it's best if you take your men and leave Mr. Carruthers's range."

"Take this turncoat with you," Carruthers said, pointing at Dan. "I won't answer for what will happen to him if he's not cleared out of the bunkhouse by the time I get home."

"Don't bother," Dan said. "I was going to quit anyway."

❧

Amanda slapped him as hard as she could.

"What's wrong with you?" Gary demanded as he

grabbed hold of Corby's desk to keep from losing his balance. "Have you gone crazy?" Instead of answering him, Amanda slapped him again. Broc stepped forward when Gary drew his arm back to punch Amanda.

"Lay one finger on your sister, and I'll break both your arms."

"She hit me."

"You're lucky. If you were my brother, I'd have castrated you."

"I know you don't like working on the ranch," Amanda said, her breath unsteady from anger and exertion, "but I would never have believed you would intentionally try to ruin your own family by giving our cows to Carruthers."

Gary blanched. "I didn't—"

"Don't attempt to deny it," Broc said. "All of Carruthers's cowhands backed him up."

Cornered, Gary changed his story. "I was afraid Sandoval would steal them. I knew Carruthers would keep them safe."

Amanda rolled her eyes. "I can't believe I'm related to anyone stupid enough to believe that."

"It's more likely he was trying to ingratiate himself with Carruthers so his daughter would pay him some attention," Broc said to Amanda before turning to Gary. "Do you realize Carruthers was going to put his brand on all the calves this morning? If we hadn't stopped him, by this time they would have been his."

"But because you put the cows on his land, the sheriff couldn't do anything about it," his sister told him. "Because you cut the ground out from under us, the sheriff won't believe anything I say in the future."

"The only good thing to come out of this is that we found the cows and were able to get most of them back," Broc said. "You have to help us find the rest of them."

"You can't make me," Gary said.

"Then the sheriff will," Amanda said. "He's not happy that you caused all this trouble."

"Carruthers won't let you on his land."

"He will because it's the only way he can clear his name of suspicion," Broc replied. "And he means to do that so he can keep on trying to ruin your family."

"He's not trying to ruin us," Gary declared. "He just wants to buy the ranch. If you would stop trying to pin everything on him—"

"Then what?" Amanda asked. "Priscilla would fall in love with you for solving her father's problems, you'd be married in a huge wedding with all the town invited, and you'd live happily ever after with at least a dozen perfect children to perpetuate the Liscomb heritage?"

Gary's expression turned mulish. "I don't see why you think that should be so impossible."

"It's impossible because she's not interested."

"If you'd stop blaming her father for everything, maybe she wouldn't run away every time I try to speak to her."

"Well, I can't blame her father for everything now, can I? I have to blame my own brother instead."

Gary had the grace to look chagrined. "If I had thought Carruthers was going to put his brand on our calves, I wouldn't have taken them to him."

"No, you'd have taken them to Sandoval instead. Do you hate the ranch that much?"

"Yes!" The word exploded from Gary. "I begged Pa not to buy it. Hell, he didn't know any more about ranching than the rest of us. It probably would have failed anyway."

"It's not going to fail," Amanda said. "I'm not going to let it."

"How are you going to do that?"

Before Amanda could answer, the door opened and Corby entered the room. "What's going on in here? I can hear the shouting in the saloon."

"They're having a family conference," Broc told him.

"Then what are you doing here?"

"I asked him to be here," Amanda said.

"Why? He's just a stranger in town for a few days."

"I asked him because he's my foreman."

Corby took the news so badly that if his hair hadn't been greased down, it might have stood on end. "Why didn't you tell me you'd hired a foreman? I told you I'd take care of everything."

"Only if I married you," Amanda reminded him, "but I'm not ready to get married."

"When will you be ready?"

"I have no idea."

Broc noticed faint spots of color bloom in her cheeks. Did that mean she *had* been thinking about marriage, maybe to him? That seemed too much to hope for, but those spots of color had to mean something.

"I don't want him in my office," Corby said, indicating Broc.

"Why?" Amanda asked.

"I don't trust him. He tried to steal money from

you. How do I know he won't try to steal from me? I sometimes have large sums in my safe."

From the way Corby preened, Broc decided he'd said that to demonstrate how important he was.

"I'll wait for you outside," Broc told Amanda.

"You're scheduled to perform in about ten minutes," Corby reminded him.

"I'll just step out the back door for some fresh air. I like to clear my lungs before I wade into that gray haze."

"I'm leaving," Amanda said. "If I stay here, I'll be too upset to sing."

"Get back to the bar," Corby told Gary. "Gil needs help. The place always gets crowded when it's time for Amanda to sing."

Gary left the room as quickly as possible.

"You ought to ask for a percentage of the bar," Broc said to Amanda. "Those men wouldn't be here if it weren't for you."

"You'll have to start doing more if you want to keep them here," Corby said, anxious to avoid any discussion of paying Amanda more money. "The other saloons are getting their own singers."

"Not as good or as pretty as Amanda," Broc reminded him.

"No, but they're more friendly with the customers."

Amanda swelled with indignation. "I refuse to allow anyone to take liberties with me."

"I don't want you to," Corby assured her. "I'm just telling you there's competition."

"No one plays as well as Broc," Amanda said, "or sings duets like he does."

"I know that," Corby said, "but I'm paying you a lot of money to keep the customers here."

"I think we can come up with something," Broc said. "Give us a couple of days."

"Good. Now it's time to sing."

❧

"I hear you're going to search Carruthers's range," Dan said to Broc. He'd been standing at the bar all through the evening, but he only spoke to Broc outside. "I'm surprised he agreed."

"He didn't have much choice after the sheriff changed his mind about looking for Lazy T cows."

"You know he won't give up, don't you?"

"I never expected he would. What are you doing now?" Everybody in Cactus Bend knew Carruthers had ordered Dan off his range.

"Just hanging around. Would you like to ride with someone who knows that range better than Carruthers himself?"

Broc admitted to being a bit surprised. "You offering yourself?"

"Who else would I be offering?"

"The way Carruthers feels about you now will be nothing compared to the way he'll react if he thinks you're working for Amanda."

"I don't care what he does."

"You got a reason for putting your neck in a noose?"

Dan laughed. "Yeah, I have a reason, several of them, but I'm not sharing more than to say I want to see that Amanda gets a fair chance to find her cows. You know Carruthers will cause as much trouble as he can."

"Then the best way you can help would be to convince the sheriff to ride along with us. Our credibility isn't too high with him right now."

"Sorry, but I thought Amanda knew about Gary bringing the cows. He said it was her idea."

"Gary is a proven liar. The sheriff isn't sure about Amanda and me."

"I think I know a few things that might convince him to give Carruthers a closer look," Dan said.

"I gather you're not sharing those things, either."

Dan laughed. "Maybe one of these days."

"From your expression, it all has something to do with a woman."

"I'm leaving. A few more minutes, and you'll know everything without me saying a word."

Broc didn't know everything, but he was certain of one thing. Dan had the look of a man in love. Broc knew because that's the way he felt.

❧

Carruthers's men were fanned out like a cordon with Carruthers astride his mount about ten yards in front. Broc was relieved Dan had been able to talk the sheriff into joining them.

"What are you doing here, sheriff?" Carruthers asked. Broc could tell he was thrown off balance by the sheriff's presence.

"I know it makes a rancher nervous to have strangers riding all over his land. I thought it would be best if I came along to make sure these folks don't do anything to upset you or your cows."

Broc didn't know what Dan had told the sheriff,

but this was a very different approach from the one he'd taken just the day before.

"I don't want to put you to any bother," Carruthers said. "Me and my boys can take care of things."

"I'm sure you can," the sheriff replied, "but I'd appreciate it if you'd let me ride along for a while. I used to be a cowhand. Once in a while I miss it."

The sheriff was making it hard for Carruthers to refuse.

"I know you've got a tough job," Carruthers said. "I don't want the citizens of Cactus Bend to blame me for keeping you from your work if something terrible was to happen back in town."

"I got two deputies who can handle anything I can," the sheriff said.

"I'm sure they can, but nobody respects them the same way they do you."

The sheriff turned his head a little to the side and stared at Carruthers for a moment. "You wouldn't be trying to keep *me* off your range, would you?"

Carruthers's temper slipped out of control. The muscles in his face contorted, his skin grew dark, and his eyes flashed what looked like uncontrollable rage. "I don't want anybody on my range," he exploded, "especially those two." He stabbed a finger at Broc, then at Dan. "Get them out of here now."

The sheriff waited a moment. Broc presumed he was as curious about the change in Carruthers as he was. The man's color faded, his muscles relaxed, and the fire in his eyes dimmed until only a tiny spark remained.

"Broc is the Lazy T foreman," the sheriff said. "It's his job to take responsibility for any cows we find.

Since no one other than your crew knows anything about your range, Dan has volunteered to make sure we don't get lost. You've got a lot of land out there."

"I've ordered my men to ride with them every step of the way," Carruthers said. "They put a rope on even one of my cows, and I'm hanging them for rustling."

"If you don't have anything else to say, I need to—"

Carruthers cut the sheriff off in midsentence. "I'm warning you," he said to Broc and Dan. "Step one foot wrong, and you're dead men."

"As I was about to say," the sheriff continued, "I think it would be a good idea if everyone gave up their guns."

Broc had noticed all of Carruthers's cowhands were armed today.

"My men are not giving up their guns on my own land." Carruthers glared at Dan.

"They won't need them with me here."

"What about when you leave?"

"I'll be here all day. Have one of your men collect their guns."

That was welcome news to Broc.

"You can't force me to ride without a gun on my own land," Carruthers shouted.

"I'm asking," the sheriff said.

"And I'm refusing for me and my men."

But his men had already started giving up their weapons and didn't look eager to take them back. Broc thought Carruthers looked angry enough to shoot the whole bunch. He'd be glad when this roundup was over.

"You have an incredible voice," Broc said to Priscilla. "I was so flabbergasted I could hardly play."

Priscilla looked so thrilled, Broc was afraid she might start crying with happiness.

"I've seen you in church, but I've never heard you sing," Amanda said.

"Papa doesn't like me to sing where anybody can hear me."

Broc was so tired, he had half hoped Priscilla wouldn't show up. Their day of rounding up strays had been one of the most difficult and tension-filled of his life. With Dan's help, they'd located most of the missing cattle quickly. There were so many, the sheriff had enlisted some of Carruthers's men to drive them back to Lazy T range. That was just one of the things that had caused Carruthers to fall into a rage.

Carruthers had stayed with them the entire day, badgering the sheriff, haranguing his men, and threatening Broc and Dan. Amanda was the only one spared his verbal abuse, but some of the looks Carruthers directed toward her were nearly as hate-filled as those he reserved for Broc and Dan. It got so bad, the sheriff had to position himself between Carruthers and the Lazy T riders. Dan had insisted that they ride to every part of the range where he'd seen Lazy T cows. It appeared that all of those cows had simply strayed from one range to another as longhorns usually did, but for some reason seeing them rounded up and headed back to their home range infuriated Carruthers more than the hundred or so that Gary had moved.

"I never touched that bull," he'd shouted when

Amanda demanded an explanation of why cows bearing Carruthers's brand had calves by her stud bull. "I can't help it if he gets out and breeds with my cows."

Amanda had been left without a leg to stand on because the bull *had* gotten out several times. Broc figured Gary was responsible for that, too.

Carruthers's parting shot had been a demand that he and his men be allowed to search the Lazy T. That meant tomorrow would probably be just as tense and tiring as today. Fortunately, the sheriff had said he'd ride with them again. That news had plunged Carruthers into another fit of rage. It was a testament to how desperate Priscilla was to sing that she'd come into town.

"Do you really think my voice is good enough for the professional stage?"

"Your voice is good enough for just about anything you want to do," Broc said, "but you need a lot of training. You sing like you don't know what to do with your voice."

"Will you help me?" Priscilla asked.

"I'll do what I can to help you get used to your voice and get it under control. Once your voice is in shape—it's a lot like being in shape to ride, run, or do anything physically strenuous—you'll need to find a vocal teacher who can prepare you for the kind of career you want. Do you have something else you want to sing?"

Broc couldn't understand why Carruthers didn't realize his daughter had a truly remarkable talent. How could any father hear that voice and not realize his daughter had been blessed with an outstanding gift?

The note she was holding now was like liquid gold. It poured from her with such ease, with such full-bodied resonance, he wanted to stop playing and just listen. Amanda sat with her eyes closed, an expression of wonder on her face, as Priscilla's voice soared in the little church and—

The sound of doors being flung open caused Priscilla's voice to break off with a squawk. Broc turned to see Carruthers striding down the center of the church, a look of pure fury on his face.

Sixteen

"HOW DARE YOU DISOBEY ME!" CARRUTHERS SHOUTED. "I'll flay the hide off you for this."

Broc had seen Carruthers angry, but he'd never seen the man like this. It took only one glance at her father to turn Priscilla from a smiling, happy young woman into a frightened, cowering child. Amanda reached Priscilla first, positioning herself between Priscilla and her father.

"What are you so upset about?" she asked Carruthers. "Priscilla was only singing for me."

Carruthers was so furious, even the veins in his neck stood out.

"I don't care if she was singing for God," he thundered. "I told her if she sang so much as one note outside the house, I'd burn every piece of music she owned."

"She has a beautiful voice, quite a remarkable gift." Amanda held her ground despite Carruthers's attempts to reach his daughter. "You should be proud of her."

"Why should I be proud of something that makes her want to parade herself in front of a lot of strangers like a common hussy?"

"With a voice like hers, there would be nothing common about anything she did."

"I'm not interested in the opinion of a woman who earns a living by displaying herself in front of a lot of drunks. I intend to make sure my daughter understands I won't let her do the same. Now get out of my way."

When Carruthers reached out to push Amanda aside, he came into contact with Broc instead. "Lay one hand on Amanda, and you'll be carried out of this church. You're too upset to think straight right now. Why don't you take a few minutes to calm down?"

"This is all your fault!" Carruthers raged at Broc. "Priscilla has always been a sweet girl. She would never have gone against me if you hadn't encouraged her."

Broc decided not to tell Carruthers the meeting had been Priscilla's idea. "I just offered to play for her, not encourage her to sing for anybody else. Oscar can't do her justice."

"I intend to see she never sings another note," Carruthers stormed. "Now get out of my way."

"Not until you calm down."

Broc was ready for the attack. He blocked the man's punch and hit him three times in quick succession. Carruthers wasn't weak or cowardly, but he hit the floor with a thud.

"I'll kill you for this," Carruthers threatened through lips that were split and beginning to bleed. "I'll feed your carcass to the coyotes."

Broc rubbed his sore knuckles while he tried to figure out what to do next. The sheriff wasn't going to be happy about what he'd done. The sound of the church door opening caused him to look up. Dan Walch came striding down the aisle toward them. He stopped a few feet away from where Carruthers lay.

"I heard he'd come after Priscilla. I got here as soon as I could."

"What can you do? He fired you."

"I don't care what you do with him. I'm here to make sure Priscilla gets home safely."

Broc turned to Priscilla, but the words he'd meant to say were never uttered. The look on her face was clearly that of someone deeply in love. He turned and encountered the same look on Dan's face. Hell, he thought. Things are complicated enough without this.

"Getting her home safely is the easy part," Broc said. "It's keeping her safe that's the problem."

"You can't protect her if you're not with her," Amanda said, "and Carruthers isn't going to allow you anywhere near his house."

"I'll shoot the damned bastard if he sets one foot on my range," Carruthers said through rapidly swelling lips.

"She can stay in a hotel," Dan suggested.

"Not without someone to stay with her." Amanda turned to Priscilla. "You're coming home with me."

"She's coming home with me," Carruthers shouted.

"No, she's not," Dan said. "And if you so much as touch her, you'll answer to me."

Broc was beginning to feel it would have been easier to just go to jail. How could he have guessed that notifying the Liscombs of an unpaid debt would land him neck-deep in a whole mess of troubles? Now he had a love-struck couple on his hands when he didn't know what to do about his own situation.

"I'd better see about getting Amanda and Priscilla home. Don't argue," Broc said, when Dan started to disagree. He looked down at Carruthers, who was now in a sitting position. "You need to explain this situation to the sheriff. He's the only one who has a chance to fix this without anybody getting hurt."

"Okay, but I'm coming out to the Lazy T afterward." He turned to Amanda. "I'll work for you without pay. I just want to make sure Priscilla is safe."

They continued to discuss a few logistics despite Carruthers's shouted threats to kill all of them. "Do you want me to do something with him?" Dan asked Broc when they were ready to go.

"Just make sure he doesn't follow us."

"You can be sure of that." Dan turned to Carruthers. "Get up, you hateful old bastard. You're defiling this church just by being here."

"I'll make you pay for this," Carruthers said as he struggled to his feet. "I'll make all of you pay."

❧

Priscilla's move to the Lazy T had several unexpected results, not the least of which was Gary's return home. Priscilla helped Amanda's mother with the cooking and cleaning while Dan proved himself an invaluable cowhand. Not only did he know as much as Broc about ranching, he was able to coax Andy into taking a genuine interest in his work.

The most unexpected aspect of Gary's return was that he started working on the ranch again. Amanda decided he could only have forced himself to do something he hated so much because he was desperate for a chance to see and talk to Priscilla as well as keep an eye on Dan.

"Can't you see she's in love with Dan, and he's in love with her?" Amanda had asked her brother less than an hour after he returned home.

"She hardly ever saw me, but she saw him all the time," Gary had said. "Now she'll get to see me as much."

Amanda had given up after that.

Mrs. Liscomb had been very cool about opening her home to Priscilla. Amanda wasn't sure whether it was that Priscilla was the daughter of the man who was trying to ruin the Liscombs, or that she was the daughter of the woman her mother hoped to supplant as the leader of Cactus Bend society, but her attitude had undergone a dramatic change when Mrs. Carruthers descended on them the next morning. The woman's weeping over her husband's cruelties had caused her mother's resistance to thaw. It melted completely when Mrs. Carruthers hugged her mother and praised her as an angel of God, a beacon of hope, a bastion of courage. It didn't hurt that Mrs. Carruthers assured her that Priscilla would be more than happy to do her share of the cooking and cleaning. It became an honor to give the girl temporary asylum when it became clear Mrs. Carruthers now considered Amanda's mother her best and closest friend.

Priscilla was happy because she could see Dan at meals and could sing whenever she wanted. And Amanda was happy, too. For the first time in her life, she had a woman her age to talk to about the thoughts paramount in her mind. "What does it feel like to be in love?" she asked Priscilla the first evening she didn't have to sing in the saloon.

Priscilla giggled. "It makes me happy. When I think about Dan, I tend to giggle like I did just now."

Thinking about Broc had never made Amanda giggle. In fact, her reaction had been quite different. She wondered if she had the courage to mention it to Priscilla.

"Dan doesn't care that I'm so tall." Priscilla giggled again. "He's so big, I seem small to him."

Amanda decided they weren't very different. Priscilla didn't want to be seen as a giant, and Amanda was tired of feeling like just a pretty face. "Has he asked you to marry him?"

Priscilla blushed. "No. He thinks I'm too good for him. We get so little time together, I haven't had an opportunity to convince him I don't care if he isn't rich. We wouldn't have had a chance to talk at all if Papa hadn't assigned him to drive me to town whenever I came without Mama." She sighed. "He's such a sweet man. He thinks I'm beautiful." She laughed. "I'm built too much like my father to ever be beautiful, but I don't contradict him when he tells me he thinks I'm prettier than you." She laughed so hard she fell back on the bed where they'd been sitting side by side. "That's when I knew he really did love me."

That made Amanda wonder whether she'd been able to convince Broc she didn't care about his scars.

"You're in love with Broc, aren't you?" Priscilla asked.

"Is it that obvious?"

"It is to me. He's in love with you, too."

"How can you tell?" Despite the kisses they'd shared, they'd never spoken of love.

"He looks at you the same way Dan looks at me. His face softens and his eyes grow luminous." She leaned over and whispered. "I can tell Dan *wants* me." She giggled. "Isn't it wonderful to have that effect on a man?"

Amanda wasn't sure. She'd been wanted by so many men, she'd been hoping desire wouldn't be part of Broc's feeling toward her. Now that she thought about it, she wondered if that was unnatural. Surely a woman would hope the man who loved her would want her body as much as he wanted the rest of her. She hadn't realized until now that she had feared seeing that look in Broc's eyes. "Do you want to have that effect on a man?" she asked.

Priscilla sat up, her smile rapturous. "Of course I do. Don't you feel the same?" Her excitement faded. "You're so gorgeous, every man wants you. Does that make you feel a little bit hunted?"

"Yes!" Amanda was ecstatic she'd finally found someone who understood how she felt. "I guess that's why I'm always having dreams of being chased by some wild animal."

"Do you ever dream of being rescued?"

"Sometimes. Recently."

"Who rescues you?"

Amanda felt a smile begin to grow. "Broc."

Priscilla grinned. "That proves you're not afraid of him."

Amanda realized that even before the kisses, she had always felt comfortable with Broc. Even when she doubted him because of the issue with the debt, she felt safe around him. Most important, she wanted to be with him. Part of her reason for insisting that she would begin riding every day was to be with Broc. She liked talking to him. She liked performing with him. Most of all, she liked the moments when they could be together long enough to steal a few kisses. They never talked about the future, but she decided that would have to change. She was in love with Broc, and she didn't mean to let him walk out of her life.

❧

"Taking part in plays is not demeaning," Broc said to Mrs. Liscomb. "Members of the British aristocracy stage them in their mansions all the time." Broc had known Mrs. Liscomb would oppose his plan to stage a skit for the saloon. He was about to abandon the idea when Mrs. Carruthers arrived.

"Let's see what he has in mind," Mrs. Carruthers said. "It might not be so bad."

Mrs. Liscomb didn't look happy, but she wasn't willing to oppose Mrs. Carruthers.

"I'm thinking of a simple plot about a good guy rescuing a maiden in distress from the bad guy."

"I want to be the bad guy," Eddie declared.

"Who'd be afraid of you?" Gary scoffed.

"I would," Dan said. "Eddie can be really fierce."

Eddie threw out his skinny chest with pride. "I can beat up any old villain," he told Gary.

"No, you can't."

"Yes, I can 'cause Broc and Dan will help me."

"I thought I'd be the villain." Broc turned his

scarred face toward Eddie. "One look at this, and anybody would be scared to tangle with me."

Eddie looked confused. "I don't think you look scary."

"I don't, either, and I don't want you to do it."

Broc turned to Amanda. "Why not?"

"I already told you."

"What did you tell him?" Eddie asked.

Amanda hesitated. A glance at Priscilla gave her courage. "I told him I thought his wounds were visible proof of his courage. I also said I thought it was extraordinary that he had the inner strength to face the world knowing how so many people would react."

"I agree," Priscilla said.

Broc wasn't sure how he got the next words out, but somehow he found himself saying, "I appreciate that, but it makes sense to use any advantage we have." He paused, then smiled. "I'm going to play the hero *and* the villain. Hopefully, that will turn this into a comedy."

Gary protested. "You can't be two people."

"It just takes a little imagination, a cleverly made costume, and a little face paint."

"Can I wear face paint?" Eddie asked.

A slow smile spread over Amanda's face.

"Do you know what I'm going to do?" Broc asked her.

"I think so."

"What?"

"One side will be the hero and the other the villain." Broc felt a surge of warmth. It was silly to let something so inconsequential make him feel mushy inside, but he couldn't help it when it came to Amanda.

"I want everybody to have a part," he said.

"I'm not acting in no play," Gary declared.

"Nobody wants you to," Eddie said. "You're a terrible actor."

"You've never seen me act, because I've never done it," Gary said.

"That's why you'd be terrible," Eddie stated, proud of his deduction.

"Naturally, I won't take part," Mrs. Liscomb said.

Broc had plans for Mrs. Liscomb but decided to ignore her just now. He turned to Priscilla. "I'd like to start with you."

"Me!" Priscilla looked both shocked and pleased.

"My idea is that you and Amanda will stroll on the stage together. You'll be telling her how you long to meet someone special. You can sing the song you sang for me yesterday."

Priscilla turned to her mother. "Do you think I should?"

Mrs. Carruthers thought for a moment. "I don't see what would be wrong with that as long as I'm there. You did say you wanted all of us to take part," she said, turning to Broc.

"I'd like you and Mrs. Liscomb to have a brief conversation about young people falling in love and some of the complications."

"Should it be amusing?"

"I hope so."

"I can't do that," Mrs. Liscomb objected. "What would people think?"

"They'll think what we tell them to think, Grace," Mrs. Carruthers said. "After all, we're the most influential women in Cactus Bend."

"What about me?" Eddie asked. "What do I get to do?"

Leaving Mrs. Carruthers to convince Mrs. Liscomb, he turned to Eddie. "After Priscilla leaves, the hero shows up, he and Amanda sing a duet, then he goes off leaving Amanda to sing by herself."

"I asked about me," Eddie reminded him.

"You get to run on and tell her the villain is coming. Then you run off to find the hero."

"I want to fight the villain," Eddie said.

"You can't. The hero's supposed to do that."

"But you can't fight yourself. I think Gary ought to be the villain. I can fight him."

"I'm not acting in any stupid play," Gary asserted.

"I want you to be the announcer," Broc said to Gary.

"I'm not being any announcer." He stopped. "What's an announcer?"

"He comes on before the play starts to tell the audience what they're going to see. After that you can go back to the bar if you want."

Gary looked stubborn, but Broc knew trying to force him to agree would only have a negative effect. "Okay, let's start with the mothers," Broc said. "Your dialogue should go something like this."

He outlined a conversation not unlike what any mother would say when complaining about a daughter falling in love and being virtually useless. Mrs. Carruthers took to the role enthusiastically and embroidered it with some of her own contributions. Words had to practically be forced from Mrs. Liscomb, but at least she didn't refuse to take part. Priscilla sang so beautifully Broc decided he might work up a skit featuring her. Eddie performed his part with relish and begged for more. Broc then showed how he planned to play both the hero and the villain. There was a good deal of laughter and some doubts about how it would work, but Mrs. Carruthers volunteered to make a cape for him that very afternoon.

"I know exactly how to achieve the effect you want," she said, apparently pleased with the notion she had in mind.

"That's the idea of the show," Broc said to Gary. "Think you can introduce us?"

"I can do it," Eddie piped up. "Let me."

"Anybody can do that," Gary said.

"I was really asking whether you *would* do it."

"I'll have to ask Corby. I won't do it if he thinks I shouldn't."

"Okay. But if you can't, Eddie gets to do it."

A jubilant Eddie was certain he had the part, but Broc could tell Gary wasn't happy about letting his little brother have so much of the limelight. This was one time jealousy might work in his favor.

❧

In the mysterious way that all small towns have when it comes to spreading news, it seemed every man in Cactus Bend knew there was going to be something special at the Open Door Saloon that evening. A few women showed up with their husbands. Corby didn't know whether to be pleased or nervous. It was possible that having women become regulars at his saloon could drive a lot of his regular customers to look for a saloon where their nightly enjoyment wouldn't be inhibited by the sensitivities of the delicate sex. For the single men, leering at the waitresses and giving them an occasional pat as they passed close by was the highlight of the evening.

"I've never seen the place so full," Dan Walch said to Corby.

"I don't know about having those women here," Corby said, indicating a group who'd commandeered a table for themselves. "Some of the men don't like it."

"Maybe not, but *some of us* get tired of looking at the same old ugly faces night after night."

"They're not young."

"They're not men. That's what counts."

"Your show had better be good," Corby said, twisting around to glare at Broc. "If it's not, I won't pay Amanda her percentage of the bar." He glared at the table of women. "With them here, we may not make as much as I expected."

"They'll go home early," Dan said. "If the men are in a good mood, they'll drink even more."

"Aaron Liscomb told me women would never set foot in my saloon so I didn't have to worry about them."

Broc believed women were gradually taking more control of their lives and demanding to be included in areas that men had previously considered all-male domains. If Corby didn't learn to change with the times, his business wouldn't last. Mrs. Liscomb didn't realize that by owning a ranch managed by her daughter, she was at the forefront of change, and Broc didn't mean to tell her. The shock would be too much.

"Get started," Corby said to Broc. "The men are getting fidgety."

Gary looked nervous when he mounted the stage, but he managed to explain the play without confusing people too much.

The men were shocked when the first people to walk out on the stage were the two most respected women in Cactus Bend, but Mrs. Carruthers took command of the stage as if she'd been acting all her life. She led the mumbling Mrs. Liscomb through their dialogue, managing to make Mrs. Liscomb's bumbling efforts as funny as her lines.

The men didn't know how to react when Priscilla appeared on stage, but it didn't take more than a few notes of her song before every voice was silenced. She was close to the end of her song when the doors to the saloon opened with a loud crash, and Carruthers stormed in.

"You damned bitch!" he shouted at his daughter. "I'll show you what happens to a daughter who doesn't obey her father."

Carruthers's entry was so unexpected and his progress through the crowded saloon so rapid, he had almost reached the stage before anyone was able to react. There were too many people between Broc and Priscilla for him to prevent Carruthers from grabbing his daughter's wrist and yanking her off the stage.

The only reason she didn't fall was that Dan Walch somehow managed to force his way through the crowd. He caught Priscilla with one arm while he used the other to land a punch in Carruthers's face.

The man acted as though he didn't feel a thing. "Whore!" he screamed at Priscilla.

Several men had gotten over their shock sufficiently to try to restrain Carruthers, but he still didn't let go of Priscilla. Mrs. Carruthers's shrill shouts only added to the confusion. Aiming for the straining muscle in Carruthers's forearm, Broc brought his fist down with all his strength. His blow paralyzed Carruthers's muscles, and the rancher lost his grip on his daughter's wrist. Dan pulled Priscilla toward her mother while several men wrestled Carruthers to the floor.

"He's drunk," someone said.

"It doesn't matter," another said. "He shouldn't mistreat a woman, not even his own daughter."

Broc didn't doubt Carruthers had been drinking, but this was the attack of a crazed man capable of doing dangerous, possibly tragic things. Broc was convinced Carruthers was mentally unstable. Why else would he think no laws applied to him? Why would he attempt to harm his daughter with a saloon full of people watching? Why was he shouting threats at Corby, vowing to close him down, burn him out, for letting his daughter sing?

"Put him in jail long enough for him to calm down," Dan said to the sheriff, who'd been summoned by the noise. "If he tries to hurt Priscilla again, I'll kill him."

Dan stood with one powerful arm around Priscilla, who looked happy to be there.

"Shut up, man. Can't you see there are women

here?" the sheriff asked Carruthers when he continued to shout profanity.

"I think he ought to see a doctor," Broc suggested.

"I agree." Mrs. Carruthers had made her way to the front. "He hasn't been himself recently."

The sheriff had been reluctant to take action against the most powerful man in the area, but now, he didn't have any choice. "I'll take him over to the jail and have the doc look at him."

It took four men to help the sheriff drag Carruthers from the saloon. A shouted "Bitch!" was the last word they heard from him.

It took several minutes for everybody to settle down. Even after they had reclaimed their seats, they didn't stop discussing what they'd seen.

"I want you to sing your song again," Broc said to Priscilla.

"She can't do that," Amanda said. "She's too upset."

"If she wants to be a professional singer, she'll have to learn to perform regardless of what's happening in her personal life. The audience only cares about what it has paid to see." Broc knew he was being harsh, but it was the best way for Priscilla and everybody else to put the ugly scene behind them.

Priscilla swallowed, patted Dan's arm, then stepped away from him. "Okay, I'll do it."

"Are you sure?" Amanda gave Broc an angry glare.

"Broc is right. I can't let anything keep me from performing."

When Broc announced that Priscilla would start her song again, the men gave her a rousing round of applause. Their response when she finished was so enthusiastic, she had to sing the last verse again.

Broc was pleased for Priscilla, but he was relieved the audience was back in the mood to be entertained. Now their show had a chance of being successful.

Their duet was well received, but Broc knew the success of the show really depended on his being able to carry off the two parts. He had been careful to keep his good side to the stage during the duet. He wore a white hat, a white shirt and string tie, black pants, and boots. From that side he looked like the perfect romantic hero.

Amanda's solo was beautifully sung and loudly applauded. The clapping only stopped when Eddie rushed on stage shouting that the villain was coming. The little ham added to his lines by drawing a lurid picture of what the villain would do to Amanda. They practically had to yank him off the stage.

When Broc appeared as the villain, he entered from the opposite side of the stage which showed the wounded side of his face. That side of his hat was black, and a black cape covered his white shirt, giving him a totally black silhouette. The audience gasped when they saw him.

Amanda recoiled in horror when Broc demanded that she marry him or he would foreclose on the family ranch. She begged for mercy, but he was relentless. When Amanda sank to her knees, Broc crossed behind her and turned, exposing his heroic side. The hero promised to protect Amanda, save the family ranch, and vanquish the villain. He pantomimed a punch.

Changing sides of the stage, Broc exposed his villain side. Pantomiming stumbling back from the force of the hero's blow, he made terrible threats and punched at the hero. Broc crossed back behind Amanda and exposed his hero side, then stumbled from the force of the villain's blow. Finally understanding what Broc was doing, the audience started to laugh. The more times Broc changed from hero to villain and back to hero again, the harder they laughed. Some even started to cheer for the hero and others for the villain. When the villain was finally overcome by the hero, Broc did his best to make his death scene a comic masterpiece before scrambling up to sing a final duet with Amanda.

The men whistled, shouted, and stomped. Some even threw coins on the stage. The women clapped just as enthusiastically. It amused Broc that Corby seemed caught between *pleasure* that the show had been so successful and *anger* that it had been so successful.

The women left after the show was over, and the men reverted to their usual practice of drinking themselves silly before wandering off to their beds.

"Amanda, I want to see you in my office right now."

Amanda laughed at Corby. "You don't have to increase what you're paying me. We'll do the show every night for the same amount."

"That isn't what I want to talk about."

"Then what is it?"

Broc didn't understand why Corby looked so unhappy. His saloon was packed with men in a mood to stay longer than usual to talk about the show and

Seventeen

AMANDA WONDERED HOW IT WAS POSSIBLE TO QUES-
tion what had been said when she had heard each
word perfectly clearly. "Let's go to your office," she
said. "Either you're not feeling well and need to lie
down, or you've been drinking too much of your own
whiskey and don't know what you're saying."

"I know exactly what I'm saying."

"Then you're going to have to explain it to me and
Broc."

The office was a monument to Corby's opinion of
himself. When her father had occupied it, the room
had contained little more than a desk, a chair, and a
cabinet for his records. After her father died, Corby
had asked advice from several ladies in town. Now
he had pictures on the wall, an armchair for visitors, a
carpet, and a table with a lamp.

Amanda couldn't believe Corby was serious. It
would be impossible to carry on without Broc. He was
the heart of the show, its creator, and its producer. All
of them simply did what he suggested.

She wished her mother and Mrs. Carruthers were

still here, but Mrs. Carruthers had been anxious to take Priscilla home. Amanda's mother had been equally insistent that Eddie needed to be in bed. Eddie had objected strongly but was overruled.

"Now tell me why you want to do anything as stupid as firing Broc," Amanda said when the door closed behind Corby.

"How can you ask a question like that when you heard what Carruthers said?" Corby asked.

"Pay no attention to Carruthers. He was angry at Priscilla for disobeying him. He thinks singing in public is beneath her."

Corby spun around to face Broc. "Did you know that?"

Broc nodded.

"And you persuaded her to sing anyway?"

"Her mother approved," Amanda reminded him. "Nothing should have happened."

"Something *did* happen," Corby nearly shouted. "Carruthers promised to burn the saloon to the ground."

"I doubt he'll remember his threat when he sobers up."

"You can ignore him," Corby shouted. "You don't own the saloon he intends to burn down. I'm never going to let his daughter set foot inside my place again. I'll lock the doors if she or her mother comes near here."

"Everybody loved Priscilla," Amanda reminded him.

"I did without her before, and I can without her again." Corby turned on Broc. "And I can do without you."

"Don't be ridiculous," Amanda said. "The show won't be the same without him."

"I don't want a show," Corby said. "I want you to go back to waiting tables and singing a few songs. I'm putting Oscar back on piano. I want everything to be like it was before."

"I can't go back to things as they were before," Amanda said. "I can't make enough money to keep the ranch going."

"You don't have to worry about that," Corby said. "I'll take care of everything when we get married."

Amanda looked at Broc, but his face was devoid of expression. Seeing him head-on, the stage paint making his disfigurement even more apparent, she was surprised once again how little his scars affected her. It was Broc's face, the face of the man she loved, and she couldn't imagine him looking any other way.

Her own thoughts stunned her. She liked Broc more than any man she'd ever met. She enjoyed being with him, being kissed and held by him. She readily acknowledged that she had started to depend on him, to turn to him when she had a question. She never hesitated to put herself in his hands because she had complete confidence that he would protect her. But when had her feelings turned to love?

Wouldn't she have noticed something so important as that? Had she been so busy worrying about finding the missing cows, making enough money to pay wages, and trying to keep her mother and brother happy that she hadn't had time to pay attention to her own feelings?

"It doesn't make any difference if he fires me,"

Broc said to her. "I was only going to be here for a few more days."

Amanda jerked her thoughts back to the most immediate problem. "It does make a difference," she insisted. "You're the reason all of this happened...the songs, the duets, the piano, the skit. Without you, I'd still be waiting tables."

"That's what he wants you to do. You don't need me for that."

Amanda could feel Broc pulling back, withdrawing from her emotionally. She couldn't let that happen, not until she told him. But what good would it do if he was leaving? Would he come back if he knew she loved him? She didn't have time to sort through the thoughts bouncing around in her brain. She could deal with everything else later.

"I don't want to go back to waiting tables," she told Corby. "After listening to Broc, everybody in the saloon knows Oscar is an awful pianist."

"It's my saloon, and I decide who does what," Corby announced. "That means Broc is fired, and Oscar is back at the piano."

"Then I quit, too." She hadn't meant to say that, but the words were out before she could stop them. She was furious that Corby would fire Broc, but she was certain he would change his mind. He didn't want to lose her. He was just jealous of Broc.

"Don't quit," Broc said. "You have to think of your family."

Why did she have to think of her family all the time? When was somebody going to start thinking about her? It seemed everyone expected her to be responsible for everything, to solve every problem. Eddie was the only one who ever offered to help.

Broc, on the other hand, had volunteered to help with the ranch and with her work in the saloon. Now Corby was trying to force her to turn her back on him. She couldn't do that. She didn't know what the consequences would be to her or her family, but she would *not* work another evening, not even another minute, without Broc.

"You should take Broc's advice," Corby said, "and think of your family."

"I am thinking of them. I'm *always* thinking of them."

"If you were, you would have married me long ago," Corby told her.

"I've told you several times I'm not ready to be married," she said to Corby.

"I'll wait, but I'm getting impatient. A man in my position needs a wife and family."

He puffed out his skinny chest, and Amanda wondered how he could be so blind as to attempt to impress her with Broc in the same room.

"I wasn't being truthful," she continued. "I won't marry you because I'm not in love with you."

"I know that, but admiration and respect are much more important in a marriage than love. And financial security is most important of all. I can provide that."

Corby didn't understand that she didn't want her marriage to be like a business agreement. She wanted it to be hot and passionate. She wanted to miss her husband when he wasn't around. She wanted to long for his touch, to ache for his presence, to be haunted by his smile. She wanted simply thinking about him to make her so happy she would smile, even break out in unexplained laughter. She wanted to *want* to cook for him, to take care of him when he was sick, to make love with him and bear his children, to nourish his body as well as his soul.

"I don't agree with you," she said. "I think love is the most important quality to look for in a marriage. Without that, it might as well be a business arrangement."

"But that's what a marriage should be, a sensible arrangement between two like-minded people."

Amanda turned to Broc. "Do you agree with Corby?"

"Why are you asking him?" Corby demanded. "No woman's going to marry him."

She didn't bother to attempt to explain to Corby why he was wrong. He wouldn't have understood.

"All the things Corby mentioned are important," Broc said.

Amanda's heart sank. How could he think that? Had she fallen in love with a man just like Corby?

"See, he agrees with me," Corby said.

"A few years ago I might have agreed with you," Broc corrected him, "but I don't now."

"Why?" Corby asked.

"I saw four of my friends overcome tremendous odds to make good marriages because love made them want to be with their wives so much they were willing to do whatever it took." He turned to Amanda with a smile that caused her heart to skip a beat. "I agree with Amanda that a marriage without love is not worth having."

"Is that what you were saying?" Corby asked Amanda.

She looked at Broc rather than Corby. "Yes. That's exactly what I was saying."

She had wondered what Broc felt for her, but now she saw the answer in his eyes. He loved her as much as she loved him. She had hoped, she had dreamed, but she'd never been sure. Now the realization of his love filled her heart with so much happiness, she felt she could hardly breathe.

"You're in love with him, aren't you?" Corby's shocked, horrified voice penetrated her cocoon of happiness.

"Yes, I am."

"He's nothing but a common cowboy with a face that will give you nightmares."

"I love his face," Amanda said.

"Do you mean that?" Broc looked desperate to believe her but afraid to leave himself open to hurt and disappointment.

"How many times have I told you I think your face is a testament to your courage and integrity?"

"I was afraid to let myself believe you."

"You're crazy!" Corby yelled at Amanda. "If you marry him, you'll be the laughingstock of Cactus Bend."

"You're wrong," Amanda said. "Everyone will be jealous of me, because they'll see I have found something wonderful."

Broc took Amanda's hands in his. "I never thought anybody could feel that way about me. I know what I look like, but—"

Amanda pulled one hand from his grasp and caressed his disfigured cheek. "I can't imagine you looking any other way." She withdrew both hands and stepped back. "But you're leaving in a few days."

"I have to go to jail, but I'll come back if you want me to."

"He's going to jail!" Corby's voice sliced its way between them. "You're thinking about marrying a criminal?"

"He's not a criminal," Amanda said, her gaze still locked on Broc. "He just got into a fight."

"How many people did he kill?" Corby's voice dripped with sarcasm.

"None," Broc said. "I broke a man's arm for heckling me about my face."

"Are you willing to marry a man who'll be jeered at by everyone who sees him?"

"No person of character would jeer at him," Amanda said. "If they do, they'll have to answer to me."

"Get out of my office!" Corby shouted. "Out of my saloon! Out of my town! You'll never work for me again. Gary, either. I wouldn't give either one of you a job if you were on the street and penniless."

His cruel words shattered Amanda's aura of happiness. "This has nothing to do with Gary. He doesn't even like Broc."

"I'm glad to know he has more sense than his sister, but I don't want any Liscomb here ever again." He marched over to the door, flung it open, and waited for them to leave.

Amanda let her gaze settle on Corby for so long he started to fidget. "I used to think you loved me, but

now I know I was just another piece of property, something to enhance your standing in the community."

"I don't need you," Corby said, angrily. "I can do
without you just fine."

"Good, because you'll have to."

Amanda walked out of the office and out of the
saloon without stopping. The magnitude of what had
just happened didn't hit her until she reached the
street. "What am I going to do?" she asked, turning to
Broc. "Now we'll lose the ranch for certain."

◈

"Corby would never have fired me if you hadn't made
him so mad," Gary shouted at his sister.

"Don't you care that he fired Broc and told me I
had to go back to waiting tables?" Amanda asked her
brother.

"What's wrong with that?" Gary demanded. "It's
what you used to do." Gary turned so sharply in his
striding about the parlor, he sent one of their mother's
small rugs skittering across the room.

"With you gone, I needed the extra money I made
singing."

"Well, now you still need it and don't have any
way to get it," Gary said. "That's how much good
falling in love with him did." Gary indicated Broc
with an angry jab of his index finger.

"What are you talking about?" their mother
demanded. She'd listened with only mild concern
while Gary accused Amanda of ruining the family, but
the possibility Amanda had fallen in love riveted her
attention.

"Amanda told Corby she had fallen in love with Broc," Gary said. "And he said he's fallen in love with her, too."

"Amanda, tell me this isn't true," her mother pleaded.

"I think it's wonderful."

They turned to see Priscilla standing in the doorway.

"You shouldn't have been listening at the door," her mother said sternly.

"I was on my way to the kitchen when I heard what Gary said. I think Amanda is really lucky. Broc is a wonderful man."

"But he's scarred," her mother said.

"I'm big, ungainly, and not pretty like Amanda," Priscilla said. "Does that mean I don't deserve to be loved?"

"I love you," Gary said.

Everyone ignored him.

"I didn't mean to interrupt," Priscilla said.

When she turned to leave, Gary repeated, "I love you." He half rose out of his seat to follow her. When she didn't turn around or answer him, he slumped back. "This is all your fault," he threw at Broc. "It wasn't like this before you got here, telling us we were in debt, riling Carruthers until he's even more angry at you than he is at us. Now you've turned Corby against us as well. Anything else you want to do before you go off to jail?"

"I wish *you* were going to jail instead of Broc," Eddie said to his brother.

"I know you don't mean that," his mother said.

"Yes, I do," Eddie replied. "Broc lets me ride with

him and never tells me I'm stupid or says I'm too little to do things."

Gary erupted from the chair. "Go to hell, all of you," he shouted on his way out of the house.

"Gary Livingston Liscomb, come back here this minute," his mother ordered.

Gary didn't slow down. The sound of the back door slamming was proof he had no intention of obeying his mother's summons.

For a time no one spoke. Finally, her mother looked at Amanda and asked, "What are we going to do now?"

"I'm not sure. I never thought Corby would fire Broc after the skit was so successful. He tried to blame it on Carruthers's threats to burn him out, but it was really because he's jealous."

"If you had married him, we wouldn't be in this trouble," her mother said.

"No, it would be worse. You'd be faced with running a ranch that you know nothing about, because you're too proud to be connected with a saloon. Meanwhile, I'd be tied to a man I don't love, one I'm not even sure I like."

"I don't like him," Eddie said.

"Do you like anybody?" his mother snapped.

"I like Broc," Eddie said with a big grin.

"I know that. Do you like anybody else?"

He thought for a moment. "I like Amanda and Leo. That's all."

Eddie wasn't aware of what he'd done, but his mother looked stricken.

"What do you think we ought to do?" Amanda asked Broc.

"You've got just one crop of calves on the ground and another to be born next year. Do you have anything you can sell so you can hold on for at least two more years?"

Every eye in the room focused on one or more pieces of furniture before gradually settling on her mother, who squirmed under the collective gazes before she raised her eyes to face them.

"It would be pointless to sell my furniture," she said. "I'd never get half of what it's worth. Besides, it's Amanda's inheritance."

"I don't want your furniture." Amanda realized immediately she should have said she didn't *need* the furniture, but she couldn't retract her words now.

"This was my mother's furniture," her mother intoned. "Your father hauled every piece of it from Mississippi because he was certain you would value it as I have."

Amanda didn't value the furniture, and everybody knew it. "It's not a question of whether I value it or not. It's a question of being able to hold on to this ranch, of having a way to support all of us, of having something to leave Eddie and Gary as well as me."

"I want the horses," Eddie said. "Gary can have the cows."

"There is another possible solution," Broc said.

"What?" her mother asked.

"You could sell the bull. By using the calves you have now and the ones you'll have next year, you can still upgrade your herd."

"Do you think that will work?" her mother asked.

"It depends on a number of things, but you have to do one thing before anything else."

"What is that?"

"You have to find out for sure whether you owe money to Ella Sibley. If you do, the judge will sell the bull for you."

The familiar sinking feeling was back in the pit of Amanda's stomach. She had managed to put the debt out of her mind because she was certain it was a mistake, but if a judge had proof to back up his belief, then he could do what he wanted with their property.

"Of course we don't owe that woman any money," her mother said. "My husband would have told me. He never kept anything from me."

Amanda wondered how much of that was true. Her mother never kept anything from the family. She considered her wants to be of sufficient importance that everyone should know of them, but her father had played his cards close to the vest. He always said a businessman couldn't be successful if everyone knew his secrets.

Amanda asked Broc, "How can we find out the truth?"

"I have to be back to Crystal Springs in a couple of days. I can go see Mrs. Sibley. If I learn anything useful, I'll find a way of letting you know."

It took Amanda only one second to make her decision. "I'll go with you."

❧

Ella Sibley was a charming, elderly lady who lived in a modest but comfortably furnished house two blocks from the main street in Crystal Springs. "My husband liked to ranch, but I prefer living in town," she told Broc and Amanda with a warm smile. "I'd rather have neighbors who talk than moo."

The moment Amanda entered Mrs. Sibley's house and was welcomed with a cup of coffee and two sugar cookies, she was certain the debt was real. The flowered paper on the walls, the lace curtains at the windows, the starched crochet decorating the room, even the several daguerreotypes divided among three tables in the room—everything spoke of a woman who lived her life with integrity and a welcoming smile. Her powder-white hair and diminutive stature made her look like everyone's grandmother.

"That must make it a bit uncomfortable living in Texas," Broc said.

"Not at all," Ella said with one of her charming smiles. "There are a lot of men who want nothing to do with cows."

"It's a good thing not everyone agrees with you," Broc said with an equally charming smile, "or Texas would still be as broke as it was when the war ended."

Despite her distaste for cows, it soon became apparent Ella knew quite a bit about cows, ranching, and Texas. She was as interested in what Broc and his partners were doing on their ranch south of San Antonio as she was in what his friend was doing on his farm in California.

"Do you think your friend in California would adopt me as his grandmother?" she asked with a twinkle in her eye. "You make his farm sound like a perfect place to live."

"I'm sure he'd love to have you." Broc laughed. "And there's a nice little town where you can get away from the smell of cows."

"I'm sure I wouldn't notice the smell after it was filtered through acres of flowering fruit trees in bloom." She sighed. "I can still remember an apple tree next to the house where I grew up." She walked over to a window and pulled back the filmy curtain. "I've planted apple trees all around the house. I don't care if they have any apples as long as they bloom every spring."

It was impossible for Amanda not to like Ella Sibley. She felt guilty when she realized she wished her mother was more like Ella.

"There's something important we need to talk to you about," Broc said.

"I knew there had to be," Ella replied with a sly grin. "Beautiful young people don't waste their time with an old woman unless they must."

"Then the young people in Crystal Springs are missing an invaluable opportunity," Broc told her.

"You're a charming young man with a silver tongue," Ella said, smiling even more broadly. "Now tell me your business. I expect you'll be more honest when you talk about that."

"It's really my business," Amanda said. "Broc just got caught up in it by accident."

Ella was too much of a lady to betray her curiosity, but Amanda knew she must be curious.

"I allowed myself to lose my temper when a man here in Crystal Springs took exception to my face," Broc said.

"Felix Yant," Ella said with disgust. "I heard about what he did. I wish you'd broken more than his arm."

Broc grinned. "I think the judge agreed with you, but he couldn't say so. He said I didn't have to go to jail if I could collect the debt owed you."

"It's my family that owes the debt," Amanda said, "only we don't know anything about it. Before my father died, he told us he had no debts. Broc and I came here hoping you had some document that would help us solve this mystery."

"It's no mystery," Ella said. "Your father bought our stud bull after my husband died. I was to be paid fifty dollars a month until the total was paid. I was paid for less than a year. Then the payments stopped."

"Do you have a bill of sale, a written agreement, or something we could look at?" Amanda asked. "My family has nothing."

"How odd," Ella said. "Of course you can look at the agreement. I gave the judge the original, but he returned it two days ago. I'll get it for you." Ella walked over to one of the tables bearing the daguerreotypes. She set all of them aside, lifted the top of the table, and took out a paper lying on top. "You're fortunate you didn't ask for it a month ago. It would have taken me hours to find it."

"Let Broc see it," Amanda said. "My father shared a lot with me, but nothing to do with business." She watched uneasily as Broc took the document and began to read through it. She wasn't reassured when his gaze intensified, and his lips pursed in an expression of anger.

"The bastard!" he muttered. "The thieving, lying bastard."

Eighteen

"WHO'S A BASTARD?" AMANDA ASKED.

"Yes, tell us both," Ella said. "Nothing exciting has happened to me since a longhorn hooked one of our cowhands' pants and ripped them from top to bottom. The best-equipped young man I've ever seen."

Broc sputtered with laughter but sobered quickly. "Your family doesn't owe Mrs. Sibley one cent," he said to Amanda, "but Corby Wilson owes her seven hundred dollars."

"Corby? Why does he owe her money?"

"It's not clear from this document, but my guess is that your father didn't have the cash to pay for the bull, and Corby didn't have the cash to pay for his share of the saloon, so Corby assumed the debt for the bull in exchange for your father's share in the saloon. Did Corby pay you directly?" Broc asked Mrs. Sibley.

"No. The payments were sent to the bank. The bank president would tell me when a deposit had been made."

"Do you know how it was made?"

"It was always cash."

Amanda didn't know much about banking, but she could figure out that neither the bank president nor Mrs. Sibley had any way of knowing who'd actually made the payments. They only knew if money had been deposited. "If Corby's name is on the document, we have nothing to worry about," Amanda said.

"But Corby's name *isn't* on this paper," Broc said. "It simply states that twenty-four payments of fifty dollars will be made—one each month for two years—by an agent appointed to make the payments on Aaron Liscomb's behalf. The bank president in Cactus Bend said he had no knowledge of this transaction. The only possible explanation is that Corby was to make the payments. Did the bank president say your father had made any significant deposit two years ago?"

"No. He said my father didn't trust banks."

"Unless you have some other explanation, that leaves Corby."

Amanda was so stunned, she could hardly think. Corby had said many times that he owed every bit of his success to her father, that he wouldn't be where he was today without Aaron Liscomb. How could he possibly renege on a promise he'd made to his former partner? How could he have done this when he professed to love her, had asked her to marry him, promised to take care of all the problems on the Lazy T? Would he have forced her family to sell the ranch? Would he have forced all of them to work in the saloon or diner?

It shocked her to realize that at one time she'd considered marrying Corby, might still have done so if Broc hadn't come along.

"Unfortunately, there's nothing in the document that proves Corby assumed the debt," Broc said. "Without that, I don't know that we're any better off than we were before."

"Yes, we are," Amanda declared, a fire burning in her belly. "When I get through with Corby Wilson," she said to Ella, "he'll be glad to pay every cent he owes you."

"What do you propose to do?" Ella asked.

"I'm going to confront him with what he's done and tell him he has to pay you what he owes."

"You have no proof," Ella reminded her.

"There couldn't be anybody else. Everybody will know that."

"It's not a matter of what everybody knows," Ella said. "It's what you can prove. And if your friend has read the document correctly, you can't prove anything."

Amanda turned to Broc, hoping he had some brilliant plan to prove Corby owed the money, but Broc simply shook his head. "She's right. Without something that says otherwise, the person who owns the bull owes the money."

"I'll kill him!" Amanda said. "Carruthers threatened to burn him out. I'll help."

"I can understand how you feel," Ella said with a hearty laugh, "but killing him won't help. You still won't have the money to pay for the bull. If you burn the saloon down, neither one of you will have any money."

"I'm just so angry I don't know what I'm saying," Amanda said.

She stood. She couldn't subject Ella to any more of her temper, and right now, she thought she would explode if she couldn't work off some of the rage that burned through her. What an odd time to discover that even though she'd complained about being responsible for the ranch, she wanted it, didn't mind working to make it successful. Owning the Lazy T gave her the opportunity to make a marriage of choice rather than one of necessity. It had given her the chance to find a man like Broc.

That was another sin to add to Corby's list. Unless he would agree to repay the debt, he would be responsible for Broc going to jail. Amanda could forgive him many things, but she couldn't forgive him that.

"Thank you for seeing us," she said to Ella. "I hope we haven't upset you."

"Not at all," Ella assured her. "I have too little in my life to interest me. You've given me my most entertaining afternoon in years. I'd love to be able to say you didn't have to pay the rest of the money, but unfortunately I need it to live on."

"I wouldn't accept if you offered," Amanda said. "You deserve payment, and I'll see you get it."

"Please let me know how things work out. I feel somehow responsible."

"Please don't. Thanks for the coffee and the cookies."

As soon as they were outside, she turned to Broc. "What am I going to do?"

"We're going to find a way to prove Corby owes that money."

"How?"

"I don't know. In the meantime, we're going to have a nice dinner and take a walk in the moonlight."

∽

Amanda felt she should try to keep her mind focused on finding a solution to her problem, but it was difficult to think of anything other than Broc's nearness. Walking in the moonlight with the man she loved was not a situation likely to keep her thoughts centered on anything beyond Broc. Besides, she had tomorrow to worry.

"Are you feeling better?" Broc asked.

"As long as I don't think about Corby, I'm fine. I'd much rather think about you." She probably shouldn't have been so direct, but she was tired of restraint. She was tired of responsibility. She was tired of thinking of others first and herself later…if at all.

"I'd much rather think about you, too," Broc said. "I don't find Corby nearly as attractive."

Amanda giggled. Usually she would have been embarrassed. According to her mother, ladies didn't giggle, but she didn't feel like a lady, at least not a grown one. She felt like a girl who'd fallen in love for the first time and couldn't believe it had happened to her. She thanked whatever lucky star it was that prevented her from marrying Corby simply because it was the easiest and most practical thing to do.

"What are you going to do after you get out of jail?" She was afraid of the answer, but she had to ask.

"It depends."

"On what?"

"Many things, but mostly you."

They'd enjoyed a quiet dinner in a little restaurant where no one knew them. After they'd walked every street in Crystal Springs, they ended beside the spring that gave the town its name.

Dark clouds obscured the moon, but lights from the main street and the homes nearby provided enough illumination for them to see each other. In the shadows she was able to imagine he was the perfect young man he'd been before the war. She wished she'd known him then. She could easily imagine him as the hero in a romantic comedy. Even now, he was her idea of a perfect hero.

"Do you want to sit?" Broc asked.

Someone had been thoughtful enough to place several benches around the source of the springs. Amanda could imagine young couples coming here on sultry summer afternoons, resting in the shade of the tall maples and walnuts that shaded the springs. She was certain others preferred moonlit evenings when a soft breeze could give birth to romance in even the most jaded soul. Even with the moonlight now partially obscured by clouds, the evening had worked its magic on her. She wanted to stay here forever, to hide in the safety of this moment, to stretch it out until it encompassed the rest of her life.

"I'll sit if you'll sit next to me," she answered.

Broc chuckled softly. "I was planning on it."

She sat down. Broc settled down next to her and placed his arm around her shoulders. Amanda didn't wait for an invitation to lean into his embrace.

"Will you come back?" she asked.

"Are you sure you want me to?"

"Yes."

"It won't be easy."

"Why?"

"To use a common term, I'll be a jailbird. That's

not something a woman should have to accept in her husband or for her children. Your mother doesn't like me now. She's going to hold me responsible if you lose the ranch or the bull. Gary will blame me for that, as well as for Priscilla not liking him. You won't be able to ignore the way people react to the way I look. Can you imagine what it would do to our children to be teased and taunted about their father's scarred face? I have eight brothers and sisters. I know how cruel children can be."

"I don't care."

"Maybe you'll be able to ignore your family because they're adults and should know better, but the things that can happen to your children will tear you apart. You may not think so now, but I know."

Amanda had to convince Broc to come back to her. Together they could figure out how to face the future. Whatever the difficulties, they would be easier with him at her side. Maybe he didn't know it yet, but anyone who dared badger or make fun of him for his looks would have to deal with her. She wouldn't hesitate to tackle anyone who dared tease their children. Longhorn cows had been known to kill wolves in defense of their calves. Amanda didn't see any reason she should be less protective.

"I don't want to talk about any of that tonight," she said to Broc. "I want to think about the present and let the future take care of itself."

"Do you think it will?"

He sounded unsure of himself. It hurt her to realize the extent to which his injury had undermined his confidence in himself, the depth of his fear that no one would ever be able to love him. That was something she could do for him. She could love him year after year, his face growing more dear to her with each passing day. She could give him children who would think he was the most wonderful father in the world, capable of slaying all dragons and solving all problems. She would surround him with so much love, he would forget his face wasn't perfect.

In her eyes, it was.

"We'll have problems like everyone else," she said, "but we have something they don't, something so strong and so deep it will see us through any difficulty."

It bothered her that he didn't respond. She had to teach him to be optimistic again. In order to do that, she suspected he would have to get over his fear of facing his family. That was something she'd figured out without his telling her, but it was a battle for another day. This night was made for romance, and she didn't intend to waste it.

"Kiss me."

In the beginning, stealing moments for kisses had been exciting, something they did because they enjoyed it, because their kisses could say things they were reluctant to put into words. It was like stepping out of the real world for a few minutes. It was a time to feel young and free, to allow herself to be filled with love and hope.

Though she was certain Broc's feelings for her hadn't changed, his kisses had been different lately. There was a hesitancy to them, a bittersweet sadness because he was the cause of all her troubles. That feeling had intensified after Corby fired him, and she quit in response.

"Kisses won't change anything," Broc said.

"I don't want you to kiss me because I think it will make things better. I want you to kiss me because you want to, because you love me, and because I love you."

Broc chuckled softly. "Any more reasons?"

"Hundreds, but they're all I need."

His kiss was gentle, but she didn't want gentle. She wanted him to overpower her, to sweep her away with the strength of his love, to overwhelm her senses until she wasn't aware of anything except him. She wanted to feel he couldn't get enough of her, that he was going to devour her inch by inch. She wound her arms around his neck and kissed him the way she wanted him to kiss her.

Broc didn't need an explanation to realize she needed more than he was offering. Or maybe he'd been holding back, wanting to make sure her feelings for him hadn't changed. She thought she'd made that clear, but apparently actions were easier to believe than words. She didn't intend to leave any room for doubt.

She leaned forward, her breasts pressed hard against his chest, and kissed him with so much force she was certain her lips would be bruised. She reached deep inside herself in hopes of blasting through the last remnants of his reserve, his hesitation, his doubt. She was determined that by the time this night was over, there would be no barriers between them.

It took only seconds before she could feel his resistance begin to dissolve, the distance between them lessen. Broc took a breath, seemed to gather himself. Then his arms tightened around her, nearly crushing her with the ferocity of his embrace. From somewhere deep inside her came an answering response that leapt forward with the speed of a startled antelope, with the explosive force of an angry bull. It was as though the two of them were trying to hold on to each other so tightly nothing could ever tear them apart. More than that, she was trying to make Broc believe nothing could ever dent her love for him, that she wanted to be with him no matter what might happen in the future.

She wanted him to understand that he *was* her future.

Broc broke their embrace. "I shouldn't be kissing you where anybody could walk up and see us."

"What's wrong with that? I love you, and you love me."

"My mother would say I'm endangering your reputation. Your mother would say I've ruined you."

Amanda tightened her hold on Broc. "I'm not my mother, and this isn't Mississippi before the war. This is Texas. Everything is different here."

"Only because everything is so unsettled. In a few years, it will be the same all over again."

"In a few years, we'll be an older, respectable couple. People will be used to us kissing. They'll know we're not ashamed of our attraction to each other. We'll probably have half a dozen children to prove it."

Broc's bark of laughter was so spontaneous, it drew an answering laugh from Amanda.

"You'll never be a leader of society with that attitude," Broc said.

"Society will have to accept me the way I am. I'm in love with you and don't care who knows."

"When did you turn into such a rebel?"

"When I met you."

Broc's smile faded. "What have I done to make you love me so much?"

"Simply being who you are."

"Being *who I am* has brought you nothing but trouble."

"And a great deal of happiness." Amanda's arms tightened around him. "Do you realize if you hadn't gotten into that fight and been sent to Cactus Bend to collect that debt, I might have married Corby?" She shuddered. "Nothing could be worse than that. Now kiss me again."

Broc kissed Amanda with great thoroughness. She wondered how many women he'd practiced on before the war. Whoever they were, he'd learned his lessons well. She offered a silent *thank you* to the universe.

She broke the kiss. "That wasn't bad," she said. "Do you think you could kiss me so well, every memory of Corby would be wiped from my mind forever?"

"I don't know, but it's a challenge I'm willing to accept."

Broc didn't succeed in obliterating Corby's existence from her memory, but it was an experiment she hoped to repeat as often as possible. Broc's kisses weren't simply lips meeting lips. Neither were they merely an outward expression of their inner feelings for each other. They invited her to become part of him. It didn't matter whether they were gentle, fierce, demanding, or sharing. Every one brought forth an answering response from her. She felt paired with him, bound to him, balanced with him, two souls coming together to face the future as one, indivisible and inseparable.

Just being in his arms and knowing he loved her was the most wonderful feeling she'd ever experienced. She tried not to lose sight of the fact that she ought to be thinking of his happiness as much as her own, but it was impossible not to concentrate on soaking up the wonderful feeling of being wanted and needed for who she was as a person, not for what she looked like or for what she could do.

Broc sensed the presence of another couple before she did. She felt something inside him grow still—tense. "Someone's coming."

She knew she shouldn't feel angry, but she resented this couple's intrusion into the first evening she'd ever been able to spend alone with Broc. There must have been a dozen other places the couple could have gone. Why did they have to choose this one? *There should be a rule that says a second couple can't come to this spot until the first couple has left.* Even when she could hear their voices coming closer, could hear the crunch of gravel under their feet, she didn't want to release her hold on Broc. It would be like losing him all over again.

But there was no point in trying to hold on to a moment that had come and gone. She didn't know which of them was made more uncomfortable by the approach of other people, but it didn't really matter whether it was Broc's scar or her mother's oft-repeated rules of propriety. Either one was enough to dissipate the mood that had enabled her to feel she and

Broc were alone in the world. She allowed her arms to drop from around him and he moved back a step.

But he didn't let go of her hand. That meant a lot to her.

"It's getting late."

She felt as if the evening had just started. "We just got here."

Broc laughed softly. She loved that sound. There was something comforting and warm about it. It was a special way of communicating that existed only between them, something he shared with her and no one else.

"We've been here nearly an hour."

It couldn't have been that long. In an hour, she could have extracted a promise from Broc to come back to her the minute he was released from jail. They might even have figured out a way to make Corby pay off the debt if she'd been willing to waste those precious minutes thinking about anything but how much she loved Broc. "It doesn't seem half that long to me."

He showed her his watch. "It keeps on ticking off the minutes no matter how much we'd like time to stand still."

The other couple came into view and stopped when they saw Broc and Amanda.

"Sorry," the young woman said. "We didn't know anyone was here."

"We were just going," Broc said.

"Don't let us chase you away," the young man said, but it was obvious he was relieved they wouldn't have to share the spot.

"You're not," Broc said. "It's a lovely evening. Enjoy it."

The couple moved to the side of the path to allow Amanda and Broc to pass. They walked hand in hand in silence until they reached the first street. Amanda hesitated, hoping Broc knew of another romantic spot, but he turned in the direction of their hotel. She followed but had already made up her mind their evening wouldn't end yet.

The light coming from the homes they passed had seemed friendly before, almost as though it was reaching out to her, enveloping her in warmth, encouraging her hopes. Now the light felt distant, retreating behind walls that could not be penetrated. It seemed like a metaphor for Amanda's fading hopes for the evening.

She would not give up. She had until tomorrow to convince Broc she couldn't live without him, that he didn't *want* to live without her. All she had to do was make him believe that when she looked at him, she only saw the person behind the scars. It had been that way from the beginning.

"We should leave early tomorrow," Broc said as they approached the hotel.

"Okay." She didn't care about tomorrow. Only tonight.

"We have to think of a way to force Corby to pay that debt."

"I know." She would think about that tomorrow.

They entered the hotel and passed the desk. The clerk looked up and mumbled good night before going back to the book he was reading. There was no one else in the lobby or on the stairs. Broc paused when they reached the door to her room. "I had hoped we'd find there was some mistake, but at least we know

Corby's the one who's responsible for paying the debt.
I'll give it some thought tonight and see if I can come
up with a way to force him to honor it."

"Forget about Corby."

"I'll be happy to forget him as soon as I figure
out—"

"I don't want you to think about Corby tonight."

"What do you want me to think about?"

"Me."

"I do that all the time." His soft chuckle banished
any lingering guilt over what she was about to do.

"Then show me."

"How?"

"Make love to me tonight."

Nineteen

BROC LOOKED SO STARTLED, AMANDA WAS AFRAID HE was going to refuse. She'd never asked a man such a question, never even considered the possibility that she would.

"I don't think you realize what you've just asked me to do," Broc said.

Despite his shock, he hadn't refused. She still had a chance. "I know exactly what I'm asking." She blushed. "I don't know all that's involved, but I know it means I love you and want to be with you."

Broc looked around. There was no one in the hall, but he said, "We really can't discuss this here."

"I don't see anything we need to discuss." Amanda reached for the door to her room, opened it, and stepped inside. Broc didn't move. "I'm not going to force you." She didn't know where she'd found the courage to say that. She was acting like a strumpet, at least what her mother said a strumpet acted like, but she didn't care. She had a horrible feeling that if she lost Broc now, she'd never get him back.

Still, he hesitated. "If anyone saw me enter or leave your room, your reputation would be ruined."

What kind of reputation did she have? What kind of reputation did she want? She wasn't sure, but she knew no reputation could make up for the absence of Broc in her life. "There's only one reputation I want, that of being your faithful and loving wife."

"We have to take things one step at a time," Broc said, "and that's several steps down the road."

"At least come in and talk to me." She held the door wider. Her heart pounded; the muscles in her legs and shoulders tensed; she held her breath, waiting. She sighed in relief when Broc walked through the door to take a position against the wall as far away from the bed as possible. She crossed the room on shaky legs to take a seat in the only chair in the room.

She opened her mouth only to discover she didn't know what to say. Talking about things that could separate her from Broc was pointless, because there was nothing that powerful this side of death.

"Do you love me?" She knew the answer, but she could never hear it often enough, especially when he was standing across the room from her.

"You know I do."

"I love you, too, but it's hard when you keep pulling away from me."

"I'm not pulling away. I'm just keeping a certain distance."

"Sometimes the reason isn't as important as the distance itself."

"The only reason I keep any distance between us is to protect you."

"I don't need your protection as much as I need your love."

"You have that. You'll always have it."

"Do you believe I love you?"

"Yes."

He'd hesitated. It was only a brief faltering, but it was as important as if it had been ten times longer. He still feared it was impossible for anyone to love him. Unless he believed in her love, he wouldn't come back to her after he got out of jail—wouldn't stay after he found a way to force Corby to pay off the debt.

She stood. "Come here."

He didn't move. "I can hear what you have to say from here."

"You can't *do* what I want you to do from there."

"If I can't do it from here, I probably shouldn't be doing it."

"You think it's okay to hold my hand or kiss me, don't you?"

"Yes." He sounded as if he didn't trust where she was going.

"It's no worse than that."

There was that low chuckle again. One of these days she was going to tell him just what it did to her. Then maybe she wouldn't. She wasn't sure she wanted him to know how much power he could have over her.

"I never thought of holding your hand or kissing you as *worse*. I've spent hours figuring out how to do it again."

"Then come here."

When he approached reluctantly, she held out her hands.

"Take my hands."

He did. She didn't know whether she found their strength or roughness more significant, but together they characterized a side of him she found very appealing. There was no polish to his strength, no glittering sheen to blind her to a weakness or flaw. It was naked and honest, there for anyone to see who could look past the scars.

"Now put your arms around me."

Again he complied with uncharacteristic tentativeness. It made her sad.

"Now I want you to kiss me like *you* want to kiss me, not the way you think it's proper to kiss me, not even the way you might think I want to be kissed."

She was relieved to feel all trace of tentativeness disappear. His arms wrapped around her so tightly she couldn't take a deep breath. More important, he pulled her against him with none of the hesitation he'd shown moments before. From shoulder to thigh, she could feel the tautness of his muscles, the rigidness of his body. His kiss was satisfyingly hard and thorough.

She started to tell him that allowing him to do something she wouldn't permit any other man to do proved she loved him, but she decided it would be better to show him instead. She tilted her head to one side to expose her neck and shoulder to his lips. After a brief moment of hesitation—she wondered what arguments raced through Broc's mind—the temptation proved too great. He scattered a line of kisses from her ear down her neck to her shoulder.

Much to Amanda's surprise, Broc found a spot just at the base of her neck that nearly rendered her incapable of standing. She'd had no idea that any spot on her body was so sensitive, or that something as simple as a kiss could come close to causing her to collapse. She clung to him for support. He took that as a sign of encouragement and intensified his efforts. Not certain of how much longer she could remain standing under this assault, Amanda tilted her head to the other side.

She was relieved—and disappointed—that Broc found no equally sensitive spot on the other side of her neck. But she was able to enjoy the sensation of his lips on her neck, to revel in the electricity that skittered about under her skin, the tantalizing tremors that traveled to the extremities of her body, the heat from his closeness, the feel of his hands on her back.

She usually avoided any sort of closeness with men. Listening to some of the women who worked in the saloon talk about the pleasure they found in the company of men had made her worry there might be something wrong with her. Being with Broc had proved she was no different from the other women. She'd just needed to find the right man.

And everything about Broc had felt right from the beginning, so right and natural she hadn't been aware she was falling in love until it was too late to pull back. Not that she *wanted* to pull back. Being in love with Broc was the most wonderful experience of her life. Some days she felt so happy it was hard to keep from smiling and laughing when there was nothing to smile or laugh about.

Yet this happiness was in jeopardy, because he didn't believe anyone could love him the way he wanted to be loved, the way he *had* to be loved, before he would commit his life to her. He saw only obstacles to be overcome. But having found what would make her happy, she wasn't about to let anything—or anyone—cause her to lose it.

Broc was making it difficult to keep her thoughts focused. His lips were no longer brushing lightly over her skin. His kisses had become more intense, had grown more aggressive. Had she known kisses could be aggressive? Had she guessed she would like that best of all? She'd never allowed anyone such liberty or herself so much enjoyment. Now that she had, she didn't want to stop.

She undid the top two buttons on her dress so she could slip it down far enough to give Broc access to her shoulder. Her shoulder wasn't as sensitive as the spot at the base of her neck, but it was responsive enough that she wanted to bare the other shoulder. When she had trouble with the next two buttons, Broc undid them for her.

Her self-control was dissolving with the speed of ice sizzling on a hot stove. She was beyond resisting. She was beyond mere acceptance. She wanted more. She needed more. She demanded more.

But the right words—assuming there were some—wouldn't come. Instead she reached up and pulled his head so deeply into the curve between the base of her neck and her shoulder, she feared she might suffocate him. Rather than pull back or gasp for breath, Broc nipped the skin at the base of her neck and raked her shoulder with his teeth.

Amanda was certain she'd dissolve on the spot if he

did that again. He did, and she didn't dissolve. Instead she pivoted so he could do it to the other side.

Her purpose in encouraging Broc's attentions had been to prove to him she loved him without reservation, but she was proving something to herself as well. With the right man, everything was better. Everything felt right.

It seemed only natural for her dress sleeve to slip down her arm until she was able to pull her arm free, or for Broc to blaze a trail of kisses from her shoulder to her palm and back again. It seemed only natural for her to want him to do that with the other arm as well. It seemed only natural when he complied.

She tried to think of what she could do to give Broc pleasure, but his kisses were making any kind of thinking nearly impossible. All she wanted to do was sink into the sea of sensation that his lips were creating, to let the waves wash over her until she was beyond wanting to think, but she couldn't abandon control just yet. She had to make him believe she loved him despite his scar.

It took a conscious effort to summon the energy to raise her hand to cup the side of Broc's face. The scarred side. He tried to pull away, but she wouldn't let him. The look he gave her was laced with pain and full of questions.

"Why are you pulling away?"

"I don't want you to touch me there."

"Why not? It's part of you."

"No, it's not. It's this horrible thing that has destroyed the person I used to be."

He was so upset he was shaking, but she didn't drop

her hand. "I wish I had known you before the war, but I was a little girl, and you were a grown man used to dazzling women with your handsome face. Neither of us would have given the other a second thought."

He looked as thought he wanted to deny that but knew he couldn't.

"I've never seen you without the scar. I'm not haunted by what you used to look like because that wouldn't be the face of the man I fell in love with." She caressed his cheek. "This is the face I love. Your scar reminds me you were willing to fight for something you believed in, of the strength it took to endure such terrible pain, the courage it takes every day to face rude curiosity and thoughtless cruelty. It reminds me how proud I am that you have chosen to love me."

"How can I believe that? I see my face in the mirror every day. I know what I look like."

"There's no mirror in the world that will let you see yourself through my eyes. When you see yourself, you're seeing what you lost. When I look at you, I see only what I've gained. You are the most wonderful man I've ever met. I still find it hard to believe you exist, even more that you could love me."

She could only guess how difficult it was for him to believe what she said, but she wouldn't give up. He was teetering on the edge, half hopeful and half fearful. If she failed to convince him now, she might never get another chance.

Standing on her tiptoes, she kissed his scarred cheek. "This is part of the man I love. There's no way I will ever be afraid of it or ashamed of it. I won't cringe or turn away when I see it. I won't apologize for loving you, or allow anyone to pity me, because I know I have more than they have, more than they'll ever be able to understand. I'm proud of the man you've become since that awful day. I'm sure you've always been a wonderful person, but for me, you're a miracle."

His face crumpled, and for a moment she thought he was going to cry. "You don't know how much I want to believe that." His voice was as unsteady as a newborn calf, choked and scarred by powerful emotions.

"You don't have to believe it all at once. Just a little bit, only as much as you can manage. I have the rest of our lives to make you believe all of it."

He didn't move; his gaze didn't waver. It was as though he was trying to see into her very core, to make sure she meant every word she said. She knew this was a crucial moment, that he stood at some kind of precipice, but she didn't know what more she could say to help him cross the black and bottomless crevasse that yawned at his feet. She raised her other hand to his unmarked cheek, cradled his face in her hands.

"When I first met you, I noticed your scar. I was aware of it, but it didn't bother me. Now I don't see it anymore because I don't see you in parts, nor do I see only the surface. What I see of you comes from inside and is projected out. It wouldn't matter if both sides of your face had been scarred. It's only your face. It's not your kindness, your courage, your intelligence, or your willingness to put others before yourself. Those things are what make you the man I am proud to love, the man I will always love."

A strangled sound escaped Broc, a sound not unlike something breaking apart. She wasn't sure whether it was the anguish of disbelief or the emergence of hope, but it was laced with pain. His head sank slowly until it rested on her shoulder; his arms closed around her. He remained motionless for so long, she started to worry that he didn't believe her, that he had slumped against her in defeat.

"You give me more credit than I deserve." He raised his head until he looked directly into her eyes. "I begged my friends to let me die. I didn't want to go through all that pain only to have to live as a monster for the rest of my life, but they forced me to live, to get well, to come to Texas with them. I didn't even have the courage to face my family. I wanted them to remember me the way I was, so I talked my commanding officer into reporting that I had died in the attack."

Amanda couldn't imagine what he must have endured knowing no matter how much love and support his friends could give him, the rest of the world would look on him with shock, even revulsion.

"There was never any question about my going back on the stage. That part of my life was over. I had been given what I thought was ample proof no woman could love me. I told myself the smartest thing to do was never to allow myself to develop feelings for any woman, that if I should feel any attraction, I should get the hell out as fast as I could."

"But you couldn't leave this time, or you'd go to jail."

"Even without the threat of jail, I couldn't have left." His bleak look softened into a thin smile. "I fell in love with you so fast, I didn't have time to run. I cursed myself, decided to settle for a few kisses, then spend the rest of my life reliving the times I held you in my arms." His smile broadened. "Even when you seemed to enjoy being with me, I wouldn't let myself believe you might fall in love with me. I told myself you were only being kind, or indulging in a mild flirtation."

Amanda stiffened. "Do you think I allow men who flirt with me the same liberties I've allowed you?"

"I know you wouldn't. That's why I started to believe it just might be possible you did love me."

She relaxed and leaned against him, her head on his shoulder. "When did you finally believe it?"

"I'm not sure."

She raised her head so she could look at him. "But I thought—"

"I kept my distance, because I worried that loving you might not be the best thing I could do for you."

He was afraid that their marriage would lead to unhappiness. She would not panic. He loved her, and he believed she loved him. More than that, he loved her so much he couldn't leave even when he tried. He just needed more time to realize that whatever his fears about their future, they could and would face them together. It wouldn't always be easy, but they would succeed because they would be together.

"Loving me is, and always will be, the best thing you can do for me." She slid her arms around his neck and pulled him into a kiss. She wouldn't let him go until he believed that. He kissed her with so much passion she wondered how he could even think of leaving her.

It was the kind of kiss she spent her nights dreaming about. But she wanted much more. She'd dreamed

of being held in his arms, of sleeping next to him, of
making love to him. She'd dreamed of the sons and
daughters they would have together, the times they
would laugh together, the times they would sit quietly
without words because none were needed. She'd
never had dreams like that about Corby or any other
man. Only Broc, and she had every intention of turning them into reality.

Breaking their kiss, she gently and firmly directed
him to the side of her neck. He found that sensitive
spot so quickly, she was caught off guard. The low
moan that escaped her caused him to pause.

"Don't stop." She was begging, but she didn't care.
As long as he could find that one sensitive spot, the
world could go away.

It was a disappointment when he shifted his attentions to her shoulders, but she wanted to explore his
body, and she couldn't think when he was concentrating on *the spot*. She'd always admired his physical
appearance, but the brief times they'd had together
hadn't allowed for much more than being held in
his arms. Now she wanted to run her hands along
his arms from wrist to shoulder, over his back, and
down his sides. She wanted to feel the power of his
thighs against her, to cup the swell of his bottom in
her hands, feel the heat of his desire through the fabric
of her dress.

She'd never thought a woman could want a man in
this way. But now she wondered how she'd gone so
long in ignorance. Had she thought all the talk she'd
heard from the other waitresses was just their imagination? Or wishful thinking? Had she assumed because

she couldn't experience it, they couldn't, either? If so, the joke was on her, but it wasn't a cruel joke. It was a wonderful, spectacular revelation.

It got even more spectacular when Broc moved his left hand to cover her breast. The tidal wave of sensation that rocked her body caused her breath to be locked in her lungs before escaping in a low moan. She hadn't known being with a man could feel like this. She wondered if it felt the same for Broc.

According to the other waitresses, men were obsessed with being with women. It was all they talked about, all they thought about, but Broc had never acted like that. It had been one of the things that attracted her to him. The waitresses also said men cared little for a woman's feelings, only their own. She looked into Broc's eyes, but he seemed focused on her reaction to his touch.

His touch was gentle yet firm, insistent without being forceful. It was as though he was asking permission to touch her, to please her, to take her on a sensual journey. She would never have considered accepting such an invitation from another man, but she couldn't refuse when it came from Broc. She didn't *want* to refuse.

When his right hand moved to cover her other breast, she found it harder to think. She didn't really want to think, just allow the sensations that flowed from his touch to envelop her whole being. She was being swallowed up by a slowly growing lassitude coupled with a nervous energy that made her feel like she was going to jump out of her skin. She didn't know how the two could exist at the same time, but it didn't seem important to come up with an answer.

When he lowered her dress enough to free her breasts from her shift, it became impossible to think. She would never have suspected her breasts could be so sensitive, or that she would enjoy the touch of his rough skin on her tender flesh. She gasped in surprise when he gently brushed her nipples with his fingertips.

"Did I hurt you?"

"No." How could she describe the most exquisite feeling she'd ever experienced? When Broc leaned down to take a firm nipple into his mouth, Amanda's strength deserted her.

"I think I'd better lie down."

Twenty

"ARE YOU ALL RIGHT?"

Broc looked so worried, Amanda struggled to summon the energy to tell him she was more than all right. She was wondrously, gloriously, fabulously perfect. She just hadn't been prepared for such perfection. Unable to find the right words, and fearful her weak smile was short of the assurance he needed, she nodded her head.

"Are you sure?"

"Yes." One word, and she was exhausted, but not so tired she couldn't place his hands back on her breasts. When he hesitated, she found the energy to pull him down until his lips touched the soft mounds. She arched her body against him, hoping he would suckle her nipples again.

He did.

She wondered if his body was as sensitive as hers, even decided to find out, but she couldn't force her limbs to move. Broc's attentions were draining the last bits of willpower and self-control from her as efficiently as a bee draws nectar from a blossom.

When he took her nipple between his teeth and bit down with a gentle, insistent pressure, her last coherent thought snapped like a fragile twig. With a sigh, she surrendered unconditionally to the sensations that were overtaking her body.

She was in a daze, her body floating, buoyed by the currents flowing through her with ever-increasing speed, with growing turbulence. Broc's hands were everywhere, touching, caressing, kneading. She heard moan after moan and knew they came from her, though she didn't recognize the sound as her own voice. She thrashed about in the bed, inviting his touch, reveling in what it did to her. She wanted him to touch her everywhere at once, to neglect no part of her body. She wanted it all, everywhere, now.

When she felt his fingers part her flesh and enter her body, she believed she finally did have it all. She had no idea when he'd removed her dress or her shift. Somehow her shoes and stockings had disappeared as well. She lay naked before him, open to his touch, defenseless against her need for him. Yet it was more than that. She reveled in his touch. His rough hands on her. His seeking fingers inside her. His warm breath against her hot skin. Broc had transformed her body into a tactile battlefield where she was the winner in every encounter, where she eagerly awaited the next engagement, where she anticipated the escalation in intensity even when she wasn't certain she could endure any more.

But there was more. There seemed to be no end to the things Broc could show her, the levels to which she could ascend, the need her body had for his touch.

She was like a starving person who'd been denied food. Enough was not enough.

She wasn't sure she could stand it if his loving went on much longer. She had no idea what Broc was doing to her body, but she felt like a spring being wound tighter and tighter until she was certain she would break and shatter into a million pieces. Yet she didn't shatter. She exploded like a Chinese rocket.

"Broc!" The word was a cry of release rather than a name. Even as she began to descend from the heights, as the pieces of her shattered being began to coalesce, she wondered if it could happen again. She wanted it to happen again. She needed it to happen again.

She panicked when Broc withdrew from her. She felt abandoned, forsaken. Cold. She collected her scattered thoughts just enough to focus her gaze on him as he undressed. Although she'd been around men her whole life, she'd never seen one completely naked. Her mother was obsessive about the rules of propriety that decreed a woman should know nothing about the male body before marriage. And she made sure Amanda knew a proper young woman wasn't supposed to find it attractive.

Once again she failed to measure up to her mother's standards, because she liked what she saw very much. She'd always admired Broc's broad shoulders and strong arms. They felt wonderful when she was wrapped in their embrace. She'd had trouble admitting to herself that she liked the look of his backside as well as his powerful thighs, but that was a secret she enjoyed privately. It felt all the more thrilling because it was forbidden. Just thinking about his butt could cause shivers to race up and down her spine.

Now she had something new to add to her collection of images. Propriety strictly forbade a woman to have any interest in the swell of a man's pants, but what she saw now wouldn't fit inside any pair of pants she'd ever seen. How could that possibly fit inside her?

"I won't do anything to hurt you," Broc said. "If something makes you uncomfortable, let me know, and I'll stop."

As he joined her on the bed, moved above her, she could only wait. She felt his fingers enter her again. In seconds she felt the familiar sensations start to build and spread. Her muscles relaxed as her apprehension eased, and her body sank back into the bed. Then she felt something large and warm press against her.

"This will feel even better than my hand."

There was no pain. No real discomfort, but she felt herself being stretched until she was certain she could stretch no more. He backed away, and the tension eased. Yet a moment later, he drove so deeply inside her, she gasped in surprise.

"That's it," Broc said in a strangled voice. "Now it's only pleasure."

He moved inside her with slow, even strokes. The feeling of fullness that was uppermost at first began to fade as her body gradually moved into sync with Broc's. Before she knew it, it was no longer her body joined with his. They were one, each sharing the other's pleasure, each contributing to the other's excitement.

Then it happened all over again. Amanda started

to lose contact with the world around her, even with her own body. She became a swirling collection of sensations that built upon each other until she felt she was being held together by a mere thread. Broc started to move faster, each stroke going deep before almost withdrawing, then plunging in again. Her jaw went slack, and her mouth fell open. She could feel a scream beginning to build inside her, but she felt incapable of uttering any sound.

She was vaguely aware that Broc's breathing had become more labored, that his body was becoming rigid, that his strokes were starting to be uneven. She wanted to ask if anything was wrong, but she couldn't. She was approaching the edge. She could feel the scream pushing its way from deep inside her, getting closer and closer every second. Then with only the barest of warnings, it burst from her throat to be swallowed by Broc's kiss.

❧

Broc didn't know whether to berate himself for letting his emotions get control of him, or simply to let himself enjoy being in love and being loved. It would be so easy to do that, but he would be ignoring his responsibility to protect Amanda from all harm.

Despite his misgivings, it was impossible to deny the pervading sense of contentment, the nearly giddy feeling of happiness he got just from watching her sleep. A woman loved him. The woman he *loved* loved him in return. She was a beautiful, talented, wonderful woman who could have married virtually any man she wanted, yet she'd chosen him. There were a hundred reasons why he should be castigating himself for allowing this to happen, but he would have time enough for that tomorrow. Right now, he wanted to be selfish, to think only of himself, of his happiness.

She loves me.

That thought kept running through his brain like an endless refrain. Saying it over and over again didn't make it any less incredible. Why would this woman want to love him? What was there about him that could attract her interest, hold it, and turn it into something as wonderful as love? He didn't know a whole lot about ranching. She certainly wasn't going to let her head be turned by his music or his playacting. She was too intelligent for that, yet something had caused her to fall in love.

There was no point in torturing himself. She loved him, and he loved her. He didn't have to understand it. He just had to accept it. He lowered himself back down to the mattress very carefully so he wouldn't wake her. He needed to sleep. They would go back to Cactus Bend tomorrow. He needed to focus all his energy on figuring out how to prove Corby Wilson was responsible for the debt to Mrs. Sibley. Once he had done that, he would have time to consider whether Amanda's future would be better with or without him.

If he failed, he'd be facing the same question from jail, a position that wasn't likely to provide a favorable answer.

∾

"What the hell do you mean the bull is gone?" Amanda wasn't in the habit of swearing, but she was so shocked, so exasperated, so furious, the word just burst from her. "If you let it out again, I'll beat you to a pulp." She and Broc had arrived at the Lazy T mid-morning to discover all hell had broken loose.

"You can't do that." Gary was belligerent, but he was also scared.

"I'll do it," Eddie said.

"And I'll help you," Leo said.

"He'll have help from a lot of quarters," Broc said.

"I didn't let the bull out, okay?" Gary said.

"How can I believe you?" Amanda asked.

Gary dropped his head. "I was in town trying to talk Corby into giving me back my job."

"You should have been here."

"I hate this ranch," Gary shouted. "I hate every minute I have to spend here."

After the number of times he'd let the bull out before and lied about it, Amanda wasn't sure she could believe Gary this time. The animal couldn't have gotten out on its own. "If you didn't let it out, then someone stole it."

"Who would be that stupid?" Leo asked. "Everybody in three counties knows that bull."

"Did you check the fence?" Amanda asked.

"Every foot," Leo said. "He didn't break through the fence."

"Then someone let him out." Broc's accusing glare settled on Gary.

"Who would do that besides Carruthers?" Amanda asked.

"Sandoval," Leo suggested.

"He wants the ranch as badly as Carruthers,"

Amanda said, "but I heard that after seeing our calves, he decided to buy his own bull."

"It would be cheaper to take yours," Leo pointed out.

"Could Corby Wilson be responsible?" her mother asked.

The news that Corby was responsible for the debt had hit the ground like a bombshell. Gary didn't believe it. After having encouraged Amanda to marry Corby, her mother was too shocked to say anything. Eddie had devoted his energies to thinking up new and hideous ways to torture Corby. Leo offered to maim Corby if he didn't come up with the money.

"I can't see any reason for Corby to let the bull out," Broc said. "He doesn't know we've figured out he's responsible for the debt. Besides, getting rid of the bull wouldn't cancel the money owed."

The sound of horses approaching the house drew Amanda's attention. She looked out a nearby window. She didn't know the two riders well, but they had a reputation for being shiftless, willing to bend rules, and not above looking for ways to get around the law. "I'll go see what they want," she said. "You keep trying to figure out what to do about the bull."

As Amanda watched the two men dismount, hitch their horses, and climb the steps to the porch, she unconsciously compared them to Broc. They fell so far short it was pathetic. One was so thin he was shapeless. The other thought more about food and beer than he did his personal appearance.

"Howdy," the thin one said. "It's a little warm for this time of year."

"It's been a long while since I saw you at the saloon, Bryce," Amanda said. "What are you doing out here?"

"We've been out of town," Purdy said. "Just got back yesterday."

"What caused you to ride this far out?"

"We got some information on a fella folks say has been hanging around your place," Bryce said.

The two men worked for the Reconstruction government. Its only purpose seemed to be to give unprincipled scoundrels the means to pry money out of honest people any way they could. When it couldn't do that, it threatened to cause trouble with the police or the army. The reputation of both forces was so notorious Texans would do virtually anything to avoid being the focus of their attention.

"There are no men *hanging around our place*," Amanda stated impatiently. "This is a ranch. Everyone here works."

"It doesn't matter what he does," Purdy said. "We have reason to arrest him."

"Who are you talking about?" She couldn't imagine they meant Leo or Andy. Dan had worked for Carruthers until recently, and Broc had never been in Cactus Bend before.

"We have information a man named Broc Kincaid has been working to reestablish a Confederate government in Texas."

That was such an absurd accusation, Amanda couldn't stop herself from laughing. "No one in his right mind would try anything like that."

"The information came from a reliable source, a spy for the Union during the war."

"Broc has been in California. He couldn't possibly have had anything to do with such a stupid plot. Besides, the war has been over four years."

"Some people can't seem to accept that."

Bryce cast his partner an uneasy glance. "We're only here to see this Kincaid fella and ask him some questions."

"Purdy said you were going to arrest him." Amanda didn't trust either of them.

"We got to ask him some questions first," Bryce said. "What we do depends on what he says."

"But we'll probably arrest him," Purdy said. "We can't have nobody plotting against the government."

"*Reconstruction* government," Amanda reminded him.

"It's the government of Texas," Purdy insisted.

"It's a gang of thieves sent to rob and plunder."

"Careful," Purdy said, his weasel-like smile back in place. "A person who didn't know you might consider that treason."

"Only a member of the Reconstruction government."

"You got to let us come in," Bryce said. "If you don't, we'll have to send for the army."

"What's going on?" a stern voice demanded.

Amanda turned to see that Broc and her mother had come out onto the porch. "These men say they have to talk to Broc about plotting against the Reconstruction government."

"That's absurd," Broc said. "I haven't been in Texas. And if I had been, I wouldn't have done anything that stupid."

"We have information from a reputable source," Purdy said.

Broc replied with cool confidence, "There's no one who could make such an accusation against me because it isn't true."

"It's someone who knew you during the war." Purdy was clearly enjoying his feeling of power. "He's known every move you've made since then."

"Purdy says the man was a spy for the Union during the war," Amanda told Broc.

Having expected Broc to laugh in Purdy's face, Amanda was shocked to see Broc lose color, his expression change from calm indifference to anger in a matter of seconds.

"Was this person Laveau di Viere?" Broc asked.

"That's exactly who it was." Purdy appeared to think Broc's response was proof of his guilt.

"Laveau di Viere fought for the Confederacy," Broc said.

"He was a spy for the Union," Purdy said.

"For three years he was a member of a Confederate cavalry troop that raided Union supply depots, blew up trains, stole payrolls, did anything we could to disrupt Union forces," Broc stated. "When he realized the Union was going to win the war, he betrayed his troop. He murdered the lookout, stole his best friend's money, and left us to be murdered in our sleep. He's a liar, a thief, a cattle rustler, and is wanted in California for kidnapping and attempted murder. He's an outcast even to his own family."

Purdy grinned. "I wouldn't expect you to speak highly of a man of principle."

"The only *principle* Laveau adheres to is improving his situation by whatever means possible."

"We're wasting time," Purdy said. "You got to come with us."

"Why?"

"To answer questions about this charge," Bryce said.

"Laveau has been following the surviving members of our troop ever since the war, trying to do anything he could to discredit us or cause trouble."

"You'll get your chance to speak."

If Purdy's sly grin was any indication, Amanda felt certain he'd already decided Broc was guilty. "What will happen to him?" she asked.

"That'll be up to the army to decide." Purdy appeared to enjoy considering the possible punishments. "If he's guilty, he'll go to jail. If the charges are serious enough, he might be hanged." He stepped toward Broc.

"I'm not going with you," Broc said. "You don't care that Laveau is a liar. I doubt you'll make any attempt to discover his reputation or verify his statements."

The sound of a rifle being cocked drew all eyes. "It's time for you boys to leave." Dan had emerged from the house, rifle pointed directly at Purdy. "You've got no business here."

Purdy's smile was sinister. "No point in kicking up a fuss. If you don't come quiet, you'll come hard. The army will take a dim view when I tell them about what's happened here today."

"I don't think you'll do that, Purdy Beamis. In

fact, I think you and Bryce will go back to Cactus Bend and never say a word to anybody about why you came here."

Amanda wasn't the only one who was surprised by her mother's words.

"Begging your pardon, Miz Liscomb, but we can't do that," Purdy said. "We got our duty to do."

"I guess you do," Amanda's mother said, "but you'll understand if I feel the same way about my duty."

Purdy's smile stayed in place, but it faltered a bit. "I don't know what you're talking about."

"Just yesterday Mrs. Carruthers was explaining to me the way the ironclad oath is being applied by the army these days," her mother told Purdy. "She said it's interpreted to mean that anyone who's ever been a mayor, school trustee, clerk, public weigher, even a cemetery sexton during or *before* the war is disenfranchised. I would think that would also include being barred from working for the Reconstruction government. Your bosses might be angry that you and Bryce have lied to them about fighting for the Confederacy."

Purdy's smile bloomed again. "I *never* fought for the Confederacy."

"You and Bryce both signed up when Texas seceded. My husband saw you. I remember him saying two more worthless soldiers would be difficult to find." Her mother stepped forward until she could look Purdy directly in the eye. "If a Union army captain were to begin to look into your activities during the war, I don't think it would be difficult to convince him that your loyalties were still with the Confederacy, maybe even that you spied for Texas during the war. My husband said you delivered guns and supplies to Texas troops."

Purdy had never had much color, but now he looked white. Bryce had turned a dull red.

"Mrs. Carruthers told me that the man in charge of the army in Dallas has a reputation for being the most diligent officer in Texas for finding hidden sympathizers. And for being most severe in handling their cases."

"He wouldn't believe any accusation made by a woman," Purdy said.

"Don't be a fool," Bryce said. "He'd believe anything said against a Texan. Only last month he—"

"I know what he did," Purdy said.

"Then you know what he'd do to us if he found out we lied to him."

"I know both your families," Amanda's mother said. "I have no wish to cause them any heartache. All I ask is that you forget everything this Laveau person said. No one can believe the word of a traitor."

Purdy was angry at having to back down, but it was just as clear Bryce was anxious to leave as fast as possible. "I had my doubts about his accusations," Bryce told her mother. "He seemed to be going out of his way to provide information."

"He went all the way to California to cause trouble," Broc said. "He wouldn't hesitate to cross half of Texas."

"We can overlook it this time," Purdy said, "but if he comes back again—"

"We'll know not to believe a word he says." Bryce directed his gaze and words at Purdy. "Sorry to have bothered you, Mr. Kincaid."

Amanda strove to calm her nerves as she watched Purdy and Bryce mount up and ride away. Broc's narrow escape from the jaws of the Reconstruction forces had her heart beating double time.

"Thank you," Broc said to her mother. "Everything Laveau di Viere said was untrue, but that wouldn't have stopped the Army. The actions of some officers have been nothing short of criminal."

"You told me you didn't like Broc," Eddie said to his mother. "You said you hoped the judge would put him in jail. Why did you help him?"

It took her mother several seconds to regain her composure, but when she did, she turned to Broc rather than Eddie.

"I haven't been fair to you. I was angry at you over this business of the debt, but you've behaved very well. Though I don't like Amanda spending so much time with you, I do appreciate your efforts to help us with the ranch. It's a great misfortune that your face has been so badly disfigured. It gives you quite a hideous appearance."

"Mother!" Amanda couldn't believe her mother would say something so cruel.

"I was about to say that people are likely to be quite mistaken in their estimation of his character. As I was." Her mother turned back to Broc. "I'm sorry for the things I've said and done. I'm quite ashamed of myself."

Amanda wouldn't have believed this could be happening if she hadn't witnessed it. Her mother *never* apologized or admitted she could have made a mistake.

"You don't have to apologize, Mrs. Liscomb,"

Broc said. "You've been under a great deal of stress. It's understandable that you would distrust anyone who threatened to make your situation worse."

"I didn't just distrust you. I disliked you. I can't forgive myself for that."

Before Amanda could think of something to say, another rider came into view.

"That's Russell, one of the hands on Carruthers's ranch," Dan said.

"What could he be doing here?"

"Whatever it is, it can't be good," her mother said. "I was not mistaken in my assessment of Carruthers's character."

As he drew close, Amanda noticed Russell's horse was lathered. Whatever the reason for his visit, it had caused him to ride hard. He rode his horse up to the porch before stopping. He spoke to Dan without dismounting.

"Charlie told Carruthers he saw the bull that belongs to these folks down by the lake the creek makes when it rains." He glanced briefly at Amanda before turning back to Dan. "Carruthers grabbed his rifle and rode out. He said he was going to put an end to this problem once and for all."

Twenty-one

DAN HAD SHOWN THEM THE SHORTEST ROUTE TO THE swampy area where Carruthers had tried to brand the calves.

"Surely he doesn't intend to shoot the bull," Amanda said to Broc.

Probably not, but Broc had reached the conclusion Carruthers was mentally unstable. In his opinion, no sane man would attack his daughter in public or destroy her music just because she wanted to sing. "Ask Dan. He knows the man better." The three of them were riding abreast, with Russell on his tired mount trailing behind.

"His wanting to buy your ranch has gotten to be about more than adding additional land to his spread," Dan said. "He's like a child who's been denied something he wants. He'll do anything he can to get it."

"I don't see how killing the bull would help him do that," Amanda said.

Broc did. Getting rid of the bull would ruin the Liscombs.

Several cows with calves were grazing in the

meadows bordering the creek and the lake when they arrived, but they saw no sign of Carruthers or the bull.

"Maybe he couldn't find the bull," Amanda said.

"He could have changed his mind." Russell had caught up once they stopped. "Maybe he was just mad and said the first thing that came to mind."

"He has always had a tendency to fly off the handle when things don't go his way," Dan said.

"I hope you're right," Broc said, "but I'll feel better once we find the bull and get it back in its pasture. I think it's time we put a padlock on that gate."

The words were hardly out of his mouth when he heard rifle fire. It was quickly followed by three more shots.

"That many shots makes it sound like someone is hunting," Amanda said.

"They'd better not let Carruthers find them," Dan said.

"I think we ought to check out the rifle shots," Broc said. "If it is a stray hunter, we need to warn him about Carruthers."

The rifle fire continued sporadically while they skirted several dense thickets of trees, vines, brush, and swamp grass. They found Carruthers on a small rise of ground surrounded by a marsh thick with bulrushes. The bullet-riddled carcass of the bull lay less than ten yards away.

Amanda gasped. "My God! He did kill the bull."

Even as they rode toward him, Carruthers shot twice more into the carcass of the dead animal. He seemed unaware of their existence as they rode up.

"I don't think he's in his right mind," Broc said. "I'm going to try to get the rifle away from him."

"Let me," Dan said. "He hates you so much he might turn the rifle on you."

Broc wasn't sure Carruthers liked Dan any better.

"Maybe I ought to try," Amanda said. "He has no reason to want to hurt me."

Broc wasn't willing to risk it. Amanda's family owned the land Carruthers wanted. And Amanda was responsible for Priscilla's singing in the saloon and having a place to stay when her father was furious at her. "Do you have a rifle?" Broc asked Russell.

The young man nodded.

"If you think Carruthers is about to shoot one of us, get him first."

The man blanched but nodded.

It turned out to be no problem to disarm Carruthers. He shot the bull once more but didn't object when Broc took the rifle from his hands.

"That's one problem taken care of," he said to Broc.

Broc couldn't resist asking, "How is that?"

"They *have* to sell me the ranch now."

Carruthers acted as though what he'd done was of no more consequence than getting rid of a lobo wolf that had been preying on his calves. Broc looked at the bullet-riddled body of the bull. "Why did you need to shoot it so many times?"

"It wouldn't die," Carruthers said. "It kept getting up. I had to keep shooting until it would stay down." Carruthers got up from where he'd been sitting on a decaying log. "I've got to go see Grace, tell her the bull is out of the way so she can sell the ranch to me now."

Carruthers started walking, but he wasn't headed in the direction of his ranch house or his horse, which was ground-hitched a few yards away. Broc handed Carruthers's rifle to Dan. He took the man by the arm and guided him toward his horse.

"What are you going to do?" Dan asked.

"Take him home," Broc said. "It'll be up to his wife to decide what should be done next."

It was as if another man had taken possession of Carruthers's body. There was none of the belligerence, the violence, the anger that could blaze into hatred, but Broc had had enough experience with soldiers who had gone into shock to know Carruthers's mood might change at any time. It was important to get him home and send for a doctor.

"What's wrong with him?" Russell asked. The boy looked as bewildered as he was shocked.

"I'd guess he's lost contact with reality," Broc said.

"What caused it?" Amanda asked.

"Maybe he felt so strongly about everything, his mind couldn't hold up under the strain."

But what could make Carruthers—a man with the shrewdness and doggedness to claw his way to a position of wealth and influence—suddenly go crazy? Why would he keep shooting the bull long after it was dead?

"What will happen to the ranch?"

Broc thought that wasn't an appropriate question, but he figured Russell was too young and too shocked to be thinking clearly. "That will be for Mrs. Carruthers and Priscilla to decide." A thought occurred to him, and he glanced over at Dan. "I expect one of the first things they'll do is rehire their foreman."

It amused him to see Dan color.

The ride to Carruthers's ranch house was uneventful. Carruthers talked the whole way, often saying things that made no sense or were unconnected to his previous remarks. The thread woven through his rambling was that the elimination of the bull would solve everyone's problems. He seemed to believe he had behaved like Solomon in finding a solution that was best for everyone. Broc reflected that the outcome wouldn't have been any different if he'd cut the bull in half rather than shooting it.

Mrs. Carruthers came out to meet them when they reached the ranch house. Carruthers didn't wait for Broc to help him dismount. He threw his leg across, slid from the saddle, and ran over to embrace his wife.

"I'll get the Lazy T now. The bull is dead."

It took several minutes to guide Carruthers inside. He refused to go to his bedroom, but he did allow himself to be settled into a deep chair by the window.

"What happened?" his wife asked.

Broc was relieved and pleased when she turned to Dan rather than to him.

"He killed the Liscombs' bull," Dan said. "Shot it at least a dozen times after he knew it was dead."

Mrs. Carruthers looked at her husband, then back at Dan. "Do you think he's all right in his mind?"

"No."

"Will he get better?"

"I don't know. Broc has more experience with this sort of thing than I do."

"He could suddenly snap out of it, go in and out, or never recover," Broc said when Mrs. Carruthers turned to him. "It's most likely, however, that he'll recover if he gets plenty of rest. But this is only speculation. I'm not a doctor."

She turned to Dan. "Will you come back to work for us?"

"Of course."

Mrs. Carruthers's relief was obvious. She turned to Amanda. "I'm so sorry about your bull. I don't know anything about my husband's financial matters, but I hope we'll be able to buy you another one."

Broc thought it best if he and Amanda left as quickly as possible. The decisions Mrs. Carruthers had to make could be better made without them.

"What are you going to do now?" Broc asked Amanda as soon as they were back in the saddle and headed home. "If Carruthers recovers, he'll never replace your bull. If he doesn't, Mrs. Carruthers might not have the money to buy another."

"And that's only half the problem. Gary says there isn't anything about the debt among Papa's papers."

"That doesn't make any sense," Broc said. "Even if your father didn't trust banks, he would have made a record of a transaction of that importance. Where did he keep his cash?"

"He didn't have any when he died." Amanda laughed. "He always said if I needed money, I could depend on Mother's secretaire, which was his idea of a joke. He knew Mother would sell everything in the house before she would part with that desk. It's supposed to have been owned by a distant English ancestor who claimed to be minor nobility. I think it's a story somebody made up."

"Which still leaves us with the problem of how to prove the debt belongs to Corby."

&

"If you don't give me the money right now, I'll shoot you in the center of your black heart."

"I don't have that much money."

Corby gaped at Mrs. Liscomb with wide, frightened eyes. She was furious, and she held a gun pointed at the center of Corby's chest. She had backed him into a corner in his office, his thin, shapeless frame making him look more like a piece of room decoration than a human being.

Standing just outside the office door, Broc listened to the exchange in astonishment.

"Then find it. I don't care where. Just get it."

"I can't go into the bank and expect them to hand over seven hundred dollars to pay for a dead bull."

"If you'd paid for it, it wouldn't be dead."

"You can't prove that."

"Maybe not, but that won't much matter if you're dead."

Broc would never have dreamed this overly decorous Southern lady could turn into a gun-wielding madwoman, but he should have known better than to underestimate the fury of a mother when she believed her family was threatened. He would have liked to see Mrs. Liscomb terrorize Corby a bit longer, but the look in her eyes made him decide to intervene.

"I wouldn't mind seeing him dead, either, but we wouldn't be able to get the money out of him then, would we?"

Mrs. Liscomb's fury didn't abate. "It would be worth it. My husband trusted this man. I encouraged my daughter to marry him."

"I still want to marry her," Corby said. "I told her I'd take care of the ranch, of everything."

His words served only to stoke Mrs. Liscomb's anger. Corby's eyes grew wide with fear when she jammed the gun into his breastbone. "I'd work in this saloon myself before I'd let her marry a loathsome piece of frog spawn like you."

For a nice lady, she had a deadly way of phrasing insults. "I have no objection to your shooting Corby. Personally, I'd like to start with his legs and work my way around his body, being careful to avoid hitting anything that could actually kill him, but Amanda and Eddie wouldn't be very happy to have to visit you in jail."

"We could force him to open his safe," she said. "He must have seven hundred dollars in there."

"That would be robbery," Corby said.

"Which would be only fair since you've robbed us," Grace pointed out.

"I never took a cent from any of you," Corby protested. "I paid Amanda more than twice what I paid anyone else."

Mrs. Liscomb prodded him with the gun barrel. "Then fired her when she brought in more money than you've ever made in your miserable life."

"Carruthers threatened to ruin me, to burn down the saloon."

"You're a coward, Corby Wilson. A liar, a thief, and a yellow-bellied coward. You deserve shooting, but you're not worth going to jail for."

Broc grinned. Apparently Mrs. Liscomb had picked up a few Texas-style insults. She was still pressing the gun against Corby's chest when Amanda rushed into the room.

"Mother, what are you doing?"

"Trying to force this poor excuse for a man to honor his obligations, but apparently Texans don't believe in honor as much as people brought up in Mississippi."

"I already said—"

"Silence!" Mrs. Liscomb poked Corby so sharply, he grimaced. "I've heard more than I want out of you."

Broc was sorry for the mess Amanda's family found itself in, but the crisis seemed to be working wonders on Mrs. Liscomb.

"You might as well let him go," Amanda said.

"I'd much prefer to shoot him."

"I think this would be a good time to renegotiate Amanda and Gary's contract," Broc suggested. "I believe you've got Corby's full attention. They don't actually have a contract, but I think it would be a good idea to put the agreement in writing this time. That would eliminate the possibility of Corby firing them any time he fell into a jealous fit."

"I would never be jealous of a disfigured man like you," Corby shouted.

Mrs. Liscomb poked him again. She appeared to like the way his eyes widened in fear each time she dug into his ribs. "That's because you're not smart enough to know Mr. Kincaid's a hundred times the man you'll ever be."

Broc was beginning to like Mrs. Liscomb more and more.

"I don't want to work for Corby," Amanda said.

"I think once you've had time to *look into things*"—Broc hoped she noticed his emphasis—"you'll change your mind."

Amanda gave him a hard, questioning look. "Only if he'll agree to hire Broc as well." Her expression didn't change.

"I don't want him," Corby said.

Mrs. Liscomb poked him again. "You don't get any say in this."

"It's my saloon."

"I wouldn't be too sure of that. Broc will find a way to prove you lied. Then I'll take you to court. By the time I tell the judge all the pain and heartache you've put me and my family through—I believe my appearing in court in widow's weeds with tearstained, powdered cheeks will make a powerful impression—you'll be lucky if he doesn't give me the saloon outright."

Broc nearly laughed aloud at Corby's expression. It might be worth a few weeks in jail to see that confrontation.

"Gary gets his job back, Broc plays the piano, Priscilla gets to sing if she wants, and we can do any skit Broc writes." Amanda looked Corby in the eye. "Those are my conditions. None are negotiable."

Corby glared at Broc. "He said he was leaving."

"He'll be back."

The way Amanda gazed at him tore at Broc's heart. How could he tell her that the best thing he could do for her might be not to come back?

"Carruthers won't let Priscilla come near the saloon," Corby said.

"Carruthers is too ill to leave his bed," Broc told Corby.

"He could still burn me out when he gets well."

"He won't be allowed to leave the house for weeks to come," Amanda told him.

When Corby was slow to respond, Mrs. Liscomb prodded him again. Broc was worried that one of those times she was going jab him too hard, and the gun would go off. If she did shoot him, he hoped a judge could be persuaded to believe it was an accident caused by extreme emotional stress.

"You think my daughter is a liar like you?" Mrs. Liscomb poked Corby so hard, Broc steeled himself to hear a gunshot. "We don't make agreements we don't intend to honor. Broc can write out the contracts for you."

Broc was finding that being transformed in a matter of minutes from a distrusted and disliked interloper to a magician who was expected to pull any trick out of his hat was a bit disconcerting. He didn't know what Mrs. Liscomb would decide he could do next, but apparently, she saw no limit to his talents. A pity she wasn't right.

"If you don't hire us, we'll work for your competition," Amanda said. "We have to work for someone, because we need the money."

"But what's the point? You don't have a bull," Corby reminded her, "so the ranch will fail anyway."

"They have his calves," Broc pointed out. "In a couple of years, they'll have dozens of young bulls with his blood."

"But we need jobs until then," Amanda said.

Mrs. Liscomb poked Corby. "Tell her you agree."

"Okay." Corby's ribs must have been getting really sore because he gave in more readily than Broc expected. "But I've got to read the contracts before I sign them."

Mrs. Liscomb poked him again. "And after you read them, you'll sign them, right?"

"I'll sign them," Corby said, "but I'd much rather marry Amanda. I'd take care of everything, and she wouldn't have to work."

Broc wasn't sure Corby had enough money to do all he said, but he was relieved neither Amanda nor her mother showed the slightest interest in his offer. It didn't take long to put all the pertinent information down on paper. Mrs. Liscomb continued to hold Corby at gunpoint. She didn't lower her weapon until Corby had read and signed the contract.

"I'll tell Gary," Amanda said. "I'm sure he'll want to start tonight."

"I think you and Broc should wait until tomorrow," Mrs. Liscomb said. "You'll need time to decide what you want to perform." She picked up her purse and put the gun inside.

"I'm relieved to see you put that gun away," Broc said. "I was afraid you might poke Corby a bit too hard, and it would go off."

"It's not loaded," Mrs. Liscomb said. "I couldn't figure out how to put the bullets in it."

❧

Amanda was convinced there was something in Corby's office that would confirm he had agreed to pay for the bull in exchange for her father's share of the saloon. The only problem was figuring out where he'd hidden it. She hadn't wanted to work in the saloon, but in addition to needing the money, it had provided her with several opportunities to search Corby's office when he was busy talking with his customers. So far she hadn't found anything of interest except money. Each time she entered his office, she had to tell herself she couldn't take the money just because he owed it to Mrs. Sibley. Despite the injustice of what he was doing, that would be stealing, and she would not lower herself to Corby's level.

In the meantime, she had to be especially careful. When Broc was in the saloon, Corby was so jealous of him he wouldn't let Broc out of his sight, but Broc had finally gone back to Crystal Springs to start serving his jail time. That made it even more difficult for Amanda not to take the money. If Corby had agreed to pay the debt, Broc wouldn't have had to go to jail, so it was Corby's fault Amanda was separated from Broc. It was Corby's fault that the ranch was in trouble, that the bull was dead, that her mother still faced the possibility of having to sell some of her precious furniture.

It would serve him right if Amanda stole his money and Carruthers burned him out.

But she wasn't a thief, and Carruthers was heavily sedated.

Where should she search next? She had begun by going through Corby's safe. It had taken a bit of persuasion, but she'd convinced Gary to leave it unlocked when he went to get cash for the bar. She'd found money, deeds to the saloon and diner, and some other important papers, but she found nothing about the debt to Mrs.

Sibley. She wished she could have read all the documents thoroughly—she was sure she'd have found something to hold over Corby—but she didn't have time.

Next she'd gone through the large cabinet that stood at the back of the room. Her father had kept his records there, as well as odds and ends from the saloon or the diner, but she had found nothing in the cabinet that had any connection with the sale of the saloon or the bull. She'd even checked behind the two pictures to see if Corby had installed a secret safe.

The only piece of real furniture in the room was the desk. Her father had bought it from a family moving farther west who needed the money and didn't need the extra weight. She'd rarely seen Corby do more than relax in the chair, so she'd saved it for last. Except for two drawers on either side, it didn't seem to have any places to hide papers.

She sat down at the desk, pulled out the first drawer, and scanned its contents. No papers there, just odds and ends like ink, pens, blotters, extra paper. The second drawer was empty. A third held Corby's bank records. Maybe they would give her the information she needed. If she could find something that showed he'd paid any money to Mrs. Sibley, it could be used as evidence that he owed her still more.

She quickly thumbed through the receipts, but she couldn't find anything that had Mrs. Sibley's name on it or that could be proved to have been payment for the bull. There must be something here. There *had* to be. She'd just missed it. She started through everything again, concentrating so hard, she didn't hear the door open.

"What are you doing?" Corby demanded.

Twenty-two

AMANDA CURSED UNDER HER BREATH. HOW COULD SHE have been so stupid as to have let herself be caught? She needed to think of something that was incriminating but wouldn't cause Corby to guess what she was really after.

"I was looking to see if you had as much money as you claimed. If I should decide to accept your offer of marriage, I need to know you can support me."

That was a weak excuse and so far from the truth, it cost her dearly to utter the lie. Corby's gaze remained angry and suspicious, but she could see an element of doubt—or maybe she should call it *hope*—make its way into his eyes. He wasn't a stupid man, but he had an enormous ego that required constant massaging. Since he was convinced a man's measure was determined by money and prestige, maybe he would believe she thought the same thing.

"Your mother said she wouldn't let you marry me."

"She was upset. She doesn't want to live in poverty any more than I do."

"You can't be living in poverty with what I'm being forced to pay you and your brother."

"It will take nearly everything we earn to pay for the bull."

His expression turned angry, even pugnacious, a look that wasn't attractive on his thin face. "Your mother tried to make me pay for that bull. She even held a gun to my head."

Every time she thought of Broc's uncontrollable laughter when her mother confessed she hadn't known how to put bullets in the gun, she started laughing. If she even cracked a smile now, Corby wouldn't believe a word she said. She thought of being married to Corby, of having to face him on their wedding night, and she lost any desire to smile. "As I told you, Mother was upset."

Corby wasn't through yet. "Do you think I'm a liar and a thief?"

Maybe it was silly to balk at lying at this point, but she'd prefer to find a way around it. "I was upset. You'd just fired Gary and me. Carruthers had just killed our bull. I've had time to reconsider my opinion since then." She *had* reconsidered her opinion of him. It had gotten worse.

"You could have told me what you wanted to know. I'd have given you all the proof you could want."

"I'm enough like my father to like to prove things for myself."

"Are you satisfied now?"

She breathed a sigh of relief. It was amazing how a person could be so focused on something he wanted that he could blind himself to everything else. "I don't know. I didn't find any record of outstanding debts, but I didn't find anything showing you have a bank

342   LEIGH GREENWOOD

balance, either. I know the saloon and diner are worth more than enough to pay our debt, but you wouldn't have a way to support me if you sold them."

She knew she'd escaped discovery when Corby's frown turned to his trademark grin, the one that grew out of his belief he was one of the three or four most important and influential men in Cactus Bend. Corby crossed over to the safe, unlocked it, reached inside, and pulled out a roll of bills.

"Here's all the money you need to pay off the rest of your debt."

She knew that. Even now she itched to snatch the money from him.

"The saloon and diner generate more than enough income to support a wife and family."

She knew that, too. Half the income from the two businesses had been sufficient to support her family.

Amanda put the papers back in the drawer, closed it, and got to her feet. She had to get out of this room before Corby could press her for a commitment. "That's all I needed to know. Now I'd better get back to work. I don't want you to think I'm not earning my keep."

"You won't have to work after you marry me," Corby said.

"But I'm not married now, so I do need to work." She rounded the desk and headed for the door. "You'd better come watch. I want you to realize just how much better the entertainment is when Broc is here."

That comment would needle him so much he would forget about anything romantic. For that matter, Amanda wondered if Corby was capable of being romantic. He'd never said anything romantic. He'd never done anything romantic. He'd never even thought of their marriage in terms of love. He insisted that he loved her, but Amanda doubted he was capable of love or understanding how important love was to her. If he hadn't lied and cheated, she would have hoped he'd someday find a woman who could teach him how to love. Now, however, she hoped no woman would be forced to live with a man like him. She never would, not even if her family had to sell every piece of furniture in the house, every calf, every cow. Some things were worse than poverty.

Amanda wasn't sure how much longer she could stand it. She spent her days working on the Lazy T and her evenings working in the saloon, but she couldn't stop herself from thinking of Broc, wondering what was happening to him, wondering when he would come back, *if* he would come back. She had asked him to write but wasn't surprised when no letters arrived. What could he have to tell her? Not much of interest was likely to happen when you were locked up in a jail.

She had coerced Corby into giving her an advance on her salary so Broc could take Mrs. Sibley a small payment. She'd hoped that would encourage the judge to reconsider his decision to send Broc to jail, but apparently it hadn't worked. She'd even talked Gary into giving their mother half his salary in exchange for not being required to work on the ranch. Her mother had been surprised, but Amanda knew Gary hated the ranch with a depth of feeling her mother couldn't

understand. What other reason could he have had for
letting the bull out so many times when he knew how
important it was to the survival of the ranch?

Today was one of those rare days in Texas when
a steady rain had turned the prairie into ankle-deep
mud, making it virtually impossible to work outside.
Leo and Andy were holed up in the bunkhouse cleaning saddles and bridles, and repairing any equipment
in need of fixing. Eddie was helping her mother in the
kitchen. Amanda had swept every room in the house.
Now she was dusting and polishing her mother's precious furniture. Remembering her father's admonition
to "look to the secretaire" if they ever found themselves in a difficult position, she scowled at the intricate
piece of furniture that stood tall against a background
of flowered wallpaper like an aristocrat trapped among
the hoi polloi, its inlaid woods, beveled glass, and tiny
brass knobs making it the focal point of the room.
Her mother had been too grief-stricken after her husband's death to be of any help in settling his affairs, so
Amanda had been the one to go through every drawer
and cubbyhole. She'd thumbed through every book,
read every piece of paper, without finding anything
useful. Now she glared at it, daring it to live up to her
father's promise.

"Haven't you finished dusting yet?" her mother
asked.

It was impossible to *finish* dusting in Texas. By the
time she finished with the last piece of furniture, a new
layer of dust had begun to settle on the first. "Yes, I'm
done."

"Then what are you doing standing there?"

"I keep wondering what Papa meant when he said I was to look to the secretaire if we were in trouble. I read every piece of paper in it without finding anything helpful."

"Did you look in the secret drawer?"

It was hard to describe the effect that question had on her. She felt as if the ground had fallen away from under her at the same time she felt an upsurge of hope. "What secret drawer? Papa never said anything about a secret drawer."

"Of course not. It wouldn't have been secret if he had."

Amanda bit back the response that sprang to her mind. "You never said anything about a secret drawer."

"I was too upset when your father died to think of it."

"He's been dead over a year. Why didn't you say something about it before now?"

"I don't know. I guess I didn't think it was important."

Swallowing another response she decided not to utter, Amanda shrugged in defeat. "I don't see how knowing there's a secret drawer in that secretaire is going to help us when we don't know where it is or how to open it."

"You forget this used to be my father's desk," her mother said. "He showed me where it is and how to open it."

Amanda's tingle of excitement was tempered by her doubt the drawer could contain anything that would solve their problems. "Can you open it now?"

Her mother shrugged and walked over to the secretaire. She opened it, reached under a decorative piece of wood that fronted the base of the row of cubbies, and pushed something that caused the piece of wood to slide less than an inch forward, revealing itself as the front of a long, shallow drawer. Her mother gripped the drawer with her fingertips and pulled it open.

Some papers occupied the right corner of the drawer, but Amanda's eyes were drawn to the gold coins scattered across the majority of the drawer. She didn't know how much money was there, but she was certain it was more than enough to pay off the debt on the bull.

It took a moment for her to catch her breath, to calm her racing heart, before she could speak. "Did you know about this?" she asked her mother.

"Your father never discussed business with me."

"Why didn't he tell you about the contract for the bull? Why didn't he tell you about the money? You said he told you everything."

Her mother looked abashed. "He might have, but I didn't want to know. My mother taught me it was unsuitable for a lady to interest herself in anything beyond the household accounts."

Amanda's grandmother could never have anticipated a war that would change the way her daughter would have to live. "Well, you need to be interested in everything now. Let's see how much money we have here."

Why had her father not told anyone about the money? They could have sold the secretaire and never realized what was hidden inside.

"What are you doing?" Eddie's eyes grew wide

when he saw the gold coins. "Where did you get all that money?"

"It's Papa's money," Amanda said. "I mean it's our money. Papa hid it in the secretaire for us."

"Did you know?" Eddie asked.

"No."

Eddie studied the coins a moment. "Do we have enough to buy me a horse?"

Her mother paused. "You have three horses."

"They're no good. I want a horse like Broc's."

"Have you considered selling your three horses for one really good one?"

Clearly Eddie hadn't, but he was apparently giving it serious consideration now.

By the time Amanda and her mother finished, they had counted more than two thousand dollars. Her head was spinning from the double shock of finding so much money and realizing the future of the ranch was assured. "I think we ought to put it in the bank," she said to her mother.

"Your father never trusted banks," her mother reminded her.

"And because of that, we nearly lost the ranch. What if you'd sold the secretaire?"

"I never would."

"But what if you had? What if lightning had struck the house and it had burned?"

"Does gold burn up?" Eddie asked.

"No, but it can be lost or stolen. I think we ought to put the money in the bank. It's what Broc would do," she said when her mother looked doubtful.

Her mother wasn't convinced, but she shrugged.

"You know more about all this than I do. Do what you think is best."

Amanda gathered up the coins and put them back in the drawer. "I'll ride into town as soon as the weather clears. Right now, I want to see what's in these papers."

Amanda moved to a window to take advantage of the meager light coming through. The first sheets of paper were deeds to the ranch, the saloon and diner, and several bills of sale, including one for the bull. There was some tax information, business records, and several other sheets that she put aside to be read more closely when she had the time. The last document stopped her in her tracks. Certain she must have misunderstood something, she went back to the beginning and read the entire document over again. Nothing changed. She had understood every word. She was so angry she had trouble breathing.

"What's wrong?" her mother asked. "You look white as a sheet."

"The son of a bitch! The goddamned son of a bitch!"

"Amanda Liscomb!" her mother exclaimed. "I will not have that kind of language in my house. I can't believe those horrible words actually came from your mouth."

"If you had read what I've just read, you'd be cussing, too."

"Nothing could make me lose such control of myself," her mother stated with a kind of stiff-necked pride that inflamed rather than cooled Amanda's anger. She thrust the document into her mother's hands.

Her mother read it through with such painful slowness, it was all Amanda could do to keep from taking the document and reading it aloud. Her restraint finally had its reward. When her mother reached the end of the document, she raised stunned eyes to her daughter.

"Show me how to put bullets in that gun. I intend to shoot that man."

⤮

Amanda burst into Corby's office, pointed an accusing finger at him that still shook from anger, then turned to the sheriff, who had followed in her wake. "Arrest that man for a liar and a thief. He has refused to pay his debts and tried to steal my family's share of the saloon and diner."

Corby couldn't have looked more surprised if the ghost of his dead partner had climbed out of his grave to accuse him. "You've been very worried and probably working too hard," Corby said, "but that's no reason to start acting like your mother. I don't know what has gotten you so upset, but I'm sure if we—"

"*This* has gotten me upset." It was all Amanda could do to keep from shouting as she waved the document in front of Corby. "You told us Papa had sold you the diner and the saloon. That was a lie. And you never said anything about agreeing to make Papa's payments for the bull—even when you knew that judge in Crystal Springs was trying to collect the debt from us."

Corby lost color but didn't act like a man caught in a web of guilty lies. In a way, he actually seemed relieved. For a moment, Amanda had a horrible feeling something still more shocking was about to be revealed.

"I wasn't trying to steal the diner or saloon from you," Corby said. "You might say I was saving them for your family."

"How?" Amanda was so flabbergasted by his attitude, she couldn't find words to express her feelings.

"Your father didn't want to buy that ranch," Corby told her. "He only bought it because your mother wouldn't give him any peace."

Amanda hated to admit Corby was right, but all three children had been witness to her mother's relentless campaign to force her husband to find a more respectable way to make a living.

"Your father loved towns and people," Corby continued. "He didn't know anything about cows and didn't want to learn. He was afraid the ranch would fail, so he was determined to hang on to the saloon and the diner for his family. We agreed that after he was gone, I would get his share of the income from the business until his debts had been paid off. After that, the income would revert to the family."

"Why didn't he tell us that?" Amanda asked. "Why didn't *you* tell me?"

"Your father knew he was sick. He wanted to make sure there was someone to take care of you and your family after he was gone. I was his partner, and I wanted to marry you. I was the logical person to be his confidant."

Amanda felt like the stuffing had been pulled out of her. She didn't want to believe Corby—she still didn't believe he'd acted ethically—but too many things made sense. Her father didn't trust his family enough to tell them about his illness or his businesses. He didn't trust anyone when it came to money. "What about paying for the bull?" That was one thing Corby couldn't explain away.

"I told him he was paying too much, but he insisted it was the only way the ranch would be a success. When he died, I figured I'd paid enough, so I didn't pay any more."

Any court of law would declare Corby guilty on several counts, but somehow he'd managed to slither beyond the range of her outrage. She didn't agree with what he'd done, but according to Corby's own twisted thinking, he'd performed admirably. Even worse, it appeared her father had been the one to put the ideas in his head. Amanda felt the ground had been washed from beneath her feet.

"You have signed a contract to pay Mrs. Sibley a specific amount of money," the sheriff told Corby. "You have to pay it whether or not you think it's a fair price. As for the rest, I would prefer you work out your differences with Amanda and her family," he said, turning to Amanda. "As I see it, he hasn't done anything illegal. Basically he withheld the same information your father withheld."

Amanda wanted to scream that Corby deserved some kind of punishment. He'd used their ignorance to try to force her to marry him, to keep her and Gary working in the saloon, to lock her family in a perpetual state of anxiety. Added to that was her sense of personal outrage. Corby said he loved her and wanted to marry her. Yet he thought so little of her as a person, he had attempted to coerce her into marriage. She was nothing more than a business arrangement.

She wanted to hit him so hard in his smug, self-righteous face that his nose would end up behind his left ear. If he had owned up to the debt, Broc wouldn't have had to go to jail. He wouldn't have had another reason to think he was an unsuitable husband for her. If Corby hadn't been so jealous, Broc would still be working with her at the ranch, working with her in the saloon, becoming so much a part of her life he could never think of leaving.

"I want a full accounting of everything the diner and saloon have earned from the day my father died," she told Corby. There wasn't much more she could do. It was clear the sheriff wasn't going to arrest him. "I want to know down to the penny how much you owe my mother, and I want you to see that seven hundred dollars is paid to Mrs. Sibley as soon as possible." She turned to the sheriff. "If he hasn't done everything by this time tomorrow, I want you to arrest him and put him in jail."

"I think you need to allow him a little more time," the sheriff said. "I expect the information you want will take a while to gather."

She supposed the reason Tom Mercer was such a successful sheriff was his habit of looking for a way to peacefully solve disagreements. For once, though, she would like to see him lose control and lock Corby in jail.

"I will have to explain all of this to my mother," Amanda told Corby. "If you don't want her to learn how to put bullets in a gun, you'd better have that information and money ready when she comes banging on your door."

"Amanda, your mother can't—"

She turned to the sheriff. "Whatever you're about to say, save it for my mother."

With that she turned and strode from Corby's office.

❧

It was a good thing Amanda's horse traveled the route between the ranch and town so often he could do it on his own, because Amanda's thoughts were consumed with impotent anger. Corby had put her and her family through months of fear that they'd lose the ranch, weeks of stress over a debt he should have paid, and forced her to work in the saloon after long days at the ranch. What gave him the right to decide what was best for her family?

But if Corby hadn't tried to welsh on his debt in the first place, Broc would never have come into her life.

Thinking of Broc improved her mood but didn't relieve her anxiety. It was impossible to think of him without smiling, without feeling an upsurge of hope, without remembering his kisses or how wonderful it felt to be held in his arms. For the first time in her life, she had someone who thought of her first, someone who loved her without expecting her to do anything to earn his love. He didn't even require that she be beautiful.

She tried to find words that could describe how she felt, but every word that came to mind failed in one or more ways to encompass the breadth or the depth of her happiness. Or to take into consideration the sadness, the regret, the sheer anger that she felt every time she thought of Broc being hurt because of his scars. She ached to protect him, to strike back at anyone who dared treat him as anything less than the wonderful man he was. It wasn't his fault other people were too shallow to see beyond a surface imperfection.

Remembering their night in Crystal Springs caused heat to flood her body and make her squirm in the saddle. At least a dozen times a day the memory of his lips on her breasts would cause her to forget where she was or what she was doing. What could she say to her mother or Leo to explain why she would suddenly be lost to her surroundings? Why she didn't know how to respond to their questions?

She couldn't explain to herself why Broc's love had affected her so profoundly. She'd always hoped to be loved, had anticipated it would be wonderful, but she hadn't expected love to transform her life. It was hard to understand, impossible to explain, how she could feel more grounded, yet at the same time feel less in control of herself. Even more surprising, this state of confusion didn't worry her. It bewildered her, yes, but it brought so much joy and hope that she welcomed the confusion, even embraced it, because it meant Broc was an integral part of her life.

She was so lost in thought she didn't notice the approaching horseman until he was practically upon her. She was surprised to see it was Carruthers. She had thought he was still confined to his bedroom. He looked up, a puzzled expression on his face. Priscilla had said her father had periods when he didn't even know his wife or daughter.

"You." The single syllable indicated surprise rather than anger.

"How are you, Mr. Carruthers?" She didn't know what else to say. She couldn't very well tell him he ought to be at home where people could make sure he didn't hurt himself. She wondered if anyone knew he was gone, or if they were already out looking for him. Maybe she could coax him into going back home. "How is your wife?"

"She asks about you. She hopes you'll come for a visit so she can repay you for your hospitality to Priscilla."

"That's nice of her. I'll try to find time to drop by in a day or two."

"You're not doing anything now," Carruthers said.

Amanda wasn't in the mood to pay a social call. "I need to get home. I have things to discuss with my mother."

"It won't take long. Besides, my wife has something she wants you to take to your mother."

Amanda didn't want to go anywhere with Carruthers, but he appeared to have gotten over whatever it was that had caused him to go a little crazy. He seemed almost afraid she wouldn't accept his invitation. Rather than take a chance that refusing him might cause a relapse, she decided she could spare an hour. She wanted time to cool down, and a visit with Priscilla and her mother might be just the distraction she needed. "Okay, but I can't stay long."

Carruthers nodded and turned his horse, coming around behind her. The sharp blow to her head was totally unexpected. Just before darkness closed around her, she heard Carruthers say, "What was good enough for your bull is good enough for you."

⤢

Broc rode with a loose rein, his mind too busy wrestling with conflicting thoughts to care if his horse stopped to graze on a particularly inviting patch of grass. Ironically, the judge in Crystal Springs was responsible for a large part of his indecision.

Broc had made up his mind that if he went to jail, he wouldn't return to Cactus Bend. He couldn't bear to saddle Amanda with a jailbird for a husband. But the judge hadn't sent him to jail. Broc didn't know whether it was the partial payment he'd brought Mrs. Sibley, or Mrs. Sibley's intervention on his behalf, but Broc had spent a week traveling with the judge, sitting through all the trials, taking notes on the proceedings, and keeping a record of the judgments. He had done so well, the judge threatened to sentence him to a lifetime of being his personal assistant. Instead he'd let him go with a parting admonition to forget his scars.

Broc found it incredible that Amanda wasn't bothered by his disfigurement, but he was sure she couldn't have let him make love to her otherwise. Memories of their loving had dominated his dreams every night since. He would wake up in a cold sweat, his body shaking from the intensity of his need for her. He could chide himself for letting the physical attraction between them influence his thinking, but he couldn't help himself. From the beginning, it had been difficult to hold Amanda in his arms and not think of going much further. Now that they had, his love for her encompassed every part of her being.

But would her life be more difficult if he married her…or if he didn't?

He'd spent weeks trying to answer that question without coming up with any answer. He'd never felt so stupid, so frustrated, so unable to see his way. He wished he could talk to his friends, but he had to answer this question for himself. It was his life. No one could live it for him.

He was almost relieved when he saw a horse without a rider up ahead. He hadn't gotten much closer when he could make out a man lying on the ground. He was relieved to see the young cowhand turn his head in his direction when he rode up. The cowboy was bleeding, but hopefully the bullet hadn't hit any vital organ. "What happened?" Broc asked as he dismounted.

"It was Carruthers." The boy grimaced in pain, but his eyes were clear.

"What about him?"

"He was with Amanda Liscomb," the boy said. "When I asked him what was wrong with her, he shot me."

So many possible explanations exploded in Broc's head at the same time, he couldn't begin to sort through them. "Do you know what was wrong with her?"

"It looked to me like she had fainted."

"Was he taking her home?"

"I thought so, but if he was, why did he shoot me?"

That was exactly the question Broc was asking himself. "Which way did he go?"

"In the direction you came from."

Broc felt a chill knife through him. He hadn't seen anyone for the last two hours.

"Let me help you mount up," Broc said to the boy. "I'm taking you to the Lazy T. If Amanda isn't there, I'm going to turn this county inside out before the sun goes down."

Twenty-three

BROC KEPT HIS TIRED HORSE IN A GALLOP THOUGH THE animal was lathered and his stride labored. Amanda hadn't been at the Lazy T. He had wanted to leave immediately, but Mrs. Liscomb had detained him long enough to explain about the money and the contract with Corby. He would settle the score with Corby later. Right now his only thoughts were of finding Amanda. Carruthers had shot his own cowhand merely for asking what was wrong with Amanda. Broc didn't want to speculate on the state of the man's mind or what it might drive him to do to Amanda.

When he pulled his exhausted horse to a stop in front of the Carruthers ranch house, Dan was waiting for him at the bottom of the steps. Priscilla and Mrs. Carruthers rushed out of the house.

"I have every man on the place looking for the boss," Dan said before Broc could speak. "One of them may have already found him."

Knowing that a dozen men were already looking for Carruthers did little to alleviate Broc's fears. The man didn't need a lot of time to kill Amanda, only the opportunity, and he'd had more than enough of that.

"Have you heard back from anyone yet?" He dismounted.

"Only to know where he isn't."

"He has Amanda. He shot his own cowhand when the boy asked why Amanda couldn't stay in the saddle by herself."

Mrs. Carruthers's hand flew to her mouth. "Did he hurt her?"

"I don't know, but I've got to find them as soon as possible."

Broc and Dan helped the young cowhand out of the saddle.

"Bring him into the house," Mrs. Carruthers said. Once up the stairs, the young cowhand was able to walk on his own.

"Do you have any idea where he might go or what he'll do?" Broc asked Dan.

"None. He's been doing so well recently that the doctor thought he had recovered."

"I need a fresh horse," Broc said.

"Take any one you want, but I think we ought to wait here. One of my men will find them."

Broc knew that was good advice, but he didn't think he'd be able to take it. If anything were to happen to Amanda, he'd never be able to forgive himself for standing around waiting. Yet if he rushed off in an aimless and likely futile chase, he'd have to depend on someone else to rescue Amanda. He couldn't do that, either.

Hell! Being in love was about all the reason a man needed for staying a bachelor.

Dan took the reins of the cowhand's mount. "Let's get you a fresh horse."

"How long ago did you send the men out?" Broc asked as they hurried toward the corrals behind the large bunkhouse.

"About half an hour. He couldn't have been gone long. Mrs. Carruthers had collected the dishes from his lunch a short time earlier."

Broc quickly stripped the saddle and bridle from his horse and turned it into the corral. He allowed himself less than a minute before choosing a dappled gray. When the animal proved too skittish to be roped easily, he settled for a sturdy pinto gelding. Dan chose a strapping dun with black markings. It took only a few minutes for the men to saddle their respective mounts.

"I can't wait here doing nothing," Broc said to Dan.

"I'll come with you as soon as I tell Mrs. Carruthers we're leaving."

The two minutes it took Dan to go to the house and come back seemed more like two hours. He tried not to let his imagination get out of control, but just thinking of what Carruthers could be doing to Amanda nearly drove him crazy. How could she have let Carruthers near her? Didn't she know the man was crazy?

"Let's ride north," Dan said when he'd returned and they'd mounted up. "That's the biggest part of our range."

Dan's suggestion made as much sense as anything else, but Broc felt they might as well have been riding in circles. Carruthers controlled thousands of acres. They could ride for hours and not see anyone. They could ride for days without covering every part of the range. The man could be anywhere. He could be hiding in any one of a hundred thickets. He could be crouched down in a grove of trees. He could be out of sight in a dip behind a low hill. No one knew for sure he'd actually come back to his own land. He could have headed north, south, east, or west.

He could be anywhere!

It was all Broc could do to keep from striking out at Dan in frustration. Why hadn't he kept a better watch on Carruthers? Why hadn't the doctor known the man hadn't recovered? Why hadn't anyone seen him leave? Was he the only one who understood how dangerous Carruthers could be?

He'd always found the Texas prairie bursting with life. Today it seemed dead. Boring. Devoid of interest. He was wasting his time. Carruthers wouldn't be here. It was too open. He needed a place to hide.

Broc refused to allow himself to think of the things Carruthers might do. He had to tell himself Amanda was intelligent and courageous, that she would figure out a way to outwit Carruthers. Maybe she already had. It was possible that at this very moment she was on her way home, or already there.

One thing he did know for certain. If—no, *when*—he got Amanda safely home, he'd never leave her again. Marrying her might not be the best thing he could do for Amanda, but beyond a doubt it was the best thing for him. Knowing her safety and happiness were in the hands of someone else would drive him crazy. He might as well put a gun to his head now and put himself out of his misery.

No, he was marrying Amanda as soon as he could get her to a church. It was too bad if Mrs. Liscomb wasn't happy about the prospect of a son-in-law with a mangled face. Better Broc with his mangled face than Corby with his mangled character.

But first he had to find Amanda.

Call it intuition. Call it a hunch. Call it anything you want, but Broc was suddenly sure that whatever Carruthers intended to do, he was going to do at or near the place he'd shot the bull. That was also where he'd tried to brand the calves.

"I'm heading to the spot where the creek makes a lake when it floods," he said to Dan.

"That was the first place I had the boys look," Dan said.

This news was a blow, but Broc couldn't shake the feeling that the swampy area was where Carruthers would go. "He could have arrived later."

"Somebody would have seen him. That's open land."

True, but no one knew it better than Carruthers. He'd claimed the land more than twenty years ago and ridden it every day since. "I still have to check it out."

"You're wasting your time."

Possibly, but he was wasting his time riding around without a clear objective in mind. "Where can I find you later?"

"I'll find you. It'll be easier."

It was a relief to be on his own, but as he rode across the prairie, it gradually assumed an ominous character, as though it were in league with Carruthers to hide Amanda from him. Thickets became impenetrable tangles of vines; sharp-thorned bushes tore his flesh. Groves of trees guarded their shadowy recesses from the revealing light of the sun. The endless prairie laughed at his puny effort to expose its secrets. Even the cows ignored him.

Broc shook his head to rid himself of images that threatened to undermine his confidence. He would check out the swampy area. If Carruthers wasn't there, he'd just have to decide what to do next.

Broc didn't notice anything at first. Nothing seemed different. Then he realized he didn't see any cows. The grass was richer here than in other parts of the range, and cows always gravitated toward the richest grass. Even the birds were quiet. Broc looked into the thicket where he'd hidden before, but there was no sign that anyone had been there since. The ashes of the fire built to brand the calves lay undisturbed. The spot where the bull had been killed had been cleared. It looked as if no one had been here for days.

Broc wasn't sure what made him look across the flooded marsh to a small bank that separated the marsh from the swollen creek, but what he saw caused his breath to catch in his throat and his heart to thump with relief. Amanda was seated on the small rise of ground barely inches above the surrounding water. She was tied hand and foot, but she appeared to be okay because she was struggling against her restraints. Her horse, wet and mud-caked, grazed some distance away, but Broc didn't see Carruthers or his horse.

Movement out of the corner of Broc's eye caught his attention. He turned to see Carruthers in a small boat rowing toward Amanda. Broc couldn't figure out why

Carruthers had deposited Amanda on the rise of ground or why he was rowing toward her with what looked like a bundle of debris in tow, but he wasn't going to wait to find out. He rode his horse into the lake.

His original plan was to stay away from the deep part of the lake—there was always the possibility of quicksand—but that would mean Carruthers might reach Amanda before he did. He didn't know what Carruthers was trying to do, but he knew it couldn't be good.

Amanda's gaze had been focused on Carruthers, but the noise Broc's horse made splashing through the shallow lake caught her attention. Broc wasn't close enough to tell whether her expression was one of relief, surprise, or concern, but he had no trouble understanding what she shouted to him.

That bundle of what looked like rubbish Carruthers was towing was a nest of cottonmouth moccasins. He apparently intended to tow them to the rise where he'd left Amanda. He intended for the snakes to kill Amanda.

Broc urged his horse through the water faster, but Carruthers spotted Broc and started to row harder. At the present rate, Carruthers would reach Amanda first. Broc didn't know how to stop snakes, but he did know how to stop Carruthers. Though he had plenty of reasons to dislike Carruthers, he wouldn't kill the man.

Hitting Carruthers at this distance and wounding him instead of killing him was a big risk, but he couldn't let Carruthers tow those snakes to the mound. Once they swarmed on dry ground, there would be nothing he could do to save Amanda.

Broc pulled his horse up, but the animal fidgeted so much, throwing his head as well as shifting his weight from foot to foot, that Broc couldn't get a steady shot at Carruthers. Broc was left with the choice of taking any shot he could get or letting Carruthers reach the island before him.

The horse stood still for a split second, but it was enough for Broc to fire a single shot.

Carruthers's body jerked. The oars fell from his grasp, and he slumped over in the boat. Broc didn't know whether he was dead, mortally wounded, or hurt just enough to stop him, but he couldn't take the time to check now. Urging his horse forward, he headed toward Amanda.

The first words out of her mouth when he reached her were, "Did you kill Carruthers?"

"I hope not." While he untied the ropes binding her hands and feet, he glanced over at the boat and was relieved to see Carruthers move. A moment later he sat up, a look of dazed confusion on his face. "Why was he trying to kill you with those snakes?" Broc asked Amanda.

"He thinks I'm his mother. Apparently she belittled him all his life. If I understand his rambling correctly, she once threatened to set a snake on him if he didn't do something she wanted. He was trying to get back at her."

Broc had finished untying Amanda. "Why did you go with him?"

"He said his wife wanted me to take something to my mother. I was on my own horse and in the open. I thought I'd be safe. Unfortunately, I didn't pay attention when he turned his horse around."

Broc pulled Amanda to her feet. "Can you stand?"

"I don't think so."

Broc picked her up and mounted her on his horse.

"What about Carruthers?" The rancher was sitting in the drifting boat, the nest of snakes still attached.

"Dan has his whole crew combing the ranch. I'll send someone for him."

Broc mounted up behind Amanda and rode his horse back into the lake.

It gave Broc a nasty feeling in the pit of his stomach to think how close Amanda had come to a prolonged and painful death, but now that she was safe, he could feel the muscles in his shoulders and the back of his neck begin to relax. The problems with the Lazy T and Corby had been solved. Nothing stood in the way of the kind of future he'd never dared let himself hope to find.

"I'm sorry I was so stupid," Amanda said, "but Carruthers acted so normal, I figured it was okay to ride with him." She leaned back into Broc's embrace. "I was afraid no one would find me. I thought you were in jail, and no one knew I had been kidnapped."

"Dan said his man looked here first but didn't see anyone."

"Carruthers saw him coming and hid me in the same thicket you used when he was trying to brand my calves. He knocked me out again." She raised a hand to the back of her head. "I've got two bumps the size of goose eggs. Am I bleeding?"

Broc leaned down and kissed the bumps. They were nowhere near the size of goose eggs, but he guessed the pain made them feel as though they were.

"I don't see any blood, but I'll get the doctor to look at it."

"I don't want to see a doctor. I just want to go home." She twisted in the saddle. "You have come back to me, haven't you?"

Broc kissed her cheek. "Yes, I've come back."

Amanda turned back around. "I was afraid you wouldn't after going to jail."

"I didn't go to jail. The judge made me his secretary instead."

Broc had angled his horse across the lake so they came out close to where Amanda's horse was still grazing. "He looks a little dirty, but he's dry." Broc slid off his horse. "We ought to hurry home. Your mother is worried to death about you."

Amanda looked back at Carruthers. "We can't leave him."

"Dan will send someone for him."

"We can't leave him. I know he tried to kill me, but I'm sure he wouldn't have if he hadn't been sick."

Broc wasn't certain he believed that, but he wasn't going to argue. He just wanted to get Amanda safely home. Carruthers was struggling to get to his feet, but his balance was off so much he couldn't stand up without rocking the boat wildly.

"If he falls into the lake, the snakes will attack him," Amanda said.

"If I get close enough to help him, the snakes could turn on me," Broc pointed out.

"You'll think of something," Amanda said, "but we can't leave him."

Broc wanted to argue, but he knew Amanda wouldn't leave until Carruthers was safe. He smothered a curse. "Dismount. I'll need both horses."

Amanda dismounted and handed the reins to him. With a second muttered curse at the incomprehensible nature of women, he drove both horses back into the lake. "Sit down!" he yelled at Carruthers. "I'm coming after you."

For a moment, Broc thought the man was going to fall headfirst into the lake, but some instinct for self-preservation seemed to have surfaced, and he sat down. By the time Broc reached the rise, Carruthers was trying to stand once more.

"Cut that snake nest loose," Broc called to Carruthers. "I'm going to toss my rope to you. Catch it, and I'll pull the boat in."

Carruthers sat down but made no effort to get rid of the snakes.

"Get rid of the nest," Broc repeated. "I don't want to drag it here along with you."

"I can't," Carruthers said. "It takes two hands, and I can't use my right."

"Are you sure? Have you tried?"

"It's my arm. I ought to know if it won't move."

Carruthers sounded perfectly sane to him. He couldn't blame Amanda for thinking the same thing.

"Throw me the rope," Carruthers said. "I think I can catch it."

It took four tosses before Carruthers caught the rope. Broc kept a wary eye on the snakes as he pulled the boat closer to the rise. "Can you get out of the boat by yourself?" he asked Carruthers. "You're going to have to wade the last few feet so the snakes don't get any closer."

"I'm not sure."

"Stand up slowly, then give me your hand." He could see at least a dozen snakes in the water behind the boat. Pushing off with his good arm, Carruthers rose to his feet. The boat rocked under him when he stepped forward, but he was able to grab Broc's hand before he lost his balance. "I'll help you into the saddle so we can—"

The man had no sooner set both feet on solid ground than he reached for his gun. If he hadn't had to reach across his body, he might have been able to get it out of his holster before Broc could stop him. Frustrated in his attempt to draw his gun, Carruthers threw himself at Broc, causing them both to go down on the wet ground.

Up to this point, Broc had had a little sympathy for Carruthers, but that was a thing of the past. He grabbed Carruthers by his injured shoulder and threw him off. Much to his surprise, Carruthers didn't appear to have felt a thing. He struggled to his knees to attack Broc again. Broc paused, trying to decide how best to subdue Carruthers without doing further injury to his arm, when he noticed one of the snakes had slithered onto the rise. Several others were following.

He had to get off the rise before the snake could strike. Time for hard decisions. Broc drew back his fist and slammed it into Carruthers's jaw. The man lurched but didn't fall.

A second snake crawled out of the water.

Broc hit Carruthers harder. The blow stunned him

into immobility. Broc dragged him to his feet and over to the horse. "Mount up before the snakes kill us both."

Carruthers responded by throwing his weight backward. Broc nearly went down. With or without Carruthers, Broc had only seconds to get off the rise. He didn't like Carruthers, but couldn't square it with his conscience to leave the man to certain death. He hit Carruthers with the butt of his own gun. The man sank to his knees. Broc grabbed him under his arms and with a superhuman effort, managed to get him across the saddle of the nearer horse. One of the snakes had come so close, Broc had to kick it away. Another struck at him, but its fangs were deflected by his leather boots. Broc sprang onto his saddle and drove the horses into the lake only inches ahead of the snakes.

He still wasn't safe because the snakes followed him.

Broc had no idea how fast cottonmouth moccasins could swim, but he knew he couldn't afford to let them catch him or his horses. Fortunately, the horses seemed to be as frightened of the snakes as he was, and they lurched through the water.

Broc would never have believed it, but the snakes could swim as fast as the horses could run through the water. As they ran, sometimes through water nearly chest deep, the horses kicked up such a swirling wake the snakes couldn't reach them. Broc was certain every snake from the nest was in pursuit.

Carruthers was slipping off the saddle. If the man fell into the water, there would be nothing Broc could do to save him. Damn the man. It would serve him right to be caught in his own trap. Uttering curses he hoped Amanda would never have occasion to hear, he grabbed Carruthers by the belt and pulled him out of the saddle and across his own horse. For a moment, he thought the extra weight was going to sink his horse so deeply in the muddy lake bottom the snakes would have a chance to catch up, but the frightened animal summoned the energy to lunge forward and stagger out of the water.

Still the snakes followed.

"I'll catch your horse," Broc called to Amanda. He didn't know how long the snakes would follow, but they seemed just as fast on the ground as in the water. "When I bring him to you, ride like hell! Half the snakes in Texas are after us."

Broc had to push his horse to catch up with Amanda's riderless mount, but he managed to catch the animal and lead him back to Amanda. Meanwhile, the grass appeared to be alive with snakes fanning out in all directions. Her horse was too spooked by the snakes to stand still. Broc couldn't help because it was all he could do to stay in the saddle and hold on to Carruthers.

"Hurry. I've never seen so many snakes in my life."

Amanda managed to get one foot in the stirrup before her horse panicked and galloped off, leaving Amanda perilously balanced over the body of the horse. Her hold on the reins wouldn't do her any good unless she could get her other leg across the horse and sit down in the saddle. She was safe from the snakes now, but if she lost her balance, her foot would be caught in the stirrup and she'd be dragged to death.

Inventing new curses as fast as the words could

leave his mouth, Broc urged his tired and overburdened horse into a labored gallop. Try as he might, he couldn't gain on Amanda's horse. He was on the verge of dumping Carruthers on the ground when he saw a rider top a rise in the distance. He waved to the man, indicating Amanda's runaway horse.

Perversely, the moment help arrived, Amanda's horse slowed down, and she was able to get into the saddle. Breathing a sigh of relief, Broc slowed his horse to a walk as Amanda doubled back to meet him.

Carruthers stirred. "Don't twitch a single muscle, you son of a bitch," an exhausted and thoroughly out-of-temper Broc told him, "or I'll hit you so hard your brains will end up in Oklahoma."

∽

Amanda settled back into the circle of Broc's arms. It was the kind of soft evening that would become a wistful memory during the heat of summer, and she was enjoying it on her front porch with Broc rather than in Corby's smoke-filled saloon. Now that the need for money was no longer pressing, she would have to decide if she wanted to keep performing, but that was a decision she would make later. And with Broc. She suspected he enjoyed performing even more than she did, but tonight something else was in the forefront of their minds.

"Are you sure you want to stay here and marry me?"

Broc held her a little tighter and kissed the top of her head. "Of course I want to marry you. Why do you ask?"

Being kissed on the top of the head reminded her of what her father used to do when she was a little girl and he was tired of putting up with her. She knew it was Broc's way of reassuring her, but it still annoyed her. She'd have to show him some places she'd prefer to be kissed.

"So much of what you've done since the war has been because of your wound." She felt him stiffen and turned to face him. "Mama told Mrs. Carruthers she thinks you're better looking than Corby." She laughed. "If Mama can forget your scars, anybody can."

Broc's eyes took on that glazed look they got when he didn't want to talk about something.

"Now that the family has half the income from the saloon and diner, Mama and Eddie don't need me. I'll perform with you if you want. If you don't want to sing or act yourself, you can write skits and direct them. Mrs. Carruthers would like for you to be Priscilla's manager. You said yourself she has the voice for a major career. I'll go with you anywhere you want to go. I just want you to be happy."

She didn't like it when Broc silenced her, but being silenced with a kiss wasn't a bad thing. Especially when one kiss turned into several. Especially when those several kisses left her breathless and unable to put together a rational argument. Or wanting to do anything but have him kiss her again. She sighed and leaned her head against his chest. "You don't want to talk about it, do you?"

"I'd rather spend the time kissing you."

She looked up and smiled. "So would I, but you deserve to be the happiest man in Texas."

"Being in love with you has already made me the happiest man in Texas. How could I not be when the most beautiful woman in the state is offering to do anything within her power to make me happy?"

She would have liked to believe his claim, but she knew his wounds haunted him like a specter dogging his footsteps, staying just out of sight until he was most vulnerable. Somehow she had to make him believe that given time, people would forget the scars just as she had.

"Though I liked Corby—Papa and I both made a huge mistake there—I resisted marrying him because I knew I wouldn't be happy unless I loved my husband and he loved me. I love you, and you love me, but you'll never be really happy until you are convinced the people you love don't care about your scars."

Broc kissed the end of her nose. "Eddie never has, and these days your mother actually smiles when she sees me. Now that Gary feels like a full partner with Corby, he wouldn't care if my whole face had been shot off. And before you say it, Priscilla thinks I can do no wrong, and Dan is the best friend I have. Have I missed anybody except the sheriff? He doesn't care what I look like, just that I've made him look bad because he refused to believe what we found out about Carruthers and Corby."

"No, I don't think you've missed anybody in Cactus Bend. Since Mrs. Sibley and the judge continue to sing your praises, I think you've got Crystal Springs covered as well."

Broc's arms tightened around her. "Good. For the record, I don't want to go back to performing. It's what I did growing up. It's what I thought I'd do for the rest of my life, but now I enjoy being a cowhand. I think I'll like being the boss even better. I'll give Priscilla what advice I can, but I intend to stay right here with you. And Eddie. And your mother. And Gary. With everybody in Cactus Bend. Even Corby. Now, isn't it time we talked about a wedding?" His gaze grew heated. "After that we can talk about how many children you'd like to have."

Further discussion was postponed while they explored various satisfactory ways to kiss. Amanda would have liked to continue the exploration, but she needed to ask him something first.

"One more thing," Amanda said when she could catch her breath.

Broc frowned. "Okay, but this is the last inter-ruption. I saved up a backlog of kisses while I was in Crystal Springs. I plan to use all of them tonight."

"Before we start planning the wedding, I think you ought to go home to see your family."

Twenty-four

BROC GAZED IN DISBELIEF AT THE THRONG OF PEOPLE gathered around him. What had been planned as an ordinary family picnic had turned into a celebration involving every member of his family, extending to in-laws as well as nieces and nephews. They had spread out over the lawn of an abandoned riverside plantation. While some of the children played among the burned-out ruins of the house, the men sat talking and smoking in the shade of magnolias and water oaks. Small children and babies played or slept on handmade blankets. At the back of two wagons, several women were laying out food that would feed a group at least twice as large. There were already skinned knees and scratched elbows, but nothing had been able to dampen the festive atmosphere.

Knowing he was the focus of this celebration had probably shocked him more than learning he was alive had shocked his family. He had spent the last two days answering nonstop questions about the war and his time in Texas. That had been easy compared to explaining why he'd allowed his family to think he was dead. He wasn't sure his mother would ever forgive him. She still teared up whenever she looked at him.

"You've got to come, or Uncle Vernon is going to sing again," one of his nephews begged. "Grandma says no one was ever as good as you."

"I'll be there in a little while," Broc said. "Right now I want to relax a bit. I've been singing for the last hour."

"That's 'cause nobody wants to listen to anybody else now you're here." The boy blushed and turned to Amanda. "I didn't mean we didn't want to listen to you. It's just..." He seemed lost for words.

"You haven't hurt my feelings," Amanda said with a smile. "I know I can't sing as well as Broc."

"But you're awfully pretty."

"Watch it," Broc teased. "She's my girl. No poaching." Amanda's beauty had blossomed once the cares of the last few months had been washed away. She was radiant in her happiness.

The boy, who couldn't be more than seven, blushed. "I'm too young, but you'd better watch out for Wally. He hasn't stopped staring at her since you got here."

Wally was the youngest of Broc's siblings and the only one who wasn't married.

"Why don't you remind Wally I changed his diapers?" Broc said. "That'll take the starch out of him."

The kid grinned. "He'd knock my block off."

"Not if he couldn't catch you. I get the feeling you could outrun him."

"Everybody can. Uncle Wally likes to eat as much

as he likes girls." He turned serious. "Promise you'll sing so Uncle Vernon won't?"

"I promise. Now go get some of that fried chicken before Wally eats it all."

"He's a cute boy," Amanda said. "He's got the Kincaid look." She glanced around. "All of the children bear a strong family resemblance. I hope our children do, too."

"Our children are going to have the Liscomb look." Broc brushed Amanda's cheek with his lips.

"Only the girls. The boys are going to look like you."

"You won't have any children to look like either one of you if you don't stop talking about it and get married."

Broc turned to find his mother had come up from behind them. During the eight years since he'd gone off to war, she had grown thin, her hair streaked with gray. Broc thought she was still beautiful, but fine lines marred a complexion that had once been nearly flawless. Light shone in her eyes, but the twinkle was gone. Today tears flowed down her cheeks. Broc had exhausted his resources looking for ways to apologize, so he simply held out his hand and drew her down to sit next to him.

"We can't get married until Rafe's family gets here from California. His half brother Luis says if we get married before he arrives, we'll have to do it all over again."

They might have to get married twice anyway. They'd planned the wedding for Texas because that was where Amanda's family and his friends lived, but his family wanted to attend. Now that he'd been restored to them, they wanted to be part of his life again. The reception his family had given him was still hard for him to believe. Not one person seemed bothered by his scars. Once his parents had gotten over the shock of learning he was alive, the news had spread to the rest of the family with the speed of a Texas prairie fire. Within hours, every member of the clan had descended on the parental home, each new arrival wanting to hear the story of Laveau's betrayal. Rather than recoil from Broc's injuries, they'd been ready to organize a family militia to help hunt down Laveau di Viere.

It was equally surprising to learn the family had dropped out of show business after he joined the army. His mother had said, *It was your talent that kept us going. I never realized you thought that was the only reason we loved you.*

There was a lesson there that Broc told himself he must never forget with his own children. He must not become so focused on success that it appeared to be more important than the people in his life. He knew nothing was more important than his love for Amanda. He wanted to make sure his children felt he loved them just as much.

"I don't care where you get married as long as I can be there," his mother said. "I've missed too much of your life already."

Broc's throat tightened, but he forced the words out. "That was my fault, not yours."

"Whose fault it is doesn't matter anymore." She patted Broc's hand, then got up. "You don't have to sing again if you'd rather not."

"Sammy made me promise."

His mother laughed. "He says Vernon sings in the cracks." She grimaced. "He's right." Her expression softened, and her tears started again. "I hope I never meet Laveau di Viere, because if I do, I might kill him. I can never forgive him for keeping you away from us." She wiped her cheeks. "Now I won't say anything else to make me cry. Your father says if I don't stop crying every time I see you, it will drive you away again."

"That won't happen. There's no better proof you're happy I'm here."

His mother shed a few more tears, leaned over to kiss him, then hurried off to referee an argument over how many lemons were needed for the lemonade.

As he watched her go, Broc wondered again how he could have misjudged his family so badly. Had he disliked his face so much that he believed everyone else would feel the same way, or was it just that people like Felix Yant made him forget not everyone was narrow-minded and cruel? Whatever the reason, he would never feel that way again.

"I'm glad you talked me into coming here," he said to Amanda. "I would never have done it otherwise."

Amanda squeezed his hand and leaned into him. "I knew you'd never be really happy believing your family didn't want anything to do with you."

"The only person who really matters is you."

"I hope I'm the one who matters *most*, but I'm not the only one. I don't even want to be. Everyone you love, everyone who loves you—they all matter. You might be surprised just how many that adds up to."

He still found it hard to believe people like the

judge, Mrs. Sibley, Eddie, even Leo, had never been bothered by his face. Most of all, he was thankful it didn't matter to Amanda. He could have endured anything as long as she loved him, but it was much better knowing she wasn't the only one.

"I'm still grateful. I would never have had this—" he gestured to the thirty-one people gathered here because of him—"if you hadn't forced me to come."

"You wanted to come. You just needed a reason, and nothing brings a family together better than a wedding."

Maybe he had wanted to come, but he would never have had enough courage without Amanda's support. He owed her so much. It was her love that made it possible for him to believe others could see past his injury. That had given him back himself. He was a person, not just a disfigured face.

He was a man named Broc. "I love you," he said.

"I know."

"I mean I love you in ways I never thought possible. I can't imagine being without you. There is no *me*. Just *us*. I want to touch you all the time. I want to see your smile, hear you breathe, smell your hair, taste your skin when we're making love. Then I want to do it all over again."

"I'll remind you of this when we have our first argument."

"I'll only argue because I love you."

"What if Luis insists we get married a second time?"

"I'll marry you every week for the rest of my life if you want."

"I'll settle for being loved every day. I don't think you can afford that many wedding dresses."

About the Author

Leigh Greenwood is the award-winning author of over fifty books, many of which have appeared on the *USA Today* bestseller list. Leigh lives in Charlotte, North Carolina. Please visit his website at leigh-greenwood.com.

Enjoy this sneak peek into
Rosanne Bittner's epic,
Ride the High Lonesome,
coming November 26, 2019!

August 1869

KATE DUCKED INTO THE TALL GRASS AS SOON AS SHE
heard men's voices. She slowly crawled to get close
enough to listen, then parted the dense, yellow blades
to see five rough-looking men gathered around a
lonely, half-dead cottonwood tree. One of the men
raised up in his stirrups and flung a rope over the
biggest branch left on the leafless tree, while another,
guarded at rifle point, sat astride his horse with his
hands tied behind his back.

Dear God, are they going to hang *that man?*

In the distance, about twenty head of cattle and
a pack horse grazed, unconcerned about the terrible
event about to take place. All five men shouted at each
other, but Kate could distinguish only bits and pieces
of their conversation.

"Hang…son of a bitch!"

The man whose hands were tied was angrily and
desperately yelling back at them. "I didn't steal—"

"Makes no difference—"

"Murdering bastards!"

If she were a man, with a weapon and a horse, Kate could at least ride down to the site to see what was going on and maybe talk the men out of the hanging, but whether what was happening below was lawful or lawless, what could a thirty-two-year-old woman, with nothing more than the clothes on her back, do against five men? She didn't even dare show herself. This was pure outlaw country. There wasn't a man around who could be trusted to help and not harm.

Was the poor soul about to be hanged innocent or guilty? And did it really matter in this lost world of lawlessness? All around them, massive and endless mesas stood guard over a valley that stretched so far into the distance that she couldn't even see the end of it. It would probably take a week of nonstop riding to escape this place. How many weeks would it take to flee on foot—her *only* way out?

She'd never seen such big country, such endless horizons, nor had she ever felt so far removed from civilization…so dreadfully and completely alone. She'd read somewhere that canyons and strange rock formations like this were formed by water cutting a path through the land—probably a million years ago, when dinosaurs roamed the earth. She felt caught up in that past. Did civilization still exist beyond this vast chain of buttes and mesas?

She watched with a sinking heart as one of the men led under the noose the man with his hands tied and placed the rope around his neck. Kate put her head down, unable to look. Strangely, the worst part of this was wondering how close she might be to food

and water, to men who might be able to help her find
her way out of this god-forsaken country and back to
safety. But she'd rather die from thirst and hunger than
to suffer the things four desperate, lonely men might
decide to do with her if she showed herself. They
might even kill her for witnessing what they were
about to do.

She heard more shouts and strained to hear the
doomed man swear his innocence.

"I *paid* for those cattle!"

"Thief!"

"Rustler!"

"*You're* the outlaws!" he snapped.

Kate jumped and almost cried out when a gun
was fired. A couple of horses whinnied, and she felt
literal pain in her stomach at the thought of what had
just happened. Everything grew quiet, until one man
yelled loudly, "Goddamn it! He isn't dead yet,"

"He *will* be in a couple more minutes," someone
answered.

"Let the son of a bitch suffer."

"Let's go!"

Kate hadn't watched any of it. With her ear to the
ground, she heard the pounding of horses' hooves,
a sound that seemed to carry like thunder for miles
through the earth She'd learned from the wagon train
guide how to listen for oncoming horses or buffalo
this way. That guide was dead now, along with all the
others she'd traveled with—even two children. She
would always remember the guide telling her that out
in this land a man could hear the thunder of horses'
hooves from miles away. Too bad old Gus hadn't

listened to the ground the day of their attack. They would have had more time to circle the wagons and prepare for a fight.

As the thundering began to fade, she raised her head slightly. She heard whistles and shouts that sounded more like war whoops, but they sounded far away.

She dared to lift her head higher. Three men were charging after the cattle in the distance, while one kept trying to grab the hanged man's horse. It kept rearing up and yanking itself away, until finally the fourth man rode off after the others, who'd already stolen their victim's pack horse. Kate thanked God they were all riding away from her rather than toward her. She noticed then that the hanged man's feet were still kicking, and she grasped her stomach at the awful sight. "God have mercy on his soul," she said softly.

She again looked into the horizon of dry, yellow grass. The four men were still riding hard behind the cattle. They headed around the bend of a mesa, and soon men and cattle all disappeared. When Kate turned her attention back to the hanged man, she noticed that his feet were *still* moving. "Oh my God!" she groaned.

Did she dare get up? Outlaw or not, she couldn't bear the fact that the hanged man was suffering horribly as his last bit of oxygen left him. He couldn't possibly be a danger to her at the moment. He was, after all, just one man, and he would likely die before she could reach him. Besides, she needed his horse and supplies. A canteen hung from his saddle horn, and she saw a rifle strapped to his gear. The saddlebags lying over the horse's rump were surely full of needed supplies. A gun belt lay on the ground. The horse and its supplies were her only hope of staying alive and finding her way out of this cruel, unforgiving country.

It was now or never. She couldn't let the hanged man suffer any longer, and she had to grab his horse before it decided to run off. She stood up, lifted the long skirt of her dress, and started running through the tall grass. The sole on her right shoe had loosened from so much walking, and she stumbled as she ran.

Everything around her was rocky and steep and treacherous.

Finally, she reached the horse, which had already wandered several yards from where its owner still hung. She grunted as she climbed into the saddle, so weak she barely had the strength to pull herself up. She didn't bother to shorten the stirrups. She just let her legs dangle and kicked the horse into a hard run, heading for the hanged man. She reached his limp body and gasped when she heard a horrible gurgling sound come from his lips. His face had turned purple, but his feet jerked gently in a sickening signal of dwindling life.

The man's eyeballs rolled back. Kate desperately searched for a way to get him down, then noticed that though he wore no gun, there was a knife in his belt. She leaned over and yanked it out of its sheath, then reached as high as she could and grabbed the end of the rope near his head.

She strained to vigorously cut at the rope, and finally the knife sliced through. The hanged man's body fell with a thud onto a sandy patch of ground.

Two

KATE DISMOUNTED THE HORSE AND QUICKLY TIED IT TO a low branch of the hanging tree. She knelt beside the suffering man, who was still choking and gasping for breath. She yanked the rope from around his neck and threw it aside, noticing he was a big man, tall and solid. Could he even breathe?

He made a chilling gagging sound, and although she didn't know him, she wished she could take away his misery. "Mister? I want to help you."

He couldn't find his voice to reply.

Kate scrambled to retrieve the knife she'd dropped and then hurried back to where the man lay. She rolled him to his side and cut the ropes that held his wrists together. She pulled one arm forward and gently rolled him onto his back, then pulled the other arm out from under him. She reached under his neck and helped him arch his head back to open his airway as much as possible.

He gasped in ugly grunts, a deep, grating groan that made Kate ache for him. "Try to relax," she urged. "You're getting air, so relax and slowly breathe in, mister. Keep breathing and let your throat open back up." She sat down and moved her legs under his head to keep it raised, then began massaging the sides and back of his neck, trying to relax his muscles while at the same time avoiding the scraped, blood-tinged skin where the rope had produced an ugly ring around his throat.

He struggled to put one hand to his chest and dig the other into the sand. His chest heaved as he forced himself to breathe in, over and over.

"That's it," Kate told him. "Just breathe." She studied his face, noting the purplish hue had eased. His skin was tanned, and the outer corners of his eyes were creased from weeks, months, maybe years of sun exposure. Who was he, and why was he out here? Was he guilty or innocent of rustling cattle, or maybe something worse? Could she trust him once he reclaimed his breath and strength?

As she wondered, she observed him still. Beyond what must be only a day-old beard, his features were strong: square jaw, straight nose, full lips, a prominent brow. The high plains were cool today, and he wore a wool jacket over broad shoulders. His hair needed cutting, but what man out here *didn't* need a haircut? Towns with barbers and bathhouses were hundreds of miles apart, and in between, there was little access to water. Even so, this man didn't smell of someone who seldom washed. She'd encountered that nose-twisting odor too often during the trip out here, and now she wondered about herself. After walking for three days through dry, hot country, she had no business worrying about someone else's hygiene.

For the moment, her priority was to get this man back to normal breathing. His dark-brown hair was almost shoulder-length, and she brushed errant strands from his face, wondering if it was the thickness of his hair at the sides and back of his neck that had protected him from the rope. His hair and the collar of his jacket might have saved his life.

She shivered, the air suddenly chilling her. She remembered others telling her that the weather could change in an instant in high country, and that sometimes it even snowed this time of year. She was afraid to leave the man on his own yet, so she just hunched closer and kept coaching him to breathing. As she bent closer to stay warm, he opened his eyes and looked straight into her eyes.

They were inches apart. They just stared at each other a moment until Kate suddenly straightened, not sure just how aware the man was of his surroundings, or of her.

"Do you know where you are?" she asked him. "Do you remember what just happened?"

He kept staring at her as though she were a creature from another world, confusion and pain in his gaze. "You…an…angel?" He gasped the words in a deeply strained, grating voice.

Kate rubbed the sides of his neck again. "No," she replied. "You are indeed alive, mister, and I'm lost out here. My name is Kate. I came across that awful hanging and hid until those men left. I saw that you were still alive, so I cut you down."

The man gasped again and made a sickening choking sound, then turned sideways and coughed up blood before turning back and relaxing his head on her legs again. He swallowed. "Sorry."

"You can't help it."

"Your...dress."

"It's already torn and filthy. You can't hurt it. Just relax and keep breathing. Don't get up yet. What's your name?"

He gasped for his next breath and bent one knee, then opened his eyes again and just stared at her a moment, still looking confused. He was silent, as though he wasn't sure of his name, then closed his eyes again. "Luke," he grunted. "I...need...water."

"Oh, of course! Can you sit up?"

"Try..."

"See if you can help me scoot you against the tree," Kate told him. "You're too big for me to do this by myself." She helped get him to a sitting position, then moved behind him and grasped him under the arms, pulling at him while he used one leg to help push himself backward until he could lean against the tree. He started gasping for breath again, and Kate hurried over to his horse, taking a canteen from where it hung around the pommel of the saddle. She knelt beside him and uncorked the canteen, holding it to his lips. "Here. Try to drink, but be careful. You don't want to start coughing if you can help it. I imagine it would hurt to cough and might even injure your throat even worse."

She tipped the canteen a little and let some water dribble into his mouth. He took hold of it then himself and took a bigger swallow.

"Be careful," Kate warned.

Luke lowered the canteen and closed his eyes again, taking a deep breath.

"Mister, I have to drink some of this, too. I've gone all day without water. The one canteen I managed to salvage three days ago ran empty last night."

Luke watched her as she took a long swallow of water.

"I hope you have more than just this one canteen," she told him as she recorked it and wiped at her lips.

"One…more," he managed to choke out. "Inside… that satchel…tied to my…horse. Don't want…other men to see it. Out here…men steal…water…horses… money…cattle…anything." He groaned with pain then, grasping at his throat and bending over to take more deep breaths.

"Is that what those men were doing?" Kate asked him. "Stealing your cattle?"

Luke nodded. "Bastards! I'll…kill…every last…one of them!"

Kate wondered just how many men Luke had already killed. He seemed to have no qualms about killing four more. Maybe he would have no qualms about hurting or killing her, too. "First you have to learn to breathe again and get your strength back," she told him, hoping kindness would save her. "I saw another jacket tied to your supplies. Do you mind if I put it on? I'm cold."

He studied her a moment, looking her over in that way a man had of telling a woman he liked what he saw. Kate scooted away a little, wondering if she'd gotten herself into worse trouble by helping him.

"Sure," he answered. "You…saved…my life, lady."

Kate rose and walked to his horse, untying the

sheepskin jacket and pulling it on. It was far too big, and its sleeves hung down over her hands, but the sheep's wool lining brought welcome warmth. She walked over to where Luke's gun belt lay and picked it up, taking it to the horse and hanging it over the pommel of the saddle. She hesitated then, wondering if she needed protection. She took out the heavy six-gun and dropped it into a pocket on the jacket.

The gun weighed down that side of the jacket awkwardly, but she had no choice for the moment. This was dangerous country, full of dangerous men. She turned to see Luke watching her.

"No need...for that," he managed to tell her.

Kate walked around to gather some pieces of dead wood from under the tree. *We'll see*, she thought. "I'll build a fire," she said aloud. "It will be dark soon, and it looks like we have no choice but to camp here for the night."

"I'm...grateful," Luke said. "I...owe you."

"You don't owe me a thing. I might have saved your life, but you've saved mine just by being here. I'm hungry and worn to the bone from walking, and I was getting desperate and terrified. I'm completely lost, so you need to live in order to help me find my way out of this godforsaken country."

Kate glanced over at the tree to see the man had slipped sideways and was lying on the ground again. She grabbed a blanket from his horse and hurried over to bunch it up under his head and helped him lie flat. "Don't die on me, Luke," she said. "I'll never find my way back to civilization without you. I hope you know where you are and how to find help."

"Don't…steal my…horse," he whispered, his eyes closed. "Don't…leave me here without a…gun and…a horse."

Kate couldn't help feeling sorry for him. She leaned closer. "I need that horse, but I also need the man who owns it," she told him. *Unless I can't trust him.* "So I won't steal it. Besides, why would I ride off after just saving your life?"

She rose and walked back to her little pile of wood, then looked out at the violent landscape that was growing dimmer as the sun set. In the distance she saw a herd of wild horses running through the valley, so far away she could see them, but could not hear them. She got on her knees and put her ear to the ground.

The guide had been right. She could hear their pounding hooves, even though they were unshod and so far away she could barely see them in the evening's dim light. She raised up to watch them disappear into a deep shadow created by the sun settling behind a grand mesa. Somewhere in the unreal landscape; a wolf howled, its cry echoing across the valley.

"Can you eat?" she asked Luke.

He just lay there, making no reply.

Kate fished through the man's supplies and found some biscuits. She ate two and decided that would have to do for now. She remembered someone telling her once that a person shouldn't eat too heavily on a severely empty stomach. Maybe it was when she'd helped with wounded men during the war…that awful war that had robbed her of everything she'd ever loved.

She checked Luke once more, touching his shoulder. "Luke? Are you okay?"

He opened his eyes. "Just...cover me and...leave a canteen," he choked out.

Kate did as he asked, taking another long drink first. She left the canteen near Luke, then laid out his bedroll near the fire. She found leather straps for hobbling the horse, led the gelding out to better grass, and wrapped his front legs into the straps. She took Luke's rifle from his gear and walked back to the fire, where she practically collapsed onto his bedroll. Exhaustion overwhelmed her as she crawled inside the bedroll, thinking to rest just a few minutes and then check on Luke again. She figured she shouldn't let herself sleep too hard. After all, Luke was yet a stranger, and for all she knew, he still could be dangerous. He could recover faster than she anticipated.

She laid the rifle and Luke's six-gun beside her and closed her eyes. *Where in God's name am I,* she wondered, *and what kind of man am I with?*

Three

SOMEONE NUDGED KATE AWAKE. SHE GASPED AND reached for the rifle she'd left beside her the night before, but it was held in place by a big, booted foot.

"Don't be…shooting me out of fear." The words came out in a grating rasp. "I'm just giving you time… to get your bearings."

Kate blinked and jumped to her feet to face Luke, who stood there in the early morning light with his six-gun in hand. Kate felt mortified. Rather than sleep just a little, she'd apparently slept through the night and wasn't even aware that Luke was up and better and had possession of both guns.

"I—you—"

"You're fine," he told her. He'd already strapped on his gun belt, and he slipped the six-gun into its holster. "I just don't want you to shoot me from being startled awake," he repeated.

Kate noted his eyes were bloodshot, and his entire neck and part of his jawline were bruised. His long hair was in disarray, and his beard was badly in need of a trim. He stepped back, taking his foot off the rifle, then leaned down to pick it up. "Sometimes when a person is lost and scared, he or she will shoot at anything." He took out his hand gun again and handed it out. "Take this…if it makes you feel better."

"It's okay, I guess." Kate pushed a tendril of her hair behind her ear, thinking she must be as much in need of a bath and clean clothes as Luke. She was suddenly too aware of how she must look. Her red hair always tried to go in six directions at once. Now it was disheveled from the wind and sullied with dust and grit.

She looked around the camp, realizing Luke had rebuilt the fire.

"I…I intended to get a fire started…make some coffee or something before you were even up," she told him, realizing only then that the man was taller than she'd first surmised—certainly big enough to have his way with her if he so chose. Yet he'd offered her his six-gun. "I didn't think you would be up and around so soon."

"Don't worry about it. I aim to get going soon as possible and get my cattle back." He re-holstered his six-gun.

Kate frowned. "But you must be in terrible pain. You should rest another day. And I need to find a way to civilization. I need a horse of my own, supplies, clean clothes. I was hoping you'd lead me to a place where I can get those things before you go after those men."

Luke shook his head. "I can't let them get too far ahead." He sniffed the air. "There's clouds hanging in the west. Look like rain clouds, something you don't see out here often." He cleared his throat and choked a little. "It's going to get colder instead of warmer. There's no predicting the weather in this country. We'll warm up a little and rest up more…just to get the ache out of our bones. Then we'll need to get going. I aim to go after the men who hanged me. I want them dead and I need to get my cattle back. Or my money. Both, if possible. You needing to ride with me will slow us down, so the earlier we start, the better."

"Where will we go?"

"There's a town a good thirty-five miles north of here called Lander. I'm sure that's where those men are headed. We'll find a good place for you to hole up while I ride to Lander and get what's mine. It will all go faster if I do this alone. I'll also get the supplies we need—food, clothes, and a horse for you."

Kate watched him look around for more firewood. "I don't even know your last name," she told him.

Luke kept his rifle in one hand and leaned down to pick up an unburned stick. He stirred the coals under the fire. "Bowden," he answered. "Luke Bowden. How about you?"

Kate helped pick up more wood, glad he'd mentioned finding her a horse and supplies, and doubly glad to realize he seemed to know his way around this country. "Kate Winters."

They both laid more wood on the fire at the same time, momentarily raising their heads and looking into each other's eyes. After helping nurse wounded men during the Civil War, Kate knew enough about men's pride to know Luke Bowden was feeling more than a little shame at how she'd found him, at the mercy of other men, a noose around his neck, hanging, kicking, and dying.

"I reckon I owe you my life, Miss Winters. Or is it Mrs.?"

"It's Mrs.," she told him. "My husband was killed in the war." She quickly rose, feeling a little embarrassed at their faces being so close. "And I suppose you do owe me, but I can't take too much credit, Mister Bowden. I didn't want to see you suffer, but I also needed your horse and supplies. The wagon train I was with had dwindled down to only three wagons because of sickness and breakdowns along the way. We were headed for Oregon when we were attacked by a gang of ragtag soldiers and renegades, probably leftovers from the war. I never even got a good look at them. The three men I traveled with—a preacher and two farmers, plus the guide—they hid me under a blanket beneath my wagon." Kate wanted to cry at the memory. "They were all killed. All supplies stolen. The wagons burned. Mine collapsed right on top of me. By some miracle I was able to burrow deeper into a little dip in the ground, and I just let it burn around me. The wagon bed didn't burn, and I was able to crawl out after the awful men who attacked us rode off with our small remuda of horses and the supplies. They killed the oxen." Her heart ached at the memory of the friends she'd made, including the rugged old guide who'd taught her to listen to the ground. "I just started walking, hoping I'd find someone to help me."

Luke shook his head. "Why in hell did your guide

leave so late in the year for Oregon? It's too late to get over the mountains. It's already snowing up there."

"We were going to lay over in Utah at a Mormon settlement."

"The fact remains, you're in outlaw country now, and you won't find much help among the kind of men who live out here. They call this the Outlaw Trail. Runs from Canada practically all the way to Mexico." He fanned the flames with his hat. "You've likely figured out that men come here to hide from the law. No lawman will show his face in this country."

Kate knew it to be true, but her heart fell a little more at hearing it. "Are *you* an outlaw, Mister Bowden?"

Luke managed a light laugh. "Depends on what you consider an outlaw. Once I catch up to those men who hanged me, I reckon I'll end up being called a murderer. Just rest your mind that I'm no woman-beater and I don't kill men without good cause. And I sure as hell wouldn't harm someone who just saved my life, so get that worried look off your face. And call me Luke, not Mister Bowden. Can I keep calling you Kate?"

"Of course."

"Well, Kate, grab that blanket you slept with last night. Sit by the fire for a while. We'll eat a couple of biscuits and then leave."

"Luke, it's a terrible thing you went through yesterday. I think you should rest one more day."

He shook his head. "No, ma'am. Time is of the essence. Those sons of bitches—pardon my language—but they stole what's mine and tried to kill me. A man doesn't forget something like that." He coughed again and rubbed at his throat. "I want to hunt them down." He coughed again. "I'm sorry, but that comes first, and I'll travel faster alone. I know a place where you can stay and wait. I'll leave you food and water and blankets."

Kate rubbed at her eyes. "Right now, I need to you to look away while I go behind that big rock to… well…"

"Everybody needs to pee when they wake up, ma'am. I already took care of my own needs. Go ahead. Then get over here and warm yourself more. I'm surprised you were able to sleep at all with only my old coat and my bedroll to bed down with. It gets damn cold in this country at night. You must kind of hurt all over after what you've been through." He met her gaze. "How long ago was the attack?"

"Four days, I think. I've been wandering so long and was so hungry and thirsty and worn out, I lost track. I'm afraid I ate some of your biscuits last night."

"No problem."

Kate wanted to ask so much more. Where was he from? What was he doing out here herding cattle by himself? Where was he headed when the outlaws stole his herd? Was he married? Did he have family somewhere? Was he even telling the truth about not being an outlaw and not being a threat to her? And how did he think he was going to take on four men all by himself?

She stood up and walked to the boulder, glad it was just big enough that he couldn't see her kneel behind it and lift her skirts.

Just as she started to rise, a quail fluttered upward from where it was hidden in tall grass. Kate gasped in surprise and quickly pulled up her drawers. She jumped and let out a little scream when a gun went off. She hurried around the boulder to see the quail drop to the ground some distance away.

Luke turned to her, rifle in hand, and nodded. "Our supper," he told her. "Now if we can find some water, we won't starve or die from thirst."

Kate walked back to the fire while Luke walked off to find the quail he'd shot. *Well, Luke Bowden, you are apparently a strong and able man when it comes to survival. And at least you seem to know this country.*

Whether or not he could be trusted was still to be proven. Right now, he was weak and grateful. Men changed when they got stronger, and she was already aware from some men's attitudes and remarks what some men thought a widowed woman needed. She prayed Mister Luke Bowden was not a drinking man, or that a meaner side would not show itself as he grew stronger. Right now, he was all the hope she had of getting out of this place alive.

Four

LUKE BUTTONED THE COLLAR OF HIS WOOL JACKET closer around his neck, then pulled his left foot from the stirrup. "Put your foot in the stirrup and climb up behind me," he told Kate, reaching down for her.

"Are you sure you should be doing this?" Kate asked. "You don't look good. Getting hanged isn't like having a cold or something. You're seriously injured."

"I'll manage."

His voice was so pitifully raspy that Kate couldn't help feeling very sorry for him. She threw a blanket over the horse's neck, then grasped Luke's hand and put her left foot into the stirrup. "Are you sure this isn't too much weight for your horse?" she asked.

Luke helped hoist her up, and she settled in behind him, surprised and impressed with how easily he'd pulled her up. He was a strong man, but she couldn't help worrying how easily he could use that strength against her.

"You don't weigh much," he replied. "Ole Red will be fine, especially since we managed to make up a travois from some of those tree limbs to carry the supplies separate." Luke handed her the blanket she'd draped around Red's neck, and she laid it over her legs and huddled against his back.

Luke had been right. Even though it was still August, the morning had already grown colder instead of warmer, and the sky was getting darker instead of brighter. She could hardly believe the change in the weather, after sweating so much the past four days.

She had no choice now but to wrap her arms around Luke's solid middle and hang on tight as he kicked his horse into motion. She glanced back at the doused camp fire they had shared, wondering where on earth life would take her from here. Although Luke Bowden was a complete stranger about whom she knew almost nothing, she was grateful to have finally found some kind of help.

She'd smoothed the wild curls of her hair back at the sides as best she could and secured it with the three combs she'd managed to hang on to after the wagon attack. That day her hair was piled on top of her head with several combs. It had fallen down, section by section, as she walked mile after mile, looking for help, not even knowing which direction she'd taken. She desperately needed a bath, a real bed, and a decent change of clothes.

"Tell me again where we are going," she said.

"A town called Lander, but I need to find a decent place for you to wait while I take care of the men I'm after and get the supplies we need. There's a cave where men sometimes hole up on the way there. Hoping to reach it by nightfall."

Kate looked around at nothing but more wide-open

valley surrounded by miles and miles of the same high, flat-topped cliffs. How a man found his way in country like this, she could not imagine. It seemed impossible there could be a town anywhere even remotely close, and everything looked identically empty and endless. She saw no signs of life. She did see trampled grass ahead of them. The stolen herd of cattle had left an easy path. She looked down at it when the horse stumbled.

"Easy there, Red," Luke soothed.

Kate noticed the quail he'd shot was bouncing against the horse's rump, where Luke had tied it upside-down after gutting and beheading the bird to let the blood drain as they rode. The travois, tied to the back of the saddle, dragged and bounced behind the horse and made scratching and tearing sounds as it was pulled through the grass and over patches of gravely ground.

"Luke, we can't travel like this for more than a couple of days. It's too hard on the horse and too awkward for us."

"I am well aware of all of that," he answered, his voice hoarse.

"I'm sorry," Kate told him. "Are you sure you know what direction we are going?"

"North. Trust me. I used to hunt in wild country with my pa a long time ago. Learned how to track things. Besides, I've been living out here the past couple of years. I know this country, and I know north from south."

Kate wondered why he'd chosen to stay in such desolate country, but she didn't ask. It was too hard for the man to talk, and it really was none of her business anyway. They rode a while in silence. Kate looked up when she heard the cry of an eagle and saw the big bird floating on an air current, making it all look so easy. She thought how, from above, she and Luke Bowden must look like nothing more than two specks against the yellow grass, no bigger than bugs against a landscape so magnificently vast.

Red plodded along, his riders rocking back and forth with the horse's gait, the horse snorting and tossing his head at times. Luke had given the animal a little water before they left, but the poor animal needed more. All *three* of them needed more.

"Who were those men who hanged you?" Kate asked Luke, feeling she needed to break the awkward silence in spite of how difficult it was for Luke to talk.

"I'll explain later," he answered.

A cold wind suddenly picked up and rushed through the valley with surprising speed, making Luke duck his head. Kate lowered her own head behind his broad back, feeling guilty that she could use his body as a shield while Luke had to take the brunt of it. A light, cold rain began to fall. It was soon mixed with snowflakes, then solid snow.

"So it's true," Kate muttered. "It *can* snow in August."

"This country is higher than you think."

They plodded on, bent against the wind and snow, still able to follow the tracks of Luke's cattle in spite of the fresh snow that would normally have covered them. The trampled grass left an indention that, even snow-covered, was easy to follow. They continued the miserable ride for what seemed hours, stopping once behind a huge boulder for shelter. They ate another biscuit each and drank a little water while letting Red rest. It was late afternoon when Luke drew Red to a halt and stared intently at something. He pointed and leaned back, talking close to Kate's ear because his pain kept him from yelling above the howling wind.

"There's the cave," he told her. "We'll hole up there."

Kate nodded, thinking how good it would feel to get out of the wind. She shivered into the sheepskin jacket as Luke headed across to the east side of the valley. It took far longer to reach the cave than Kate first expected, but she was learning that nothing in this wild land was ever as close as it looked. The wind and snow let up a little as they drew closer.

They were perhaps a half mile from the cave when Red stumbled, and his front legs seemed to collapse. Both Kate and Luke went flying forward into the snow. Luke quickly rolled away and got to his knees. He noticed Kate took a moment to answer. She rolled over, holding her head.

"You okay?" Luke asked.

Kate finally managed to sit up, wet snow on her face. "I think so."

Luke noticed a spot of blood on a snow-covered rock. "Jesus," he muttered. "Sit still a minute." He reached over to Red. The horse whinnied and stood up again, shaking his mane and stumbling slightly.

"What happened, boy?" Luke got up and checked the horse's legs. "I think he's okay—just worn out," he told Kate. He walked up to her and reached out a hand to help her up, then frowned. "Ma'am, your forehead is bleeding."

Kate put a hand to the painful spot. "I hit my head on that rock."

He put an arm around her waist and helped her toward his horse. "Put some snow on it," he said as he grabbed the reins. "The cold will slow the bleeding. I'll find you something to hold against it." He let go of her and turned back to Red and ran his hands over the horse's shoulders and front legs again, then checked the ground around them. "There's a big hole here," he said, pointing to a spot just behind the horse. "The snow hid it." He turned back around to see Kate crumple to the ground as her legs went out from under her. "Kate!"

Kate tried to gather her thoughts and steady herself, but a terrible dizziness made that impossible. She fought a black fog that scattered her thoughts as Luke gathered her in his arms.

"I'll get you to that cave," he told her. "I'm sorry, but I'll have to drape you over Red unless you think you can sit up on the horse."

Kate couldn't find the words to answer him. She was aware of being draped over a horse's back and covered with a blanket. "I know this is uncomfortable, but we have to get to the cave," Luke said. "I'll lead Red so he doesn't step into anymore holes. I don't want to put my weight on him till I'm sure he doesn't have an injured leg."

Kate instinctively reached down with her hands and grabbed the right stirrup, hanging on to it to keep from slipping backward off the saddle. The slow walk the rest of the way to the cave seemed to take forever.

"It's just ahead now," Luke told her.

His voice was the last thing Kate remembered.

Also by Leigh Greenwood

Night Riders

Texas Homecoming

Texas Bride

Born to Love

Someone Like You

Texas Pride

Heart of a Texan

Cactus Creek Cowboys

To Have and to Hold

To Love and to Cherish

Forever and Always

Christmas in a Cowboy's Arms

No One But You

Longing for a Cowboy Christmas